Like Eban

By

P L Jenkinson

Like Eban by P L Jenkinson

This story is a work of fiction. All aspects of this work, whether invented by the author or any real places which are mentioned within, have been used fictitiously.

ISBN 9780995799127

This book is dedicated to Chris Radley, one of the nicest, kindest, bravest and most inspirational men I know. This one's just for you Radders.

My enormous gratitude goes to Nicky Wilkinson for her hard work, skill and brilliant advice offered in the editing of this novel, you're amazing.

Many thanks to Steve Bruce from the National Records of Scotland offices in Edinburgh, for his very helpful advice on Scottish laws regarding adoption.

Thanks are also due to Steve Dodds for his valuable advice on some of the legalities mentioned in this story.

Thank you to Ray Graham for his technical help with the front cover.

Finally; I will always be grateful to my brilliant, supportive and amazing friends and colleagues. You hold me up when I struggle, you comfort me when I'm sad and you kick me up the backside when I need it. Much love.

Prologue

The cup shattered into several large shards, as it made contact with the wall above the filing cabinet. The hot coffee it had contained splattered across the top and ran down the wall at the back. To say that Detective Inspector Mike White was furious was the biggest understatement of the century.

"What the hell happened? How the fuck did y'let it happen? Christ almighty heads are going t'roll for this I tell ya!"

"I'm really sorry we, er…he had us all convinced, not just us, the doctors too…"

"Not good enough! Get it in a report, right now! I want t'know from the thread to the bloody needle, how the hell did this happen? There'll be necks on the line over this. D'ya understand me? An' I'll be making sure

6

it's your scrawny, piss-taking necks before it's mine, get it!"

"Sir," Detective Sergeant Radley interrupted him, "as an overview, it seems as though he'd planned the whole thing. Right from the charge that was brought against him in prison, to the fact that he's got an allergy to the drug codeine. He knew what it'd do to him but he took it anyway. No-one knew about his reaction t'codeine 'til staff at the hospital accessed System One an' it was on his medical records. He knew what he were doing Sir. He made himself ill on purpose. He must've done some research because he knew exactly how to behave an' to answer the doctors' questions. It wasn't foreseeable Sir."

"Are you pulling my bloody chain? Why wasn't it foreseeable? He's a damn head-case, an' now he's a damn head-case on the loose somewhere…Find him!"

Three weeks earlier

"It's not what happens to us in life that matters Chris, it's how we choose to deal with what's happened that counts." Ray Graham rested back into his chair as he shuffled the papers he was holding into some semblance of order.

"Yeah, well this *is* how I choose t'deal with it," Chris said with an increased agitation in his tone.

"You're not a happy man Chris. You need to understand that your life will always be a reflection of the choices you've made, good or bad."

"Have you swallowed a book o'fucking clichés or summat? 'Cos y'sound like a right wanker."

Graham let out an exasperated sigh. "Look, like it or not, I'm here to help you. To advise, to guide if you like."

"Well fucking guide this!" Chris threw the tea from his mug over Graham and got to his feet. "I'm not interested mate, okay?"

The two uniformed prison warders who'd been standing sentry suddenly lunged forward and grabbed an arm each pressing Chris's face up against the wall, a team effort that saw him cuffed again in a matter of seconds. One of them pushed his head forward as the other slightly lifted the handcuffs that held his wrists tightly locked together behind his back. This caused him to stoop and walk in such a way as the guards dictated, a well practised manoeuvre and an effective way of getting him out of the interview room and back to his cell quickly. He'd not attempted to fight against what they were doing, he didn't see the point. Besides, he was sick to death of listening to the meaningless drivel that was projectile vomiting forth from the moustached mouth of that bloody social worker or counsellor or whatever the hell he was.

Back at his office, Ray Graham had compiled his report and was ready to forward it on, but something held him back. He wanted to talk to the police officer in charge of Chris's case first so he decided to give him a call.

He explained that he was about to file his review, but that there was something he wasn't entirely comfortable with. "Don't get me wrong, I can handle having a cup o' tea thrown at me, it's not that," he clarified. "It's just that, well, I've spent the best part of the past month with Chris Hartley, trying to get somewhere with him and each time I speak to him there's this undertone that I can't quite put my finger on. I think there's something more going on than I feel qualified to work with. In my opinion he should have a proper psychiatric evaluation."

This suggestion hadn't gone down too well at the other end of the phone. More cost, more time wasted. When all the police wanted was to get the bastard off the streets. The Crown Prosecution Service had more than enough to make their case anyway, but now that these concerns had been raised, there was a duty of care. They had to be seen to cover all bases and if Ray Graham was going to document his concerns and they were then blatantly overlooked, it could leave one almighty loophole for the defence to jump through. Justifying why a psychiatric evaluation hadn't been utilised after it had been suggested would be far harder than just going ahead with it.

"Fine," the Sergeant said reluctantly. "I'll sort it. Leave it with me."

Back in his cell, Chris was laid on his bunk staring at the wall on the far side from him. The anger hadn't subsided at all, though for all intents and purposes he appeared calm. Which served a purpose because it hid the fact that there was still unfinished business.

Chapter One

Clive's grasp on modern technology was much akin
to that of many people of his generation. He thought it a
marvellous thing on the one hand, yet he was awe-struck
if not a little fearful of it on the other. However, he was
in this instance completely taken with the photobook of
Robbie and Lynsey's wedding day.

Ten weeks had passed since the day itself, but the
DVD and pictures of the day had only just arrived by
courier that morning.

"In my day y'just got a pile o'photos t'stick in an
album. Or if y'were flushed an' could afford one o'them
posh photographers, ya'd get the album ready-made
like," Clive marvelled. "Now look at it. All printed in a
book like it's proper published. These are wonderful

pictures Robbie, she's done a grand job that photographer lass hasn't she?"

Lynsey smiled as she unpacked the framed prints they'd ordered too. There was one of the two of them standing with Clive and Rich, Robbie holding a picture of Annie in his hand. "Here," Lynsey said as she passed the picture to Clive. "This one's for you Clive. We thought you'd like it."

It was an eight by ten in a subtle, chrome frame. It was beautiful and Clive found he couldn't speak as he looked at it. The picture of Annie had also been an eight by ten and so was big enough that her lovely smile could be easily made out in this one. He maintained his composure as he looked back up at Lynsey. "Thank you lovey," he half whispered. "I just know she'd be so, so happy an' proud of y'both."

"Now for the big one, eh Lyns?" Robbie picked up the large parcel that they'd left until last. "This should be the canvas we ordered." He ripped away the strip along the 'open' line and the thick cardboard package opened like a book, allowing him to slide the poster-sized canvas out from its protective layers.

Lynsey gasped. "Oh that looks so much more striking than I thought it would. I mean, I knew it'd look good, but I'm blown away Robbie."

He stood it on the table, resting against the wall. She was right, it was a stunning picture of the two of them having their first dance. Emily, the photographer, had caught the moment perfectly: The movement in Lynsey's gown, the way they were both looking at each other, the lighting, it was all so perfect. Even Robbie felt a little rheumy-eyed as he looked at it. It had been a brilliant day, though he wished his mum had lived to see it. He was at least content in the knowledge that she'd be happy for him. He liked to think that both of them, Mona, his real mum and Annie, the woman he'd only ever known as Mum, would both be watching over him, both have seen him on his wedding day, both proud of the man he'd become.

Robbie had spent much of the past few months since Annie's death just *getting on with it* so to speak. It had been easy to allow himself to become pre-occupied in the lead up to the wedding, but now that the whole thing was past, thoughts of Eban Whithorn and the file of information that Dredger had left for him were creeping into his day more and more.

Old Gregor Scoular. Robbie missed the old duffer. It was strange because in the grand scheme of things, he'd not actually known the old man for very long at all. Yet, he still felt a sense of loss at the thought of not seeing him again. He'd had a strong connection to Dredger that seemed to run deep, though God knows why.

There'd been some more of Michael's memories that had surfaced in the months since Annie's death, but not many, not as many as he'd have liked. There were people he'd remember, though not always their names nor their context in some instances too. For instance, he'd remembered that the butcher's son was a chubby wee lad, but in his head, he'd be convinced that his name had been Justin, when it had actually been Kelvin. Thankfully he still had Joe to help with such things. Joe McStay, Robbie's last link to his old life in the Isle. All of those people who'd gone to so much trouble and such lengths to help him all those years ago, and Joe was the only one left. Everyone else all dead now, or left the village for pastures new many years back. Of course Eban was still alive too, still hanging in there…unfortunately.

There were so many questions he'd liked to have asked Eban, so many answers he'd have demanded, but even if the vile old cripple could tell him things, could he really trust what he might have to say? Probably not.

Robbie had been finding it hard to reconcile with himself. He thought that irrespective of what Eban Whithorn had done in the past, that he was an old man now. Completely dependent on others for his every day care, no longer able to communicate, to express his needs. Though no-one could say with any certainty how sharp Eban's mental state was, Robbie was convinced that his father knew what was what. At least, he hoped his father knew what was what, because that other part of himself, his unforgiving, vengeful side, wanted Eban to know what each day entailed for him. He wanted that locked-in syndrome to be an excruciating torturous existence. Being unable to say if he was in pain, was hungry, needed the toilet, everything. Robbie knew that the *right* thing to do, would be to forgive, to sympathise even, but he just couldn't. He felt a certain shame in these dark thoughts, but he couldn't shake them, not yet at any rate.

"Penny for them?" Lynsey caught him off guard.

Robbie smiled back at her. "It's nothing, really. Just drifting off, chilling, y'know how it is?"

She put her arms around his waist and pulled herself in close. "Ya can't fool me Robbie McAndrew," she said. "I've seen y'looking at that envelope Joe gave ya. I think maybe it's time, don't you?"

"Time for what?" he asked, trying to appear nonchalant.

"Time you opened it up an' dealt with what's inside, that's what." She gave him *that* look. The one that told him to not even bother trying to deny it.

"You're amazing," he told her as he leant in for a kiss.

"I know, that's why y'married me," Lynsey laughed as she dodged him. Wriggling out of his grasp, she went to the desk where she pulled open the heavy bottom drawer and took out the large manila envelope that had remained untouched since the day of Annie's funeral. "Here," she handed it to him, "we both know that things are starting t'keep you awake at night again don't we? I hope y'know I understand Robbie? We all do an' so would Annie. Whatever's in this; I think y'should deal with it soon, while ya've still got someone who can answer things for ya."

"D'ya mean Joe? While Joe's still alive?" It had seemed a cold thing to think of at first consideration, but he knew she was right. If there was anything in there relating to the Isle of Stennoch and Robbie's real parents, then Joe was the only one left who'd be able to clarify anything for him; if anything were to need clarification that was.

***

Lynsey's sister, Natalie, had moved back to Leeds, she'd moved in with Mark Pallister just after the wedding and the two sisters were going on a shopping trip. Before she'd left, Lynsey had carefully placed the manila envelope on the coffee table in the living room by way of a huge hint for Robbie. It made him smile when he'd come across it later that morning. She knew him so well.

He remembered the feelings he'd had that day when Annie had brought round that old box. The one that changed his life forever because that had been the day that he'd found out that Robbie McAndrew was a long dead baby in a grave somewhere and that he himself, was in fact Michael Whithorn. That Annie was his Aunt and not his mother and that Mona, his real mother had likely died at the hands of his father, a bloody Vicar for

God's sake. He didn't mind admitting that he had reservations about what might be lurking in this envelope on his coffee table. He wasn't sure just how much of a head-fuck one man could reasonably be expected to take, but he knew he'd look anyway. He despised the very existence of his father, but he also had a morbid fascination to know more about him, because no-one seemed to know anything about Eban before he'd arrived in the Isle; until Dredger had done what Dredger did best.

Elizabeth and Martin Whithorn, Robbie's half siblings, who'd have thought? There'd been absolutely no mention of Eban having a marriage previous to the one to Mona Cummings, Robbie's mother, or Michael, to give him his true name. And after reading Dredger's letter to him on the day of Annie's funeral, it seemed to suggest that Eban's first marriage had never formally ended; that he'd married Mona bigamously. A reckless thing to do for any man, but ridiculously stupid for a Minister of the Free Church of Scotland.

Sitting down, Robbie pulled the contents of the envelope out onto the sofa beside him. Much of the papers had 'Dumfriesshire Police' printed at the top of it, mostly photocopies of handwritten notes. There were other scraps of paper that had quite clearly originated from church offices as well as registry offices. There they were; two photocopies of birth certificates for Elizabeth Mae Whithorn, born 17th February 1961 and Martin John Whithorn, born 21st October 1962. The father's name was recorded as Eban Whithorn, though there was no mention of him being a Reverend. In fact, his occupation was stated as being 'labourer'. So they were born before Eban was ordained into the Free Church of Scotland then. Their mother was named as being Maevis Whithorn with 'housewife' written under occupation for her. In amongst the rest of the papers was a copy of the couple's marriage certificate too, which if correct, showed that they had married when Maevis had been five months pregnant with Elizabeth. Her maiden name looked like it was double barrelled: Parker-Tait, though the handwriting wasn't the clearest.

What Robbie came across next took some absorbing. He thought he'd misread the name at first, then the date but as it turned out, he'd read both correctly. There were two other certificates; a birth certificate with the same dates on it that were on the one for Martin, but the name is what threw him, Michael James Whithorn. The other photocopy was of a death certificate for Michael: died 3rd December 1962. The first thing that struck him of course was that his father, their father, had been sick enough to call him Michael too. The second realisation was that Martin had been a twin, until his brother's death that is. The cause of which was given as 'failure to thrive', whatever that meant. All of this occurring a good ten years or so before he'd been born himself. So what had happened in the meantime? Where were these people now? The county registry mark on both the marriage certificate and the birth certificate for Elizabeth, was Lanarkshire, but the twins' birth certificates and Michael's death certificate were marked as Larne in Northern Ireland. So somewhere between 1961 and 1962 Eban had moved his family from Scotland to Ireland.

Robbie also came across copies of the correspondences which had passed between the Reverend Jacob Whithorn and the various retirement and care home facilities that had been looking after Eban. One document stood out among the others. It was letter headed from some sort of clinic and was addressed to the bishop. Typewritten, but with the scrawl of a ballpoint across the top which read *Enclose this copy for Jacob please.* The reference line read *With regard to our recent assessment of Rev. Eban Whithorn* and was dated 19th July 1996. The content was somewhat vague, but seemed to imply that Eban's mental health was in question. Words like, dissociative and psycho-pathology were mentioned, but Robbie wasn't too sure if this was something diagnostic or if this particular letter was just one in a number. Something that didn't make much sense on its own but was probably part of a bigger picture.

Still, it had given him a starting point because several of the letters from care homes were addressed to either the bishop, or to Jacob himself. There was nothing that Dredger had been able to get hold of that came from recent years. The most recent letter was one from the home that Eban now resided in, though it appeared to have been sent just after he'd been admitted there. It talked about a respite period and how, after further assessment and discussion, it had been decided that it would be better for the patient, Eban, to remain at the facility rather than be returned to a previous care home, which was apparently less able to meet his needs.

The one thing that the documents did provide though, were the contact details for the Reverend Jacob Whithorn, Eban's brother. There were details there too for the bishop. Robbie took note of them, but decided that he'd only contact the bishop if all else failed. He didn't trust the church, nor did he think they'd be particularly forthcoming with any information he might ask them for. These were modern times and definitely more difficult for them to close ranks around one of their own, but none-the-less, he didn't hold much by way of confidence in them.

At the bottom of the pile was a small photograph; an old black and white, head and shoulders shot of a young woman. Robbie didn't recognise her and wondered if she were Maevis, Eban's first wife. '1959' was the only thing written on the back, no name, nothing.

Now that he'd looked at this stuff, well, most of it anyway, Robbie found himself pretty fired up again. When Annie had died it had broken his heart and he didn't want to be bothered about anything at the time. He was going to marry the love of his life and wanted to focus on that. Nothing else had seemed important to him, but now that the dust had settled somewhat, that curiosity, that morbid fascination was taking him over again. He needed to know. He wanted to know about that part of himself that had come from Eban. The man was a mystery, almost as if he'd just landed in the Isle of Stennoch back then. No past, no history, he was just there. And even though Annie, Dredger and Joe had all agreed that they thought he'd come over from Ireland, none of them was entirely sure, though Dredger told him that Eban spoke with a sullied Scottish accent, meaning that elsewhere had left its mark in his diction. Something that could have occurred due to his own travels or perhaps due to his parents' travels when he was a child. If they really had been missionaries, then at least that would make some kind of sense.

Robbie knew he should wait for Lynsey before doing anything, but she'd be hours yet. He decided to sound his brother Rich out instead. He could be hot-headed when it came to dealing with his own shit could Rich, but he was usually pretty sensible about other peoples'.

Chapter Two

"So what did he have t'say then?" Rich asked. He was sitting in the passenger seat of Robbie's parked car, outside his tattoo shop on Briggate.

Robbie sighed and took a few pensive seconds before replying with regard to the telephone conversation he'd had with Dieter Richter, the care home manager where Eban lived. "Not a great deal really. Says the old bastard's had another mini-stroke since I were there, but not much else has changed."

"Does he believe your story then? He still thinks yer Eban's nephew?"

"Yeh, why wouldn't he? It's not like there's anyone to put him right is it?" He pushed his fingers back through his hair, he was a little anxious. "I feel like I shouldn't give a fuck Rich, but part o' me just can't switch it off."

Rich tried to reassure his brother. "Look, I'm no expert Robbie, but whatever y'think o' the old twat; he is *your* father. He might never o'been yer dad, but biologically I mean. I'd be surprised if y'weren't curious. Where did he come from? Who was he before he met Mona? No-one's that fucking twisted without there being some background."

Robbie felt suddenly defensive. "Doesn't matter about his background; there's no excuse for the stuff he's done!" he snapped.

"I never said there was." Rich bounced it back. "I didn't mean it that way. I meant that he didn't just start being a twat when he arrived in the Isle o' Stennoch. He can't have done. He must have form somewhere, some kind o'trail of devastation that's likely left marks somewhere if y'get my meaning."

Robbie conceded. "Yeh, sorry. There's part o'me that doesn't want t'know, but then I can't switch that off either."

"Then do it. Find out what y'can. Whatever y'find out is history now isn't it? It's not like there's anything y'can change, but if it helps you understand, helps ya put it t'bed an' move on, then just do what y'need to, but don't let it take over yer life this time. Y'know I'll help if y'want it. An' I bet Lynsey's not got a problem with it either has she?"

After thinking for a moment more, Robbie reached round to the back of the driver's seat and brought the dog-eared manila envelope back onto his knee. "I asked Dieter if Eban's brother had visited. I wanted t'bring him up in case anything's happened, y'know, like he might o'died or something. He told me he hadn't visited, said he were quite old himself, so probably not up to it. I had t'blag it a bit. Said I had his address from years ago an' wondered if it'd changed."

"An' have ya?" Rich asked. "Got his address?"

"Only what's on some o'these letters that Dredger left me. Dieter didn't seem t'know much. Just said he'd not been informed of any changes, but that he wouldn't necessarily expect t'be. Said the Bishop'd be the one t'know anything like that. I just told him t'pass on my regards to *Uncle Eban* an' said I'd probably visit in a few weeks. Didn't really know what else *to* say."

There was a sudden bang on the passenger side window, startling the brothers. It was Damo, one of Rich's apprentices. "Are you coming back in any time soon?" he shouted through the glass. "Only yer client's waiting an' I want t'go for my dinner."

"On my way," Rich responded with a wave of his hand as if to dismiss Damo, who just rolled his eyes and went back into the shop.

"I'll sort it," Robbie said. "I think I'll ring the number on this letter, see if it's still live, ask if he lives there."

Rich looked a little concerned. "An' say what? *Hello, are you the mad bastard's brother?* Ya need t'know if it's the right person first, without it sounding all weird or suspicious. Ya'll have t'make something up. Here, pass it t'me, I'll do it."

He took the letter from Robbie and pulled his mobile from his pocket. "Look," he said, "ya need t'do this to hide your own number." He keyed in 1 4 1 before he dialled the rest of the number. "That makes the incoming call show up as unknown or withheld or whatever."

Robbie took the phone from him. "No, I'll do it. I'll think o'something. If he's not well it'll probably be someone else that answers anyway." He pressed *call* on the handset and waited.

It rang four times before someone picked it up. "Hello," said the male voice at the other end. His voice sounded wheezy with a deep tone to it.

Robbie's eyes widened and he quickly glanced round at Rich before speaking. "Erm, hello. I was wondering if the Reverend Jacob Whithorn still lived at this address we have on our system for him?" Robbie read off the Northern Irish address from the top of the Bishop's letter he was holding.

"Yes, that's correct," the man confirmed.

"Could I speak to him please?" Robbie asked, not that he'd any idea what it was he might actually say.

"You *are* speaking to him. Can I ask who *you* are?"

For the briefest of moments, Robbie was stunned. He hadn't expected Jacob Whithorn to still be at that address and he certainly hadn't expected him to answer the phone, to hear his voice. He panicked and hung up quickly. "That was him," he said to Rich. "Fuck, I never expected that."

"So what now?" Rich asked. "Will y'ring him back or what?"

"Don't know, not sure. I might write to him maybe."

Another bang on the window from Damo disturbed them. "Rich, come on mate."

"For fuck sake!" Rich stormed. "Alright, I'm coming!" He turned back to Robbie as he opened the car door. "Let me know what ya've decided."

***

Lynsey got home just as Robbie was finishing a phone call. She'd a couple of bags with her, though according to her that was nothing compared to the amount that Natalie had bought. She noticed the pained expression on her husband's face and pushed for a reason.

"I'm going to Ireland," he told her. "Tomorrow."

"You're what?" Stunned by this sudden revelation, she dropped her bags down beside her and walked further into the room. "Since when? Why?"

"I've found Jacob Whithorn. I want t'go see him; face t'face," Robbie explained.

"Christ, I've only been out a few hours Robbie. How's this all happened so fast? Has he invited ya?" Lynsey was struggling to make sense of how so much could happen in such a short time. "He can't possibly have got his head round you being his nephew. He'll think y'should be dead, they all think Michael's dead."

"I know. I didn't tell him. His address is in this stuff Dredger gave me; there was a phone number so I rang it. I never thought he'd actually answer, but he did."

"What did y'say to him?" she was blatantly worried.

"Not much," Robbie told her. "I bottled it once I knew it were him. I hung up."

Lynsey's sense of puzzlement only deepened. "I don't get it Robbie. If you've not told him anything, if he doesn't know who you are, then how come you're going to Ireland? Ya can't just turn up on his doorstep, surely?"

"Well I've just booked a flight t'Belfast for tomorrow, so I guess I can," he replied, though he was cautious to say it in a way that wasn't going to instigate an argument. He'd thought about asking her to go with him, but he'd no idea what to expect when he got there, or indeed what kind of reception he might get and he didn't want to have to worry about her as well as himself. To be fair, he'd not got the faintest idea what he'd say when he got there either. He'd not thought any further ahead than getting on a plane. All he'd assumed thus far, was that Jacob, whether he'd approved of the situation or not, had been complicit in protecting Eban, in covering up the things he'd done. That knowledge in itself, would on the surface, deem it reasonable to think that Robbie's reception in Ireland might not be the warmest.

"I want to go with you," Lynsey insisted.

"No. Absolutely not. I'm sorry Lyns, but I just need t'do this myself. My head's in bits at the minute an' I don't want to have t'worry about you as well as everything else. I love ya Lyns, y'know that don't ya? Just trust me, please?"

She could feel her heart racing at the thought, but she knew her husband. Once he'd made his mind up about something, he was damn near impossible to budge.

"I'm not some kind o'weakling y'know; this isn't the dark ages Robbie. I *can* look after myself believe it or not."

Robbie got to his feet and went to put his arms around her. "I know that love," he said softly, "but I don't want to end up being a moody twat cos things get a bit heavy for me like they did last year when we went up t'Scotland. I just need t'be able t'get my head round things without worrying that I'm hurting anyone's feelings."

"But yer hurting mine now Robbie."

"You know me better than I know myself Lyns. You know I'll be fine. I've knocked our Richard back too, he wanted t'come, but I just want t'do this myself. Please don't take it the wrong way."

Relenting, though making a point of it, Lynsey pulled away from him and retrieved her bags from the floor in the doorway. "I suppose I'd struggle t'get the time off work at such short notice anyway," she said. "Will y'ring Joe McStay first an' tell him? He's the only one who's met Jacob. An' you can be the one t'tell Clive, because I'm not."

He smiled, if only to himself. He knew her so well and could see what she was doing. "Trust me Lyns."

"But you have no idea how it felt when you'd gone missing last year after being attacked Robbie; what we went through. It was awful."

Still smiling, he drew in a deep breath. "I'll ring ya every day, ten times a day, fifty if it makes y'feel any better."

"Every day? How long d'ya plan being there?"

Robbie could hear the rising panic in her voice. "Two or three, that's all an' I promise I'll check in with ya…lots, okay?

Chapter Three

Turning left out of Belfast City Airport onto the Sydenham Bypass, Robbie followed the road round onto the A55 and headed away from the city. Newtownards was only about ten miles east of Belfast and according to the built-in Satnav in the hire car, shouldn't take him more than twenty minutes to get there. Having said that, he was a bit more old school when it came to finding his way around. He preferred to use the directions he'd plotted himself, along with good old-fashioned road sign reading. Satnavs had got him into trouble on more than one occasion. Not that he ruled out their use, he just didn't like to rely on them solely.

It wasn't too long before he found himself taking a left onto the A20, Upper Newtownards Road. He soon passed the large gated entrance to the Stormont Estate with the Parliament Buildings visible off in the distance up the long, straight driveway.

Once he'd passed a sign for Dundonald High School and the turning for a small industrial estate, he seemed to leave the built-up outskirts of Belfast behind as he drove on through the more rural farm land; agricultural for the most part, though sheep occupied the odd field on his journey too.

The light was beginning to fade somewhat, not yet dark, but low enough that some of the other traffic on the road had put on their headlights. Robbie's original intention had been to go straight to the address he had for Jacob Whithorn, but now that he was actually entering Newtownards, he was beginning to have second thoughts. He wanted to see where it was, maybe catch a glimpse of the old man, but anxiety had begun to build in the very pit of his gut and he wasn't feeling too confident any more.

Circular Road; he knew he was close now. He pulled over to the roadside, opposite a school, Regent

House Grammar. It was hard to know what was bothering him more, hard to differentiate. Was it the thought of meeting Eban's older brother, his own uncle? Or was it mixed feelings of resentment, that Jacob should have done more?

He realised he hadn't really thought things through properly. Jacob would believe that Michael Whithorn was dead just like everyone else did. Could Robbie really risk telling him the truth? After all he didn't know anything about him. According to Joe, other than exchanging pleasantries with Jacob all those years ago when his parents had married, no-one knew him, he was an enigma. What if he was just like Eban? Cut from the same cloth? It was dawning on him that he really hadn't thought this through at all. He should have taken more time instead of jumping on the first available plane and finding himself in the middle of god-knows-where on a mission he was ill-prepared for.

He never used to be this impulsive but ever since the mugging and the head injury he'd sustained, something inside him had changed. Not the fundament of his personality, but little things, like this, like being more willing to take risks than he had before, a little more reckless. He'd lost count of the times Lynsey had brought it up over the past year. *Think how you'd feel if I did that* she'd say to him and she'd be right. He found that he had to keep reminding himself of her words at times, in order to keep a lid on things. If he'd have arrived home one day to find her packing a bag, stating her intention to fly to Belfast the next day for this kind of hair-brained reason, he couldn't imagine he'd be too enamoured about it either.

Looking to his left, there was a car park attached to the school. Beyond that were the backs of some red-brick semi-detached houses. Robbie knew that somewhere within that housing estate he'd find the Reverend Jacob Whithorn. Maybe he lived in one of the houses that Robbie was looking at right then, who knows. His heart was pounding and part of him just wanted to turn tail back home to Leeds and the comfort of Lynsey, his new wife, his best friend, but then he'd come this far already and he knew he'd regret it if he didn't carry on while he'd got the chance.

The street lights were all warming up now and he was tired. Taking out the email confirmation he'd received, he began to input the address of his B & B into the satnav: *The Old Schoolhouse, Bowtown Road, BT23.* He was only tracking at four minutes away, not far. He put the car in gear and indicated to pull back out. He had to wait for a mother with a push chair and two unruly boys in tow, to finish crossing the road in front of him first.

"Michael!" she yelled as she passed the front of the car. Robbie jumped, suddenly feeling momentarily vulnerable, until he realised she'd shouted at one of her boys who was lagging behind. Relieved but still a little shaken, he drove off. He was tired and getting hungry and the thought of a couple of pints was quite appealing too, so he followed the road up to the traffic lights which were red. There was a Renault showroom opposite, quite big, he'd keep an eye out for it again, a good landmark so he wouldn't get lost when he came back.

He turned left and noticed that what he'd thought would be Comber Road changed into South Street. He'd not noticed that when he'd looked at the map to plan his route, he'd thought it was all called Comber Road. It appeared that it was Comber Road right up to the Circular Road junction where it changed to South Street. A brief glance at the satnav confirmed it.

The first part of South Street was an odd mix of newly painted, terraced cottages on the left and semi-derelict ones on the right, like half the street had been given a face lift, but the other half had been left in ruin. It soon gave way to shops on both sides though. Another couple of minutes and a left turn after a fire station found Robbie on Bowtown Road. The Old Schoolhouse was right on the edge of the built up area at the junction with Ballyreagh Road. There was a small car park to the rear in what would've once been the school playground no doubt. It didn't resemble anything like a playground any more, but it was nice and the building itself was still very much like an old fashioned schoolhouse apart from the big conservatory that now wrapped around from the back to the side overlooking farmland. The school itself had been undoubtedly replaced by the Castle Gardens Primary that was pretty much diagonally opposite and a much bigger building than the old one.

He was met at the door by a middle-aged woman who introduced herself as Paulette. She'd a soft voice with a very brogue accent and she liked to chat, that was clear enough. By the time she'd shown Robbie up to his room, he'd pretty much learned the bulk of her life story. She wasn't native to these parts, though her husband, Barry, he was. Theirs had been a mixed marriage as she was Catholic and Barry a Protestant, which had resulted in her family disowning her years ago and she'd not seen them since. They'd three daughters and two sons, all grown up now and doing really well for themselves, seven grandkids and one on the way.

"And here we are Mr McAndrew; this is you. Breakfast's half-seven 'til nine." She'd barely taken a breath between reeling off her family tree and pushing the room key into his hand.

"Er, thank you," Robbie called after her as she scuttled off across the landing.

As Robbie dropped his bag onto the bed, he remembered that his mobile phone was still in flight mode. Fishing it out of his jeans pocket, he quickly remedied this before dropping that too onto the bed and going into the en-suite bathroom to freshen up.

Paulette had left a neatly laminated A4 sheet on the bedside table, which detailed checking in and out times, breakfast, fire escape assembly point, as well as informing guests to dial 9 for an outside line and what the call costs were. *There are no pets allowed in any of our rooms, but there is free wifi.* Erm…okay.

Checking his phone, Robbie noticed that he'd got three text messages and two missed calls from Lynsey. A missed call from Clive and a text from Rich.

"Let me know when you land," the text from Rich read.

"FFS answer your phone Robbie," Lynsey's last one read. She'd left a voice mail to much the same end too.

To be fair, he *had* promised to call her as soon as he'd landed. He'd just got caught up sorting out the hire car and everything, he'd simply forgotten.

He braced himself for a bollocking and rang her back. "Lyns, before y'go off on one, I forgot love, I'm sorry," he pled his case. "It were a bit rushed sorting the hire car out 'cos they were wanting t'close up for the day. An' then it took me ages t'find my licence, it were right at the bottom of…"

"It's alright," she cut him off. "I've been worried Robbie that's all. I don't like this. I don't like it at all. Is it really so important that you have to be so far away? I hate this, especially when I can't get hold of ya. It reminds me of last year, I just…I don't know Robbie, I just don't like it."

He managed to talk her down, despite his own reservations and he did manage to cover the fact that in reality, he had no idea what he was doing.

***

Ray Graham had the patience of a saint when it came to his job and the kind of ne'er-do-wells he dealt with on a daily basis. He could usually find something in everyone that he liked, some endearing or redeeming quality, but even he was struggling with Chris Hartley. He was due to attend as an appropriate adult while Chris underwent a psychiatric evaluation ahead of his upcoming day in court. He'd cancelled or rescheduled other clients in order to be there, only to have Chris tell him to *fuck off* at the eleventh hour…charming. What made it worse is that the look in Chris' eye made it plain to see that he was enjoying this game; getting a kick out of manipulating people. It was hard to keep his cool when all Ray wanted was to bite back. It showed, it must have done and Chris Hartley was more than aware of it.

Ray had dealt with a lot of unsavoury characters in his time, that was true, but there was something more than a little bit sinister about this young man. He had a string of violent robberies behind him, not to mention a list of aliases as long as his arm and Ray felt he was only a heartbeat away from taking the next step and murdering someone. The levels of violence he'd shown to some of his victims was nothing short of gratuitous. He hadn't needed to go as far as he did, but he *appeared out of control* according to his former friend and partner in crime, Dale Price.

Price had some previous, burglaries for the most part. Then he'd been foolish enough to be drawn in by Hartley, but the levels of aggression and violence employed by the latter had been too much even for a career criminal like Price. Price was a fit, athletic, young man, but he was clearly scared of Hartley. It hadn't taken much for him to turn Queen's evidence in order to get a lighter conviction for himself as soon as they'd been arrested and charged with several robberies. One in particular tipped the balance for Price, when the police told him they were going to push for an attempted murder charge on that jogger they'd robbed on the tow-path at Apperley Bridge. That was when he knew for certain that he needed to distance himself from Hartley.

Price hadn't done any of the beatings, or so he'd told the police. The problem was that he was the only one showing up on their system as having a criminal record, because his mate, Gareth Dalby, looked to be squeaky clean, until Price had given them his real name that is, Chris Hartley. Everything changed then. Price told them how he'd begged Hartley to stop, told him he was going too far. He said that Hartley had tried to drag the battered, unconscious man to the edge of the canal, to push him in and let him drown. He'd bellowed at Price to help him do it as the man was such a dead weight, but Price said he'd refused. They'd heard voices approaching and scarpered. Price paid for his refusal with a broken nose later that day.

Chapter Four

There was a ridiculous amount of traffic moving through and around Circular Road. It was about eight-twenty the next morning and apart from the fact it was rush hour, there were endless cars pulling up and dropping off teenagers on the roads around Regent House Grammar School, kids more than old enough to get on a bus and get themselves to their destination without all the hassle it caused being chauffeur-driven by over bearing parents in BMWs and oversized Audis, clogging up the roads and competing for ten-second parking spots with the Chelsea tractor brigade. Robbie was beginning to wish he'd waited another hour or so before setting off, but he'd wanted to be at Jacob Whithorn's early enough that the old man wouldn't have gone out as yet. He just hadn't anticipated the onslaught of the school-run.

He turned off, onto Rugby Gardens and parked up, deciding it would be wise to wait it out rather than attempt to fight his way through. He could feel his heart sinking a little with each minute that passed. Having psyched himself up, he'd been ready to pull up, get out of the car and knock on the door on Moray Crescent, just round the corner. In his mind's eye, Jacob would answer and he'd be able to blag him into a conversation about Eban.

He'd decided to use a cover story; he was going to say that he was a writer, doing a social research study of what made men of the church take up the dog-collar and how they felt after retiring from it. He'd already worked out his back story; he'd tell Jacob that he'd spoken to some of the retired clergy in Scotland and England and that he now wanted to speak to retirees in Ireland before taking his research to Wales. That way he could work in questions about family connections to the church etcetera. It was a last minute idea, but one he thought he'd be able to get away with; it sounded plausible at least.

Once the furore of the school traffic had died down, Robbie followed the road around to where it became Moray Crescent. As he rounded the corner he could see that he was now at the back of the school. There were hedges and a mesh wire fence running the length of this stretch on the right and semi-detached houses on the left, overlooking it.

'You have arrived at your destination', the satnav had informed him prior to beeping several times, just in case he'd not heard it…as if. Robbie's heart was in his mouth as he parked the car on the fenced side of the concrete road and took stock. There was a line of cars parked neatly in a row just on the other side of the fence, within the school grounds, staff cars no doubt. Looking the other way towards the houses, he strained to make out the number on the one opposite: number thirty-one. He was looking for number thirty-five, which was a couple of doors back. At least the damn satnav was nearly right.

Getting out of the car, he looked towards the house that was next-door-but-one. It stood out from the others, in that both itself and its adjoining neighbour were clad in a grey stone facia. All the other houses were the standard red brick same as most of the rest of the estate.

Taking a deep breath, Robbie crossed the small road and walked up the tarmacked drive to the front door of number thirty-five. He quickly ran through his cover story in his head again, just so as he wouldn't trip himself up, then he pressed the bell. He couldn't hear if it rang indoors or not, so he knocked on the frosted glass panel of the door too, just in case. He couldn't see any movement through the glass nor hear any; he'd just about raised his arm, ready to knock for a second time, when a voice to his right startled him.

"What d'ya want?" he demanded to know.

Robbie spun in his direction, taken aback somewhat. There was a young man standing there on the driveway. He'd a mop of fair hair beneath a navy blue baseball cap and he'd pale blue eyes. He looked in his early twenties, though he could've been younger given what he was wearing: jeans draped round his backside, an over-sized tee-shirt with an equally oversized hoodie, unzipped over the top of it and ox-blood coloured skater shoes.

"Are ya selling some'ing? Cos if y'are ya can feck off, we're not interested." He took a step back, in order to make way for Robbie's exit.

"I er, I'm actually looking for Reverend Whithorn? Jacob Whithorn?" Robbie chanced.

"Yer English," stating the obvious. Robbie nodded his affirmation. "Come wit' me, it's round the back, we don't much use the front door." He led Robbie round the side of the house and through an archway by the garage to where the back door had been left ajar.

"Grandai!" he yelled out as they entered. "There's some Brit fella wanting ya's."

A Jack Russell terrier came bounding into the room yapping excitedly. "Quiet now Pip!" the young host instructed. It jumped up at Robbie with its front feet, tail wagging furiously. "Get down Pip! Sorry Mister…what's yer name anyways?"

Robbie held his hand out to shake. "Robbie, Robbie Wilkinson," he lied. He'd decided to use Clive's name, just in case his own rang any bells with Jacob. "And you are…?" he tried to sound confident.

"Alex Whithorn," he announced as he reciprocated the handshake. "Jacob's me granddaddy. I look in on him, take care o'him, y'know."

"I can take care o'myself wee man."

Robbie recognised the voice in an instant. It was the same deep, wheezy voice he'd heard over the phone only a couple of days previously and the only Scottish accent he'd heard since his arrival.

Alex tutted his disdain at being referred to as *wee man*. "Grandai, I'm nearly twenty-four. Will ya not stop it wit' the wee man thing."

Jacob smirked a little; he obviously knew what buttons to press to get a playful rise out of his grandson.

"Anyways, this fella's Robbie Wilkinson an' he's here t'see ya's," Alex said.

"Is that right now," Jacob stated rather than asked for confirmation. He was a big man, even in his advanced years. Taller than Eban by the look of him, though Robbie had never seen Eban standing. He had a walking stick in his left hand, a gold wedding band on his ring finger. He held his right hand out towards Robbie in greeting. "Pleased tae meet ya," he said as he shook hands with him. He held on to Robbie's hand just that little bit more than was comfortable; his stare was quite intense.

Heart pounding, Robbie responded as calmly as he could manage. "I'm pleased t'meet you too Reverend Whithorn."

"Yorkshireman," Jacob stated. "Unmistakable accent. Interesting." It was more the way he said it, than the words themselves that left Robbie with an uneasy feeling. He put it down to nerves. "What can I do for ya?"

Alex interrupted them, giving Robbie a welcome few extra seconds to try and get his story straight. "Shall I make a brew Grandai?" he asked.

Before Robbie had the chance to decline, Jacob had accepted for the both of them. He'd not taken his gaze away from Robbie since his arrival, peering at him over the rim of a thin pair of wire-framed spectacles. A wizened forehead with overgrown eyebrows and liver spots down both cheeks.

Having been shown round into the front room, Robbie took a seat in the armchair that was on the opposite side of the coffee table from the high-backed chair that Jacob was sitting in. Alex brought a tray in with a tea-pot, a jug of milk, a pot of sugar and three sets of cups and saucers stacked on it.

"Why's there three cups?" Jacob asked him. "You're not staying are ya? I thought ya were going tae The Ards for me? Get me some shopping in?"

Alex rolled his eyes and took one of the cups and saucers away. "Right y'are Grandai," he sighed.

"Money's in the kitchen, top o'the fridge," he informed him. "An' make sure ya remember tae call in the bookies this time. I'll share my winnings with ya." His laugh turned into a brief wheezy cough. He took a handkerchief from his pocket and coughed into it, wiping his nose and mouth as he did so. "Too many cigarettes," he told Robbie as he settled back down. "Stopped them though. I've breathing problems see. Only ever inhale this bloody thing now," he said, holding up a blue inhaler, like the ones used by asthmatics. "Why don't you pour?" He pointed at the tray, indicating for Robbie to go ahead and pour the tea.

As he did so, Robbie was aware of his hands shaking a little; he hoped Jacob hadn't noticed too. "Do y'take sugar?" he asked him.

"No," Jacob replied. "Ya still haven't said why yer here son?" His stare, still firmly fixed on Robbie.

Right, this was it, Robbie thought to himself. He needed to keep his cool and stick to his story. "Well, I'm writing a study on retired clergy. I've been travelling round, talking t'people about what made them sign up in the first place and how they felt about having t'retire." He was quite impressed with himself at how convincing he thought he sounded.

"Have ya now?" It was hard to tell if Jacob had believed him or not as he sat back in his easy chair, cup and saucer in hand.

Robbie continued. "So far I've spoken t'people in the North of England, Scotland, I'm here in Northern Ireland for a couple o'days, then I'll be speaking t'some in Wales an' the South…of England, that is."

"Really?" Jacob wasn't giving anything away. "An' ya've just *dropped in* on 'em all have ya? Or is it just me that ya didn't think required a more respectful approach than you just turning up on a man's doorstep like one o'them double-glazing salesmen?"

Robbie was taken aback, he hadn't expected that, nor had he thought about how it might look, him just turning up. Stupid, stupid, stupid. He should've taken more time to think it through better. Still he needed to think on his feet now.

"An' how d'ya know where we all live? How d'ya get my address for instance?" Jacob pressed him for an answer. One he couldn't find quickly enough.

"Well, I er…I…"

"It was you rang me the other day wasn't it son? The line went dead."

It was pointless denying it. "Yeah, sorry. I tried t'ring back but it wouldn't connect," he lied…again. "I'm sorry I should've kept trying Reverend Whithorn; or d'ya prefer Mr Whithorn now?" he tried to salvage things.

The old man took a slurp of his tea before resting it back on the saucer and placing them both on the coffee table in front of himself. He drew in a deep breath as he sat back into his chair, bringing both hands up onto his chest and intertwining his fingers as he released the breath in one long, drawn-out sigh that seemed to last an age.

He dropped his chin and looked straight at Robbie over the top of those wire rims. "Well, maybe we should just do away with the formalities Robbie," he finally said. "Maybe ya should just call me Uncle Jacob; what d'ya say tae that?"

Chapter Five

"I'm not as green as I'm cabbage looking," Jacob said.

"But I…I think you've…"

"…made a mistake?" Jacob laughed, causing himself to cough again. He took out his handkerchief to cover his mouth as he did so. "We're none of us fools Robbie. I know who y'are; knew it as soon as I laid eyes on ya. Ya've a strong look o'him y'know, of yer father."

Robbie was too stunned to speak, too confused. Just what had he walked into? None of this fit or made sense. He'd planned out what he wanted to say, how he'd wanted to play it and none of it had included Jacob actually knowing who he was. Finding it difficult to believe, he started to wonder if the old man had mistaken him for someone else's son. He couldn't find any words to respond with.

Jacob leant in and picked up his cup again. "I wondered if there'd ever come a day y'know. A day like today, where you'd show up wanting answers."

"I'm sorry?" Robbie was still struggling to grasp things.

"Is Robbie the real name ya go by now son or are y'still Michael? Only I don't want tae cause offence at all."

It seemed pointless trying to keep it up; he'd been caught so much off guard that he was finding it impossible to think quickly enough. The whole situation reminded him of the first time he'd met old Dredger Scoular back in the Isle of Stennoch. "Robbie, I'm Robbie," he conceded.

"Ya took her husband's name then, Wilkinson?" Jacob asked.

"McAndrew, I'm Robbie McAndrew. Peter McAndrew was Mum's…I mean Annie's first husband, he died. Clive Wilkinson's my step-dad, kinda."

"Were they good tae ya son?" Jacob seemed genuinely concerned. "Were ya looked after well?"

Robbie looked him square in the eyes. "Yes I was, very well."

"An' do they know yer here Robbie?"

"Clive does, Mum died last year. Cancer." The lump in his throat almost caused a sob, but he managed to swallow it back down.

"I'm very sorry tae hear that son. I lost my wife last year too; it's been hard." Jacob took another sip of his tea.

"How did y'know?" Robbie finally plucked up the courage to ask, "that I'm Michael?"

The harsh and to-the-point expression that had adorned Jacob's features until now, began to melt away and a softer, more compassionate appearance took its place. "It's always been suspected in the family son. Eban thought he knew, did ya know that? My brother's always known ya weren't dead or so he once told me. When she took ya, he was all set tae raise hell about it, but we, the family that is, knew it were true that ya'd be better off an' we stood against him. The church elders knew what sort of a man he'd become, they'd known for a long time. We let them all continue tae think ya'd drowned, tae my shame I even lied tae the Bishop about it. Fed him some cock-an-bull story about it tipping Eban over the edge an' I needed tae get him away.

"Truth was, he'd tipped over the edge a long time afore that. He needed tae be stopped an' the Bishop knew that as well as anyone. I brought him back here at first, tae Ireland, but that created a whole host of other problems."

Robbie thought he knew what those other problems might be. "D'ya mean because of his other wife, not t'mention their two kids?"

This time it was Jacob's turn to look disconcerted. "You know about them?" he asked. "I didn't think Mona's family knew about them. He never told us he was going tae marry Mona y'know; we found out through the grape-vine so tae speak. I went over there tae try put a stop tae the wedding. It was bigamous, immoral not tae mention illegal. That's why I was there on the day."

"So why didn't y'stop it then? Why let it go ahead?"

Jacob let out a sigh as he paused for a moment. "Because he lied tae me son. He swore on the Holy Bible an' all the saints he could bring tae mind, that he'd divorced Maev, his first wife. He was so bloody-minded about it, so convincing that I questioned myself, questioned her honesty.

"Ya see, my brother was always on the outside, if ya catch my drift Robbie, always sly, always planning, but he's also a very clever man an' a master manipulator. A good looking fella in his youth an' a way about him that seemed tae either intrigue or scare folks. He'd set his cap at Maev, an' the more her people saw through him, the more he wanted his own way, an' he got it, but he never loved the girl. He became quite cruel an' sometimes violent, but she had the benefit of us, the Whithorns. We couldn't stop him, but it made him uncomfortable knowing we were witnesses tae his behaviour.

"My mother felt he'd benefit from turning tae the church, like them, like me I suppose, an' so he did. He was trained and ordained here in Northern Ireland, then he took up a post in Scotland, just outside Glasgow tae be exact. Told us he'd send for Maev an' their children when he was settled. He visited them a lot, back an' forth, but eventually it petered out. I think Maev was quite relieved in some ways, but it caused her a lot of hardship too. She'd no family support of her own as they'd disowned her years before when she'd married Eban an' she was too proud tae go back cap in hand tae them, proving them right all along. Then we found out he'd taken the post at the Isle of Stennoch; I only got tae know because I'd attended a Protestant convention in

Belfast about programs tae help kids from deprived inner city areas. There was a Bishop from New Galloway there. I overheard him telling someone that they'd finally replaced an old Minister; I forget if he'd died or just retired now, but his parish had been left wanting a while. Anyway, *the Reverend Eban Whithorn, a promising young man,* is what I heard him say. That's how we knew where he'd gone."

Robbie frowned. It was difficult to take in all of this information about his father, when he'd gone most of his life never even knowing he existed.

Jacob was aware things were awkward. "Look Robbie, tae cut a long story short, he'd never told the church he was a married man. Told them he was single an' by the time I found out he planned tae marry Mona it was too late. Time had passed, he an' Maev were estranged by then, an' even though he'd seen her only a few months afore, he still scared her. She dreaded his visits an' his threats. He still turned up occasionally, even after he'd married Mona y' know."

"Why the hell didn't anyone speak up then?"
Robbie couldn't get his head around how things could've
been allowed to decline in such a way. Why his wife,
his legal wife, or indeed Eban's own family at the very
least, wouldn't intervene to stop this from happening.

Jacob removed his spectacles and rubbed his sunken
eyes. "I'm sorry son. Yer right of course. We
should've done more I know. I don't know what tae say
tae ya about it; what excuses we might've had. Only that
my parents were very religious folk, Missionaries,
community leaders, prayer leaders. They were the sort
of folk that other folk looked up tae, turned tae in a time
of need. An' rightly or wrongly, they bent over
backwards tae protect their reputations. They did what
they thought was the right thing for Eban, but when
things got beyond their control, they felt they could do
no more than sweep it under the carpet, a kind of damage
limitation tack I suppose. Something I'm in part guilty
of too I know, but times were different then, society was
different then. The scandal that was looming would've
ended us all."

Robbie could feel a burning in his chest, emotions confused with reactions and both of them fighting for restraint. "So you knew what sort of a man he was; you knew what he was capable of an' you just *let* him loose on other people? You let him marry my mother knowing full well what sort of a life she'd have?"

"My parents prayed for your mother every day they were alive Robbie. Yes, we knew what sort of a man he was, but no, we did *not* know exactly what he was capable of. We hoped that if we left him tae his new life that it'd be the making of him. Mona's family seemed happy about the union; I thought that maybe he'd finally settled, that he was finally with a good woman that he loved an' wanted tae make a life with. He'd convinced me of a divorce with Maev an' I didn't find the truth out until much later."

"An' when y'did, why didn't y'do something then? Why not tell the Bishop at least?"

"Look, I know it's hard for ya tae understand son, but things really were different back then. There was the shame it would've brought tae so many including yer mother an' her own family. Maev didn't want anyone finding out that her husband had abandoned her an' married another woman, an' my parents were mortified. My mother was never the same until the day she died, blamed herself for it all ya see."

"Why would she blame herself? She was your mother as much as his an' *you* don't seem too bad for it," Robbie noted.

Jacob looked uneasy. He removed his glasses and rubbed the bridge of his nose where they'd been sitting. "I'm tae take it ya don't know then," he said rhetorically.

Robbie was nothing if not perplexed by that. "Know what?" he asked.

"Eban, the reason my mother blamed herself is because she'd been the one tae bring him intae the home. He's adopted ya see son." Noting the astonished expression on his guest's face, Jacob explained further. "He was four or five years old. My parents were in the Glasgow region as part o' their calling as Missionaries.

She, my mother that is, used tae organise days out an' treats for the underprivileged, especially the children. Anyway, one o'her regular haunts, if ya can call it that, was an orphanage in the area."

Robbie could feel his heart pounding at this new revelation; he'd had absolutely no idea. He found he couldn't help but hark back to the conversation he'd had with Dredger when the old man had tried to put him off from finding Eban. *There'll be more questions than answers*, he'd warned him, or words to that effect. And he had the feeling now that what Jacob had just revealed was only the tip of a very big iceberg.

"Are ya alright son?" Jacob interrupted his thoughts. "Shall I go on?"

Robbie nodded, but just as he did so, the telephone beside Jacob began to ring. The old chap excused himself as he answered it. While he was talking, Robbie got up from his seat and wondered towards the window. He'd believed Jacob to be a blood relation and though he knew he could get some answers to some of his questions, he couldn't help but feel a little disappointed in the knowledge that apart from Eban himself, he'd still not met anyone who could be described as an immediate blood relative. Oh he knew who his family were and he loved them dearly, that would never change, but this was a more basal feeling, something deep inside of him that felt the need to know more about his own DNA, his roots, about why his life had taken the turns that it had done.

Looking out of the window to his right, across the back gardens, he could see some sort of tower in the distance. It looked odd; right up on a hill that could be seen above the rooftops of the nearby houses. It reminded him of a castle's turret, but no castle to go with it. That's why it looked so odd sitting there on the hilltop all alone.

"That's Scrabo Tower," Jacob's deep wheezy tone brought him back to the present. "It was built in 1857 so I believe. Warring Charlie's memorial tower. Charles Stewart tae be precise, an old Marquis from round these parts." He drew in a deep breath before releasing it slowly. "That was an old parishioner of mine Robbie, well his daughter actually. He's no' well an' he'd like tae see me. He's in a hospice no' too far away. I'm sorry son, but I must go tae him."

It seemed very odd seeing such compassion from Jacob, when his brother was not only dis-compassionate, but damn right cruel. Though the fact that they weren't related by birth could explain a lot. "Of course," Robbie said, though he was aching to find out more; he knew he'd have to wait for now.

"Where are ya staying?" Jacob asked.

"The Old Schoolhouse on Bowtown Road."

"Oh aye, Barry an' Paulette's place isn't it?" Jacob asked. "Will ya still be there tomorrow Robbie? We've a lot tae discuss I think son."

"Yeah, I'll be there. Shall I leave my mobile number with ya?"

"Aye, write it on the pad beside the phone for me. I'll ring ya t'night son okay?"

Robbie wrote down his number as requested and shook his Uncle's hand. "Thank you," he said.

"What for?"

"For being so understanding I suppose. This can't be easy."

"I think it's easier for me than it is for you son," Jacob sighed. "There's more ya should know, but tomorrow'll do."

It must've only taken Robbie about five minutes or so to drive back to the B&B. He sat in his car outside for a while first, before deciding against going in. He didn't want to be alone and was really beginning to regret not bringing Lynsey with him. The past year or so had been so full of traumas; there'd been so much for him to get his head around and Lynsey had always been there for him. They'd been together for such a long time and he couldn't understand why they'd not married sooner, but he was glad they were married now, glad that she was his wife now because he couldn't imagine going through this without her support. All of those emotions he'd undergone over the past twelve months were something he thought he'd come to terms with. He still felt guilt that he was using the identity of his dead cousin, that his wife was known as Mrs McAndrew, when, if things were as they should've been, she'd be Mrs Whithorn.

Michael Whithorn; the name he was born with, the name he should be known by but wasn't. Through no fault of his own and without any control, he'd become Robbie McAndrew, because in order to conceal him from his abusive father, his mother's sister, Annie, felt she'd no other choice. A fact that when it'd first become apparent had made him feel physically ill. He hated the thought that he'd grown up hiding behind the identity of a dead child, his own cousin, but he'd had time to come to terms with that. He'd had time to learn that it had been a necessary evil when all else had appeared to be futile. But to find out that even his original name, his true name, Michael Whithorn, was one he'd been given by his father, Eban Whithorn, who unbeknown to anyone else, had used the same name as a previous child he'd had, a twin who'd not survived infancy, it was deplorable. Eban had basically fathered four children in all, two of which had the same name, Michael; Robbie's original name. It only served to stir up all of those feelings again.

It was ridiculous and he knew it deep down, but he couldn't shake the feelings of inadequacy. Difficult to explain why, but it was almost as if he weren't worthy of an identity of his own, as if he'd not mattered enough. Being born into the identity of a dead half sibling, then being raised in the identity of a dead cousin. The truth was, his real mother, Mona, couldn't possibly have known about Eban's past or the other Michael Whithorn. She was blameless; Eban however, must've thought it to be some kind of sick joke. Logic told Robbie that all of this had been beyond his knowledge at the time, let alone his ability to have any control and it made him feel angry. Angry with himself mostly, that he'd wanted to matter enough to Eban. Why? The man was an evil son-of-a-bitch who didn't deserve space in Robbie's head, let alone anything else. This was why he was missing his wife right now, he could tell her these things and she'd know what to say.

***

Listening to his voice-mails as he crossed the Headrow in Leeds, Ray Graham, the man loosely described as a 'social worker type' by Radley, came to a stop just outside the town hall. The traffic was noisy and he wasn't sure he'd heard the last message properly so he pressed number one, on the keypad to listen again, this time blocking off his other ear from the noise. His heart sank as he absorbed the information he was hearing and his headache suddenly worsened.

A serious expression on his face gave away both his annoyance and the fact that he was growing weary of something. He called his office to speak to a colleague.

"Hi Debs it's Ray. Listen, I'm going t'forward an email on to you hun. Would y'mind printing off the attachment for me? I'm not going t'be back in the office for an hour or so yet an' I'll need to grab it an' run if

that's okay? Yep, yeh, I'll do it now from my phone.
Thanks Debs you're a life saver."

It only took a minute to forward the email then Ray continued on his way to the Crown Court building. Two girls that were on his books were due in court for a preliminary hearing. He didn't need to be there, but they'd asked to speak to him before they went in. After that he'd be free to get that print-out before his next appointment. He could peruse it at home later but he knew it meant he'd have to head back to the prison to speak to the so called Chris Hartley again in the morning.

Chapter Six

Robbie needed to think, he needed to get his head
around this new information and he wanted to wait until
he knew Lynsey would be on her lunch break so that he
could call her, partly to keep her posted, but mostly just
so he could hear her voice. He started up the car again
and put it into gear, moving off with no real destination
in mind. He carried on along the Bowtown Road,
heading east away from Newtownards. He wasn't on the
road for long. About fifteen or twenty minutes was all it
took for him to find himself on the coast in a small
village called Millisle, bigger than the Isle of Stennoch,
but small none-the-less. He stopped on the Main Street
and bought himself fish and chips from a place called
McClements before driving on. Turning off left next to
an old Masonic Hall towards the sea-front, he soon
found himself tucked out of the way in what looked like

some sort of car park. He wasn't sure if he was trespassing or not, but he couldn't see any signs to indicate if this was private land. Besides, there was a little church at one end, so it must be access and parking for that. There was no other way people could get to it unless they walked along the beach.

Robbie took his fish and chips with him as he walked through a gap in the wall and headed for the sea front. He sat on the sea wall and ate his food. The constant sound and movement of the waves gently washing up only ten or so yards away was almost hypnotic. It was a pleasant day now, cool but sunny for the most part; it was calming. One thing he had noticed was the distinct lack of gulls swooping in to relieve him of his chips. They were around here and there, but none were paying him much attention. He'd seen a programme once about gulls and how their thieving ways were learned behaviour, usually taught to them inadvertently by clueless tourists. He wondered if that was why they weren't bothering him, because they hadn't learnt to around here; no tourists maybe, just locals.

Looking out to sea, he knew that as the crow flies, it'd probably be no more than fifty miles if that to the Isle of Stennoch on the southern Scottish coast from where he was. If it were possible to drive over the water he could probably be there in just over an hour. So near and yet so far.

He found a litter bin for his rubbish then took his phone out to check the time: twelve-thirty. Lynsey should be on her lunch break by now. He continued to walk slowly along the front as he called her.

"Hi, you're through to Lynsey McAndrew," the disembodied voice said. *"I'm unable to take your call just now, but please leave a message and I'll get back to you."*

Robbie sighed. "Hi love, it's only me. I just wanted t'check in with ya that's all. I'll catch y'later; love you."

He'd no sooner put his phone back in his pocket, when it began to ring and his brother, Rich's name flashed up on the display. "Hey buddy, how y'doing? Everything okay?"

It was a relief to hear a familiar voice. "Hiya bro, yeah I'm okay thanks. Only I er…I'm not exactly the surprise visitor over here that I thought I would be. Jacob knew who I was straight away, said the whole bloody family suspected Michael wasn't dead, including Eban."

"What the fuck?" Rich sounded stunned. "How? I mean…well I don't know what I mean but Christ Almighty Robbie. What's going on? Are you alright? What've they said t'ya?"

"It's okay Rich, I'm fine. I've only met Jacob so far, oh an' a young lad, his grandson, but he didn't know who I was. Come to think of it, he must be some sort of cousin o'mine. Anyway, old Jacob's been fine, but there's no family resemblance at all an' y'know why?"

"Go on," Rich pressed.

"Because Eban's not a Whithorn by birth, he's adopted, that's why."

Rich made some noises of confusion and disbelief before jumping in with more questions about Eban's provenance that Robbie was as yet unable to answer. He explained what he knew so far and that he was going to see Jacob again the next day.

"Rich can y'ring Clive an' ask him t'speak to Joe McStay? See if there's anything it brings t'mind for him. It might jog his memory," Robbie asked. "I wish Dredger were still around. I can't help thinking that he might o'known more than he let on."

"Don't start getting paranoid Robbie," Rich was having none of it. "He seemed t'go out of his way for you. An' think about it, if he knew Eban had been adopted, why would he withhold info like that when he's been so upfront with all the other stuff he gave ya?"

"I know, I know y'right. It's just that he seemed t'know how things'd pan out that's all. He were the one who told me that chasing all this stuff up would lead t'more questions. Like he knew what were coming."

"Ya said yourself Robbie, the man had a way about him. Maybe he *did* know things'd get complicated, he just didn't know how or what, if y'see what I mean?"

Robbie knew his brother was right about Dredger. If he'd known any of this, then he'd have surely told Robbie himself, if not in person, then at least it would've been included in with the rest of the paperwork he'd given him. The old sage had been a copper, and a bloody good one according to Annie and Joe. They'd both borne testament to the fact that you couldn't have pulled the wool over Dredger's eyes for love nor money. It was more likely that he'd sensed things were bigger than they'd seemed where Eban Whithorn was concerned, that there was more rot to seep to the surface. Robbie could sense it too; this revelation that Eban had been adopted by the Whithorns was just the beginning. He just knew there'd be so much more to come.

It was after three before Lynsey returned his call. "I'm sorry, I was in a meeting," she told him. She sounded down.

"Is everything okay love?" Robbie asked. "Ya don't sound too good."

"I'm fine, honestly." She wasn't and he knew it but didn't want to push her. "So, how have things gone so far? Have y'met Jacob Whithorn yet?"

Robbie went on to explain the day's events so far, but her interest in what he had to say was strained at best. Something was bothering her but she wasn't letting on; it was her tone that made it obvious to him. He couldn't tell if she was upset or angry and he didn't want to risk the latter in case it ignited an argument, not while he was so far away. She was attempting interest in what had happened, but there was a distance in her voice too, something he couldn't quite put his finger on.

"When are y'coming home?" she asked him.

He was wary of how to answer her in case he pissed her off. "Erm, it kinda depends on the outcome tomorrow I think love. Y'see I don't know what else I'm going t'find out."

"Okay, let me know," was all she replied. No argument, no questions, just *okay.*

Robbie assumed her to be upset about him coming to Ireland without her, though she'd seemed alright when he'd spoken to her the day before. And she wasn't backward in coming forward when it came down to saying her piece if she was upset with him. He told himself that whatever it was couldn't be that important or she would've said, but he decided to text his brother anyway, just to see if him or his wife, Jodie might give Lynsey an impromptu call, just in case.

He felt restless, as if he wanted to just get on and find out as much as he could, but he knew he'd need to wait, to pace himself. Robbie was the kind of person who would take on a project and then blitz it until he'd finished. Having to be patient and wait for someone else's input and dance to someone else's tune, wasn't the easiest of tasks for him. He'd just met Jacob but he didn't really know him from Adam. What if he were lying? What if he'd just said that Eban was adopted to try and absolve himself and his family of any responsibility for the old bastard's actions? He'd seemed okay, he'd seemed plausible; after all he was still technically a vicar too…but then so was Eban.

***

Jodie had just ordered her caramel latte at the Costa on Albion Place when Lynsey arrived. "Shall I make it two? she asked her.

"No thanks," Lynsey said, "I'll have one o'them berry smoothies instead please."

It was nice to see Jodie again; they didn't meet up often enough really. Jodie was one of the most together people that Lynsey knew. She was so stylish, way out there, but stylish none the less. She'd countless tattoos, several piercings and her hair seemed to have changed colour every time Lynsey saw her, but she carried herself with such confidence that she was accepted with respect wherever she was. She certainly turned heads, but she'd just smile at the gawpers and say hello.

The two of them embraced. "Bloody hell Lyns, I don't think we've seen each other since a fortnight after

the wedding. Sisters-in-law now y'know, we need
t'make more of an effort."

It lifted Lynsey's spirits to see her. It's not that they
were each other's best friend or anything, but they'd
always got on and Jodie had been an absolute rock when
Robbie had been missing. Always made time for them
despite having her and Rich's kids to take care of, not to
mention the tattoo studio to help run, but Lynsey was
under no illusion.

"He's rung ya then? Robbie?" she thought it better
to get rid of the elephant in the room first thing.

Jodie's initial look of *rabbit in the headlights* soon
gave way to a wry smile of acceptance. "Rich, he rang
Rich. He said y'seemed a bit down, felt guilty for
shooting off so ridiculously fast and that he was worried
you were pissed off with him, which I wouldn't be
surprised if you are. I'd be pissed off with him in your
shoes."

"I like your hair by the way," Lynsey deflected the
question, though she did genuinely like Jodie's hair,

which was currently jet black with big chunks of copper and purple through it and longer on the right than it was on the left.

"Thanks," Jodie sighed as she sat back into her chair, half closing her eyes as she probed Lynsey's face for clues of what was going on. She decided not to beat about the bush. "Okay. Spill?"

Now it was her sister-in-law's turn to feel caught in the headlights. "What? What d'ya mean? Look, I know Robbie's worried, but that's just Robbie isn't it? I'm fine, honest."

"Really?" It wasn't hard to note the air of disbelief in Jodie's voice. "I can run down a list of likelihoods if y'want, but it'd be quicker just t'say."

They both laughed before Jodie began her questioning again. "Are y'pissed off with him? Is it that simple?"

Lynsey smiled back. "I'm not pissed off with him, no. Well, not really. This is something he needs t'do. Ever since it all kicked off last year, I knew there'd be things he'd need t'find out, questions he'd want to ask. Wouldn't we all? No, I understand why he's away. Doesn't stop me worrying about him, but I do understand."

Jodie glanced at the tall glass containing the dark red-purple smoothie in Lynsey's hand. "You love caramel lattes. On a health kick are we?" she pried. Lynsey didn't respond, but nor did she meet her eyes either.

Leaning forward onto the table, Jodie grabbed Lynsey's forearm, a big grin across her face. "Oh my god; you're up the duff aren't ya? You are! You're pregnant?"

Lynsey didn't need to reply this time, the flushed colour in her cheeks gave away the answer to that question, but Jodie was struggling to maintain her excitement.

"When did y'find out? How long? I mean, how far gone are ya? Does Robbie know? No, no, of course not. Silly question, sorry. Are you okay? Is everything okay?" She was like a machine gun firing off a couple of hundred rounds a minute.

Raising her hands in a fend-off motion, Lynsey gestured for her to calm it down. "Woah, Jodie, it's not the Spanish inquisition y'know," she laughed. "Yes, alright yes, I'm pregnant. I found out this morning an' I think I'm probably six to eight weeks, okay? And no, Robbie doesn't know yet."

Try as she might, Jodie couldn't prevent her obvious excitement at the news. "How are y'feeling? You are happy about it aren't ya hun?

Lynsey shrugged. "I'm not sure t'be honest Jodie. I think so, but it's not something we were anticipating. I had t'change my contraceptive pill a few weeks back, the other kept giving me migraines. It must've happened then. Then there's the fact that I've still been on the pill, I've still been drinking etcetera, not t'mention the fact that I'm no spring chicken, so I'm a higher risk. I just don't know what t'think yet. I want t'be happy, but I don't know how things are going t'pan out. And I don't know how Robbie's going t'feel. He's had so much t'deal with lately, it might be too soon. We've never really talked about kids.

"Please don't say anything Jodie? Don't tell Rich, not yet. It wouldn't be fair him knowing before Robbie. I need t'talk to Robbie before I get myself in too deep. I want him t'come home, but he'll know something's wrong if I push him to. And besides, he's going to have t'sort all this Eban shit out at some point isn't he? Might as well get it out of the way sooner rather than later."

Jodie took a big slurp of her latte and a moment to digest the news before she agreed to keep her silence around Rich, and the next hour was spent in deep discussion about baby names for if it was a boy or a girl, though Lynsey was quick to mention it could come to nothing, given the conditions around conception and her being in her late thirties. Despite all the maybes and might nots though, she was finding it hard to hide her inner joy. The whole thing seemed somehow more real now that someone else was in the know too. It meant it was really happening.

Chapter Seven

Driving along the Portaferry Road, looking for the junction with George Street, Robbie slowed as he tried to make out the name of the red-brick pub he was approaching. Simply and unimaginatively called The Junction Inn, he pulled into the car park. This was where Jacob had asked to meet him, in the car park, not in the pub itself, which, given that it was still only half-nine in the morning, was locked and shuttered up.

There was a blue Ford Fiesta and a white Honda Civic parked to the side of the building, but other than that, his was the only car there. He rested his head back onto the seat and closed his eyes. He was so tired and he'd not had much sleep. Most of the night had been spent staring at the ceiling; he just hadn't been able to switch off the constant scenarios that were playing out in his mind. It had been a mistake coming here alone. He missed Lynsey and he was really feeling Annie's loss again now too, having no-one to back him up or just to go through the day's events with and if the previous day were anything to go by, those events could get quite big.

A swift tapping on his driver's side window startled him back to wakefulness. It was Jacob. "Sorry, didn't mean tae make ya jump son. Shall I get in?" He indicated towards the passenger side.

"Erm, yeh, sure Jacob, get in." It wasn't quite the meeting he'd expected and Robbie quickly scanned around the outside of the car for signs of anyone else, or another vehicle moving off having dropped the old man off, but there didn't seem to be anyone.

"It's a nice car ya've got son." Jacob said as he made himself comfortable in the passenger seat.

"It's not mine, it's a hire car," Robbie explained. "But yeah, it's not bad. Have *you* just walked here? I mean, I would've picked you up y'know. It wouldn't o'been a problem."

Jacob laughed, causing himself to cough. "I did indeed walk here Robbie, but only from St Oswald's nursing home. It's about fifty yards that way," he smiled as he pointed down George Street. "So you are picking me up really son."

Robbie asked if Jacob wanted a lift home in that case, but the older man shook his head. "I spend far too much time stuck in there already," he paused for a moment. "I know, the golf club!" he proclaimed. "I haven't been there in an age. I'm still a member an' they do a nice breakfast y'know. Have ya eaten yet son?" he asked.

"Just some toast at the bed an' breakfast."

"Aghh, toast's not enough. Let's get a man's breakfast at the club house."

Following Jacob's direction, Robbie soon found that they were taking the same turn off that appeared to lead up to Scrabo Tower. Jacob told him he should visit while he was in town, but that he could no longer manage the trek up to it himself. The path for the tower veered off to the right but the Golf Club was straight ahead. As they drove past the entrance sign, Robbie was taken by the fact that there was a small, but healthy looking palm tree growing behind the blue sign. It seemed very out of place for Northern Ireland, a bit too exotic a plant for the climate really.

Jacob noticed him looking. "We're caught in the edge of the same gulf stream that runs down the Ayrshire coast, Robbie. Keeps us a couple o'degrees warmer than other parts."

"Reverend Whithorn, it's nice to see you again; it's been a while," the well spoken English manager said as he showed them to a table overlooking the green. "Just wave at one of our staff when you're ready to order won't you?"

Robbie was finding it difficult to start the conversation that they'd both gone there to have: Eban. He needn't have worried because Jacob stepped in to take the lead. Reaching into the inside pocket of his jacket, he took out half a dozen old photographs and handed them to Robbie, who looked them over one at a time. Jacob leant in as they perused them.

"That's my parents, just after the war that was taken I think," he elucidated, before moving on to the next one, which Robbie recognised as being identical to the one he'd seen in Eban's room. "That's them again with the three of us. I'm the eldest, then yer dad and then Mouse, Jessy's her real name, but she always went by Mouse, on account o'being so quiet y'see."

Robbie shuddered a little. "He's got this one in his room but d'ya mind if we just call him Eban? I can't think of him as my dad, I'm sorry."

Jacob was a little taken aback by his request, but more for the fact that it hadn't occurred to him rather than seeing it as anything bad. "Of course, Robbie. I should o'thought son, sorry. A little insensitive of me," he paused again. "You've been tae see him?" he seemed more than a little bit uncomfortable at the thought of that.

Robbie decided to ignore the question but wanted to know more about the Whithorns and Eban's background. "Where's yer sister now?" he asked.

Jacob looked saddened by the question, which made Robbie think that she might be dead until the old fella reassured him that she wasn't. "I still get Christmas cards an' the like," he paused, as if trying to decide what, or how much he should tell his newly found nephew, then nodded abruptly to himself before continuing. "There was some unpleasantness y'see son. Mouse then married when she was twenty an' emigrated tae Canada with her husband. She never saw my parents again because of it." A tone of shame had crept into Jacob's voice. "I don't think they ever got over it if I'm honest."

"What kind of unpleasantness d'ya mean Jacob? Did she get pregnant before she were married or something?"

"No, no, nothing like that." Jacob was clearly struggling with whatever it was and Robbie couldn't help thinking it was something to do with Eban. He was right. "The thing is…well, Mouse was only little when our mother brought Eban intae the house, so she never really remembered life before him, but I was older. I remember her being a lot livelier before he came. Growing up, she got more an' more withdrawn, then one day I noticed her flinch as he ran past her, like she was frightened he was going tae do something, I don't know, hit her or something. Anyway, I told my Ma' that I was worried Eban was picking on her, bullying her or something, but she'd have none of it. Said that Eban was a God-fearing child an' wouldn't dream of hurting his sister.

"Then one day when he was fifteen, my father walked into the back bedroom that me an' him shared, Dad was looking for me but…instead he found my sister on her knees crying, her blouse was open and Eban was standing over her with his pants round his ankles forcing her hands onto his manhood." Jacob winced at the memory. "As soon as Eban realised my father was there, he slapped my sister round the face and called her a *Satan's whore* before pulling up his pants an' pretending

tae be overcome with distress at the whole thing. I
arrived just as he was shouting his innocence at Da',
telling him how she'd come intae *his* room an' bared her
breasts before grabbing at his trousers. It was awful. I
remember the look on poor Mouse's face, her tears an'
all she was saying was *no Da' no, no, no.* It was her
birthday that day, she'd just turned thirteen an' she wasn't
a mature girl at all, not in the way my brother made out."

"Oh my god!" Robbie felt a sudden, fleeting wave
of nausea sweep over him. "Please tell me yer parents
believed her? They did, didn't they?"

Jacob shook his head. "I don't know son, really I
don't, but I believed her. The little things all made sense
after that, I looked back on how she'd changed. All the
times she'd invent things tae do, just so as she wouldn't
be left alone with him, all the errands she'd volunteer tae
do, for neighbours as well as her own people.

"My parents never seemed tae take sides. If I'm
honest I think it was a sense of denial on their part.
Times were very different back then Robbie; they were

Church people, community leaders, an' that kind of a scandal might o'finished them. Eban was their good Christian deed an' he'd backfired on them in a way that they never could've brought themselves to admit in public."

"But she was their daughter, surely they wanted t'protect her?" Robbie was disgusted.

"They did, in their own way I guess. They sent her tae stay with an old Aunt of Mam's on Uist, in the Western Isles. I think they thought they were doing the right thing, but tae her it must've felt like a punishment, being sent out tae the middle o'nowhere tae nurse an old maiden aunt she'd never met before, when her tormentor was allowed tae stay in the family home while her parents prayed their way tae saving his tainted soul. I think my mother carried the guilt; she'd been the one tae insist he needed the love of a good, God-fearing family like ours. I'm not so sure my father would've adopted him if my mother hadn't have insisted. So I think she felt him tae be her responsibility."

"An' what about Mouse? How long did they make her stay away?" Robbie's sympathy for the Aunt he'd never met was immense.

Again, Jacob shook his head. "She never came home son. My parents went out tae visit her a couple o'times, but she'd make sure tae be out, helping the crofters with lambing or else collecting peat for the fires. Turns out she got on quite well with the old Aunt, Violet I think she was called. Anyway, when the old girl died, she left her small holding tae my sister. Mouse married a local man an' they left for Canada. She never saw nor spoke tae my parents from the day they sent her tae Uist until the day they died."

"What about you? Ya said you'd believed her?"

"I did. She invited me tae her wedding on the proviso that I didn't tell our parents until after it was all over. She stayed in touch with me, but she wasn't ever the same. An' tae my shame, I didn't feel able tae stand up tae my parents where Eban was concerned. I think that they knew that I knew, if ya see what I mean? But none of us dare speak of it. He wasn't right, there was something underlying in his personality that just wasn't right, but back then there was little understanding, let alone social acceptance of damaged people like there is now, so brushing the problems under the carpet was how my parents dealt with it at the time. They were of the *make do an' mend* generation Robbie, an' tae my shame, by remaining silent for fear of their feelings, I somehow ended up complicit in the whole sorry affair an' I'm sorry son. I'm so very sorry that I closed my eyes tae things too, because a whole lot o'trouble could've been avoided if one of us had spoken out, I'm sure."

Robbie sighed, not quite sure how to answer or indeed how he should feel about this. Eban's whole family seem to have known that he was an almighty loose cannon, but none of them did anything about it, choosing to ignore it in the hope that it'd all go away one day. Eban knew right from wrong; he must've done because he knew that what he'd done to Mouse was wrong, otherwise why would he try to deny it, to blame her? He'd known exactly what he was doing but had cared only for his own outcome from it. He'd saved his own skin and allowed his sister to be sacrificed to do so. What a bastard!

"D'ya think Mouse was happy after she married?"

"I hope so son. I think she was. She'd six children of her own and at the last count she'd fourteen grandkids and a handful of greats too. Her husband passed away about ten years back, but I think they were very happy together. I hope they were; no-one deserved more than she did."

Looking at the next photograph, it was easy to work out who the family were. Eban was a young man in this picture, Maev, his young wife, standing beside him with little Elizabeth in front of her legs and baby Martin in her arms. They were on a beach somewhere.

"His wife was very pretty," Robbie said. "I take it this is my half brother an' sister then? Are they in Ireland in this photo? Martin was born in Ireland wasn't he?"

Jacob raised his eyebrows. "My, my, you have been doing yer homework haven't ya son? Aye, this isn't far away: Millisle, just east o'here. They lived there a wee while. Eban was being mentored by the minister at the time, something my parents arranged I think. I was already in Northern Ireland y'see, so I think they probably thought it'd do him good tae get away from his familiar ground, a fresh start."

Robbie felt a cold chill; he'd been in Millisle the day before.

"Everything was a fresh start for him as far as they were concerned," Jacob continued. "They thought once he'd married, he'd settle down; he didn't. Then they thought that once he became a father that'd do it, but that didn't either."

"How many churches are in Millisle?" he asked, hoping it wasn't the one he'd spent time by.

"Just the one. It's a small wee place y'see. Pretty little church, just by the beach where this picture's taken."

Looking at the picture more closely, Robbie could see that the backdrop of it was familiar. Jacob was right and it seemed that he'd been eating his fish and chips on the wall that was just visible to the right of Maev.

"How long did they stay?"

Jacob drew in a long breath and looked up at the sky through the large window while he thought about it. "Let me see, a couple o'years I think it would o'been. The…I mean Martin was born there ya see."

Jacob's little faux pas hadn't gone unnoticed and Robbie was quick to pick him up on it. "I need t'know things Jacob; I don't need y'hiding stuff. I already know that Martin was a twin, an' I already know that baby Michael died after a few weeks. Please don't hold things back, because chances are I already know, an' if I don't, then I'll find out. I've been lied to my whole life Jacob, an' I'm sick of it."

"Aye," Jacob agreed, "that ya have son. You're right, baby Michael died."

"Failure to thrive I think it said on his death certificate."

"Did it? Oh, well all I know is that the child wasn't feeding as he should. Maev wasn't making enough milk for the both bairns an' while Martin was doing okay, Michael just didn't, I couldn't be sure that killed the wee mite though, there were likely other factors I suppose."

Robbie couldn't understand why that would kill the child in an age where the National Health Service existed and Michael could've been helped, nor could Jacob explain why either. By the sound of it, the family weren't very close: parents in Scotland, sister in Canada and both brothers in different parts of Northern Ireland. No doubt Jacob only got to know what Eban wanted him to know, but something didn't sit right.

"Why would he call me Michael when he already had a dead son by that name d'ya think?" he asked.

"I've no idea son." Jacob sighed. "By the time any of us became aware of yer existence, the deed was done so tae speak. Maev had waited for him like he'd told her, but he never sent for her an' eventually didn't even contact her any more. When she found out about him an' Mona, God rest her poor soul, he came back then an' threatened her with God only knows what. Whatever he said to her, it shut her up an' she fled back tae Scotland tae try an' make amends with her parents. I don't think it was the reunion she'd hoped for though. Elizabeth's still there, Bearsden or Milngavie I think it was, just north o' Glasgow, or she was last I heard. It's been a while now though. But yer brother, Martin; well…are ya sure ya want tae hear this son?"

Robbie let out a deep breath. He didn't want to hear it, but he needed to. "I'm sure."

"He's dead now son, Martin's dead, I'm sorry." Jacob tried to gauge Robbie's response to this, but couldn't.

Robbie remained expressionless. Though he'd felt a pang of some description at the news, the reality was that he and Martin had never known each other. "No need for sympathy on my part, I'm sure he didn't even know I existed."

"Oh but he did," Jacob confirmed. "He knew alright."

"How did he die?"

Jacob took his handkerchief out of his pocket again and coughed into it, before taking a sip from his glass of water. "He took his own life son. He wasn't well ya see. Bad blood some folk'd call it if ya don't mind me using that expression?"

"I don't get what y'mean Jacob."

"Let's just say he was more like Eban than anyone would've liked, just not enough tae survive this world."

Robbie's puzzled expression let Jacob know that he was confused by that last statement.

"The thing is Robbie, he'd a lot o'problems. Yes, him an' his sister knew about you because their mother made sure of it. Argh, ya know what kids are like sometimes. I think the top an' bottom of it was that

Martin was a handful an' he'd blamed his mother for his father not being around. Not that he could've remembered too much about him. Maev blew her stack one day an' told 'em why he wasn't around.

"Anyway, he turned up here one day, just like you've done, wanting answers. I could only tell him what I knew. Back then your mother was already in the ground an' you'd gone…missing, shall we say. So there were no conclusive answers I could give the boy. I know that he tracked Eban down at some stage, but the kid was already on a downward spiral. It did him no good meeting up with his father again after all those years had passed. Eban was very bitter about life by then, the whole world was tae blame for everything. Couldn't see his own part in it."

"Is that when Martin killed himself?"

"No, no, he'd a girlfriend was expecting twins when all this happened. He went off an' changed his name by deed pole then married her. His boys were nine years old when he hung himself. Apparently they found his body. Doesn't bear thinking of does it? Poor wee boys.

"He was angry at the world, like Eban was, an' took it out on those around him. I think he felt guilty about the things he did though, unlike Eban who probably wouldn't know guilt if it jumped up an' poked him in the eye. Anyway, I think Martin most likely couldn't see any other way for himself."

"Did y'meet them? Martin's wife an' the twins?" Robbie probed. "What were their names?"

"No son, I never did. But I believe she's called Catriona, a good old Gaelic name that."

"Whithorn?" Robbie had never thought about the name's origin before.

Jacob reached for the photos that were still in Robbie's hand and sifted through them before handing one back of a dire looking young woman, who was standing next to a rather stern looking nurse of some kind. "No Robbie, Martin changed his name as I said. He changed it tae Richards after the woman in this picture. This I believe is Martha Richards, Eban's natural mother. Martin got it intae his head that their family name should be as *God* had intended it. So when he found out the truth about his father's birth, he changed his name tae what he thought it should've been. He was a lost soul Robbie; he'd all sorts o'fanciful ideas by the sound of it."

"How d'ya know all this if they didn't keep contact with ya?"

"Because after Martin's death, his mother raised hell about it. I learned some things from Eban himself and the rest from, or via the Bishop. She'd gone tae town with the blame for her son's suicide, laid it squarely at Eban's door, which o'course involved the Church."

"Who'd helped t'cover things up, just like they did over my mother's suffering an', it seems, over my supposed death. Fucking unbelievable! I'm sorry for swearing Jacob, but it's not right, none o'this is right." Robbie had to put the brakes on himself in order to stem his rising ire.

Chapter Eight

Once he'd arrived back at the Old Schoolhouse Robbie had calmed down enough to call his wife and update her. There was something in her tone that wasn't quite right, but he just didn't feel he had the energy to push her about it, so he just let her talk. "Joe wants ya t'visit the Isle o' Stennoch Robbie. He told Clive his arthritis is playing up an' he isn't up t'visiting us. If you've done in Newtownards I think y'should consider it." There was something matter-of-fact about the way Lynsey worded it, that made it come across more as an instruction rather than a suggestion.

"Well I don't think there's anything more t'be gained by me staying here if I'm honest love. Jacob's been pleasant enough, an' I know that strictly speaking, he's family, but he served a purpose. There's nothing more I need t'know from him, an' even if something

114

crops up, I know where t'find him now." Robbie knew that he sounded quite cold in what he was saying but the truth was he didn't know exactly how he felt about Jacob and the rest of the Whithorns. He seemed a kindly old gent, but the fact remained that he'd seen the destruction in his own brother's wake and done nothing to prevent recurrences. Robbie couldn't help but feel that Jacob and his parents, Robbie's own grandparents, had turned a blind eye to the things Eban was doing, more concerned about what the neighbours might think than the utter devastations he was responsible for.

His head was telling him to be rational, to think about it, to accept that what was done, was done and there was no changing that fact. Yet his heart mourned for the losses he'd suffered, the preventable losses that would've never happened if there had only been an intervention by someone who'd known the truth all those years ago; and clearly the Whithorns had known. The Isle villagers weren't listened to, but Reverend Jacob Whithorn would've been, as would the Bishop at the time. The mother he still struggled to remember fully, the childhood friends, his very identity, all sacrificed because the Whithorns and the Church couldn't bear the scandal.

"I'd rather come home first Lyns. I know it's only been a couple o'days, but I've missed ya."

"I'll meet y'there Robbie. I'll book us in at the Solway Harvester again. Why don't y' forget the return flight an' get the ferry to Stranraer instead?" she suggested.

Robbie agreed and the two of them arranged to meet at the Harvester late the following day. Lynsey would have to go into work first and said she wouldn't be able to set off before mid-afternoon.

It wasn't as expensive as he'd thought it was going to be for the ferry. Paulette let him use her computer to book online. It was only around thirty quid for a single from Belfast to Cairnryan in Stranraer, looked like a two and half hour journey, or there abouts.

He felt he should see Jacob again before leaving too, though it wasn't out of any sense of obligation. It was because he wanted to make sure that the lines of communication between them were kept open, just in case. He was feeling very confounded about Jacob. On the one hand he liked him, he was a decent old fella, but on the other hand he felt a deep resentment at his inaction when it had been needed, something there was no excuse for. It felt a little mercenary, but he wanted to keep Jacob on side, though he'd no desire to play happy families with him.

It was evening when Robbie found himself sitting in the car on Moray Crescent, a few doors down from number thirty-five. The light was just turning as the sun melted away behind the school buildings. He'd seen Alex leave about five minutes previously, with his dog, Pip.

Jacob was standing in his kitchen as Robbie walked up the drive and so saw his nephew arrive. "Come in son, it's not locked," he called as he dried his hands on the tea-towel. "I didn't expect tae see ya again so soon."

"I've just come to say my goodbyes. I'm leaving in the morning," Robbie told him.

"Ah, I see," Jacob sounded a little disheartened. "I'm sorry if ya've been upset by the things I told ya son. It's not easy I know, but there's been enough lies told over the years. The truth will always out, as they say, an' I'd rather it be told now that age has taught me what happens when it's not."

Robbie felt a brief pang of guilt for feeling badly towards the old man, but he tried to keep things in perspective. "There's not a lot t'say about it t'be honest. I'm grateful you've been so open, but I'm not sure where I go from here."

Jacob walked towards the living room door, beckoning for Robbie to follow him. Once inside, he got his address book out from the sideboard drawer. It looked old and dog-eared, and it was stuffed with pieces of paper that didn't belong to it. He began to flick through it. "I don't know if she'll still be there son, but somewhere in here I've got an address for Maev, or at least it's the address she initially gave us when she went back home tae Scotland. Her folks were from Bearsden as I recall, or was it Milngavie? They're pretty much side-by-side I think. Though tae be honest Robbie, it's been so many years now, I couldn't even be certain she's still alive."

"Isn't that where y'thought Elizabeth was?" Robbie asked him.

"Aye, that's right, but only because at the time she was living with her mother. When Martin had come tae see me, he told me that Elizabeth had married, but it was all over in the space o'six months and she'd returned tae Maev."

"Did Maev not re-marry?"

"Well she couldn't, could she? She's legally married tae Eban tae this day." Jacob seemed flustered.

Robbie asked if he knew what Elizabeth's married name might be, but he didn't. Instead he wrote down the address in Bearsden where he'd last known his sister-in-law to be. He handed it to Robbie. "I don't have the address that Maev moved tae, but I remember this one being a big detached place off the Baljaffray Road on the Bearsden outskirts. If ya do manage tae find them son, just bear it in mind that they're innocent, they've had it rough too y'know. An' if ya do find them…please tell them how sorry I am."

***

"A Mynah bird! That's what y'put me in mind o' lad." The detective was sitting at the opposite side of the table from Ray Graham and his abhorrent ward, Chris Hartley.

Ray looked nervous. He knew what was coming, but Detective Sergeant Chris Radley looked anything but, in fact he looked decidedly pissed off.

"What the fuck you on about?" was all Hartley offered up.

Radley leant his elbows on the table as he shuffled around some papers he was holding, before settling on one in particular. "Well," he finally said, "it seems that

120

one Christopher James Hartley is a deceased person whose identity you stole for your own reasons."

"Fuck off!" Though he was betrayed by a smirk creeping over his face. "Is that all ya've got y'sad bastard?"

"Indeed it's not my little Mynah bird because it seems that, excellent as it is, your local West Yorkshire accent is fake isn't it? You're a mimic, just like a Mynah bird."

The smirk began to wane a little as a scant look of realisation replaced it briefly. "So?"

"So…Ya've impressed me," Radley wanted to drip feed this revelation, so that he could read the response easier. "It can't be easy to hide a Glaswegian accent like the one you must have…Kester? Or would y'prefer me to be more formal? Mr Richards, maybe?"

Richards burst out laughing, a real howling, belly-laugh to the point where tears began to be squeezed free from his eyes. It went on a good couple of minutes before he calmed down, though his accent had become one more familiar to himself when he did. "All these fucking months an' you's lot could nae even work out who I am. Useless bastards I tell ya!" He leant in towards Radley. "I guess some poor fucker's for the high jump for letting this slip past ya all eh?" He turned to face Ray. "An' as for you, ya psycho-babble twat, nae fucking idea have ya?"

Radley continued his course. "There'll be someone arriving tomorrow, who'd like to discuss some outstanding offences in the Glasgow region that have your name stamped all over them."

"Which one?" Richards snorted.

"The real one Kester."

Richards began to pretend he was scared, shaking his hands in front of himself in a mocked fear. "Och, see how scared I am. Please don't let them take me away officer…hah!" he sneered.

"Kester, please." Ray Graham interrupted. "You're really not doing yourself any favours. Just co-operate. I can't help you when you're being like this."

"Then don't fucking try! You're a wanker anyways!" He turned towards the door. "Oi, monkey, open the fucking door, I wannae go back tae my cell."

Radley waved the guard away. "Not so fast Kester. We'll not be much longer, I promise, but y'have to understand ya've made our job somewhat more difficult by yer obvious deception fella, an' there's one thing bothers me if I'm honest."

"Go on then, enlighten me?" Kester mocked him.

"Well, given the fact that we now know the kind o'things you were up to north o'the border too, I can't help but notice that there's one particular offence that stands out from the rest. In fact, if it wasn't for the fact your DNA was at the crime scene an' we've a witness to it, I'd be tempted t'be looking elsewhere for the perpetrator of the violent robbery on that jogger last year."

Kester stared back at him blankly. He knew what Radley was getting at, but he wasn't going to help him.

Radley only paused long enough to draw breath. "You're a conman, a liar, a thief an' though using yer fists isn't exactly alien t'you, the level of violence you used on an unarmed, unprepared man seems incredibly excessive. Even when it was obvious that he'd lost consciousness, you continued. You tried to kill him; why?"

"Well maybe I was just having a bad day," Kester snarled. "Now, I want tae go back tae my cell."

Ray Graham stood up and walked over to the window as Kester was escorted from the interview room. "I don't know where t'go with this lad Sergeant, I really don't."

Radley gathered his paperwork together before pausing to answer him. "I don't doubt it Mr Graham. There's something decidedly creepy about the lad an' I certainly wouldn't want t'run into him in a dark alley if I'm honest," he sighed. He sympathised with Ray, but didn't relish the awkwardness of his own workload having now increased somewhat. "I'll speak t'the copper that dealt with the case, Sergeant Bashir apparently, see if there's anything I've missed, then I'll chase up getting that psych evaluation bumped up the list. I want it as a priority now, before he gets too much chance to think up more shite t'pull the wool over our eyes. He's a slippery customer this one."

"And quite the chameleon too," Ray added.

"Very much so. Shame he chose the wrong side o'the fence eh? We've officers deep under cover who're not as good at it as he is," Radley quipped before saying his farewell and leaving.

Ray stared out of the window for a while, pondering on the events of the last hour. All that time he felt he'd wasted, trying to build up a rapport with a young man who didn't exist. He briefly wondered who the real Chris Hartley had been and how his family would feel, knowing that his name had been exploited in such a way. If he were being completely honest, he was finding it hard not to feel a certain amount of intimidation at the thought of having to continue in his role with Kester

Richards. The young man had run rings around him so far, something that would no doubt continue despite his true identity now being known.

Chapter Nine

The ferry journey had seemed to pass in no time and even though the crossing from Belfast had been a little choppy to say the least, Robbie hadn't felt any ill effects from it. The Stena Line ferries seemed pretty robust for such voyages. Though it had to be said, he'd overheard two people in conversation up on the deck. Neither of them lived there anymore, but it turned out that they both had roots in Milngavie. One was informing the other that they still had family near Lennox Park and the other talked of Allander Water. Robbie wasn't sure what he thought he might hear from eaves-dropping, but the fact that they were talking about the very place he knew he'd likely be visiting in due course, meant that he found it incredibly difficult to drag himself away from them. The distraction they'd become was probably the reason the journey had seemed quicker than it was.

Disembarking at Cairnryan hadn't taken too long, despite an army of school kids that were being shepherded through arrivals by a couple of frazzled looking teachers. He'd had to leave the previous hire-car which meant he'd need to get another from Stranraer. He'd made the mistake of hiring from a small company when he'd arrived at the airport in Belfast, which meant having to return it to them. This time he'd hire from a big, national company like Enterprise or something. That way he could pick up the vehicle in Stranraer and leave it in a different city when he'd done.

The sign post at the ferry terminal junction with the A77, pointed right to join the A75 and the destination he was heading for, but he couldn't help but notice that it also pointed left toward Girvan. How close he must be to Eban right now. For the briefest of moments, he almost turned the wheel towards the left, before deciding on a more sensible course and indicated right instead. The temptation to just turn up, to push a few of the old man's buttons had been very briefly almost overwhelming. But he was angry and upset about the new information he'd got from Jacob and he didn't want Eban to have the satisfaction of seeing it in his face. Plus, he wondered just what else there was to learn too and there seemed no real point in confronting his father until he had more to go on. Did adopted children feel this way he wondered? Going through life knowing that the story of their origin was out there somewhere. Feeling like Robbie did, that with each handkerchief pulled from the magician's hat, another would follow, over and over again until the beginning of the story had been lost or buried beneath silks of varying colours.

Robbie hadn't been to the Isle since early the previous year when he'd been there with Annie too. He'd not been there since even though he felt he should've done, especially as he'd wanted to pay his respects at old Dredger Scoular's grave. He knew that Joe McStay was holding onto some of Dredger's things for him, but he'd just not been in the frame of mind that would allow him to deal with all of that yet.

He couldn't face the thought of driving into the village alone. It was beautiful there and part of his heart felt the tugging sensation that he knew would draw him back one day, but he just couldn't face it yet. Instead, he phoned Joe and arranged to go and see him in Cutreach. He'd go to the Isle village later, when Lynsey had arrived.

It was only a few short miles from the Isle to Cutreach and Joe was pleased to see him. "I have tae say laddie, I was a wee bit worried when Lynsey told me ya'd taken yerself off tae Ireland," he said. "No' tae mention the fact ya were away there by yerself. What if it'd o'been a hostile reception an' you on yer own son?"

"It were okay Joe, I were okay. Nothing bad happened," For some reason he didn't want to go over everything he'd learned there just yet. He wasn't averse to sharing any of it with Joe. He trusted the old fella; he just couldn't face being *advised* on what he should or shouldn't do or feel, by yet another well meaning person. So instead he stuck to the pleasantries.

***

Lynsey wasn't best pleased at being alone in the harbour facing room above the Solway Harvester Inn. Frustrated rather than angry, it wasn't that she didn't understand Robbie's reluctance to be in the Isle of Stennoch again, she just really wanted to see him. He'd asked her to meet him at Joe's, but she'd refused, partly out of fatigue, but mostly because she was pissed off at him. She'd arrived in the village a few hours ago, but it wasn't until she'd been the one to phone him, that he told her he was spending the night at Joe's, that he couldn't quite bring himself to go back there yet, not now that Annie was dead, and Dredger gone now too.

The light was fading as she sat watching the hypnotic effect of the last of it dancing on the calm ripples in the harbour, the gentle sound of mast bells as the anchored sailing boats bobbed at their moorings. It was so hard to imagine the secrets behind closed doors. Looking across to the church where, let's face it, her *true* father-in-law had once delivered the sermons was almost incomprehensible. The villagers who'd once occupied the cottages nearby would've all made their way there on the Sabbath, would've all, slowly but surely, had their illusions shattered one by one as the truth about their Minister became clearer to them, as they'd seen his wife, Robbie's mother, hiding bruises and the terror in the little boy's eyes when Eban had come home drunk again. Lynsey wondered how many times the scene in the harbour had been exactly as it was now, its tranquillity masking the truth.

She looked down to the street. Would her Robbie have played there as a child? Did he skip along holding Mona's hand saying hello to the neighbours he passed on his way? He had such a broad Yorkshire accent now, but he wouldn't have started that way. He was once as much a part of this village as the water in the harbour, but not now, not any more. His sense of belonging anywhere had been obliterated last year. None of this would've come to light had it not been for the fact that her husband had found himself in the wrong place at the wrong time. Two opportunistic thieves had robbed him of more than just his phone, they'd taken away his identity. Even though their actions had led to him finding out who he truly was, they'd left him with this loss of himself too and this new obsession that Lynsey was convinced would lead to nothing if not more heartache, but he needed to do it and she needed to be there for him. Help him or risk losing him that was the choice she faced. And at what point was she going to be able to tell him about the baby? She was an older mother, there were risks. Should she tell him anyway, even if something happened and she lost the baby? Would he cope considering everything else he was dealing with?

She'd been the one to encourage him to feed this hunger he had for the truth, but she'd never expected that he'd allow it to take over his life in the way it had, and in such a short space of time too.

She needed him now, his support and understanding. However he appeared to be blind to all else around him. Blind to the fact that his wife had a dilemma of her own that she needed help with. Lynsey felt abandoned, an after-thought and if her husband wasn't going to be there for her, then she wanted to go home to be around family

and friends, but she'd give him the benefit of the
doubt...again.

Chapter Ten

Baljaffray Road led west out of Bearsden towards Glasgow. Robbie could've driven faster, but he wanted to take his time so that he didn't miss anything. *A big detached house on the Baljaffray Road* is what Jacob had said, nothing more specific than it being on the outskirts of Bearsden, the problem was, that there didn't appear to be *any* houses on Baljaffray Road. There were several roads leading off it that seemed to be built up, in that 'leafy suburb' kind of way, but nothing that looked as if it could be accessed from the main road he was on. He'd driven up and down it three times now, from one roundabout to another and all he could think was that either Jacob had got it wrong, or else the house had been demolished.

He spotted a postal van parked up as its occupant emptied the contents of a pillar box into a grey sack. He could hear the postie whistling as he went about his task, no doubt in time to the music he seemed to have piped into his ears through the lime green ear-phones he was wearing. Though he wasn't an old fella by any stretch of the imagination, Robbie couldn't help but think he looked too old to carry off the lime green ear-phone look.

"Excuse me," Robbie announced his presence to no response. He leant in and repeated himself as he gently tapped the postie on his shoulder, startling him momentarily.

"Och I didnae see ya there, sorry."

Robbie held his hands up, palms outward in a non-threatening gesture. "I didn't mean t'make y'jump, sorry. I just wondered if ya could help me? I'm looking for a big house on this road, but I'm not sure if I've got it right or not."

Standing to his full height, the postie scratched his head, the lime green ear-phones now swinging from the collar of his polo-shirt. "Do ya no' have an address for it?" he asked.

"No, just a description." Realising that this might not come across as completely sane to this poor stranger he'd accosted, he stuck to his planned tale. "Y'see I'm looking into my family tree, an' one o'my old relatives told me that some family had come from here, that they'd lived in a big house on this road."

"Oh, right," he spent a few moments in deep thought before he answered. "I wonder if they were talking about Windyhill then."

"Windyhill?"

"Aye, Windyhill. It's a golf club just on the road there." He indicated towards the direction they were facing.

"I've been down that way, I didn't see a golf club."

The postie lifted the sack into the back of his van and slammed the doors. "Ya likely drove right past it. It's no' exactly on the road, but the access tae it is. If ya want tae jump back in yer motor an' follow me, they've a post box all o' their own up there I'm away tae empty now anyways."

As the suburban houses came to an end on the left, Robbie followed the post van up a turning on the right that looked pretty much like a farm track. Other than the shrubbery to either side, there didn't appear to be much to see, until another right turn opened up the view to a huge manor house. Bloody hell, really? Could this be the *big house* that Jacob had described? Surely not. Its white-washed walls made it look even more impressive, more like a villa of some kind. Robbie wasn't sure what he'd expected, but this hadn't been it; this couldn't be the place. He parked next to the post van and got out, still in awe of the surroundings.

"This is the only big place I can think of around here," the postie offered. "Without a proper address it's difficult isn't it?"

"Ya wouldn't know how long it's been a golf club would ya?"

"Sorry boss, I'm no' local here, I live in Glasgow. See Bearsden's just part o' my round. What're they called then?"

"Who?"

"Yer family, the folks yer looking for."

"Oh right, erm...Whithorn."

The postie shook his head. "Sorry never heard o'them."

Robbie suddenly remembered that Maevis' family name might be a better clue to give. "I think the woman's maiden name might've been double barrelled; Parker...something I think."

Raising his eyebrows the postie nodded in acknowledgement. "Could it be Parker-Tait by any chance?" he asked.

Robbie felt his heart skip a beat at the mention. "Yeh, yes I think it is. Do y'know them?"

"No' really. I deliver tae someone by that name over in Milngavie. A wee house all alone on Broadmeadow

Road, no' far from the junction with the Stockiemuir Road, heading nor-west out o'town. It's no' so far from here, a couple o'miles maybe."

"Is it easy t'get to from here?"

"Oh aye, ya just head back down towards Bearsden, when ya get tae the roundabout, go left, straight on at the next one. After a mile or so, ya'll see a sign pointing ya right towards Strathblane. It's no' far after the turning."

Robbie smiled and shook his hand. "Thanks for all your help mate, much appreciated."

"Nae bother." The postie entered the club house with a small empty bag rolled up in his hand, exiting a couple of minutes later with a half full bag that he deposited in the back of his van with all the rest. Robbie waved as the van pulled away, though he couldn't be sure if it was reciprocated as the glare of the sun prevented him seeing through the windscreen.

He decided to look around before leaving. Could this really be where Maevis came from? It was, after all, the only 'big house' around and he had noticed that there was a tendency to refer to palaces, mansions and the like as *the big house*. Though this particular pile didn't by any means qualify as either of those, it definitely couldn't be described as a suburban semi. From the outside it looked as though it could accommodate ten or twelve bedrooms over its first floor and attic, and the ground floor must have any number of reception rooms.

"Hello there, can I help you Sir?" He was greeted by a smartly dressed woman at the reception desk inside. "Are you interested in becoming a member here?" she asked him.

"Erm, yeh maybe," he lied. "I was just wanting t'look round really."

The young woman's smile seemed fixed in place somehow, her job no doubt, keep the punters happy etcetera. "No problem Sir, if you'd like tae bear with me a wee moment, I'll arrange for a member of staff tae give ya the guided tour, okay?"

"Thank you."

After being directed to sign in the visitors book he took a seat, and within a couple of minutes a man of around Robbie's age introduced himself as Lee Bainbridge and explained that he was one of the golfing instructors, as well as the deputy manager. He was certainly dressed for golf at the moment, rather than for managing so to speak, in his neatly pressed Chinos and 'Windyhill Golf Club' polo shirt.

"Do ya play a lot of golf Sir?" he asked.

"It's been a while t'be honest." Er, yeah, and then some.

"Well as ya may be aware, there's quite a few club houses around here, but we do like tae pride ourselves on being the best ya know. If ya'd like tae follow me then Sir."

The place was like a tardis, much bigger even than it had looked from the outside, though a huge conservatory had been added at some point, opening up the back of the ground floor into a large bar and restaurant area which overlooked the green. Lee went on to explain that some of the upper rooms were hired out for business or private functions, they catered for conferences, wedding parties, Bar Mitzvahs and most other social gatherings that fell under the hatch, match and dispatch umbrella, as well as running their own annual golfing tournaments where they boasted some up-coming champions among their youth teams. All very interesting…if that had been his real reason for being there that is.

"It seems like quite an old building," Robbie wanted history.

"Aye, it is. I think the original part was built around seventeen-fifty or there abouts, that's the way ya came in, through the oldest part. The rest has just been built on bit by bit over the generations I suppose."

"How long has it been a club house?" Robbie was on a roll.

"Since the nineteen-seventies I believe. It's changed hands since the original conversion though. It'd belonged tae one family for hundreds o'years apparently, rumour has it that back in the sixties, the head o'the house went an' got himself barred from the Clober golf club a few miles from here, so he set up his own right here. That's him there on the wall, the original founder."

Robbie followed Lee's indication and moved over to the elaborately framed portrait of the man in his 'country-gent' Harris Tweed, sporting the obligatory manicured facial hair to add the authoritative look. The name plate on the lower frame answered Robbie's next question before he'd asked it; *Sir Mortimer Parker-Tait, KCB.*

"Some military accolade I think, the KCB I mean. Knight Commander of the British Empire, or so I'm told," Lee explained.

"What happened to him?" Robbie asked. "How come he sold up? Cash flow problems?"

Lee pulled the corners of his mouth down and shrugged his shoulders. "No idea Sir. All I know is that at some point in the seventies he made this place a club house, but it changed hands within five years or so. Maybe he died, I don't know. I think he's got family still here abouts. Becky in reception had someone here a year or two back who was some kind o'relative, wanted tae see the old place, didnae live too far as I recall. Would ya like tae see the membership packages we've got at the moment Sir?"

No not really, but Robbie didn't want to appear impolite and he needed to keep the lie up. "I don't have too much more time at the minute, I've a meeting in Glasgow t'get to, but if you've got the information to hand and I could take it with me? I can look over it tonight then, when I've more time if that's okay?"

"Certainly, we've a folder of information, terms and conditions etcetera, back at reception. There's a couple o'wee vouchers in there too tae try an' tempt ya some more; one's for yerself and a guest tae enjoy a free meal on us in our restaurant an' the other's for you to play a round of golf for free, a try before ya buy kind o'deal."

"That's brilliant Lee, thank you," Robbie said as they shook hands.

Pulling out of the long access road and back onto Baljaffray Road, Robbie took a left towards Milngavie as he recalled the directions the postman had given him: left at the first roundabout, straight on at the second, then look out for a sign to Strathblane. It seemed as though were there to be any Parker-Taits left in the area, then that would be where he'd find them. Would they point him in the direction of Elizabeth maybe? He racked his brains as he drove, trying to think of what to concoct next. It disturbed him somewhat to think of how easily he was finding it to lie, but then what choice did he have? What else could he say realistically? *Hello, I think I'm your brother, I'm meant to be dead but I'm not. In fact my whole life's been a lie but hey, here I am.* Not bloody likely.

***

It didn't seem to take more than ten minutes or so before Robbie found himself pulling up in front of a farm gate that accessed a small cottage. It was just as the postie had described it, all on its own, surrounded by countryside. He'd passed the entrance to what looked like a big farm about a quarter of a mile back, but that was it; he couldn't see much by way of buildings of any kind, any closer than that.

He was suddenly startled by the sound of the gate rattle as a dog threw itself at it and began barking at him furiously, another Jack Russell similar to Jacob's. Though Jacob's dog Pip, had been a bit stockier and was short haired, this one was wire-haired. He heard a woman's voice shouting for someone.

"Dave! Dave!"

He couldn't yet see where she was, but he could hear that she was approaching because her calls for *Dave* were getting louder. Though Dave himself must've been deaf or something as she didn't get any answer from him.

It was only when she came into sight that he realised that she'd been shouting at the dog, Dave was the dog's name. It made him smile briefly.

"Quiet now Dave," she said as the dog jumped up, resting his front paws on her knee. She affectionately stroked his ears before nudging him away. "Down ya go now, there's a good boy."

Robbie found that he was momentarily stuck for words, for what to say or how to say it. Though she was clearly a person who loved her dog, this woman was quite formidable in appearance. He hadn't known what to expect when he'd got there, but he just didn't feel prepared anymore.

"If yer here trying tae sell me something, I'm no' interested," she half spat.

"Erm...no, no I wasn't trying t'sell anything. That's not why I'm here."

Though she was carrying a walking stick, she didn't seem to need it to help her walk at all. Robbie decided she must've brought it for protection, though her whole demeanour was quite harsh and didn't lend itself to being messed with. Could this be Elizabeth? She looked too old and certainly not what he'd imagined, but she was too young to be Maevis, providing Maevis was still alive that is. She looked to be about sixty or so, though it was possible she could've been younger. Not much shorter than he was, with short grey hair and carrying a few more pounds than her frame was built for. She'd no make-up on and the clothes she was wearing were what aged her. An old brown cardigan, half buttoned over a nylon type, cream coloured blouse and her navy blue slacks looked like they'd seen better days, they were tucked into thick woollen socks, showing just above her green paddock boots. Her hands were grubby with visible dirt under her fingernails, yellowed on one hand, her right. And her skin showed the ruddiness of someone who spent much of their time outdoors in the sun, unprotected.

"Well?" she interrupted his thoughts. "What ya doing here then? What do ya want? Is it eggs yer after?" Though her tone was hard, her accent was pretty soft and didn't quite fit in with her fairly rough exterior. If she'd have been better dressed, she'd have fit Robbie's idea of the gentle-woman farmer type. but she was unkempt. Maybe that's who she used to be, but those days had left her now.

"Eggs?"

She tapped at the gate with the walking stick, pointing out the sign that Robbie had completely missed. *Fresh laid Eggs for sale. Home-made Jams & Preserves. Enquire within.*

Brilliant, a gift of a get-out clause. "Oh, yeh. I mean, yes that's right, thank you."

"What ya thanking me for? Ya didn't buy any yet," she retorted, her voice carried the rasp of a person who'd smoked for many years. Though the nicotine stains on her fingers gave that away too.

"What preserves have you got too please?" Robbie needed a way in.

"Jams, curds, chutneys, the usual I suppose."

"Great, can I take a look?" He wasn't sure she'd go for it as she already seemed suspicious of him, but then she could be the kind of person who was suspicious of everyone.

She looked him up and down for a moment before answering. "Aye, I suppose." She instructed Dave to stay close as she opened the gate enough to allow Robbie to pass through.

He held his hand out in greeting. "I'm Robbie," he smiled at her.

"Peg," she answered without taking his hand.

Well, not Elizabeth then, which left Robbie wondering where to go from here. Was Peg related to Elizabeth on her mother's side at all? Or was she a complete randomer, someone who just happened to live in the vicinity? It could be that the Parker-Taits had lived there previously and that every now and then some junk mail made it through, still addressed to them here. That seemed a reasonable explanation as to why the postman might still think they were here.

"It was a postman down in Bearsden directed me your way, Parker-Tait he said you were called."

"Aye."

"Only he thought it was an Elizabeth Parker-Tait lived here."

"Aye, he'd be right then."

"Oh," Robbie was suddenly hopeful again. "I wouldn't mind meeting her if that's okay? If she's here I mean," he chanced.

Peg stopped in her tracks and turned to face him. "Why?"

"Well, I was just down at the golf club, Windyhill, an' they said it was private there 'til the seventies. That it was owned by the Parker-Taits. I'm just interested in the history of old buildings y'see. I thought if there was still any family about, they might be able to tell me about the old place, that's all."

"Really?" she said in a tone that told him she just wasn't buying his story. "C'mon then, preserves are in the back kitchen."

He followed her around the outside of the building to the back, where a ramshackle old porch led into the cottage. It was a typical old style farmhouse kitchen, right down to the wooden box on the floor by the Aga oven that had two very young looking lambs in it.

"The ewe didn't want 'em," Peg explained. "There's always one or two every lambing season. We hand rear them for the farmer and he helps tae fix our fencing as an' when."

We? Who did she mean by, we? The dog, Dave? He did seem like the perfect little helper, even ran back outside when she told him to after she'd forgotten the chicken feed and came back with the small basket in his chops. He reminded Robbie of one of those helper dogs, the kind that are trained to be an aid to their disabled owners, though Peg was by no means in that category. It was plain to see that she and the dog adored each other and he just lived to please her.

The tap, tap, tapping of a stick along with a shuffling sound caught his attention and he turned to see an elderly woman in the doorway behind him, dressed similarly to Peg, but at least a good twenty odd years older. She walked with a stick, the source of the tapping noise. She had one glove on her hand and was carrying the other, which she duly dropped as she changed her stick from one hand to the other. Without hesitation, Dave jumped up and ran to pick it up, bringing it back to Peg, front paws on her knee so that she didn't even need to bend too far for it. As she took it from him, one of the lambs began bleating and Dave trotted off and started to wash its face; it didn't seem to object. Robbie was in awe of this clever little pooch, he'd never seen anything like it.

"That's an amazing dog ya've got Peg. Did he take long to train?"

The old woman took it on herself to answer instead. "Never took much training, he'll do anything for a full belly an' a wee bit of a fuss. He's my Lizzie's right arm."

Lizzie? Robbie swore his heart missed a beat, Lizzie, Elizabeth not Peg.

Peg turned to the old woman, a sharp look in her eye. "This is my mother, Maev. Mother this fella wants some eggs, or was it preserves? He was asking about Windyhill, wanted tae know about its history.”

“Why?” Maev asked.

“Why indeed?” repeated Peg. “But I don’t reckon it’s for the cock an’ bull reason he gave me.”

Chapter Eleven

Taking a seat at the kitchen table, old Maev rested her stick against it. It fell to the floor with a clatter and Dave dutifully picked it up again, though he insisted on giving it to Peg, or Lizzie, or whoever the hell she was, rather than to Maev. Still, who was he to question someone else's reasons for using another name when he'd gone all his life doing the same, albeit inadvertently.

"Peg's her nick-name," Maev explained. "She used tae look after a senile old woman a lot o'years ago, who thought she were her sister, Peg. Always insisted on calling her Peg no matter how many times she were corrected, it just stuck. But I still call her the name I gave her, Elizabeth, Lizzie. Though she's no' so fond o' the latter; are ya Lizzie Dripping?"

Robbie could sense the animosity between the two women, who most likely lived together through mutual need rather than choice.

"So," Peg asked him, "who d'ya say ya are again? An' is it really eggs an' preserves yer after or something else, because there's something no' quite right about you mister."

Maev glared at him in anticipation of an answer to Peg's question. "Have we met before laddie? Ya look a wee bit familiar."

Robbie's head was swimming with excuses, but they were racing through his mind too fast for him to take a hold of one to use in this situation. What could he say? These women weren't stupid, they already knew he was lying. This woman, Peg, Elizabeth, she was his sister for Christ sake, she definitely looked older than she must be, because by his reckoning she was only ten or so years older than himself, her early fifties, not early sixties, which is what he'd taken her to be on first sight.

He decided to just come clean, to take his chances and hope it didn't all go tits-up. "Can I sit down please?"

Maev nodded and gestured towards the chair on the opposite side of the kitchen table to herself. Robbie sat.

"I'm Robbie McAndrew," he informed them. They looked to one another, then back at him with blank expressions. He continued. "At least that's the name I've always gone by, the one I'm known by, but it's not the one I was given at birth."

A look of realisation hit Peg's face and she drew in a sharp intake of breath, bringing her hand up to her forehead. Turning her back she leant against the big Belfast sink and stared out of the window.

"What? What is it?" Maev queried, half panicked by her daughter's reaction. "What's tae do? Elizabeth, what?"

Robbie swallowed hard before continuing. "My real name, that's t'say the name I was christened, is Michael, Michael Whithorn."

Maev flopped into the back of her chair, a moment of stunned silence as she stared at him, mouth agape. "No!" she shouted. Then banging the flat of her hand on the table top, she repeated herself, hitting the table hard with each word. "No! No! No!"

"Calm down mother," Peg insisted.

Robbie didn't know what to do for the best. "I'm sorry, I just…"

Maev cut him dead. "Get out!" she screamed at him. "How dare you come tae my home? Get out! Elizabeth get him out! I don't want that man's bastard child in my house! Get out!"

She grabbed her walking stick and raised it above her head as she tried to stand up from her chair. Dave was barking furiously again, not knowing what was going on. The two lambs were bleating and thrashing around in their box and Peg was trying to grab her mother's stick, to stop her walloping Robbie with it.

"Go round the front," Peg called to Robbie. "Quickly, go now!"

He didn't hang around for the whys and wherefores, he simply exited the same way he'd entered and went back around the cottage to the front. He waited a while by the gate. Dave had followed him out and they were both resting by the gate, looking back towards the house, wondering what the hell had just happened. The sound of screeching was still coming from within the walls, old Maev no doubt.

It must have scared the chickens because about eight Bantam hens appeared from the other side of the cottage, clucking their way around the front. Robbie guessed that they shouldn't be there when Dave spotted them and ran off in their direction, rounding them up and chasing them back around the building.

His heart was in his mouth and he couldn't decide whether or not to just leave, but he was afraid that if he did that, he'd never get another chance to speak to them. He was just about to open the gate and go back to his car, when he heard a couple of little yaps from Dave. He looked round to see Dave and Peg heading towards him.

"I'm sorry," he said as she approached him.

"Ya shouldn't have just turned up here like this," she scolded. "Ya should've told me before ya came inside."

"I didn't know she was there, I thought it was just you, I'm sorry. I didn't even know y'were Elizabeth at first, not when ya'd told me yer name was Peg. I'm really sorry."

What she did next took him by surprise and showed him what was beneath the harsh exterior. She walked up close to him and lifted her hand to the side of his face, touching his cheek gently, she seemed to be examining his features closely. "So you're Michael then are ya? You're my wee brother?" Her eyes looked rheumy, as if they might release a tear, though they didn't.

"I'm sorry," it was all he could seem to say in the circumstances.

"Don't apologise for who you are," she told him. "It's no fault o' yours, what happened. It's no fault o' yer mother's either. Eban Whithorn's an evil old bastard who should never've been allowed tae take a breath beyond birth, let alone grow up tae inflict his poison on innocent lives. How did ya find me?"

"I met Jacob. I went to Ireland, he told me where yer mother came from an' I just…I don't know, I just needed t'know, I can't explain beyond that, I'm sorry."

Peg remained silent for a few moments as she took his hand in hers and stretched out his fingers, then she looked up at him. "She was right when she said ya look a wee bit familiar because ya do, ya've a look o' my brother…sorry, our brother, Martin. He's dead now ya know?"

"I know, I'm so sorry, it must've been hard for you, and for your mother of course."

Peg let out a sigh. "Can ya be here again tomorrow? She goes tae the W.I. tomorrow, so she'll no' be here. Any time after half-nine an' before three, okay?"

Robbie agreed and Peg opened the gate for him, Dave trotted out to his car and waited as he got in before returning to his mistress' call. Robbie could feel that now familiar sense of mental exhaustion wash over him.

He wanted so desperately to be with Lynsey, to see his wife but he was afraid. He knew that she'd want him to give it up if only for a while, for his own health, for his sanity, and she'd be right. But he couldn't, he just couldn't let go of what he was well aware had now become his obsession. He needed to know more and more; it was eating at him and he couldn't get any respite from it.

***

"Morning Bash," Sgt Chris Radley addressed his counterpart as he walked up to Sgt Sajid Bashir's desk.

Bash stopped tapping at his keyboard and rested back in his chair for a second or two's realisation, before standing up and extending his hand. "Hey, hey, Radders mate, how y'doing? Bloody long time since I've seen *you* fella. I thought y'must o'retired."

"Cheeky twat, I'm not that bleeding old," Chris laughed, as he pulled the chair away from the empty desk next to them and sat down.

He had a green envelope folder with him that he placed on the desk in front of Bash. A sticker on the front read; *Kester Richards, aka; Christopher Hartley, aka; Gareth Dalby.* Bash picked it up and read the names as he removed the thick elastic band that was holding it together.

"Gareth Dalby?" he said. "That's one o'the scrotes that left that fella in a coma last year isn't it? Robert McAndrew? Nasty business that was, poor fella's mam died o'cancer a few month after. Poor bloody woman likely worried herself t'death. She were in bits while he were missing, nice family.

"What's with these aliases? First I've seen o'these. Which one's real? This top one, Kester?" Bash seemed puzzled but intrigued.

"Yup, Kester Richards."

"I don't get it. He checked out as Gareth Dalby when he were lifted, Chris. I'm sure he had paperwork in that name."

"He did Bash; driving licence, bank statements, even a bloody national insurance number. But when his place were turned over they found documentation in the name o'Chris Hartley. A couple o'the usual snitches named him as that an' he had more convincing documents in that name too; passport, probation records etcetera. He checked out as being Chris Hartley, but he's not. He's one Kester Richards, born an' bred in the Glasgow region, flits between the two locations, not to mention the two identities, and the two vastly different accents. That's no mean feat, an' as much of an unpleasant wanker that he is, there's a part o'me that's a little bit awe-struck by the way he goes about it."

"Fucking unbelievable!" Bash sighed, exasperated by the revelation. "This his file then?"

"It's part of it. This is the results of the psychiatric evaluation we had done on him."

"Why? Did he qualify for one? I only met him once, but he seemed fully composmentis t'me."

Radley raised his eyebrows. "Yeh, me too, but the court appointed him one o'those social worker types. I don't know what the hell he said t'make 'em think he needed one, but anyway, he got one. Bloke called Ray Graham, seems a decent sort, but it were him that wanted the evaluation doing, said there was something *not right* about Chris Hartley. Turned out he were right, he wasn't bloody Chris Hartley for one thing. Anyway, this is the evaluation. I wanted your take on it Bash. You dealt with that jogger, McAndrew, saw the extent of his injuries first hand. Was he as bad as it reads in the report?"

Bash sucked in air through his pursed lips as he shook his head. "It was awful. To be honest with ya, I don't think the report gives the full picture. His injuries were extensive, more like someone who'd been run over a couple o'times by a van, than a mugging victim. He's been left with a limp an' there's some memory deficit from the head injury he sustained. We thought he must o'fought back an' that's why he'd been beaten black an' blue, but it turned out he'd been blind-sided, didn't even see it coming. It were vicious for the sake of a mobile phone Chris, way O.T.T."

Radley rested his chin in his hand as he pondered on the assault. "There's something that just doesn't add up t'me. Have a read through that evaluation an' tell me what y'think. It's just, well...the more I've looked at it, the more questions I've got regarding that jogger."

Bash opened the file and took out the report, resting it on top of his keyboard. He leant in to read, skipping through the initial blurb to concentrate on the body of the report.

Having set a baseline standard with Mr Richards, I continued using both formal, structured and informal, unstructured, recognised and standardised methods of delivery and evaluation techniques.

First impressions. Mr Richards is a healthy looking young man in his early to mid-twenties. He is clean and tidy in appearance and gives no concern as to his ability to manage his daily routines. He does not present as a vulnerable adult. Indeed, on the contrary, Mr Richards gives me the impression that he is more than capable of taking care of his own affairs and self-care needs.

In general. Mr Richards remained calm throughout and willingly answered any questions put to him. Having said that, his contempt for the process was easy to read in the expressions he frequently showed. Mr Richards is very adept at presenting the facets that he wants to show. He is a man of very high intelligence with an I.Q. of around 149 according to the Wechsler Adult Intelligence Scale—Fourth Edition (WAIS–IV, 2008).

During testing Mr Richards displayed no characteristics concurrent with psychotic behaviour or thoughts. However, during informal sessions, I found other concerns which caused me to suspect a possible personality disorder and I therefore proceeded to utilise the Revised, Hare Psychopathy Check-list for the purpose of scoring Mr Richards against that scale.

Findings. As previously stated, I have no concerns regarding the mental health of Mr Richards. I find him to be of sound mind, well above average intellect, with a good understanding of the differences between what is right and wrong, both in legal terms and morally, within his own personal life. However, these findings are based on the fact that Mr Richards 'knows and understands' right and wrong, but he certainly has no emotional concept of them.

When offset against the facets of the Hare Psychopathy Check-list; Mr Richards scored very highly indeed. In facet 1: Interpersonal, he scored 7 out of a maximum 8. In facet 2: Affective, he again scored 7 out of 8. Facet 3: Lifestyle, his score was 7, the maximum being 10. Facet 4: Antisocial, he scored 8 out of a possible 10. With 4 out of 4 regarding other items to be measured.

The score for Mr Kester Richards is among the highest I have personally dealt with. Out of a maximum 40 points over all, Mr Richards scored 33. The cut-off score which determines if an individual can be reasonably labelled as 'Psychopath', is 25 in the UK and 30 in the US. Either way, Mr Richards falls well within the realms of that category. He is highly impulsive and volatile and an extremely skilled manipulator, a pathological liar and very criminally aware. A 'one-step-ahead' person who feels nothing for others, chillingly devoid of all empathetic response, with a constant, though controlled (probably due to intellect) undertone of severe aggression toward others.

I'm unsure if Mr Richards has undergone such tests previously; he denied he had, though he appeared acutely aware throughout that he was being assessed for this personality disorder. As he had crossed the threshold for research into psychopathy, I put it to him that this could be a positive move. He declined. As a Health Care Professional in both mental health services and research programs, it greatly concerns me that such an individual moves in normal society unchecked. Mr Richards has the capacity for great violence and though I am unaware of his past, as dictated by protocol, my own personal feeling would be that if this individual isn't already a killer that he presents with all of the appropriate markers for such behaviour.

"Wow." Bash was a tad overwhelmed by what he'd just read.

"I know," Radley acknowledged. "My thoughts exactly. Don't get me wrong, Richards is a nasty fucking toe-rag, but he's smart. All the other things he's done, there's been an intelligence to them, but this jogger just seems so messy, untidy for a mind like his. I can't help being inclined t'think that it wasn't a mugging-gone-wrong at all. I think he was genuinely trying t'kill that bloke, but why?"

Bash leant right back in his seat, stretching his arms up, hands behind his head. "Dale Price confirmed it was an unprovoked attack didn't he?" The question was rhetorical. "But yer right Chris, something's not sitting well is it? Robert McAndrew was genuine enough, so were his nearest an' dearest from what I could tell. We need t'speak to Price again, there must be something more he's got, something he could cough up on this Kester Richards. If he's that much of a fucking psycho he must've shown that before the day in question, surely. I don't know, dismembered squirrels or something sick like that. Maybe McAndrew was a practice run for him, just in the wrong place at the wrong time, while Richards honed his skill. Maybe he was building up to murder someone else, I really can't say what I think."

Radley gathered the report back up and shoved it loosely back into the folder, then re-bound it with the elastic band. "Maybe, but according to this psych chap, he's not sick is he? He's just *sick,* if y'get my meaning? And if he wanted t'practise his art, why not pick a softer target instead of one that could very well have fought back. And why did his violence escalate the more incapacitated the victim became? Are you absolutely sure the two men didn't know each other Bash?"

"Completely sure, yeh. It doesn't make sense, I know but…well, I don't know what t'say. If you get a grip of Price, I'll make contact with Rob McAndrew, okay?"

Chapter Twelve

Robbie hated it when Lynsey cried, but his last phone call to her had left her in tears, which wasn't like her, she was usually quite tough. She was still in the Isle of Stennoch waiting for him and he was still in a bed and breakfast in Glasgow, waiting to go back to Peg's once Maev had gone out for the day.

Lynsey didn't understand why he was delaying going back, or why he wouldn't let her join him and he couldn't explain. He didn't know how to put into words how vulnerable he felt, how tired, how confused. But what he did know was that he needed to do this in his own way, without the influence or input of a third party. He loved his wife wholly, but knew that she'd want him to rein things in when she saw how it was affecting him. Oh, she'd have his best interests at heart but that's not what he needed right now, at least he didn't think it was.

He promised her that he'd call once he'd spoken to Peg again.

It was hard. He knew he had family that loved him: his wife, his brother, Clive, not to mention the many friends and colleagues he had, yet he just couldn't help but feel so alone. He knew they cared, but how could they understand when he wasn't sure he understood himself. He wished his mum were still alive, Annie, the mum who'd raised him, protected him, saved him even. She'd been the only person that had lived through the lies with him, though she'd created most of them herself, he'd long since accepted that she'd done so for all the right reasons. The desire to see her, speak to her, ask her advice seemed somewhat compounded by the knowledge that it just couldn't ever happen. And as for Dredger Scoular; the two of them hadn't spent that much time together, but Robbie felt such a connection to the old man. What would he be telling him he should do right now? Hah, he'd be saying he should listen to his wife more, no doubt.

The truth was, Robbie was afraid. He knew he was letting things get on top of him and he was afraid that he'd take it out on her, that he'd snap and it would lead to further arguments and stress. Logic told him it was the wrong thing to do, but emotionally he'd gone into a kind of destructive, self-preservation mode, the 'head-in-the-sand' syndrome of ignoring the things that one really should deal with in the hope that they either go away or just self-resolve. Just for the moment, he had a single-track mind. He'd just met his sister, his real half-sister, a blood relative that had the circumstances been more acceptable, he'd have known all of his life. He should've known her and Martin, they were his siblings. He could never know Martin now, it was too late for that, but he had so many questions for Elizabeth, Peg.

***

As Chris Radley sat waiting for Dale Price to be escorted from his cell in Wakefield Prison, he began to notice how damp his jacket was. He'd been caught in a downpour when he'd got out of his car and made a run for the front gate. Procedure dictated that he be allowed through one gate at a time only, which meant that while he was waiting for the initial entry gate to close and lock automatically behind him, he was getting drenched as it was the second entry gate that would be the one to give him shelter once he'd passed through it.

The stomp of heavy boots approaching alerted him to Price's arrival, followed by the clunking of solid prison doors as two uniformed prison officers escorted their ward into the room.

"Sit down here Price!" one of them ordered, indicating to the chair on the opposite side of the table from Radley.

Price did as he was told. He looked quite meek really for a repeat offender, a petty thief with an air of vulnerability about him. Radley thought it a strange contrast of characteristics and couldn't decide if it was due to him being too thick to know when he was being used by the wrong company he'd kept, or if indeed he was very good at manipulation, much like his partner in crime…literally.

He decided to hedge his bets, not wanting to give too much away too soon and also in the hope that Price might inadvertently give away more than he'd planned to.

"Morning Dale, how're you today?" he began.

Price shrugged his shoulders, not making any effort at eye-contact. "Locked up. Shite innit."

"Unfortunately Dale, you've broken the law, many times it seems. And just like any other member of society, y'get caught, y'go to jail. It's not rocket science lad."

Price shrugged again, this time saying nothing.

"I were wanting t'talk to you about a friend of yours, Gareth Dalby. At least, that's who he was at the time of his arrest." At this point Radley could plainly see the discomfort caused by the very mention of that name. "That was the alias he used wasn't it Dale, for a while anyway? I believe you also knew him as Chris Hartley, is that right?"

"Chris Hartley yeh. Said that before in my statement, innit."

"Indeed you did Dale. Tell me, how often did yer pal use those names?"

"Y'what? I don't fucking know, do I."

"Did he have any other alias' he used?"

"Just Gareth Dalby."

"And Chris Hartley?"

Price looked puzzled, as though he were trying to make sense of the question. "I thought an alias meant it were snide?"

"It does, that's right."

"Well it were just Gareth Dalby then. That were the snide name, the other's real."

Radley decided that his initial impression of Dale Price was likely to be the correct one, the lad really wasn't that bright after all. Something Richards was clearly well aware of. Price obviously had enough about him to commit the offences, but was just the wrong side of dim, allowing him to be easily manipulated. Which was unfortunate because this had, in real terms, meant he was another victim of a master manipulator, pliable to say the least.

"Both those names are snide Dale, neither of them's his real name. Which is why I was wondering if you ever knew him to use any others? Y'never heard anyone else call him by a different name? Never saw any documents, letters in a different name?"

For the first time, Price made direct eye-contact with Radley, a marginal look of bewilderment across his face. "I always called him Chris, that's his name…at least, that's what he said. I thought…what is it then?"

"Where did 'Chris' tell you he was from?"

"Here. Leeds. Up where that old nut-house is, Guiseley or Menston, up that way. Says he used t'play in its grounds when he were a kid, before it all closed down an' got built on. Said him an' his mates used t'chuck stones at the nutters when they were out in the gardens. Told me a gang o' nut-jobs once chased them."

Wow. Radley was impressed at the lengths Kester Richards had gone to in order to create this false identity of Chris Hartley. Though being a Leeds local himself, Radley could see the historic errors in the tale Richards had woven. He decided it was probably better at this point, not to give too much away to Price. Besides, the poor lad looked like he might burst into tears; he was already upset enough at the betrayal he'd suffered, the realisation he'd been had by his pal.

"Did you ever see or hear him on the phone to someone? Using their names maybe?"

Price shook his head and looked down, clearly giving away that the real answer to that question was 'yes', but he wasn't about to say and Radley decided it wasn't that important at this point in time, and likely just innocuous contacts.

"D'ya know who Kester Richards is, Dale?"

Price sneered. "Kester? What the fuck sort o'name's that? Who is it? Is that a bloke's name or what?"

"That'll be a 'no' then I take it?" The question was more rhetorical. "Can ya tell me something though please Dale?"

"What?"

"Of all the…shall we say, activities, that you were involved in with him. How come the attack on that guy on the tow-path, the jogger, how come that one in particular was so vicious? Had the two of ya fallen out? In a bad mood? Not had a shag or something?"

"Fuck off!" Price was on the defensive, just where Radley wanted him, and so easily pliable, took no coaxing at all. He could see why he'd have his uses for someone like Richards.

"Well something made that crime different from the rest Dale, I'm just trying to ascertain what that was. Were y'both having a bad day for some reason? Was that guy just the first unlucky bastard t'cross yer path?"

"It wasn't me for fuck sake! I told them that. I were there but I never did all that."

"What did ya do then Dale? What happened?"

"It's in my statement. I've said what happened."

Radley leant forward onto the table that separated the two of them, almost to the point that his backside lifted slightly from his chair. "But I'd like ya to tell *me* all about it Dale. I'd like to know why, if it wasn't you as you've said, why did *he* do what he did to that man on that towpath, at that time?"

"He'd been watching him." Price said. "He made me follow him in town once, see where he went, that sort o' thing."

"An' was that normal for him to ask ya t'do that kind of thing? Did he often follow his potential victims?"

"No, but he said this fella was minted. Said it'd be worth our while t'know a bit more about him."

Radley sat back into his chair again and frowned. "Why did he think he was 'minted' as you say? What reason did he give you to make *you* think that the man had plenty of money?"

Price shrugged his shoulders again. "He seemed t'know him that's all."

"Explain."

"He never said, but he seemed t'know a lot about him: where he worked, his bird's name. I don't fucking know, he just did. When I saw him running down that towpath towards us, I just thought it were a coincidence. I said, '*look, it's that gadgie*'. I were surprised t'see him cos Apperley Bridge is a fair old trek from the middle o' Leeds."

"Indeed it is, it's on the outskirts of Bradford for one thing. Was it a usual haunt for y'both? Did you go there a lot?"

"First time I'd ever been down there, didn't really know why he wanted us t'go down by the canal in the first place. Truth was, I were a bit scared t'be honest. I thought he was going t'kick off at me. Thought I must've pissed him off or something. It didn't always take much. He could just turn for no reason, then other times when y'thought he'd be riled, he'd stay calm, there were no judging him. He'd go berserk as fuck over nothing, then handle it over something ya'd think he'd batter you for."

"So, the jogger was heading your way. What happened then?"

"Chris told me to twat him, just t'drop him as he passed us. I thought we were going t'rob him. I thought he'd be stunned by me hitting him, go down, we'd do the business an' fuck off, job done."

"But…?"

"But then he just started laying into him, he didn't even take any stuff. I grabbed the guy's phone off his arm-band thing. The fella got to his feet, but he wasn't quick enough an' Chris smashed him in the face with his elbow. Gadgie booted Chris in his stomach an' punched him, but he'd done it from the ground. Chris lost it an' just went berserk. I tried t'grab him, t'do a runner, but he twatted me, I were scared. Seen him lose it before, but not that bad. He were punching the fella, sticking the boot in, he even stamped on him a few times. He were already out of it, but Chris just carried on.”

“By ‘out of it’ you mean unconscious?”

“Yeh. Chris grabbed hold of one of his arms an’ a leg an’ started dragging him closer to the water. He yelled at me t’grab the other side, but I could see his leg were broke an’ I didn’t want to touch it, so I just got his arm. He were heavier than he looked, a dead weight. Chris said we had t’get him in the canal. I said he’d die if we did, he were out of it, he’d drown. He screamed at me t’do what he said or he were going to open my fucking throat. I’ll be honest, I were shitting myself. Thank fuck, we heard voices. Someone were getting close to where we were. I couldn’t see them, but I could hear them; Chris seemed oblivious though. I had to shove at him t’make him listen t’me. We ran.”

Radley was growing more and more suspicious of the connection between Richards and this particular victim. “What happened after that?”

Price pointed at his own face, indicating the kink in his nose. "He did this. He gave me a right fucking pasting. I had t'go to A&E, told them I'd been beat up by a jealous husband. I lost two teeth, he broke my nose and a couple o'ribs. I got away, did a runner."

"Why would he do that to ya? You were his mate weren't ya?"

"Don't know, he were still pumped I suppose. He said if I'd have got a grip faster, that the fucker would o'been in the canal, an' no-one would o'known. An' he took the fella's phone off me, I'd fuck all t'show for it. Taking a risk like that an' he didn't even let me keep the phone."

"How very inconsiderate of him," Radley quipped, though the sarcasm of the comment appeared lost on Price. "It all seemed a bit over the top for the sake of a mobile phone Dale. Did it not occur to you that there might well be more t'this than meets the eye?"

"What you on about?"

"Think about it for a second son. *Chris,* renders this man unconscious. Then he tries to shove his body into the canal. Even *you* knew that by doing so, the fella was surely going to die. *He* definitely knew that to do so would kill the man. This wasn't a mugging Dale, this was attempted murder an' *you* were there, *you* played a part in that."

The look of horror that covered Price's face in that instant was just the desired effect that Radley had hoped for. The realisation that he could be looking at a long stretch as a maximum security prisoner alongside some of the nastiest men in the north, rather than the few months he was serving on the low security unit, was dawning on him fast.

"I already grassed on him when I got lifted for that. Got a reduced sentence cos of it, an' he'll fucking kill me if he ever gets close enough." Panicked as he spoke, Price's eyes began to well up.

Radley knew he needed to change tack again now, become the protector. "Listen son, it's not you we're after, it's him, the vicious bastard that tried to murder that man. And might I add, though he did survive, he's not been left untouched by what happened. He still can't remember events from that day and he's got permanent scars, not all of his injuries have fully healed an' nor will they. The problem we've got Dale is this; *you* are our only witness to what happened. As I said, the victim himself can't remember. I believe ya when ya say that it were all down to Chris, but what if he tells the judge a different story? What if he says that it were all down t'you? Then it's just his word against yours. Do y'see my problem here Dale?"

Keep it simple and spoon-feed this lad. It was working. It took less than a minute for the two brain cells he had to work out that he was in deep shit here. "What do I need t'do?" he asked.

Radley nodded to one of the guards indicating that the interview was at an end. "We'll talk again Dale. We'll sort it, don't worry."

***

"Don't get me wrong," Peg told Robbie, "there were never any love lost between our father an' my mother ya know. From the way she tells it, he was always a wrong 'un. I think she were maybe attracted tae the bad-boy image when she were a girl, but the reality was something quite different. She said he were always cagey, secretive an' damn right cruel by the sounds of it. She came from money ya know, my mother did."

Robbie nodded his acknowledgement. "Hence the big house, Windyhill, right?"

"Aye, that's right. My grandparents never approved o' the match apparently, so they eloped. I were already expected ya see. Seems quite romantic on the face of it, don't ya think? They disowned her though, cut her off from her family; she'd disgraced them ya see. Eban had a bad reputation even then.

"My mother thought they might soften when I was born an' she took me tae see them. They'd a maid who answered the door. My mother standing there with me in her arms in the cold evening air. She said the maid had looked so uncomfortable because the sound of her father's voice was bellowing from somewhere out o'sight, ordering the maid tae shut the door immediately. My mother tells me how the poor wee lass looked at her so sympathetically, mouthing the words, *I'm so sorry,* as she slowly closed the door on her."

Robbie felt a pang of something he couldn't quite identify, sadness maybe, or was it guilt that he was causing Peg to recall such times?

She continued. "Anyway, we moved tae Ireland on the suggestion o'my other grandparents, Eban's lot. I forget which way round it was now, but the twins were born and Eban took the cloth." She suddenly paused as she caught herself. "Robbie, Martin was a twin. Did ya know that love?"

"I did, yeh, I've seen copies of the birth certificates an' Jacob told me too. Michael an' Martin. Michael died didn't he? Is that part of why Maev hates me so much? Because the sick bastard gave me the name of her dead baby?"

"Och, she doesn't hate ya Robbie, she doesn't know ya. She just hates what ya represent tae her. Yes, Eban's a twisted man, but my mother couldn't hold you responsible for the name ya were given, when ya'd no choice in the matter, ya were just a wee bairn back then, an innocent.

"Eban was a drinker, a womaniser, a wife-beater, a bar-room brawler an' no' much of it changed, even when he'd taken the cloth. He calmed a lot while he was being mentored apparently, but no sooner was he flying solo, than it was back to his usual antics, if ya can call it that. There was a local girl turned up all bruised with her clothes torn once. Her father couldn't get her to say what'd happened, so he took her tae church, thinking he were doing the right thing by her. My mother was there at the time, she said Eban glared at the girl, then suggested she may have been attacked by some transient trawlermen. The lassie apparently agreed, then burst intae tears an' ran out o' the church. She left the village shortly afterwards. My mother told me she knew full well who'd ruined that girl. Said she'd recognised that look he'd given her, that it was the self-same threatening look he'd give tae her if she dared defy him. The kind of a look that made ya keep yer mouth tight shut, or else.

"An' ya have tae understand Rob, back then, tae a religious family, the sanctity o' marriage meant everything. Don't get me wrong, I think if my mother hadn't have been cut off from her own, she may well have fled back here, but she'd no-one. Eban's parents were incredibly religious, they tried tae make her feel part o'their fold, but he was hell bent on going against everything that they stood for. They'd pushed him tae take up as a minister like Jacob had done; they thought it'd bring him intae line I suppose. They covered up all o'his misdemeanours, denied there was evil in him, an' when the going got too hard for them in Ireland, they encouraged him tae take up a parish elsewhere."

"And that's how he ended up in the Isle o'Stennoch? That's where my mother became tangled up in things?"

"Aye Robbie, sadly that's the truth of it." Peg leant back on the bench seat and Dave jumped up into her lap.

She petted him as he made himself comfortable. "He'd initially gone there tae be placed in a parish by the presiding Bishop. His reputation had preceded him to a point, but he was one o' them by then, an' woe betide anyone who'd accuse a churchman of any wrongdoing."

"So the church elders knew about him, even before he'd been given a post?"

"Some of it they did, an' aye, they helped tae cover his tracks. It wouldn't do for the church tae be seen in a bad light. But Eban himself pulled the wool over their eyes too ya know."

"How?"

"He told them he was a widower for a start. Gave them some sob story about his *faith* seeing him through the pain he'd endured. They knew he'd been married, but never checked up on his tale of woe. Took him at face value an' gave him a start in a small, rural parish, your parish, with a view to him taking a larger one, once he'd proved himself.

"He made several returns tae Ireland for visits, each time telling my mother that we'd be sent for when the time was right. The visits got less an' less until they stopped. My mother heard on the Whithorn family grapevine that he'd married a lassie; she was furious. She wrote tae the Bishop telling him of Eban's bigamy, an' within the week Eban was on her doorstep. He threatened her with everything he could. She said he made a grab for me, but I ran, so he caught a hold o' wee Martin, pinning him tae the floor by his throat. Told my mother that if he got the tiniest o'hints that she'd opened her mouth again, that he'd be back an' that he'd silence her permanently, and us."

Robbie wouldn't have believed it if he didn't already know of similar goings on where his father was concerned. It was an awful thing to admit to himself, but he felt partly relieved because it wasn't just him and his own mother, Mona, who'd suffered this way. He felt in some way exonerated that he and Mona hadn't caused Eban's behaviour, they'd just had to live it, just like Maev and her children had.

"Does Maev think that my mother knew he was married? Is that why she's so angry?" he asked her.

Peg placed her hand on his forearm, causing Dave to sniff at him too. "None o' this is yer fault Robbie, nor yer mother's, Maev knows that. But he'd taunt her ya see, mostly through the contact he had with Jacob an' his parents. He'd say how wonderful his life was in the Isle, how Mona was everything a wife should be, how they'd a child they loved dearly, who got the world on a plate from his 'devoted father'. She's convinced he named ya Michael as a deliberate snipe at her, an' tae be honest, she's probably right. What sane person would name their new son for their dead one, that's just sick an' a very cruel thing for my mother, me an' Martin to know.

"We'd nothing ya see. He sent us no money an' my mother had tae work hard tae keep us fed, all the time being given the impression that life was nothing but roses for you an' yer mother. She couldn't cope, she became very bitter, an' eventually had tae chance a return here tae her own people. Her mother had died by the time we arrived in Bearsden, an' she'd no' been told

by anyone, she was heart-broken. Her father refused tae
see us, but her aunt, his sister persuaded him tae allow us
the old game-keepers cottage in the grounds of
Windyhill. After a few years some folks came round an'
told us they were the new owners an' they were looking
to develop the golf course that her father had built. They
gave us notice tae quit, we had tae be gone within the
fortnight. We've been here ever since."

"What happened t'yer Grandfather? Did he ever
make it up with Maev?" Robbie was curious.

"No, never. I only ever saw him a handful o' times
an' that was accidental. I believe he took bad with
dementia. Ended his days in a care home in Glasgow
somewhere. We never visited. His estate was split
between my mother's three brothers, all dead now. One
o'them, Uncle Frank, helped us out over the years from
time tae time, but he was the only one. The fact that my
mother had lost her entire family in favour of a man who
treated her so badly, only served tae make her that much
more bitter. She came back here from Ireland, all alone
in the world but for her bairns. Made tae feel shame at

being a single mother, abandoned by her husband an'
unable tae tell the world the truth of it all. '*Yae reap wit
yae sow*', is what she was told. Very unfair o' them,
very unjust. All helped tae form her intae the bitter old
hag she's become."

Robbie looked down at Dave, fast asleep on his
mistress' lap. "Have you always known Peg? About
Eban I mean, about life for yer mother back then?"

"Aye," Peg answered, "but I've a feeling you
haven't. Yer a grown man now Robbie, ya must be in
yer forties, am I right? So why's it taken ya so long tae
do this? Why now?"

Robbie knew that the story he had to tell her was a
long one. That, but for being assaulted, he might never
have known the truth to this day. "How about a fresh
pot o' tea Peg? Because my chapters o'this bloody
nightmare don't get any less weird."

Chapter Thirteen

Pulling into one of only two harbour side parking spots outside the Solway Harvester, Robbie looked around for Lynsey's car; it wasn't there. Guessing that she'd probably gone for a drive, or to see Joe, he decided to go for a walk out onto the Cairn. The white tower was reflecting the low evening sunlight as was the sea. It was calm, with gentle waves washing against the rocks below.

He sat himself down on a bench at the foot of the tower, the one facing out to sea and watched the low light glistening on the tips of the waves. It had occurred to him as he'd walked up there, that this was the spot, over forty years ago, where Eban had overheard the grief-stricken conversation between his wife's sister, Annie, and Dredger Scoular, as they'd discussed the real Robert McAndrew, their secret son. This was the spot where the unholy agreement between the two men had been born; one keeping the other's silence, despising the very existence of one another, yet reliant on each other's compliance.

He'd not really seen the beauty in the Isle and its surrounding seascapes the last time he'd been here. Too distracted, too engulfed in what was going on at the time no doubt. But now, now he could appreciate how amazing it would have been for him to have grown up here, the place he came from. It was so hard to imagine, given how tranquil it currently felt, that so much trauma had occurred here, so many lives torn apart and ruined. It felt so peaceful now.

Just as he stood, ready to make his way back, his mobile beeped to alert him to a text message. Reception was really random in and around the village. For the most part there was no mobile signal whatsoever, but every now and again a random one made it through for no apparent reason. He looked at the message and laughed to himself. It was from the Isle of Man mobile phone service, welcoming him to their service and informing him of the tariffs for usage. He looked out across the calm water where he could just about make out the Isle of Man, given the fading light, on the horizon to the south. It was strange to think that he was closer to that than he was to Newton Stewart, the nearest major town from the village.

His phone beeped again. This time the message was from Lynsey, but he noticed the time-stamp had been several hours previously. *"Why don't you ever answer your bloody phone?"* it read. He tried to call her, but his phone indicated poor signal, so he tried to reply to the text, but that wouldn't send either. He wondered if she were back at the Harvester yet, so he made his way there. He had so much to tell her, so much information that Peg had given him. Part of him had felt a weight lifted, vindicated for the guilt he'd felt over the way his real mother and he had suffered at Eban's hands. Guilt that was never his to start with, but he'd felt anyway. Just knowing that Eban had been that way long before Mona had come on the scene, and way before he, himself had been born, released him from any irrational sense of 'why me, why us?' It had allowed him to finally see that the people in Eban's life weren't the problem, though not perfect by any stretch of the imagination, the problem was, and always had been Eban Whithorn himself.

He'd arranged with Peg that he'd go back in a couple of days, this time taking Lynsey with him. She'd said that there was so much more he should know, she wanted to tell him about Martin. She'd appeared a little cagey when he'd tried to push her on the subject, said it would keep until next time. Besides, he'd had to leave when he did as he'd taken up much of her day and Maev had been due home from the Women's Institute. She really wouldn't have been happy to find him there again.

Lynsey's car still wasn't around, so Robbie went inside and ordered a pint at the bar. Once served, he made his way round to the far side, where the till was. He recognised the woman there from his previous visit. "Hi, it's Ruby isn't it?"

"That's right, aye." She smiled at him, though clearly didn't return the recognition.

"I was wondering if ya'd seen my wife today, Lynsey, Lynsey McAndrew. We're booked in; she stayed last night but I was away."

"McAndrew?" she paused as she opened the reservations book. "Oh aye, that's right. She paid up an' checked out this morning, half-ten. Did ya not know she'd gone?"

Not wanting to look a complete twat, but feeling very much like one, Robbie attempted one of his now increasingly familiar blags. "Oh, well yeah, she said she were checking out, but I couldn't get hold of her with the dodgy signal round here, so I wasn't sure what time, that's all."

"Right y'are," Ruby said, though she didn't look all that convinced.

Robbie didn't know whether to be worried or not. Why would Lyns just leave like that? Was she angry with him after their argument last night? Had she gone home or gone to look for him in Glasgow? Oh, how could he be so fucking stupid? It was getting late, but he decided to phone Joe, just in case she was there, or at least she might have been there and told Joe of her plans.

He asked Ruby if he could possibly use the pub landline and assured her it was a local call.

It was Marie, Joe's daughter who answered. "I'm sorry Robbie, I've no' seen her. Dad never said ya were visiting again or I'd o'called at the Harvester."

"Is he there? Can I have a word please?"

"He's away tae his bed just now Robbie, but I doubt he's seen her today. He's been on a trip with the old folks club he goes tae. I only picked him up an hour ago."

Robbie made her promise to call if she or Joe heard anything from Lyns. He had to admit to being a little worried. And the more he thought about the message she'd sent him, the more concerned he felt. Just what had she been needing to tell him when she was trying to call? Had she needed to rush home to Leeds? Maybe something had happened and she'd been trying to get hold of him to let him know.

He thanked Ruby then headed out of the pub to the car. He needed to drive somewhere, where he could get some decent mobile signal and call her, or Rich. Maybe it was his step-father, Clive. Could he have been taken ill? Feelings of dread washed over him as he recalled getting bad news about his mum, Annie, while he was in the Isle of Stennoch the previous year. He tried to shake off the worry and not get too caught up in it until he knew what he was dealing with, and he wouldn't know that until he got a decent signal that meant he could speak to someone. They could've crossed paths...maybe she'd headed up to Glasgow to find *him*, just as he was heading back down.

He'd almost reached Wigtown before he found he had a consistent signal. It had been intermittent thus far, but nothing that stayed long enough to be of any use to him. It was sparse at the best of times, but always that much worse in the evenings for some reason. He knew when he'd hit a strong point because his phone went into overdrive as it downloaded stacked notifications of missed calls and text messages, not to mention his loaded email inbox.

Scrolling through them, he noticed several missed calls from a withheld number, as well as nine from Lynsey, a couple from his brother, Rich, four from Clive and three from a Leeds number that he didn't recognise. He tried his wife first, but she didn't answer. After seven rings each time, it defaulted to her voicemail, which meant she either had it on silent and didn't realise it was ringing, or she was driving. He left her a message before calling Clive at home.

"Why y'sounding so panicked lad?" Clive was concerned when he heard the intonation in Robbie's voice. "Lynsey's fine, she got home this afternoon."

"Why? We were meant t'be in Scotland. I went back t'the Harvester t'meet her an' she'd just gone."

"She tried ringing ya. Said there were a problem with the signal up there. Didn't she leave you a message? Have y'listened t'ya messages Robbie?"

He hadn't. It hadn't even occurred to him to listen
to his voicemails yet. "What's happened Clive? Why
did she need t'go back?"

Clive sighed, it was late and he was tired. He hadn't
expected to have to explain the situation, but he did his
best. "D'ya remember that copper, the one who looked
after us when y'went missing?"

"Bash, yeh I know who y'mean. What about him?"

"Well if y'kept a check on yer phone ya'd know
lad," he sounded frustrated. "He's been trying t'get hold
of ya. Something t'do with them lads that attacked ya.
Said it were urgent that y'get in touch. Any road, he got
hold o' Lynsey an' asked her to come back an' make a
statement."

"What for? That's all been dealt with hasn't it?"

"I don't know Robbie, he wouldn't tell the rest of us
too much of it. Said he needed t'speak t'you as a matter
of urgency, but not t'worry. Said he'd keep trying t'call,
but if we heard anything in the meantime, we were t'tell

ya t'contact him. D'ya want his number? I've got it here."

Robbie listened through his voicemails before calling anyone. Sgt Bashir's was first; he asked Robbie to make contact, something to do with a development regarding Gareth Dalby and Dale Price, the two lowlifes responsible for the attack he'd suffered. Lynsey's was next; *'For fuck sake Robbie! D'you ever actually look at your phone? Something's going on to do with those guys that attacked ya. Y'need to call the Police station in Leeds, Sergeant Bashir wants to speak t'you. He's asked me to attend as well, so I'm going now cos I've no idea when you're going t'be back an' I've work t'think of too. Call me!"*

Rich had left a message too, though his was more concise and to the point; *"Give me a buzz when y'get this bro, cheers."* Typical Rich, no frilly edges at all.

His phone rang again while he still had it in his hand, 'The Mrs' appeared in the display. He answered. "Lyns, I'm so sorry love. I didn't realise. I'd left my phone in the car at Peg's, then just never looked at it, 'til I couldn't find you at the Solway Harvester."

"Ya went back there?" she sounded surprised. "Well I suppose ya would've done if ya'd not listened to any messages."

"I'm sorry."

"I know, ya've said. Listen, I've had t'go into the police. Bash wanted me to go over my statement from last year. He were asking if there was any possibility that those bastards could know ya. He showed me some photos of them in case I'd seen them before. I said I hadn't, but he needs you t'do the same. He wouldn't tell me why it were suddenly so important after all this time, but something's going on."

Robbie was no wiser. He'd been shown pictures of the culprits before, he'd not recognised them then and he didn't think he'd have anything more to add. "I'm knackered Lyns. He doesn't expect me t'drive back tonight does he?"

"He won't be there now anyway. Ya might as well stay over an' drive home tomorrow. Ring him though, leave a message if he's not answering so he'll know that y'know what's going on."

"I will. An' Lyns, I really am sorry y'know. I love you. My heads been in bits again, but when I tell ya the things I've found out, ya'll know why I'm feeling better about it."

She sounded weary in her reply. "I love you too Robbie, but y'need to prioritise what's important t'ya. Ya can't keep going off on one whenever the mood takes ya. I need ya too. I know this stuff with the Whithorns is important t'ya, but it's news that's been waiting forty years or so; it's not going anywhere, it can wait a bit longer."

She was right of course, it was so easy for him to put on his blinkers and shut out everything else around him; he could become so single minded in an instant. He'd always had a tendency to, but he did have to admit to himself, that since the attack, he'd become more so.

Whether that was down to the psychological effects of what had happened, or a physiological reason, the results of the head injury perhaps, he didn't know, but he was definitely more impulsive, spontaneous in his responses to things sometimes. This obsession with the Whithorns was one such example.

Of course, everyone but Robbie would assume that the perpetrators of such an attack on him would cause his hackles to rise if nothing else, but to him…well, it was almost like seeing something on the news; it can seem bad, horrific at times maybe, but it's something that happened to someone else. That's how these fellas presented in Robbie's mind; he knew it had happened to him, but it felt like he was an observer rather than a participant. Everyone around him, his wife, his family, his friends, they all got angry and fired up whenever the situation was discussed among them. Yet to Robbie, it seemed much less relevant, much less of a distraction than the revelations he'd encountered since that day.

Bash did answer his phone. He told Robbie that there was something further they needed to discuss with regard to his attack.

"But I've already said I don't recognise them," Robbie insisted. "I don't get it, why am I having t'go through it all again? What's happened?"

"It's not something we should discuss right now Robbie. It's better that I see ya face-to-face. Lynsey said you're in Scotland. Oh congratulations on yer recent nuptials by the way. Will ya be back tomorrow?"

"Thanks. Can I leave it 'til the day after though? There's someone I need t'see up here first."

He could hear Bash audibly sigh at the other end of the line. "Erm, okay, I suppose, but don't leave it any longer please. I'll be at yours for eleven a.m. the day after tomorrow, okay. Make sure you're there please Robbie."

"I will be." And he meant it. Whatever it was sounded important. Why else would Bash be so determined to get hold of him? Though he couldn't for

the life of him think what it might be. He'd been
attacked; the guys that did it had been caught, they'd
been convicted and they'd been banged up. Job done.

Chapter Fourteen

Dave's erratic barking was the first thing to alert Robbie to something not being right the next morning when he arrived back at Peg and Maev's. He went in through the gate, calling out as he did so. Dave came running out from the back of the cottage, barking frantically, then turned and ran back in. Worried, Robbie followed him, still calling out.

"Peg, Peg where are ya? Peg."

As he rounded the corner into the hallway he could see Peg on her knees, sobbing and counting as her body appeared to be bouncing. The sound of a disembodied voice coming through the speaker phone brought Robbie to the reality of what was happening.

"Elizabeth, I'm still here," the female voice said. *"You're doing really well. The ambulance isn't far now. Keep counting with me; 1, 2, 3 ,4...1, 2, 3, 4..."*

Only then did it hit Robbie as to what was happening. Maev was in cardiac arrest and Peg was desperately pounding on her chest doing CPR. "Oh, I think I've broke her ribs. I felt them go, oh no…" she cried.

"That's absolutely fine Elizabeth. That's normal, it proves your chest compressions are just right. Keep going, you're doing so well."

Robbie rushed to her side in an instant. "Let me take over Peg, let me help!"

"Is there someone there with you now Elizabeth? Have you got someone there to help you now?"

"Aye, I have, oh thank god I have, oh Mum…"

Robbie felt more of Maev's ribs give under the pressure; it made him wince but he carried on. It was years since he'd done his first aid training at work, but he was amazed how it all came flooding back. Thirty compressions to two breaths. The instructor had been right; it was damn near impossible to keep count under the circumstances. Thirty compressions to two breaths; the words rang in his ears, over and over. The voice of his instructor came back to the forefront. 'Don't worry about losing count, it's thirty compressions to two breaths, there or there abouts, just keep going. We're here to save lives, not pass a maths exam.' Thirty compressions to two breaths. Christ this was tiring. A bead of sweat dripped from the end of his nose, landing on his hands before rolling off onto Maev's chest.

"Elizabeth, I can see on my screen that the ambulance is just outside now. Can one of you go and alert them as to where you are?"

"You go Peg, make sure they can get in." He briefly reached in his pocket and grabbed his car keys, throwing them across the floor towards her. "Tell 'em t'move my car. It's in the way. Go now Peg, quickly!"

"You're doing really well Sir. Please keep going until the crew are inside there with you. Don't stop until they tell you they're ready to take over Sir, okay?...Can you hear me Sir? Did you understand?"

"Yeh, I've got it. I'll keep going."

The sound of boots announced the crew's arrival, stomping their way in, knocking over a chair in the kitchen with their kit bags as they made their way through, Peg following on behind with a whimpering Dave in her arms. Robbie just carried on, aware that bags were being ripped open and the defibrillator was being switched on. It was only when a young woman placed her hand on his shoulder that he became fully orientated to his surroundings again.

"Are the crew inside with you now Sir?" the reassuring voice on the end of the phone enquired.

"Aye, we're here now hen, thanks," the male Paramedic replied. The emergency call handler thanked him before hanging up the call.

The woman told Robbie that she'd take over his position and proceeded to continue his chest compressions, while the bloke cut away Maev's clothing so that he could attach the sticky pads from the defibrillator. Robbie looked away. He felt he shouldn't be seeing old Maev like this; it wasn't dignified for her, though it was a necessary evil. Instead, he went over to Peg and put his arms around her.

"Thank god ya were here," she said to him.

"She's in VF!" the male Paramedic called to his crewmate.

"Good," she replied, "Let me know when yer ready for me tae jump off."

The machine made a noise, like an elongated, continuous tone, increasing in pitch to a point where it broke off to two, short, repeating bursts. "Everyone clear!" the man called.

The woman immediately knelt back on her haunches, removing her hands from Maev, as the man pressed a button. Maev's body jerked violently.

"Shock delivered. Carry on."

The two ambulance crew took it in turns to do chest compressions. Peg panicked at one point because she saw her mother's mouth move, her tongue seemed to move.

"She's breathing! Is she breathing?" she called out.

"No hen, not yet she's not. That's just a reflex in her body, but it's a good sign; it shows her brain's no' given up just yet."

Another responder arrived, just as the third shock was being delivered. This time there was a noticeable difference. The grey, paste colour in Maev's cheeks seemed to pink up. Robbie could see her throat move around her Adam's apple as she swallowed, her chest was rising and falling.

"Okay she's breathing guys. Well done, good work everyone."

Maev's eyes began to flicker and she groaned as she reached up to her face, trying to get at the oxygen mask.

The woman Paramedic blocked her from taking it off and gently pushed her hand back down beside her.

"It's okay m'love, yer safe, we're looking after ya. You just relax now."

Maev groaned again and called out for her daughter. "What's happened Lizzie?"

Peg didn't know what to say, luckily the third man who'd arrived last did. "Yer alright hen, ya'd just a funny turn is all. Yer okay now an' that's what counts."

He made it sound like she'd just fainted or something, when in fact she'd been dead for quite a few minutes. After a moment's thought, Robbie decided that he was completely right. After all, how the hell would you go about explaining to someone that they'd just died, without frightening them back off again? Nope, definitely an explanation best left for when she was actually in hospital and out of danger.

Peg thrust Dave into Robbie's arms and told him to go to the farm up the road. She said that Jack and Beryl lived there, that they'd take care of her animals until she got back. He promised to do as she asked and said he'd follow on in his car.

"We'll be going tae the South Glasgow," the paramedic called.

"He's no' local," Peg told him.

"Oh, right. Have ya a satnav in yer car?"

Robbie nodded.

"In that case, go tae yer 'points of interest', under hospitals, it's the South Glasgow University Hospital, okay?"

***

Sitting next to Peg in the relatives' room outside the Resus department put Robbie in mind of all the time he'd had to spend in hospital himself. Granted, it was a different hospital, but the smells were the same, the sounds emitted by various machines and monitoring equipment was the same, staff rushing round like blue-arsed flies. He'd no recollection of his time in this particular department at the hospital in Bradford, but he imagined they must all be very similar.

"I'm glad yer here," Peg told him. "I don't think I'd want tae be alone right now. She's a cranky old witch at times, but she's my mum. I don't have anybody else."

"What about yer nephews? Martin had kids didn't he? Don't y'see them at all?"

Peg sighed and looked away. "No, not any more I don't. Martin wasn't right for a long time before he died, he damaged them boys, I'm sure of it, their minds I mean. Their mother did her best I suppose, but tae be truthful, she wasn't in the running for mother o' the year if ya know what I mean? She'd no' been the best o' matches for our Martin, a wee bit wayward herself. I think they just brought out the worst in each other tae an extent. After he died, she spent most of her time pissed up. Them boys had a tough time. Och, Tavish has done very well for himself considering. He went tae the university, got himself a good job. He's down in

England now, Luton, it's no' so far from London ya know." She let out a heavy sigh. "But the other one…"

The door opened and the consultant walked in, taking a seat beside Peg. He was smiling. "You'll be pleased to know that your mother's now stable Mrs Parker-Tait."

"It's Miss," she corrected him. "My mother's the Mrs."

"Indeed. Anyway, we'll be moving her up to the cardiac ward soon. She'll get further, ongoing treatment there and she also needs to be seen by a thoracic specialist. You know she sustained damage to her ribs during the process of resuscitation don't you?"

Peg had stopped listening; she'd only heard the bit about her mother being stable and moved up to a ward. Everything else beyond that had blurred into one for her. She was grinning from ear to ear, but sobbing her heart out at the same time. The relief was palpable.

After seeing her mother, Robbie had offered to drive Peg back to Milngavie. He took the opportunity to find out more about Martin, the brother he'd never known.

"Jacob said Martin was troubled," he told her.

"Did he now?" Her tone indicated her indignant response to the mention of Jacob. No doubt she felt somewhat as Robbie did, in that the Whithorns could have done more to protect them all, if not prevent much of it. He decided that those feelings were likely to be more intense for Peg and her family than they were for him, simply due to the fact that she'd grown up with the knowledge of Eban's mistreatment of them, whereas at least he'd been spared that, thanks to Annie and the efforts of the Isle folk who'd been involved in saving him from it all. He'd very little memory of life before Annie had 'kidnapped' him, though that said for want of a better description, and the life he was aware of, the childhood he'd had since, had been a very loving and nurturing one. His life had been a happy one, which is probably why he'd been so devastated to discover that it had been built on lies, but the more he was finding out about Eban Whithorn and the utter destruction he seemed to create wherever he went, the more he began to consider himself lucky, blessed that he'd been spared it when Peg and the others hadn't.

"Peg, what happened to Martin?"

"Hung himself."

"Yeh, I know that. What I meant was, what happened through his life that might make him feel like that was his only option? After all, he would've been very young when Eban bailed out and left you all wouldn't he?"

She paused for a few seconds, staring out of the window. "Aye he was, but he'd memories of the occasional visits home he made. The fear it brought at the sight of our mother pinned up against the wall by her throat, blood on her face. An' then there was the way Mum was about it all."

"How d'ya mean?"

Peg let out a half laugh, half grunt. "Well you've seen for yerself Robbie. My mother became a very bitter woman. I've no' many happy memories from my childhood, just Mum ranting all the time about how *he'd* turned his back on us because *he'd* found another mug tae use, an' how they'd a wee boy of their own now. Ya have tae understand Robbie, we were brought up believing that not only had he replaced our dead, wee brother Michael, with you the new Michael, but that ya were getting all the love an' attention we weren't, not tae mention *things*. We struggled tae keep a roof an' put food on the table, all the time believing that Eban's new son had it good."

"But that just wasn't the case," Robbie maintained, feeling as though he were guilty of something, even though he wasn't.

Peg sighed, all the years of stress now showing on her face. "I know."

"So what about Martin?"

"Mum always said Martin was weak-minded, ya know, easily led, that sort o' thing. Hah, she never bloody considered that she were likely the worst offender when it came down tae that. Anyway, I suppose being the eldest son, he found it easy to be aggrieved at the thought of another son being favoured." She broke off with another sigh and narrowed her eyes. "Och, I know what yer going tae say, but ya have tae understand how things seemed tae us. Eban had planted that seed himself, telling my mother how much better his life was with you an' Mona, but she'd be the one tae never let it drop. Always going on an' on about how we had tae suffer so as the two o' you were kept in clover. Martin felt the pain o' that so much more than I did.

"He was always in fights as a kid, got himself expelled from school. He was a bully tae put no finer point on it. O' course my mother wasted no time in comparing him tae Eban, though I don't honestly think my brother was ever quite that bad. He maybe did have some similarities, I don't know. I was his older sister an' tae me he was just Martin. Anyway, things went from bad tae worse for him. He ended up on drugs, he drank, then he met his wife, another drinker. I suppose it was just a matter o' time really."

"Do you remember his twin?" Robbie was curious about the original Michael.

"Aye, o' course I do, bless his heart. He wasn't with us very long, but I remember him. What d'you know about him?"

"Only that he died as a baby; failure to thrive is what's on his death certificate."

"Hah, ya know more than me then. I remember the twins as babies, the both o' them together. Then one day there was only the one, Martin. All I was told is that Michael had been taken tae be with Jesus. I'd cried an' shouted that Jesus couldn't have him but I was slapped down an' told not tae question it. Years later when I asked my mother what had happened, she just said that he'd always been a sickly child, he was frail an' he died. Then she told me in no uncertain terms tae never remind her of it again. So I never did."

"Jacob told me Martin went over there, to Ireland I mean, asking questions about Eban an' me, long time ago though I think."

"Aye, must be well over twenty years or more. He found Eban too at some point. Jacob told him about you an' Mona, what had happened to her. At some point Martin'd visited her grave ya know, he'd seen that you were supposedly dead, but when he'd quizzed Jacob about there being no body, Jacob'd seemed cagey. Martin then told him ya might o' survived an' Jacob confirmed that tae be his own feeling too. But given that ya were most likely safer where ya were, there was no more tae be done about it."

"Eban would o' been in good health then wouldn't he? Able t'talk t'Martin I mean."

Peg drew in a long, deep breath and Robbie could almost picture her counting to ten in order to stay calm. "Martin thought he'd be welcomed by our father, like it'd be some kind of fabulous reunion. Christ he'd even changed his name by deed pole by then, when he'd

found out what Eban's surname had been at birth that is.
Called himself Martin Richards thinking it'd impress
him, but he just berated Martin, belittled him an' twisted
the knife. Martin was ten times worse after seeing him
than he'd been before, an' believe me, he wasn't great
before that.

"Martin's twins were born an' initially it seemed tae
ground him, but within a year he was back tae the black.
He'd already been in an' out o' rehab; he'd been
sectioned a couple o' times, but none of it was helping
him. It was an awful time seeing his boys grow up with
both parents neither use nor ornament. They found him
ya know, after he'd hung himself; it was the twins that
found him. He'd been there two days in the summer, so
ya can imagine how gruesome a thing it'd be for two
nine year old boys tae find their dad like that, rotting.

"Tavish had always been a quiet boy, a coper if ya
know what I mean? But his brother'd always been
trouble, like his father only with more Eban in him than
Martin'd ever had. He could be cruel, even as a boy he
was always getting in trouble at school, with the police,

with everyone. He's a real nasty side tae him our Kester has I'm afraid. Took on all o' his father's misguided perspectives, all o' his rages then intensified them. Difference is, Kester's a stronger young man now than Martin ever was; he's more control, very logical in thought, though irrational a lot o' the time, if that makes sense?"

Robbie puzzled for a moment or two. "So what're ya saying? That Martin felt some sort of animosity towards me? Despite everything he found out about that bastard, he still felt bitter towards *me?* How could he feel like that when he knew I were no more responsible for what happened than he was?"

Peg's tone suddenly became defensive. "It wasn't his fault, I told ya that. He was born *not right,* the rest was a catalogue o' circumstances. Our dad was the one tae set the ball rolling, my mother didn't help. But deep down Martin was always a powder keg, waiting tae explode. It was his own life he made a misery by it. I kept telling him that there's no controlling the past, ya just have tae deal with it an' not let it affect yer future is all, but he was obsessed an' there was no reasoning with him."

Wow, well Robbie kind of knew how that could feel, though he'd like to think that he was still capable of reasoned thought. Maybe it was a family trait? Christ he hoped not.

"Mother told me that Eban's Mum, his adopted Mum that is, would never admit tae any wrong in him, said he was troubled due tae being an orphan, said that all he needed was some discipline and a loving home. Makes him sound like a bloody stray dog doesn't it?

"She was a strong willed woman by all accounts an' them being Christian missionaries, she obviously didn't want any shame brought on the family. She'd cover things up that he'd done, fight his corner, but when he reached manhood an' had come intae his own, it became too much even for her. So as far as I know it they just buggered off on their preaching trail again, came back for the odd visit, but tae my knowledge they lived out their days at some mission in South America somewhere. I don't think they ever returned tae live in Scotland. Advised from afar, left Jacob tae keep an eye on him; fat lot o' damn good that was. From what Martin told me about his contact with Jacob, it sounds as though, once Eban's parents had found out about his bigamous marriage tae yer mother an' then you being born, they just buried their heads in the sand, put on their blinkers an' had no more tae do with him.

"Jacob told Martin that if he'd ever mentioned Eban's name tae them, that they'd just change the subject, they didn't want tae know. He'd thought it because his mother must've felt guilty, as she'd been the one tae bring the boy into their home. Doing her so called Christian duty no doubt, making herself a martyr tae her faith in the eyes of her peers. She could o' hardly taken him back for re-homing when his true nature began tae rear its ugly head now could she? Bloody typical that she could turn a blind eye tae his crimes an' abuses, but the minute he made a mockery o' the sanctity o' marriage, that was it as far as she was concerned. There was even some falling out over his sister an' they went an' took his side over their own flesh an' blood daughter. God knows what happened."

Robbie knew what had happened, but decided that it was probably better not to bring it up. Peg had been through enough by the sound of it, today included, having nearly lost her mum. "So where are Martin's kids now? Tavish wasn't it? He's the one in Luton, right?"

"Aye, a pleasant young man that, not that we see or hear from him at all. Though if I were tae be honest Robbie, I can't say as I blame him. He must feel like he grew up with the family from hell. Couldn't wait tae get away no doubt."

"An' the other one, Kester. Do y'still see him?"

"Not for a couple o' years now, though we did get yet another visit from the police a few days ago looking for him again. He used tae live with us ya see. God knows what he's been up tae; they wouldn't say. The usual crap I imagine, fighting, stealing. A man died in a robbery he'd been involved in once ya know. Kester was arrested for it, but there wasn't enough evidence tae bring the charge. But I know my nephew, an' I know what he's capable of. He's an intelligent lad, they both are, but Tavish has some humanity, a trait sadly lacking in Kester. Oh, an' he's a temper on him that boy."

Robbie didn't like the sound of this newly acquired nephew of his at all. "An' y'say he's pissed off with me as well, just like his dad was? Not as obsessed I hope?"

"Well it did him no favours living here with me an' Mum; she just couldn't let it drop. Aye she'd had a shitty life, she'd lost her own family when she'd chosen Eban over them, but that *had* been her own decision. But she held on tae the years o' denial she'd accumulated, blamed everyone else but herself. Her family, Eban's family, *you,* us, och the world an' his wife were tae blame for her unhappy lot, an' the twins had it rammed down their throats as much as the rest of us had. The problem was, that they'd had it rammed down their throats by their father too, while he was alive. Then their mother blamed their father's obsession for his suicide, the poor kids had no escape from it. Whereas

Tavish just reached saturation point an' switched off from it, Kester let it fuel him. He was seen by the education psychologist on more than one occasion, but the guy just said he wasn't ill, just angry an' that he'd probably grow out of it. He never did; he just got worse an' trust me, he's not right. It takes a lot tae scare me, but that boy scares me at times; he's just a way about him that's unsettling."

As Robbie steered the car into Broadmeadow Road, he asked if Peg needed anything before he left.

"Yer going?" she seemed genuinely surprised.

"I have to Peg. I've promised Lynsey I'll be home by tonight. Besides, I'm expected t'go over my statement about the attack. Something needs clarifying I think. Whatever it is, the police were trying t'get hold o' me for it. I said I'd be there for eleven in the morning."

"Yer going tae drive all the way back tae England *now?* Are ya mad Robbie? After everything that's happened today, ya'll likely fall asleep at the wheel. Ya can stay here ya know. Her being in hospital at least allows for that.”

“I can’t Peg, really. I’m sorry love, I hate leaving you after today’s events, but if I don’t go home tonight, I think my wife might just become my ex. I need t’go.”

She nodded her understanding of his situation. “Will ya come back at all?”

“I’m sure I will, though not without warning next time eh?” he smiled. “I’ll call at some point tomorrow anyway if that’s okay, see how Maev is, if everything’s alright?”

Again she nodded and stiffened her lips into a forced smile, the softer side of her now replaced again with the one he’d encountered when he’d first arrived at her gate. She got out of the car. “Right y’are then, thank you for the lift. Safe journey.”

Chapter Fifteen

He was shattered when he'd arrived home late the previous evening, but Lynsey had been so pleased to see Robbie, and relieved too. He'd been right, something *had* lifted in him, he seemed brighter despite the exhaustion he must've felt. It was silly him driving home after everything he'd told her had happened, but she was glad he did. Though she'd still held off telling him about the baby, she couldn't really say why, other than the fact that she really didn't know how he'd feel about it. Truth be told, she couldn't really say how *she* really felt either, not entirely. They'd never had that conversation. Kids, it'd just never come up and getting her own head around it, thinking of herself as somebody's mother, was still pretty daunting. The reality was, that she just wasn't prepared to have to deal with a negative response from Robbie, not just yet anyway.

"Just tell him," Jodie had pushed her. *"He's going t'have t'know at some point. Just get it out there chick. Even if he freaks t'start with, he'll be over the moon when he's had chance t'get his head in gear."*

Lynsey had assured her that she *would* tell him, she would…no, really she would, just maybe not today. She would need to go and wake him soon anyway. It was almost ten and she knew he'd want a shower before the police arrived to go over things again with him.

***

"Robbie, it's good t'see you again." Sgt Bashir stretched out his hand to shake, a genuine warmth in his tone. "This is my colleague an' counterpart Detective Sergeant Chris Radley," he said as he introduced the two men to one another. "Chris this is Robbie's good lady wife, Lynsey."

"It's always a pleasure Bash, but I have to admit t'being at a bit of a loss as t'why all this is necessary? Is it in case I've remembered anything else? Cos I don't think I have y'know. We could've done this over the phone, surely?"

"I appreciate the cloak an' dagger appearance of all this, but I needed for ya t'see some photos I have with me."

Radley decided it was best to let Bash lead this. He'd take a back seat while the two of them talked, see if there was anything to concern him about the way McAndrew reacted to any of the questions, or to seeing his attacker's picture. It wasn't that he was suspicious of Robbie McAndrew for any particular reason, it was just that he was a copper, and it paid to be open to these things. Though if he were to be honest, he wasn't holding out for anything new; it just needed ruling out, that's all.

"So," Bash began, "Lynsey tells me ya've been away. Scotland, wasn't it?"

"Yeh, that's right."

"Any particular reason? Business, pleasure?"

"Just felt like a break, went t'see someone I know up there."

"Good, good. Well I hope the weather stayed nice for ya Robbie. Where abouts was it y'went?"

"My friend lives in Milngavie, it's just t'the north o' Glasgow, small place."

Bash looked round at Radley, who raised his eyebrows in return. Robbie noticed the exchange between them.

"Is something wrong? What did I say?"

Bash needed to tread carefully now in order to get to the bones of his reason for being there. "Nothing, it's just a bit of a coincidence probably, but can I ask d'ya know many folk up that way Robbie? Is it somewhere ya'd say you frequented?"

"No, first time I've ever been there. Why? What's this all about?"

Lynsey began to feel a pang of concern and moved that little bit closer to her husband on the sofa. "What

coincidence? You said it's probably a coincidence.
What is?"

Radley's analytical trait had been piqued. He
relaxed back into the armchair he was in and paid closer
attention to the couple's body language.

"Well it's just that one o' the men responsible for the
attack on ya, last year Robbie, he's from Glasgow."

"But y'told us they were local, from Leeds you
said," Lynsey was beginning to worry. She wasn't too
sure what was going on, or what Bash was getting at, but
she sensed that something was coming. "You never said
any o' this t'me, when I saw ya the other day. Ya just
wanted t'know if Robbie'd remembered anything else,
talked about anything else. I've seen these pictures
already an' like I said, we don't know who they are. If
we did, we'd say. Why wouldn't we?"

Bash handed the two A4 sized mugshots to Robbie
for him to look at while he answered Lynsey's question.
"You have to understand Lyns, you each have your own
perspectives on what happened, I have to take both o'

those into account. An' though you're Robbie's wife, I still have t'deal predominantly with him, as he were the victim."

Robbie studied the two pictures he was holding in his hands while Bash and Lynsey debated why she'd not been given more information. They both had labels in the top, left hand corners. One showing a picture of a man in his twenties with dark blond hair and hazel eyes, a couple of days growth around his chin. The label at the top read; Dale Price. But when Robbie looked at the label on the other one, he physically felt his heart drop and a wave of nausea wash over him. He swallowed hard as he read the label: Kester Richards, aka Gareth Dalby, aka Christopher Hartley. Oh Christ, oh for fuck's sake. This face looking up at him from the second picture, this dark haired young man, with piercing blue eyes that was staring straight out of the photo and straight into his soul, was him. It was Kester, Martin's son, his own nephew.

He was so glad that he'd not had time to get to that part of the story with Lynsey on his arrival back home the previous night. So glad that she couldn't inadvertently give anything away. And oh so glad that she was currently keeping Bash's attention diverted away from him in case he'd given anything away himself. If they found out his connection to Kester Richards, they'd find out that he wasn't really Robbie McAndrew, but Michael Whithorn. He'd no idea the kind of trouble that might bring. At least Annie wouldn't have to answer for it now that she was dead, but what about Joe McStay? And what about Clive and Rich, not to mention Lynsey and the rest of the family? He'd been living under a false identity, granted he'd been ignorant of the fact until after the attack, but what would happen to them if it came out that they'd all known now for the past year, but conspired to keep it under wraps?

Bash might not have been paying attention to Robbie's reactions, but Chris Radley was. "Is there a problem Mr McAndrew? Only y'look as if ya've just seen a ghost, fella."

Taken aback, Robbie had to think on his feet. "No, no I'm fine, just a bit tired that's all. I were late home last night y'see. No, I were just having a good look, see if I remember seeing them that day."

"I see." Radley didn't argue the point, though he was definitely not convinced. He'd too much road work under his belt to not recognise a fake response when he got one.

Robbie should've just shut up, but he kept digging. "It's just that it still pisses me off y'see, that I can't remember what happened. I were just staring at them, trying t'make my stupid memory kick in I suppose." He knew he needed to shut the fuck up. He was nervous and convinced it must be obvious.

"I take it, it didn't then…kick in?"

"No, sorry." He was struggling to maintain eye contact with Radley, but he was making a good effort.

Bash rejoined the conversation, indicating to the photos. "Price, the blond one, told us that him an' Richards had followed you a few times. He said that he'd had the impression that Richards knew ya Robbie. Price reckons that he'd been told by Richards that you were rich. He said that Richards seemed t'know a lot about ya: where y'worked, where y'went. He knew Lynsey's name too. It just seems odd that ya wouldn't have some kind o'connection to him."

This was getting uncomfortable, but Robbie had to keep it up; he felt trapped. "Not as far as I can remember Bash. I don't recognise him, either o'them. Erm...what did he say, this Kester bloke? Has he told *you* he knows me or something?"

"Nope." Bash shook his head as he reached across to retrieve the photos. "He's a bit of a game player by all accounts. Not t'worry, I'm sure we'll get to the bottom of it."

Radley maintained his gaze on Robbie and smiled. "Oh, we'll most definitely get t'the bottom of it Mr McAndrew, y'can be sure of it."

Robbie's heart sank. He wasn't stupid; he knew that Radley knew more than he was letting on, he just didn't know what or to what extent. But that new-found sense of peace he'd returned home with just seemed to fizzle away as an almighty angst took its place, and for the first time he really felt what he presumed that Annie had felt all those years ago when she'd tried, and lied, to pass him off as her own son. Though thankfully, she'd never had to face the police under such circumstances. A much easier crime to conceal back then: no internet, no social media and no easy way for people to prove you were lying.

Lynsey came back into the living room after showing out the two police sergeants. She was wittering away about all the fuss and the fact that she'd not been told about Kester Richards seemingly knowing such a lot about them, so much so, that it took her a while to notice the distress in Robbie's expression.

He was silent, just listening to her without responding. Eventually mid-sentence, she realised something was wrong. "What is it Rob? What's wrong?"

Robbie looked her in the eye. "He's my nephew Lyns." The look of puzzlement that met him told him that she really wasn't following his thread. "That lad in the photo, the dark haired one, Kester Richards; he's my nephew."

"What? How the hell…that can't be right Robbie, no way!"

"It's true Lyns, really. It's a bloody long story, but basically it boils down to the fact that he's Martin's son."

"Martin Whithorn? As in Elizabeth an' Martin?" The same cogs were turning in her head as they were in Robbie's, though she'd a little way to go to catch up with him.

"Martin, so I'm told, put Eban on a bit of a pedestal when he were younger. Fuck knows why, probably just the lack of a father figure maybe, I don't know. Anyway, he'd tracked him down. Found out that his birth name'd been Eban Richards. Martha Richards was his real mum y'see. Martin changed his name by whatsit…"

"Ya mean deed-pole?" Lynsey asked. "He changed it to Richards by deed-pole?"

"Yeh, that's it. Elizabeth told me she thought he'd done it t'try an' impress him, but it didn't work. Apparently Eban were just as much of a bastard regardless. Martin got married, had twin boys, Tavish an' Kester, an' that's how the name came about. Martin committed suicide when the lads were nine."

Lynsey half sat and half collapsed into the armchair that Radley had vacated, her mouth agape as she tried to process the information, not to mention the implications of it all. "But if he's the same Kester Richards, then that means…"

"Yep," Robbie pushed his fingers nervously through his hair, "it means that he's known about me for an awful long time. It means that he somehow, fuck knows how but he did, managed t'find me. An' it means that I wasn't mugged love; I think he was actually trying t'kill me."

"I suppose it's possible it's a different Kester Richards." Lynsey was clinging desperately to hope, even though she knew it to be hopeless, so-to-speak.

"Come on love," Robbie quipped. "It's not exactly a Fred Bloggs kinda name is it? Just how many Kester Richards' d'ya actually think are out there? No, no way, this is definitely him. There's no chance o' this being any kind of coincidence. He knew exactly who I was an' he actually tried to kill me."

Lynsey could feel her eyes welling up, but the tears seemed almost frozen where they were because none of them spilled over. "Why?"

"Because my name's been mud t'that side o' the family Lyns. Martin apparently had major issues with my existence, thought I'd had everything he'd missed out on. I suppose his sons were fed the same crap too, I don't know."

Lynsey put her head in her hands in despondency. "Dredger were right all along; he said if you kept asking questions, more would just surface."

Robbie took her hand in his and kissed it. "I know he did love, but this lad came looking for me, an' he found me well before even *we* knew who I really am. He were coming for me regardless of all the rest love. It'll be alright Lyns, trust me, we'll be alright."

Chapter Sixteen

Robbie and Lynsey had been right about one thing: Chris Radley *had* picked up on Robbie's discomfort while looking at the picture of Kester Richards. He didn't know what it was as yet, but he had every intention of finding out just what connected the two men.

"Did y' see his reaction Bash?" Radley asked his colleague as they made their way back to the station in the pool car.

"He were a bit quiet, but I can't say I noticed a *reaction* as you put it. What did he do exactly?"

"Kester Richards' mugshot. I swear the colour drained from him when he were looking at it."

"I don't see why it would; he's seen it before after we arrested him an' Price."

Radley pondered that thought for a moment or two before answering. "But it would've said Gareth Dalby on it then I presume, wouldn't it?"

"So y'think it's the name he'd seen before then, not the face?"

"Could be Bash, could be."

***

Kester Richards was waiting at the booking desk inside Armley prison, his hands cuffed in front of himself and flanked by a guard on either side. The prisoner transport vehicle was pulling up just outside the doorway in the yard, ready to take him and three others to their respective appointments with Her Majesty's Courts.

Already a convicted prisoner, Kester was due to answer for an attack on a fellow inmate seven weeks previously. He'd stabbed the man with a home-made shank he'd taken from another prisoner earlier that same day.

He was calm, unusually so, the kind of prisoner that made the guards more than a little bit nervous to be given responsibility for. It wasn't that he'd ever attacked one of them…yet. It was just that there was something about him that almost made that a threat, something in his demeanour, his expression maybe. Whatever it was, the guards were a little on edge and he knew it. Even walking him from his cell to the warden's office, or an interview room, made them uneasy, but having to actually accompany him outside of the prison walls, into court and back again, was making them quite jumpy. They were beginning to over-compensate for their insecurities by being overly abrupt with the other prisoners; shouting at them, grabbing them and shoving them into line, they were even sniping at one another. Oh, Kester Richards was more than well aware of the effect he was having in the group, he smirked.

"What the fuck you got t'be grinning about Richards?" one of them barked at him as he shoved him to the front, nearest the door in readiness for loading onto the paddywagon. They wanted him in first, less trouble.

"Nothing," Kester replied, still grinning.

"Nothing what?" the guard yelled. "Nothing, Sir!" he demanded.

"Nothing you fuckwit." Kester glared at him, challenging him.

Luckily the guard was saved by the buzzer that indicated it was safe to open the inner door to the yard, and he didn't have to brave a comeback that he'd have been unable to back up.

It probably took longer getting through all of the security gates than it did to actually drive to the Combined Court building just off the Headrow in the centre of Leeds. Just after they'd set off, as the van was approaching the Armley Gyratory and indicating left, Kester began to up the tension.

"I think I'm gonnae puke…Sir," he informed them.

"Don't be fucking ridiculous Richards. We've only just set off an' we'll be there in less than five minutes."

"I'm no' fucking travel-sick; I puked this morning when I got up. I've gut-rot too, it's fucking agony…Sir."

"Bollocks, if y'weren't well, ya'd have said earlier…"

Before he could get to the end of his sentence, Richards had doubled over, let out a groan and vomited all over the van floor in front of himself, splashing some onto the boots of the guard beside him. Everyone else let out noises of disgust as they adjusted their positions and lifted their feet up as the stinking mulch began to run along the floor towards the back of the vehicle.

"Jesus, Richards, what the fuck have you been eating? That fucking stinks!" The guard was trying hard to stop himself from retching, as were a handful of the other occupants, guards and prisoners alike.

"Maybe it's nerves," Kester said calmly, as he spit out the remnants onto the floor.

The senior guard banged on the cab wall and shouted through to the driver to put his foot down and get them there quickly, which he did.

Once through the security gates that led under the court buildings, to the holding cells, the occupants of the transport van vacated as fast as they could, relieved not to have to breathe that enclosed stench any longer. Richards was the last one out. He looked quite pale and clammy; he looked ill.

Turning to the custody staff awaiting their arrival, the senior guard asked them to take Richards into the cells and get the duty doctor to come and see him. He might not be well enough to go before the court, but a doctor would be the only one with the authority to make that decision.

As Richards was led away, he flashed a sideways glance towards the senior guard. It hadn't gone unnoticed, though almost a defiant look, but the guard couldn't rationalise that this was anything other than a sick man. He looked ill, in fact he looked like shit.

In the cell, the duty doctor arrived to assess Kester. "Hello, I'm Dr Bower," she introduced herself. "I understand you've been vomiting and you've some abdominal pain. Is that correct?"

Kester acknowledged her query as she began asking more and more of them while attaching a blood pressure cuff to his arm and pushing a tympanic thermometer into his left ear.

"Have you any chest pain?"

"No."

"When did this stomach pain start?"

"Last night."

"When did it become this bad?"

"No' long before we set off here…agh," he groaned as he doubled over again.

"Are you allergic to any medications that you know of?"

"No."

After further examination, which included getting him to lay flat while she palpated his stomach and abdomen, she located the origin of his pain to an inch or so below his bellybutton, that was the area where he appeared to flinch more when she carefully pressed on it.

"Does this pain go anywhere else?"

"My back, it hurts in my back too, an' when I got out o' the van it started down here," he said as he rubbed along his left groin. He suddenly got up to rush over to the metal toilet in the cell, where he vomited again. That was good. She'd seen him vomit; he knew that he wouldn't be made to go into court now. He clutched at his stomach again.

"Can you describe the pain you've got please Kester?" Dr Bower asked him and his reply was enough to bring an air of serious concern to her face.

Turning to face the court officer in charge of the holding cell prisoners, she informed him that this prisoner needed to be seen as quickly as possible in the emergency department.

"We can take him round there. It's only round the corner really," the senior prison officer informed her.

She indicated to him that he should come outside of the cell with her, which he did. Quietly, she informed him of her concerns. "He's described the pain as a ripping sensation, it radiates to his back. His blood pressure, though not dangerously low, is on the low side and quite frankly he looks crap. I need to be certain that he's not having a triple A, basically that an aneurism inside his abdomen hasn't ruptured. If it has, it could kill him…fast. I'll arrange an ambulance and inform A and E of his admittance. Hopefully I'm wrong, but I don't want to be the one to take that chance. Okay?"

As the doctor had phoned ahead, the staff in the emergency department were prepped and ready for the arrival of the inbound prisoner. Something they'd seen plenty of times before, patients who were either under arrest or else already in custody would arrive, handcuffed to at least one guard. It caused problems at times as guards were often reluctant to un-cuff themselves from a prisoner, even when told to do so by the medical staff. They had a policy to follow, understandably, but occasionally the adherence to that policy was ridiculous, like the occasion they'd had a guard refuse to un-cuff, even though his ward was in a coma.

On this occasion, until they knew what they were dealing with, they allowed the guard to remain joined to Kester at the wrist. He was wheeled straight through to a cubicle and transferred to a hospital trolley, no mean feat considering he was attached to the guard the whole time. The second guard stayed close, though remained free of any shackling.

Kester rapidly lost his prison shirt and was changed into a hospital gown as a portable ultra-sound machine was wheeled into the cubicle beside him. He winced as a cold, slimy gel was deposited on his stomach and the radiographer began the search for any rogue leakage from his aorta.

Several minutes later, both the machine and its operator left and everything seemed to calm down again.

"I need the toilet," Kester informed the guards.

"I'll get them t'fetch a commode in," the second guard told him.

Just then a nurse appeared round the curtain, followed by the doctor who'd greeted him on his arrival.

"Well, whatever it is, you'll be pleased to know it's not what we thought it might be. We thought you might have a leaking aorta you see, but you don't."

Kester smiled to himself, but needed to move things on. "I need the loo."

"I'll bring a portable one in a minute," the nurse smiled.

"No way!" Kester insisted. "I'm no' using a fucking granny bog. I want tae go tae a proper toilet."

"Not going t'happen Richards. You're staying here," his guard asserted.

"I need a fucking shit for god sake. Give me a break will ya?"

"If you've had any diarrhoea then I'm afraid we can't allow you to use the public toilets Kester; it's infection control you understand," the nurse told him.

"I haven't," he insisted. "I just don't want tae have tae empty my fucking bowels behind a curtain where the world an' his wife can hear what I'm doing, an' what if it stinks?"

Reluctantly, the nurse nodded her agreement to the guard and Kester was put into a wheelchair. He had to hold his cuffed hand up and sit slightly off centre, so that the guard he was attached to could wheel him to the opposite end of the cubicles to where the nurse had directed them. Just around the corner, opposite the empty Sister's office, was a door marked *Disabled Toilet*. The door opened outwards and was big enough to fit the wheelchair through. Once inside the guard dropped the lever into place which locked them both in. Kester got out of the chair.

"For fuck sake, yer no' going tae stand there an' watch me have a shite are ya? Yer having a fucking laugh. You going tae wipe my arse for me when I'm done too?"

"You know the rules Richards."

"Aye, but look around, there's no fucking windows in here. Where d'ya think I'd be able tae go exactly? Down the bog maybe? Flush myself tae freedom?"

He had a point. Not that the guard was entirely comfortable with the idea, but nor did he relish the thought of having to be so up close to another man while he took a dump. He'd already been grossed out by this one today, when he'd vomited in the prison van. That was bad enough, having the stench of his stomach contents still lingering in his nostrils, he didn't want the stench of his bowel contents adding to it.

"Okay, but y'don't lock the door Richards an' nor do y'try an' open it without my permission either. D'ya understand?"

"Aye."

The guard fished around for the key to the handcuffs and released the one on Kester's wrist to allow him freedom of movement. "I'll be right outside the door Richards. You remember what I said."

He closed the toilet door behind him, leaving Kester alone in the cubicle while he waited outside. He leant against the door, knowing that if Kester tried to barge out, he'd not get far. He might not have that thing they'd brought him in for, but he still wasn't a well man, certainly not up to full strength.

Having heard various noises through the door over the next couple of minutes, the guard finally heard the taps being turned on and off, followed by the familiar sound of the hand dryer before it all went quiet momentarily. Then there was a soft knocking on the other side of the door.

"I'm done now," Richards called through to him.

"Right you are," the guard acknowledged as he turned to face the door again, "Step away from the door Richards an' don't try an' leave 'til I say so, alright?"

Richards agreed and so the guard took hold of the handle to open the door, but as he pulled on it, the damn thing just rattled in the frame, it wouldn't open. "Have you locked this bloody door Richards?" he called out.

"No Sir, it might be stuck I think."

"Can you give it a shove from your side?"

"Okay Sir, I'll try." On the inside of the toilet cubicle, Kester took his foot down from the wall beside the door, the one he'd been using to steady himself as he'd hung onto the rail on his side of the door, allowing the handle to be moved but preventing it from opening. He rattled the door a little, then called out that he couldn't open it either.

He felt the guard take hold of the handle from the outside again and begin to pull. He let him pull a couple of times, then on his third attempt, Kester kept hold of the rail, but allowed the door to be yanked open by the guard. The sudden release of which, knocked the man off balance, at which point Kester pulled the door sharply in towards himself then pushed it hard back towards the guard. The full force of it smashed him in the face and knocked him to the ground.

Springing into action, Kester leapt on him, dragging him back into the toilet and out of sight of any passing staff. The guard groaned. Dazed, he tried to right himself just as Kester's fist hit him full in the face, the back of his head bouncing off the floor with the impact.

After cleaning his hands, Kester took the wallet out of the guards pocket and emptied it of any cash. There wasn't much: thirty-five quid in notes and some change. He shoved the notes into the back pocket of his trousers and sifted through the change for a ten pence coin. Once he'd found what he was looking for, he briefly listened at the door for anyone passing by. It was silent. Carefully he opened the door, closing it quietly behind himself. He slotted the ten pence coin into the groove in the centre of the handle and turned it. The green 'vacant' indicator turned to the red 'engaged' one. Taking a brief look back over his shoulder, Kester then slipped through the double door beyond the Sister's office and into a corridor. He was gone.

Chapter Seventeen

Rich was doing the whole Google search thing, trying to help his brother find out how to get more information about Eban's background. There were numerous tuts and sighs as he found himself coming up against brick walls. The only thing he could find, of any use, was the National Records of Scotland at the General Register House in Edinburgh.

"Well if nothing else Robbie, I suppose they're a start. I can't find where else t'look," Rich said as he leant back with an air of exacerbation, having bounced around the World Wide Web with little to show for it. "Anyway, I feel like I'm chasing all this up on my own. Where's *your* head at bro? Yer not exactly helping. What's up?"

Robbie pondered a moment before answering. He'd returned from Scotland feeling lighter, having met Elizabeth, having discussed things with her. But now, now that familiar sense of emotional exhaustion was sitting in the middle of his chest again, it was like trying to swim while carrying a paving slab. He knew now that his nephew had found him, long before he'd known who he was himself. Did Kester really believe that this 'missing' Michael had always known who he was? Grown up in the full and complicit knowledge that he was an imposter? He supposed that in truth, Kester couldn't know one way or the other. Would Robbie feel that way if the boot were on the other foot so to speak? The fact was, that for all the Whithorns had known, Robbie might well have grown up in the knowledge of what had happened. Why wouldn't he? And how could he ever prove otherwise?

"Rich, y'know them guys…the ones who attacked me?"

"Dalby an' Price? Bastards! Yeh, what about 'em?"

"One of them, Gareth Dalby, well he's not really called Gareth Dalby, he's Kester Richards."

The penny didn't drop. Rich just looked at his brother with a half frown on his face. "Okay, and…?"

"And he's only called Kester Richards because his father changed his surname. If he hadn't, he'd be called Kester Whithorn."

Ah, finally the realisation hit Rich's face. "What the fuck?" he was stunned. Robbie could see the cogs in his mind almost visibly turning as he tried to rationalise things. "What sort of coincidence is that? I mean, what are the chances…?"

"Probably bazillions to one Rich. It was no coincidence; he came looking for me, he found me, he tried t'kill me," Robbie's voice almost gave, as if saying it out loud made it somewhat more real. "Fuck, Rich he tried t'kill me. It seems like some far-fetched bloody story-line in one o' them crappy soaps, but it isn't, it's true."

Rich couldn't speak; he didn't know what to say or how to say it. Robbie was right; it did sound far-fetched, but Robbie wasn't into fantasy, so why say it? "How d'ya know? I, I er...mean maybe he just…" he stopped himself without attempting to finish the sentence. He was out of his depth.

"That copper, Bash, he came round with another bloke from CID. Showed me their mugshots again. I didn't recognise them, but this time, one of them had a different name sticker on it. It read 'Kester Richards' instead o' Gareth Dalby. Bash said that the other fella, Price, had told them about following me for a while, about how they knew my name, where I live, work, who Lynsey is even."

"Ya mean he'd been stalking ya?" Rich couldn't quite grasp the enormity of what his brother was telling him.

"Yeh, I suppose he had. It can't possibly be anyone else Rich. Let's face it, it's not exactly the most common name, is it? He's called Kester Richards an' he's from Glasgow. One o' Martin's sons is called Kester Richards, from Glasgow. He's my fucking nephew Rich, Jesus…!" Robbie pushed his fingers back through his hair, the way he always did when stress was getting the better of him. "It's not just that Rich; he sounds radged, like Martin, like Eban. Let's face it, Eban's real mother were an inmate in the nuthouse. What if, I don't know, what if…?"

"What if what? You've inherited the psycho gene?" Rich scoffed. "Do me a favour, Rob. I grew up with ya remember; apart from running over my action man on yer trike because I'd bust yer space-hopper, what psychotic behaviour have you ever displayed then? None, that's what. Though ya did go pretty schiz on me over that space-hopper y'know," he tried to lighten the mood a little.

"I know, but it's not that. It's how I feel sometimes, how I react, y'know?"

Rich shook his head; he didn't know what Robbie was getting at.

"Sometimes Rich, sometimes I just don't seem t'feel at all, an' sometimes I feel too much, like when I went t'see the old bastard, my so called father. I wanted him t'suffer, I taunted him."

"Understandable."

"But he's a defenceless old man now Rich. He can't hurt anyone now. It wasn't like he had the option o' coming back at me. It were cruel. I were cruel, an' it shames me t'say it, but I enjoyed the fact that he were in that state an' I just kept on twisting the knife. That's not normal, an' now that I've found all this out, it's got me wondering if I haven't inherited this fucked-up gene myself, an' it scares me a bit Rich."

"Robbie, for Christ sake y'must know how stupid that sounds. Look at what's happened over the past year, look at what's come t'light. It's hardly surprising that you've felt like lashing out is it?"

"But it's all this obsession too. I can feel myself getting caught up in it, but I can't stop, not even when Lyns begs me to. I love her t'bits an' the last thing I want is to lose her, or drive her away, but I just get to a point where my head seems t'just shut her out. An' you might be right, I hope you're right an' it's all down t'this past year an' all that's gone on, but what if it's not, what if I'm not right, just like them?"

Rich wasn't sure how to handle this conversation, or what to say to try and ease the tension, but he tried. "Look, if there were ever any question as to your mental health Rob, I'm pretty sure it would o' come up long before now. Mum an' Clive would o' noticed, even if I didn't."

"Remember I took a pretty hefty blow t'the head last year Rich?"

"I know, I'm not fucking stupid, but y'were also told that these things can take ages t'come right."

Rich was right of course, but Robbie also remembered being told that he could be more prone to mood swings, outbursts, that sort of thing. He certainly didn't feel the same way he had done before the attack. Something within him had changed, something characteristic and he felt sure it wasn't just the emotional stress of finding out who he really was and where he'd come from.

The door opened and Lynsey, Jodie and Natalie walked in. Rich closed the lid on the laptop. He wasn't too sure about how much, if anything, that Lynsey's sister knew about events.

Jodie walked over and bent in to give him a kiss. He smiled as he reciprocated, before greeting Natalie and Lynsey. As he'd said hello to them both, Lynsey had noticed that he'd glanced briefly at her belly before glancing at his wife, then looking away. It wasn't much, but it was enough to tell Lynsey that he knew, he knew about her pregnancy and the only way he could've found out was through Jodie. The look on Jodie's face gave away the fact that she'd been busted. She'd promised not to say anything to Rich, but she obviously had. Lynsey wasn't happy and it was evident. Fortunately, Robbie just thought her low mood was down to him again, but Lynsey knew she really needed to tell him about the baby sooner rather than later, now that his brother knew.

***

'Bridget Jones; The Edge of Reason' was just starting on the movie channel when Lynsey sat down beside her husband that evening. The film played more as a background distraction than anything else. They'd both seen it before, and were both equally distracted from watching it properly again. They'd already discussed Kester Richards, already looked for reasons why and looked for the logic. They were both tired and both just wishing life back to the way it had been for them in the past. An impossibility that they knew could never be.

"He's going t'tell them isn't he? That I'm not who I say I am, that I'm not Robbie McAndrew." The tone in his voice was surprisingly flat, considering that the thought of being confronted by the police over his identity terrified him.

275

Lynsey sighed. "We don't know that love. Anyway, how can they prove that y'knew about it? If they do find out, how could they know whether or not yer completely oblivious to it?"

"Mum can't take the fall for this. I won't have it. I know she's dead, but if they do find out, I won't let it all be blamed on her, that's so not fair."

Lynsey neither agreed nor disagreed; she could see it from both aspects but she had something else she needed to elucidate on and it was time to bite the bullet. "I'm pregnant." Christ almighty, of all the things she'd rehearsed in her head, all the ways she could've told him and in the end she'd just blurted it out.

"You're what?" he said as he turned to look at her. Initially she'd thought she'd seen a glimpse of a smile cross his face, but it was momentary. "Really?"

"Yes, really."

"Since when? I mean, how long have you known?"

"Not long, but it's confirmed. I really am pregnant. We…really are going to have a baby."

It was all a bit much. Robbie blew out air through pursed lips as he sat back hard in his seat. He couldn't look at her, he didn't know what to say, he didn't know what to feel. He was going to be a father and it both exhilarated and mortified him at the same time. He was overwhelmed in a way that he could only describe as being on the brink of a panic attack. A droplet of sweat ran down the back of his neck as he rocked forward again resting his elbows on his knees and his head in his hands.

"Erm…are you alright, your health, the pregnancy I mean?" he forced himself to say. He didn't know what else to say at that point, his mind blank.

"Is that it?" Lynsey asked as she held back her tears. "I tell you that I've got your child inside me an' you respond as if I'm a colleague at fucking work rather than your wife!" She disappeared into their bedroom, slamming the door behind her.

Robbie knew that he should go after her, but he couldn't, he just couldn't lift himself from his spot. He'd never even considered children before. Not that he was necessarily against the idea, he just wasn't prepared. With everything else that was going on around him, he wasn't too sure of just how he felt about it either. He was scared of saying the wrong thing to her, of making things worse, if that were possible. Exhaustion suddenly hit him like a truck and sleep invaded his mind and took him away from his surroundings.

Chapter Eighteen

It was that nightmare again, the one where Eban is looming over the boy in a darkened school yard, fist raised above his head, ready to strike the terrified Michael who's cowering beneath him. Then that scream. He always woke when he heard that shrill scream. Whose scream was that? Was that his mother, Mona, was she the one who screamed? Was it him, Michael? Was this an actual memory at all, or just something his troubled mind had invented? He didn't know, but what he did know was that it was now morning and he had a crick in his neck from sleeping all night on the sofa.

The TV was still on, the curtains and blinds still closed, apart from the one in the bathroom obviously, because that was the one allowing light to stream into the hallway, confirming his night of self-imposed exile from his bedroom was now over. He listened out for signs of movement, but couldn't hear anything, just the TV movie news being delivered by some over-excited twenty-something trying to sound 'hip' and 'down with the kids'.

He walked through to the kitchen and put the kettle on, readying two cups. He'd have to face his wife at some point and it was better to do it armed with a mug of fresh made tea by way of an olive branch. It was still fairly early and although Lynsey would normally be up by now, there were no stirrings. Robbie thought she must be at least as knackered as him, probably more so. He felt bad for the way he'd reacted to her news. He should've been more supportive and he knew that. He just felt that what should be real to him was a dream and vice-versa; what should've been the stuff of nightmarish fantasy, was in fact reality, for now at least.

He swallowed a couple of Paracetamol with a mouth full of tea as he made his way to the bedroom. He knocked cautiously, not knowing what sort of reception he'd get but there was silence. She must still be asleep.

He opened the door to find the room empty. She wasn't
there at all, she'd gone.

Robbie felt a little uneasy about it, but he assumed
that she must've left for work already, no doubt avoiding
him, though he couldn't understand that she could've got
showered and ready without disturbing him. It wasn't
until he went back into the living room and sat himself
down in front of the TV, that he noticed her note.

It was on the coffee table, right in front of where
he'd been sleeping;

*"I'm glad you find sleep so easy to find Robbie, I
don't. I'm tired, physically and mentally tired. I'm tired
of walking on egg-shells around you, tired of making
allowances for you. Yes, you've been through a lot of
shit Robbie, but it's in the past now and there's nothing
anyone can do to change it, so deal with it instead of this
self-indulgent pity you seem to want to wallow in.*

*"I spent ages trying to work out how to tell you
about the baby, and how to tell you how scared I am.
I've never done this before either, in case you'd*

forgotten and I need your support. I need my husband to be there so that we can go through this together, but I'm obviously expecting too much.

"I don't know what I want right at this moment Robbie, but I do know that I don't want to be around you right now. I'm going to Mum's tonight and will probably go stay with Julie and Paul tomorrow. I don't know when, or even if, I'll be back as yet. I just need some space to get my head around becoming a mother, with or without you."

Bloody hell! Not what he'd thought he'd be waking up to. He jumped to his feet and went back to the bedroom. This time he paid more attention. Lynsey had said she was going to her mum's 'tonight', so she must've left last night, not this morning. The bed was made. At the bottom he could make out a rectangular imprint on the duvet, a suitcase? He pulled open the wardrobe doors to find that about a third of her things had gone, her underwear drawer was almost empty and when he checked the bathroom, her shampoos and other toiletries were missing too. Had she left him? The realisation crept slowly over him as his chest began to physically ache. How could he have been so stupid? How could he have just neglected her so much? For fuck sake, they'd only been married two minutes and he'd already managed to destroy it.

"Rich I think she's left me, Lynsey's gone, she left a note," his voice trembled as he tried to explain things to his brother over the phone.

"What the fuck…no way, why?"

"She's pregnant, I didn't exactly take it well."

"Oh, she told ya," Rich's voice dropped.

"You knew? You knew about it?"

"Calm down Robbie. She told Jodie, not me. The poor cow's been crapping herself about telling ya apparently. Where's she gone, d'ya know?"

"Her mum's last night. Says she's going over to her step-sister's today, Julie."

"She's the one married t'the Geordie, right?"

"Yeh, they live in Blythe. I don't know what t'do Rich, I don't know how to handle this."

"Just ring her Robbie. You *have* been a bit of a dick y'know. Just ring her an' tell her you're sorry, tell her y'love her, an' for fuck sake, think about dropping all this Eban shit Rob. You wouldn't o' been like this if it wasn't for that stuff. It's the future that counts. Why let that old bastard ruin that too?"

Lynsey's phone went straight to voicemail; she'd switched it off. She was serious about not wanting anything to do with him. He scrolled through his phonebook to find her mother's landline number.

"I'm sorry Robbie, you've missed her by about thirty minutes. She set off for Julie's early so as to avoid the rush hour traffic in the centre of town."

"Erm, is she…okay?" he asked nervously.

"Physically? Yes, but she's very upset Robbie. I think it'll do you both some good to have a bit of time apart."

"Is she coming back? I mean, d'ya think she'll come home?"

Lynsey's mother sighed. "I don't know love, I really don't. I know my daughter and I know she's got a high tolerance level; it takes a hell of a lot for her to reach that. Hopefully it's just the stress of the pregnancy playing its part, but who knows. You two need to talk, but don't push her Robbie, it won't end well if you try and force her hand."

"I know."

Totally deflated and void of anything except this dull ache in his heart where his wife should be, Robbie sank back into the sofa. He felt numb, lost even. He'd never missed Annie as much as he did right there and then, as if he'd reverted back to being a little boy in need of his mum. It was pathetic.

Rich was on his way round, in the dog-house too by all accounts. Jodie was pissed off that he'd made it so obvious to Lynsey that he knew about the baby. Truth was, Jodie felt guilty that she'd betrayed Lynsey's trust and Rich was in the firing line for it. Either way, it got him out of her way and he knew that he was probably the only one Robbie could talk to about this stuff.

Robbie had rung Lynsey's mum back to get the number for Julie's in Blythe. He'd left a message on their answer phone, asking if they'd get Lynsey to call once she arrived, so that he knew she was safe. Lynsey normally used Bluetooth when she was driving, but for the moment she wasn't taking any calls at all.

Rich arrived to find his brother at the computer; he was on the website for the National Records Office of Scotland, on the 'contact' page.

"Fuck sake Robbie, are *you* right in yer head? Yer wife's left an' you're still obsessing over this shit! What's wrong with ya?"

"I know, I know yer right Rich but I can't just walk away from it."

"Even at the expense of yer wife an' kid? Are y'mad?"

Robbie didn't quite know how to explain himself adequately. His brother was right, of course, but then he felt he was also right and the two conflicting logics just didn't reconcile. "It's because of them too Rich," he tried. "Y'know I've been stressing in case this nutter gene is hereditary, well what if it is? Especially now?"

"Rob there's fuck all wrong with ya. We've been through this."

"Yeh, well I'm maybe not as convinced as you are. An' even if you're right, it doesn't mean that I won't pass it on t'my son or daughter does it?"

Rich's look of exacerbation said far more than his words could. He took a breath and calmed his tone. "Look, let's just say yer right, which y'definitely not, but for argument's sake. So, this 'bonkers' gene is hereditary okay, you've not been affected, Elizabeth's not been affected an' by all accounts nor has this other lad."

"Tavish."

"Yeh, Tavish. So why are *you* so convinced that suddenly, after forty-odd years, yer going t'be affected by it now? An' as far as the baby's concerned, how the fuck would y'know anyway? What exactly is it that yer trying t'do here Robbie? Even if you had proof positive that the *entire* bloody family were nutters, what y'going t'be able t'do about it eh? What do y'want? For Lynsey to get rid o'the baby? Your baby?"

"No, I don't know. Look, I can't explain it Rich. I keep trying t'tell you all but I don't know how. I just *need* t'know. There's nothing I can do about it, I know that, but I *have* t'know what I'm dealing with, what I am."

"You're Robert McAndrew, or Michael Whithorn, it doesn't matter really 'cos both are just labels to identify the person, an' that person's never changed, never will." Quite profound, even for Rich.

Robbie sighed. "Help me Rich. Either help me or just walk away an' don't keep trying t'stop me. I know what yer saying but I can't let it go, I just can't."

Rich was no doctor or psychologist, but even he could see that there was no papering over these cracks. Robbie needed to deal with his demons and trying to push him into ignoring them would clearly be counterproductive to say the least. "You *do* know what yer risking here don't ya?"

"I love her more than anything, but I need t'know or it's just going to eat away at me an' I'll end up losing her anyway."

Chapter Nineteen

Robbie remained in the car while Rich went inside to drop their bags off at the B & B on Granville Terrace. They'd just arrived in Edinburgh, but Robbie wanted to go straight to the records office, despite Rich wanting to stop off and get something to eat first. He tried phoning Lyns again at Julie's, but Julie had told him that she was having a lie down, she was tired and didn't want to speak to him. "Please tell her I called."

The car jolted as Rich got back in and slammed the door shut. He handed Robbie a couple of leaflets. "Places to grab a feed. The landlady gave me them."

"Can we go t'the records place first?"

Rich sighed and reached past his brother for the satnav controls. "Right, where is it?"

Robbie scanned down the printout he had for the address. "Erm, the Legal Search Room of the National Records of Scotland is at…West Register Street, Edinburgh."

Rich punched it into their satnav and began to drive. "What is it they'll have again?"

"Adoption records for Eban, so I can hopefully find out more about Martha Richards an' her family."

"An' yer sure you'll get access t'these are ya?"

"I don't see why not, why wouldn't I?"

"A little thing called the Data Protection Act, that's why."

Robbie would have none of it. He didn't think it would apply on a case so old, nor did he think he'd have too much problem if he were wanting to look for familial medical reasons. Truth was, he'd just not really thought about it at all.

The satnav directed them right into the centre of Edinburgh, just off Prince's Street, though the traffic restrictions meant they'd had to weave their way through in a round-about manner, as cars weren't permitted on much of Prince's Street. They were both fairly awe-struck at the sights around them. Edinburgh was a beautiful city, a mixture of the old and new that seemed to marry up much more stylishly than it did in other places. Old tenement buildings that were likely the homes of hundreds of impoverished residents once upon a time, now converted to city apartments that no doubt commanded a tidy sum from today's inhabitants. Beautiful, public gardens and the famous Edinburgh Castle made this one of the most picturesque places the brothers had been.

They got to the entrance of the huge, official government building, only to find that it was swipe card only. There was a buzzer beside the sensor, so Robbie pressed it and waited.

"Can I help you?" the disembodied voice enquired.

"Yes, Erm, I'm here to look through some records," Robbie replied.

"Have you an appointment Sir?"

"No, I didn't know I'd need one."

"This is the Legal Search Room entrance Sir. I'm afraid there's no public access here without an appointment and the accompanying documentation."

"What accompanying documentation? I just wanted t'look at my father's adoption documents; we've a serious medical condition that…"

She cut him off before he'd chance to complete his sentence. *"I'm sorry Sir, but members of the public can't just turn up requesting access to sensitive documentation. We have strict protocols you know. If you'd like to make your way around to our main entrance on Prince's Street, there'll be someone who can help you there, should you need to set the ball rolling."*

"But I just…"

"Goodbye."

And that was that; no further explanations were given. What the documentation was that she'd mentioned wasn't described, so Robbie just assumed that it must be some kind of application or registration documents.

They left the car where it was and walked round onto the bustling Prince's Street as instructed. Once inside the main foyer, they made their way towards the reception desk. A woman in front of them seemed to be taking an age with whatever it was that she was there for. Eventually another member of staff came out from the room behind them and walked around the reception counter.

"Yes?" she nodded in their direction.

Robbie approached the desk leaving Rich to peruse the notice board to the left. "Hi, yeh I'm wanting to look at my father's adoption record, please? His name's…"

She cut him dead. "Is yer father still alive Sir?"

"Erm, yes, yes he is but y'see he's a very sick…"

Damn woman did it again. "I'm sorry but adoption records are locked down for a period of one hundred years under Scottish law. There's no way you can have access to them given that the adoptee is still living."

"What? Yer kidding? That can't be right. I need to see them; there's a hereditary condition I need to find out about."

"Wait here," she instructed as she came back around the counter and disappeared into the room she'd only minutes before exited from.

Robbie looked across towards the display by the entrance that Rich had worked his way round to. Palms upward, he shrugged his shoulders to indicate to him that he didn't have a clue what was going on.

A couple of minutes later the woman reappeared and gestured for him to go over to where she was. He followed her into the room where several work stations were dotted about. She led him past the first two and asked him to take a seat at the third, opposite a man who, according to the name card on his desk, was called Phil Stephens.

The man stood and reached his hand across the desk to shake Robbie's. "Hello there, Phil Stephens, And you are…?"

"Robbie McAndrew, or Michael Whithorn. I was adopted too y'see…it's complicated."

"These things always are Sir. I understand yer wanting tae find out about yer birth father's history, some medical condition is that correct?"

"Yes it is, only that woman just told me I can't. I don't understand, why not?"

"I'm really sorry tae say this Sir, but 'that woman' as ya call her, is quite correct. Here in Scotland ya see, any documentation relating to an adoption is sealed for a hundred years. Certainly if the adopted person is still alive then they can maybe petition the Sheriff Court to see the contents if a hereditary medical reason is provable. If yer birth father were dead, then you could make that petition yerself Sir."

"I don't get it, I just need t'know about his mother. He was born in an asylum, she being the inmate. There's a strong family link of serious mental illness I need t'find out about, my wife's pregnant y'see."

"I understand Sir, but the law's the law. If ya could maybe get yer birth father tae petition the Sheriff Court. If it's granted then he'd get access tae any information therein regarding his mother and the circumstances intae which he was born, providing that information was given at the time that is. There should also be a report attached that was provided by a court appointed officer known as the Curator ad Litem. They would've been the person responsible for gaining his mother's consent tae the adoption and recording any background they felt relevant. It's likely the information yer needing would be in that report, but as I said…"

"I can't get access to it."

"That's right I'm afraid. Can I ask, is yer birth father one of the affected bloodline of this condition?"

"He is."

"Then I'm really sorry I can't be of more help. It'd be a legal minefield for ya tae gain a power of attorney under such circumstances, especially as yer adopted yerself, and it still wouldn't be likely that you'd have the kind of access ya require while he's still living. I'm sorry."

"So there's nothing I can do? Nothing at all?"

"You could always try and petition the Sheriff yerself. I can give ya the relevant paperwork. If yer successful the Sheriff Court orders us tae release the documents tae them and you'd get tae view them there, not here. But I have tae be honest; I've never yet come across a case where that would happen under these particular circumstances. I'll give ya the paperwork anyway, then at least you'll know ya did all ya could eh?" He reached down and opened the third drawer of his desk, taking out the official forms. He handed them across to Robbie. "Was it here in Edinburgh where the adoption took place?"

"No, Glasgow somewhere."

"Then ya'll need tae find the sub district where his mother was living at the time and make yer application tae the Sheriff Court that covers that area."

"How the hell am I meant t'know how t'find that?"

"Unfortunately, that's not the kind of knowledge we'd possess here, but if I were you, I'd start by his mother's family name if ya know it. Go back a ways and check the census records. Providing it's not the most common name…"

"Richards, it's Martha Richards."

"Ah well, there ya go. Richards isn't a Scottish name, so it'll not be as common in the Glasgow area as some. If ya can find the family then ya'll at least find the area. Check old newspaper reports of the time too. If she was in an institution like that, then it's likely she may have had a history of petty crime or disturbing the peace, drunkenness even. If so, then these things might have been reported in the local rag. It's worth a try. Local libraries would be yer best bet there. I really am sorry that this particular avenue's closed tae ya Sir, truly I am."

***

All of the blinds and curtains remained closed in Robbie's apartment as the television burst into life. Lifting the plate containing a bacon buttie with one hand and a large mug of coffee with the other, Kester Richards walked across to the desk where he could scan between the television news and Robbie's computer. He leant back in the swivel chair as he took a bite from the sandwich he'd helped himself to. He was feeling better having had a shower and changed into some of Robbie's clothes. So what if his plans had been scuppered somewhat; he had hoped to find either one of them at home, or at least be there when they returned the previous night, but neither of them did. He'd been really pissed off about it at the time, but he didn't mind so much now, he could wait. Anyway, he'd still felt groggy from the effects of the codeine he'd taken. He was feeling more like himself now: cleaner, fresher, rested. Now he was a force to be reckoned with.

He'd spent some of the late evening wondering what Lynsey would think if she'd returned to find him in her bed. When would she notice? When she walked into the room, or when she'd slipped in beside him thinking it was her husband? He'd seen the pictures, the happy wedding day, the celebrations, the beautiful bridal gown. Oh, he'd found the said gown carefully packaged away, still beautiful, or at least it was until he'd taken a piss all over it.

It was funny really, he'd always been so careful in the past, so mindful of his moves. He was a planner, unless he was angry about something, like he had been the day before which is why he'd ended up here in the first place. No forethought, just bile for the bastard whose apartment this was. Still, best laid plans and all that. He was calmer now though, in the cold light of the new day. He wanted them to know that he'd been here; that he'd slept in their bed, pissed on her dress, spat on their wedding canvas, shit in their toilet, eaten their food and worn his clothes. He was leaving his DNA all over their home but he didn't care. Normally so careful about such things, he just didn't care anymore. He found it somewhat liberating in fact. The point that he'd stopped giving a shit about covering his tracks had snuck up on him somewhere, he wasn't sure when, but he felt free because of it. There was only really one mission he had in mind, the one thing he'd been working up to for quite some time and he'd already waited a while, so a little longer wouldn't be much of a hardship.

Picking up the phone he decided to call Kit. He needed a shag and knew she'd be up for it. She'd do anything for the price of her next fix, didn't whine too much if it got rough either and he'd been locked up a while so there was a fair chance it would. "Bring some booze an' get yer arse over here. An' ya tell any fucker ya've heard from me an' I'll make sure ya cannae speak tae no-one again, d'ya get me Kit?"

Despite his menace, she'd agreed to his terms and promised to be there within the hour. She was already shit-faced on something, he could hear it in her voice, but he didn't care. She was still tidy considering her lifestyle, still clean and relatively stylish in her dress, a good body on her and she liked a bad boy. If he hadn't have been a wanted man, he'd have probably gone out on the pull. It was always a pretty easy process for him; buy them a drink, say a few nice things, flirt a wee while, then take them somewhere quiet and fuck them. He'd generally never know their names and be walking away from them as he zipped up his jeans. But he didn't have that luxury at the present time, so Kit would have to do.

As he waited for her he clicked on the Firefox icon on Robbie's computer. "Now then, let's see what's in yer browsing history, shall we?"

Chapter Twenty

In the car on route to Glasgow the next day, Robbie decided to call Peg. He'd not spoken to her since just after arriving back home to Leeds. He'd meant to; he just never seemed to get round to it. Truth be told though, he did care. If he were being honest with himself, phoning her would've been done out of duty rather than genuine concern. There was just too much else going on for him to see Peg as having any kind of priority right now. But she's Eban's daughter and that gave her some relevance in what was happening right now; she could have snippets of information that might prove useful.

"Hi Peg, it's Robbie. How are y'doing? How's Maev?"

"Okay, she's still in Glasgow, on the cardiac ward. They've put her one o' them pacemakers in, said her heartbeat was very irregular after what happened, so it should be okay now with this in. She's improving but it's going tae be a slow process given her age. Where are ya? Ya sound like yer outside somewhere."

Robbie paused briefly before answering, not sure if he should tell her of his plans or not, before deciding that he just couldn't be bothered making up yet another lie. "I'm actually on my way t'Glasgow myself, just left Edinburgh. I've got my brother with me, Rich. Ya likely won't be in agreement, but I want t'see Eban's adoption documents, I want t'know about Martha Richards."

"What on earth for?" Peg sounded dumbfounded. "How's that going tae help anyone, least of all yerself?"

"I don't know Peg," Robbie sighed. "I have no idea, I just know that I need t'know more. I can't even explain it an' god knows I've tried. I've had all these questions from my lot too. I just need t'know, peace of mind maybe."

"D'ya really suppose ya'll gain peace of mind from knowing Robbie? Really?"

"Maybe, I don't know. My wife's pregnant, I only just found out an' it just seems so much more important to know about my bloodline now for some reason. If I'm from a family of head-cases then it scares me shitless that my baby might inherit that."

"If you're from a family o' head-cases Robbie, then so am I. But be honest now, what good will knowing that actually do? Will it change anything? No, it won't. You'll still be having a baby, congratulations by the way, an' life will still continue as it does. All yer going tae gain, is a pile o' worry ya could well do without. Leave it alone Robbie; it'll do ya no good."

"I can't. I need t'know Peg."

"D'ya know what Robbie? Yer sounding more an' more like Martin was, obsessed tae the point o' distraction. It's not healthy! Maybe there is a chance we've got some *nutcase* gene in our DNA, an' maybe there's a chance we could pass it on. But there's a fair old chance we won't too, have ya considered that? There's plenty of us that's okay ya know."

"I know, but look at Eban, his mother were insane, an' look at how Martin was, an' at how Kester is."

"Aye, but look at Eban's start in life. Is it any surprise he got a bit warped along the way? I'm no' making excuses for him, but he was never going tae be normal. Martin was just weak, an' sad though I am tae say it, he fed off my mother's bitterness."

"An' Kester?"

"Aye well, Kester's a law unto himself that one, always has been. Though I could argue that he didn't have it easy ya know. A weak minded father an' a drunk for a mother."

"Tavish had the same but he's okay."

"As far as I know Tavish is doing very well for himself, aye. That doesn't mean he has no demons tae contend with, just not in the same way as his brother thankfully."

There was nothing she could say that would sway him and Robbie was fast losing the energy to keep trying to convince her. It was easier to just change the subject. He didn't tell her that Lynsey had left him though, he couldn't face her being able to say it was his own fault, because he already knew that. Instead they discussed the baby, Maev, where he and Rich had stayed the night in Edinburgh, the weather, you name it. She made him promise to stop off and see her though, once they'd finished their business in Glasgow.

They'd left Edinburgh on the M8 motorway which, according to their satnav, made Glasgow about an hour's drive away, forty-five miles or so. Rich was busy singing along to Boulevard of Broken Dreams by Green Day. It wasn't pleasant as he was even mimicking the drumbeats. He was out of tune and loud, too bloody loud. Even his head was nodding in time to the music; it was the only thing that was in time because his singing wasn't.

"Jesus, Rich can't y'knock it off mate? My fucking ears are bleeding. Please?"

"Ya don't fancy a duet then?"

"Yer not funny y'know."

Lynsey still wasn't taking his calls. Her phone was switched off, at least that's what appeared to be the case, because it just kept going straight to voicemail. Robbie thought that there might be a problem with her phone at first because he'd missed some calls from a mobile number that he didn't recognise. He'd been ignoring them thinking it was likely to be damned PPI calls but then thought that maybe she was using a new handset, trying to get hold of him. Those hopes were quickly dashed when he'd spoken to her sister though, who'd informed him that Lynsey was fine, her phone was fine, but she still didn't want to speak to him thank you very much.

Rich had booked them into a Premier Inn this time. They hadn't anticipated needing to go to Glasgow, so it was the quickest and easiest thing to do, rather than mess around trying to find a decent B & B at short notice. Ballater Street, City Centre South. The satnav took them straight to it, though there were a few episodes of raised eyebrows as they approached.

"Gorbals!" Rich announced. "We're in the fucking Gorbals. Isn't it meant t'be dead rough in the Gorbals?"

Robbie had to admit that it wasn't the most picturesque of surroundings, though that was due to the fact that it looked more industrial than anything else. There was a big unit called McAlpine's right opposite and the whole area looked somewhat battered and bruised. The hotel itself was the smartest building around, appearing very out of place among the rest. "I don't think it's got the best reputation, but let's be honest, there's places in Leeds y'wouldn't want t'walk through on yer own isn't there?"

"Fair point."

"Besides, it'll be like a lot o' these old places, probably living down a bad rep from fifty years ago. Can't be that bad now, surely."

Robbie was even more assured that he wanted to be in that particular Premier Inn when they'd booked in at reception. He'd asked the woman behind the desk how far it was to the Sheriff's Office, and had been pleasantly surprised when she'd told him it was just around the corner.

"Och yae could be there in a wee hop, skip an' a jump," she'd informed them in her broad Glaswegian twang, though she had looked at them both a little suspiciously.

"D'ya think she thought one of us were due up before the beak?" Rich laughed as they headed towards the lift with their bags and room keys.

Turned out she'd been right; the building next to the hotel, just under the other side of the railway bridge, was the Crown Office and Procurator Fiscal Service. They crossed the road and turned right onto Gorbals Street and sure enough, there it was right in front of them. The *Glasgow Sheriff – Justice of the Peace* the sign read.

Entering the building, Robbie scanned for a general enquiries desk. Once located he headed straight over there, where a couple of uniformed thug types were manning the desk.

"Name?" one of them demanded as he'd approached.

"What? Er, McAndrew, Robbie McAndrew, but why d'ya need my name?"

The two men put their heads together and seemed to be reading something on the desk that was out of Robbie's sight.

"There's no McAndrew on the list for today!" the smaller of the two men half barked at him.

"It won't be, I'm not expected. I just wanted to ask something, that's all."

The harsh scowl they'd worn on his approach suddenly softened as their shoulders dropped in unison. "Oh, sorry Sir, my mistake. How can we help yae t'day?"

"I've got some papers from the Records office in Edinburgh that I need t'leave at the Sheriff's office. It's an application to open a sealed adoption record. They told me that I'd need to ask the Sheriff in the sub-district where the adoption took place. I just wanted to know if that'd be here or if I'd need t'go elsewhere?"

"No idea son. Sheila will know all that stuff; she's just on a break. She'll be back in five, if yae don't mind waiting?"

In reality it was closer to fifteen minutes before the elusive Sheila returned to her duties. A wiry looking woman of about sixty at a guess, she was wearing a grey skirt suit with a lilac blouse, a large brooch pinned to the top button in place of a tie. She looked quite smart, but stank of cigarette smoke as she'd brushed by them. She took up position as she all but ignored the two men who'd been holding the fort for her. She put on a professional smile, looking expectantly from Robbie to Rich and back again.

"Hi, I've got an application to view a sealed adoption record. The Records Office in Edinburgh said I'd need to submit it to the relevant Sheriff in Glasgow." Robbie wondered if she'd ever speak.

She did, finally. "I see. Well you may leave the application with me."

"But I don't know if this is the right place; they'd mentioned something about a sub-district being important."

"It is, but all of the sub-districts for births, adoptions and the like in the Glasgow region were centralised nearly a decade ago, so it's as I said, you may leave your application with me."

"Oh?"

"I'll see it gets tae the relevant department by the end of the day, I assure you."

There was something about her that made him think of the character of Miss Jean Brodie from the book by

Muriel Spark, the prim, Scottish school ma'am from the old story he remembered having to read at school once.

"How long will it be before I get a decision d'ya think?"

"Well it's very seldom that these things are even granted, I have tae be honest with you. When exactly were you adopted?"

"Oh, I wasn't, My father was. There's a medical condition y'see."

"And your father's now deceased I take it?"

"Er, no, no but he's incapacitated."

Her expression remained punitive. "Hm, then it's very highly unlikely that permission will be given I'm afraid, though I'll be sure tae submit your request anyway. Either way, it'll be weeks before they get back tae you, six to eight at the very least."

The disappointment in Robbie's expression must have been as palpable as the sense of hopelessness he was suddenly experiencing, because her tone suddenly softened. "Look, if you know anything about the adoption yourself, then there are a couple of other avenues that may prove fruitful."

"He was adopted from an orphanage in the Glasgow area in 1947."

"Glasgow's a big place. Do you know anything more?"

"No, I've a family member who might know. I can ask her, but that's all I know at the moment."

"May I suggest you take a trip tae the Mitchell Library archives on North Street in the city then? If nothing else, you're sure tae find a comprehensive list of the region's orphanages there, both current and historic."

"Will they have family records too? If I'm looking for a specific family name that might narrow it down, might it?"

"I imagine they will. As long as you're aware that you won't be able tae see anything too recent. Census records have a century long lock on them too you see."

"I know, but it's worth a try I think. Thanks for yer help, I appreciate it."

"Indeed."

Heading back down the steps outside, Rich begged Robbie to give it a rest for the day. "Please can we just chill now? I'm knackered an' I just can't be arsed with any more o' this today Rob."

He was fairly knackered himself and so agreed that they should go back to the hotel and pick up the car, go get something to eat, then give it up for the night. The library could wait. As they were passing the Procurator Fiscal building and heading towards the railway viaduct, Rich looked to his right before nudging his brother.

"Look, there's a pub built into the railway arches there, that sign says they do food. Let's go there instead o' driving; we can both have a pint or two then. It's practically next door to the hotel anyway."

Robbie agreed and so they both headed towards Sharkeys Bar, the smell of ale getting stronger as they got closer. Outside appearances made the pub look as though it would be quite small inside, but it was much bigger than expected once inside. It was busy too and it took a couple of minutes before they could get close enough to the bar to get served. Robbie had ordered their drinks, and as soon as he did, the men in the immediate vicinity had turned to look at the new faces.

The Landlady smiled as she pulled their pints. "Don't ya go minding this ignorant rabble," she joked, her inflection an unmistakable Northern Irish rather than Glaswegian though. "Not often we hear an English accent round here, is all."

The men clearly took her acceptance as their lead and turned away again, continuing their conversations. The brothers noticed that there seemed to be as many Irish accents around them as there were Scottish. An Irish pub, obviously, though the Landlady's reaction to them had led the field, and they quickly blended back into obscurity. She offered them the menus and explained that it was only bar food and not full dinners they'd be getting, but she could do toasties and chips if they wanted something hot.

Robbie had forgotten about the missed calls he'd had until he was about to take his first bite of ham and cheese toastie. His mobile began to ring in his pocket, he would've ignored it but for the fact he was still hoping that Lynsey might call. Instead it was the number he didn't recognise again.

"Hello."

"Hello, is that Robbie?" a Yorkshireman's voice. The background noise of the pub made it difficult to recognise who the voice belonged to.

"It is, who's this please?"

"It's Detective Sergeant Chris Radley. Can you talk? Only I've been trying t'get hold of ya all day."

"Er, yeh; I'm in a pub, it's a bit noisy but I'm okay to talk." His heart began pounding in his chest. He knew that this copper had the measure of him, that he knew Robbie wasn't telling him everything and it was more than a little bit worrying wondering just how much he did know. Had Kester told him who he really was? What would happen if it ever came out?

"Listen Robbie, something's happened and I need to speak with you. Where are y'now? Which pub is it? I can meet y'there."

All the lies that had come so easily to him since he'd begun his pursuit were for some reason so much harder to find of late, and the pause while he thought of one was getting too long not to be noticeable. He gave it up as a bad job. "I erm…I'm not local I'm afraid. I'm away with my brother at the minute."

"Oh right, well that explains why you've not been at home then. Can I ask, where's yer wife? Is she not with you? Is she okay d'ya know?"

There was an air of desperation in Radley's tone that was causing Robbie to worry even more. Why would Radley be so concerned about Lynsey? What the fuck was going on? "She's staying with her sister at the moment, on the east coast. We've er…had a bit of a falling out."

"She's left you?"

"No, no, she just wanted a break that's all," his heart sinking even as he said the words. "To be honest, I'm not sure, she won't speak t'me. I've spoken to her sister though so I know she's okay. Why? What's wrong?"

"Good, I have her mobile number but I think it's switched off or something as I've not been able t'get through at all. Where exactly are you at the moment Robbie?"

"Glasgow. Me an' Rich fancied a trip, a change o' scenery, y'know."

"I see."

Robbie could tell from the intonation in those two little words that Radley was suspicious.

"Well as it happens I'm in a car being driven to the station as we speak. The Glasgow train leaves in forty-five minutes an' I'll be on it. I'm travelling with a detective from Police Scotland who's connected to some of their own cases regarding a certain Mr Richards. I'll be liaising with their detective inspector in the morning."

Robbie turned to face Rich, a panic-stricken look on his face, and silently mouthed the words, *Oh fuck!*

Concerned, Rich put the remainder of his toastie back onto the plate and briefly stopped chewing what was already in his mouth. He mouthed back the word *'what?'* Shrugging his shoulders as he did so.

"Oh er, well we weren't planning on staying here, we were just passing through so t'speak."

Robbie's reluctance was something that Chris Radley just couldn't be bothered with, nor did he have the time to waste dancing around the subject. Instead he got straight to the point. "Look Robbie, you *will* still be in Glasgow tomorrow and you *will* fucking speak to me, okay! This is not a joke an' if I have to invent some charge t'have you arrested on, then I will. Am I making myself clear?"

"Very, but y'still haven't said what's happened."

"Kester Richards escaped from custody two days ago. He was on route to court. It's a long story but he's out and on the run."

"What makes y'think he's a danger t'me an' Lynsey? Surely he'll be laying low somewhere?"

"Because your flat's been turned over Robbie. I'm sorry but it's a bit of a mess."

"Oh for fuck sake!" Robbie was a bit louder than he'd intended, drawing attention to himself. Rich nudged him to remind him where he was. "I've been burgled? How bad is it? Wait a minute, how d'ya know it was him?"

"I don't know if, or how much has been taken son, but it was him alright. His fingerprints are everywhere. I don't think it was a flying visit either; I think he was waiting for you t'come home. He stayed a while."

"Christ!"

"I know there's something between the two of y'Robbie, an' tomorrow you *are* going t'tell me what exactly that is. Kester Richards, including the various guises he's used, has always been very clever, very 'scene of crime' aware. Now, t'leave so much irrefutable evidence of himself, tells me that he's getting reckless, an' if he's getting reckless it's because he doesn't care anymore."

"About being caught y'mean?"

"Precisely. I think that boy's got it in for you, an' he doesn't care what he has t'do as long as he gets what he wants: you. You have to understand Robbie, I can't say too much at the moment, but he's a very dangerous young man an' I believe y'need t'be seriously concerned about yer personal safety."

"Oh shit! Lynsey..."

"There is no doubt in my mind that he'll hurt her. I don't believe him to have any direct issue with her, but she's your wife; hurt her, hurt you. I'm sure I don't need to explain."

Robbie could feel himself start to shake as the enormity of this vendetta hit him like a truck. "She's pregnant. You have to make sure she's alright."

"Give me her sister's address and contact details an' that'll be taken care of tonight, I promise."

"I'm sorry bro, but I can't stay. If this fucking nutter even looks in the direction of my Jodie or the kids it'll be me doing time, not him." Rich had stayed the night, trying to talk himself out of worrying, but he'd not slept despite Jodie reassuring him that her and the kids were fine. "Until this bastard's caught again Robbie, then we're *all* in danger an' you need t'get yer head round that."

"It's me isn't it? The whole family's at risk because o' me?"

"It's not down t'you Rob. Yes the whole family's at risk, but it's down to him an' whatever fucking beef he's got with you. It's not *your* fault Robbie, but you have t'come clean now. You have t'tell this copper what he wants t'know, anything that'll help get the bastard locked up. This isn't just about you anymore, it's all of us under threat."

"Radley never said anything about anyone else."

"Oh come on Robbie," Rich's tone was becoming exasperated, "If he can't get t'you, he'll go after yer wife, but when he can't get t'yer wife, who d'ya think he'll go after next? Me? My wife? My kids? An' what about Clive? What about Lynsey's family? For fuck sake Rob, he's got a bloody list o' names he could pick from."

"Can't you at least hang on 'til I meet Radley later?"

"No, I'm sorry Robbie, really I am, but I just want t'get home now. I need t'be there with Jodie an' the kids. I want t'go now, sorry. You'll be okay t'get the train home when yer done won't ya? Only I want t'drive home, I'm not wasting time hanging round on station platforms."

Robbie didn't blame his brother for feeling that way. He felt that way himself about Lynsey, but at least he had the knowledge that she was safe at Julie's. The police had been round there and they had an officer in the house with them for the time being, until they had

more of an idea about where exactly Kester Richards
was now. "I'll come with ya."

"No, stay here, meet this Radley bloke. I don't
know, maybe y'can go t'that library this morning while
he's got his meeting, carry on with what y'came here for.
Y'can't keep avoiding this now Robbie, he's right. You
have t'come clean now, tell him everything."

"But what if there's some comeback? I don't know
where I stand legally. He might say I had a duty t'tell
someone the minute I found out. An' what about
everyone else: Lynsey, you, Clive? We could all have
broken the law over this."

"Well I don't know about you Robbie, but I'm
willing t'take my chances. You have t'tell him, it's the
only thing y'can do to help catch this psycho. Please?"
Rich finished throwing his clothes into his holdall before
swinging it up by the straps onto his right shoulder. He
picked his keys up from the chair by the window.
"Look, I hate leaving ya, I just…"

"It's okay, honest. I'll stay until I've seen this copper today. I'll ring ya later, let y'know my plans. Drive safely, yer not Lewis Hamilton y'know; text me when y'go home."

The brothers hugged before Rich left the room. Robbie had never felt so alone.

Chapter Twenty-One

Robbie tried Lynsey's phone again. It rang and it didn't go straight to voicemail like before.

"Hello."

"Lynsey! Thank god. I've been so worried. Are you okay love?"

"I'm fine Robbie. Got the police here, something t'do with your deranged nephew apparently."

"I'm so sorry love. I know, I've been told. I'm so sorry I've brought all this to our doorsteps."

The temperature in Lynsey's voice must've been sub-zero, though he could hear that she was fighting to stay calm, not shout, or cry. "Well ultimately it wasn't you was it, it was Annie. But hey, she can't answer for her crimes anymore so that's alright then isn't it!"

"Lynsey!"

He could understand her fear and even her anger, but she knew full well why Annie had taken him away as a child, to blame her now just wasn't fair.

She sighed heavily. "I'm sorry Robbie, I didn't mean that. Your mum was a lovely woman it's just…"

"Yer scared, angry even I know, but blame me, not her. How could she have ever known any o' this could happen?"

There was a long silence before Lynsey finally answered. "I've been advised t'stay here with Julie. Safer than going home apparently," she began to cry.

"Oh Lyns don't. I'm so, so sorry. Please let me come there, I want t'be with ya, I miss ya."

Her weeping ebbed off a little. "No, you do what you have t'do, I don't want t'know about it, I don't care anymore. I've got the baby t'think about now. *Your* crazy family's *your* thing. So you do whatever the fuck it is yer doing 'til you're happy again because I can't listen to any more of it, not right now."

"I love y'Lyns, please don't ever think I don't."

She began to cry again. At first he thought she was going to respond with the same sentiment, but she didn't. "I…oh Robbie, d'ya know what he's done to our apartment, our home?" Her words rapidly deteriorated into full blown sobs. "Did they…tell you what he's…done to my…wedding dress?" The line went dead as she hung up on him.

Filled with a mixture of grief and rage, Robbie wanted so much to be with her, to hold her, but he also wanted to hurt Kester Richards. He'd never entertained thoughts of torturing another human being before, but he was now. He imagined himself with a knife deeply embedded in some fleshy part of Richards' body, with him conscious and in pain while Robbie slowly twisted it, again and again before killing him slowly, with as much pain as was possible to inflict on someone. His own thoughts disgusted him. Was he really capable of such a thing or was this just blind rage? The fear that he'd somehow been altered by the effects of the head injury, that it'd somehow switched on the genetics within him that might make him capable of being just like them, just like Kester, just like Eban, was something that haunted him more and more.

The taxi dropped Robbie off on Granville Street, right outside the rear entrance into the Mitchell library. He didn't know what else to do with his time until Radley was ready to see him, and so decided he may as well continue with his plans, though the inner steam that had driven him up until now, wasn't anything like it had been. His mind was on his pregnant wife and family. He wanted to be with them, but also felt somewhat ostracised at the moment. He knew they didn't blame him for what was happening but was also well aware that but for him, they wouldn't have any of this trouble at their door.

Clive had been visited by the police too. He'd spoken to Robbie that morning, explained that he was going to stay with friends of his and Annie's for a week or so, that he hadn't seen them since Annie's funeral and it'd be nice to catch up. He was trying to play it down, but Robbie knew that the police had probably advised him to vacate for a time if possible. The guilt that Robbie was experiencing was crushing. He felt as though he was losing control of his life again and the rage, the rage he felt towards Kester Richards was beginning to fill his every thought. This was his own nephew, his own flesh and blood who'd tried to kill him, and was still pursuing some illogical vendetta against him. That was the problem in Robbie's eyes, the fact that he couldn't make sense of Kester's logic, he didn't understand how Kester, and Martin before him, could hold him responsible for something he didn't even know about until last year, until after Kester had tried to kill him.

The Mitchell building was an impressive piece of architecture, with two herculean type statues carved into the pillars that flanked the entrance, in a way that made them look as though they were holding up the building themselves. Various other carvings around the stonework made the building look as though it had been picked up from ancient Greece and transported somehow to the centre of Glasgow. It was just as striking on the inside.

It didn't take long to find the right department and once he'd asked a member of staff for some assistance, he was soon at his task. He decided to look from around nineteen thirty-eight onwards. He guessed that if Eban was adopted in forty-seven, then his mother could've started appearing in the local paper a couple of years or so prior to his birth. After an hour and a half he found his first *hit* in the microfiche covering the second quarter of nineteen forty.

Martha Richards aged 13, of Lasswade Close, Yoker. Was this day presented before the courts on charges of drunkenness, theft and assaulting a police officer in the process of executing his duties. Richards was spared a custodial sentence on the testimony of her father and the said police officer, Constable Stewart, who explained that he was also the girl's uncle, and that the girl was of feeble mind and prone to outbursts he felt to be beyond her control, that since the absence of his sister, the girl's mother, that these outbursts had increased, but that he felt no purpose would be served by separating the accused from her family who understood her mental state and were best placed to deal with it. Richards was duly discharged into the custody of her father.

Bloody hell; thirteen and already in this kind of trouble. There were one or two other mentions for lesser offences, minor affray. But the next entry was two years later in nineteen forty-two. This was the one that Robbie had been looking for, but blew his mind non-the-less.

Martha Richards, 15, of no fixed abode, Yoker. Was today found guilty of the grievous wounding by knife of PC McGregor who had tried to lawfully prevent her escape upon discovering her stealing from Murray's the Grocer of Dumbarton Road, Yoker. In a statement Mr Murray described the defendant as "...a clarty wee nyaff, away with my livelihood on many occasion." The defendant had been living rough these past three months following the execution of her father for murder and had been cast out by her brother whom it is described, she had stabbed maliciously with a vegetable cutting knife on two occasions. It came to light also that she had previously done the same to her father.

Described as a 'rickle a bones' and 'borderline feral' by the custodian it was felt that the defendant was not in her right mind and therefore the doctor was sent for. Upon his confirmation of this, the court felt the best course of action be that Richards be incarcerated for an undetermined duration to Glasgow Royal Mental Hospital under the care of Dr Edgar Hellmich, the Physician Superintendent, to be detained at Her Majesty's pleasure. After the hearing, Mr Murray was quoted as stating that the apple hadn't fallen far from the tree, in reference to the defendant's father John Richards who had led a less than moral existence, culminating in his hanging in recent months for the violent double murder of both Thomas and Maura McCaul in a row over gambling debts.

Robbie had discovered far more than he'd expected to, but hadn't been quite prepared to have discovered what he did. He called to a woman close by who looked like she worked there. He needed some clarifications from someone with a better local knowledge than himself. "Hi, d'ya know where Yoker is please?"

"Aye, it's about five miles north-west o' here, on the banks o' the Clyde river, not s'far from Clydebank itself as it goes."

He pointed to the parts of the text that he didn't understand. "Would y'know what these mean at all?"

She leant over his shoulder and screwed her eyes up to focus on the wording. "Well this first one, clarty means dirty, or unkempt if ya like, an' a wee nyaff is a pest, a nuisance, so it's describing the person as an unkempt little pest I suppose. Ya don't hear it so much these days, except from the old folk maybe."

"An' this other one?" He pointed to the text that read 'a Rickle a bones'. "Does this mean the same as a bag o' bones? Does it mean she was skinny?"

"Aye, it does; skinny an' wild by the look of it. Is there anything else I can help ya with here?"

"This place, Glasgow Royal Mental Hospital, where's that?"

"Och that was swallowed up by the Gartnaval General Hospital decades ago. It's on Great Western Road, but I doubt there's much if anything o' the original building; the whole place was rebuilt some years ago. It's very modern an' up tae date now."

"Okay, thank you for your help."

"Nae bother. If there's anything else, I'll be around about, an' there's a couple o' my colleagues on duty too."

It was difficult to imagine that this pathetic, scrawny creature described in the column of some obscure, obsolete local newspaper was in reality, Robbie's paternal grandmother. The photograph he'd seen of her standing next to a nurse, was clearly taken some time after these events as she looked to be better fed in the picture than the article had made her out to be. Though she still looked pathetic and a little untidy, she hadn't looked too out of place for the times.

Robbie filled out a slip of paper with the number codes of the pages he wanted to get copies of and took it to the desk. Just as he handed it over, his mobile began to ring in his pocket, much to the disgust of the librarian.

"That should be switched off on these premises Sir, or at the very least on silent. There are plenty of signs about the place."

Robbie fumbled for his phone, noticing it was Chris Radley's number before hitting the 'ignore' key, then switching it to silent quickly. "I'm really sorry, I forgot all about it. It's off now. How much do I owe ya for the copies?"

Leaning against one of the entrance pillars outside, Robbie took his phone out and called Radley back. He explained why he'd had to cut him off.

"Where are ya now?" Radley asked him.

"Outside this Mitchell Library. I were just going t'call a taxi."

"I thought you'd driven up here?"

"Oh, er yeh, we did but after y'called last yesterday, Rich wanted t'go home to his family. He took the motor."

"I see. Understandable I suppose. An' what about you?"

"I spoke t'my wife, but she doesn't want me there."

"I guess that's understandable too Robbie."

"Why? What d'ya mean by that?"

"Look fella, while ever this character has got it in for you an' is on the loose somewhere, Christ knows where, then yer a target. If he's coming after you, then yer loved ones are probably safest if they're not around you."

It made sense and Robbie knew that, but it didn't help him shake his sense of guilt at putting them all in danger like this, even though it hadn't been by conscious effort, it still felt very much as though he'd caused it. Kester fucking Richards was fast becoming the cancer in his life and he felt so out of control, not knowing where he was. It was the anticipation of something calamitous without knowing precisely what, and therefore having no way of preparing for it or forming any kind of plan. He felt like a prey animal being hunted by someone in a far better vantage point than himself.

Radley told him to stay where he was, that he'd pick him up and they'd go for a coffee. Robbie's heart sank as he agreed, knowing that today was going to be the day that this whole sorry saga would have to be told to the police. He felt a deep reluctance, but knew that for the safety of his family, especially his wife and unborn child, that he would have to, there was no other way.

Chapter Twenty-Two

A black Vauxhall Insignia pulled up next to Robbie and Radley called out from the passenger side for him to get in. He got in behind him, a little puzzled by the extra company in the driver's seat.

"This is Detective Inspector Louise Saggers, Robbie. She's my CID contact here in Glasgow; she'll be very interested to discuss Richards with us too. It seems the boy's been evading Police Scotland as much as he has us in West Yorkshire."

Robbie nodded an acknowledgement in her direction via the rear-view mirror; she did the same with a polite smile. As soon as he'd clipped his seat belt in place the car set off slowly.

He had no idea where he was or which coffee shop they were going to; he didn't know Glasgow. Radley made polite conversation with him on route to wherever it was they were headed. Had he slept well? What was the hotel like? Had he had breakfast? Along with various other trivialities.

As they drove, Robbie noticed they were passing The Winter Gardens on his right hand side. He glanced up at an approaching road sign which directed ahead for Carlyle and Edinburgh, with Stirling to the left and East Kilbride, right. The green information signs just beyond showed they were heading in the right direction for the Sir Chris Hoy Velodrome and Celtic Park football ground too.

Robbie was wondering just where they were actually going, as they'd left the city centre, when the car slowed because Saggers had indicated for a left turn. As they rounded the corner, he could see where they were for himself. The blue, chequered sign stated boldly: *Police!* Another sign to its left read: *Police Scotland, London Road.* He'd been shafted. "What's going on? You said we'd go for a coffee somewhere!"

As she parked the car in a bay marked for 'pool cars' and switched off the engine, Saggers turned to face him. "It's okay, we know how tae make coffee here Robbie. Might even route out a couple o' Garibaldis if yer lucky too." Her accent, though Scottish, wasn't Glaswegian. It was softer than that, though Robbie had no idea where she may have hailed from.

It was the first time she'd actually spoken to him for the ten minutes or so they'd been in the car. He was suspicious to say the least. "Am I being arrested or something? Why have y'brought me here?"

Radley laughed. "Of course not, it's just easier for us here. DI Saggers has got access to everything relating t'Richards here, that's all. Anything you might be able t'tell us that needs checking can be done easily if we're all here. Don't worry Robbie. Besides, you have t'bear in mind that he's been in yer home. If y'left anything lying about that might o' given him a clue as to where you've gone, then who knows; he could well be here already. Have y'thought about that?"

"Shit! My laptop. I were looking up how to view records etcetera, but if anything, that'll tell him I were heading for Edinburgh. We hadn't thought about Glasgow then, not 'til we were already in Edinburgh. Rich sorted out the hotel here. Ya don't need t'be a rocket scientist though, t'search someone's internet history."

Saggers laughed and shook her head. "We know that Robbie. How d'ya think we go about finding folk?"

She was quite a striking, slender woman, a little older than himself maybe, well presented with short cropped fair hair and brown eyes, but there was something about her that Robbie just didn't like, not that he could put his finger on anything specifically. If anything, it was probably the fact that she was holding all the cards at that moment. Obviously knowing far more about him than he did her. She unnerved him. It felt a bit like staring into the eyes of a viper, wondering when it would strike.

Robbie was shown into a room which he took to be an interview room of sorts, though it bore no resemblance to any interview room he'd seen on TV. There were two comfy sofas on opposite sides of a coffee table, plants on the windowsill and pictures on the wall. In fact, if it wasn't for the wall plaque with the Police Scotland logo on it and the words *Semper Vigilo, Always Vigilant,* there'd be no clue at all that he was in a police station.

Turning to Radley, Robbie raised his eyebrows. "Bloody hell, is this how the criminal underworld in Scotland gets treated then?"

Radley smiled and gestured for him to sit down. "Don't let it fool y'lad. I don't think ya'd find yerself in here if y'were a criminal. I think it's somewhere they interview victims maybe, a bit less intimidating for them."

Radley waited for him to choose where he was sitting, then took up position at the other end of the same sofa, inclining himself in somewhat towards Robbie.

Once Saggers had re-joined them, she plonked herself centrally on the opposite sofa, making up a triangle in effect, only the coffee table separating them.

"Coffee's on its way," she confirmed before glancing towards Radley, wanting him to take the lead. She wasn't a stupid woman and had very likely picked up on the fact that Robbie was ill-at-ease in her company for the time being. At least he'd met Radley before.

"So," Radley began, "is there anything you'd like t'tell us Robbie? Anything you feel we ought t'know?"

Robbie pondered for a moment, wondering what or how much would be *safe* to tell them. His apprehension must've been evident on his face and Radley took full advantage.

"It's just that I'm of the belief Robbie that there's more between yerself an' this Kester Richards character than victim an' criminal perpetrator if y'catch my drift? In other words what I'm saying is that *I know* that you know him."

"I don't honestly, I've never met him. Not unless y'count me getting seven bells kicked out o' me, but that's hardly a pint down the pub is it?" He could feel Saggers eyes boring into him as he spoke. It was almost a repeat of the same scene in his own apartment, where Bash had been the one speaking to him and Radley had scrutinised his every word, only this time Radley was the one doing the talking. Robbie could feel his heart pounding in anticipation, he knew he would have to tell them; it just needed to come out the right way. He wanted to know that if he were to start talking, that they would really listen to what he had to say, to his explanations. He needed to know that they would truly understand what had happened and why his path had crossed with Kester's. There was so much back-story to Kester's attack on him, much of which he was only just finding out himself, that it was difficult to know how, or where would be the right place to begin.

The coffee arrived, courtesy of a young police officer wielding a tray with three mugs and a small sugar bowl on it. He looked to be a bit nervous around DI

Saggers too. It wouldn't have surprised him to think that she had a reputation as a bit of a dragon around here or something. She thanked him dismissively without even looking at him; he took the hint and left, closing the door behind him.

Waiting until he'd lifted his mug and taken a drink from it, Saggers spoke up. "DS Radley tells me ya were lucky tae survive yer attack Robbie?"

He looked from her to Radley then back again. "Apparently so, yeh."

"Maybe you'll no' survive the next one."

Wow, that was blunt. "There hopefully won't be a next one."

"Oh I think there will." She leant forward and picked up the coffee mug in front of herself, taking a sip and giving Robbie time to mull over her comments. "Ya see, a young, physically fit man like Kester Richards, strong an' driven as he is, isnae going tae give up so easily don't ya think?"

"If he's any sense he will. I don't get what he thinks he can possibly gain coming after me. It makes no sense t'me, there's no logic…"

Saggers interjected, quite tactically. This was it, the viper strike. "Robbie, here's the facts. This Kester Richards has planned meticulously so far. He attacked someone in prison, just because he knew that'd land him in court again. He then poisoned himself, so as he'd need tae go tae the hospital, whereby he attacked his guard an' escaped. Now as an experienced police officer, on the odd occasion I've seen this kind o' thing before, an' believe me, it's rare, the prisoner has a tendency to get right the fuck away from anything an' everything. They lay low 'til they can get out o' the country or something. What they don't do, is go straight round tae their victim's home, looking for them. Ya know DS Radley here thinks he stayed the night there Robbie? Imagine ya'd gone home tae find him there, or worse, yer wife had. Imagine that.

"The point I'm making, an' I really hope I'm bloody making it now, is that yer a marked man in his eyes.

He's getting careless, too bloody careless. Kester Richards *does not* make silly mistakes, like leaving copious amounts of evidence behind. There's tons of DNA from your flat that we're confident will match tae him in due course. Now stop fucking about Robbie an' tell me the truth before I have ya charged with obstructing an investigation! Alright?"

Fuck, what a bitch. There was no softly, softly in her approach at all. Robbie took one more slurp from his coffee, then placed the mug down on the table. He leaned back, glaring at her, furious that she'd made him feel that way…vulnerable, threatened.

She read him immediately. "I'm no' here tae make friends an' influence people Robbie. An' I sure as hell won't be massaging anyone's egos. So let's just go with the facts shall we?"

Radley had come a long way and didn't want to completely piss off his best lead. "Look fella, we've all got the same goal here an' we need each other t'work towards it don't we? Now I'm not sure what it is that this psychopath has got over ya Rob, but whatever it is, if it's something illegal y'might be involved in, well we'll take those things into consideration. You'll be helping us y'see. It's bigger than you now Robbie. There's some serious charges against this lad, not just the ones relating t'you y'know."

Robbie was clearly agitated; he kept wiping his hand across his face and shifting position. Where to start? What to say? Finally he settled forward, resting his elbows on his knees with his palms together in front of his mouth as if in prayer. He took a breath. "He's my nephew."

Stunned, Radley and Saggers looked sharply at each other as they sat forwards themselves. She nodded to Radley to continue, knowing Robbie was more likely to take his questions than hers.

"He's yer nephew? Christ Robbie, he's related t'ya, an' he tried t'kill ya? You just told us that y'didn't even know him, an' he's yer bloody nephew?"

"I didn't lie; I've never met him. You just called him a psychopath. Is he?"

"It's not really something open for discussion fella, but let's just say it wasn't a flippant comment shall we?"

"It's a long story."

"We're listening."

"It's something that's gone on for most o' my life, but not something I knew anything about 'til last year, after the attack."

"You said he's yer nephew Robbie. I understood y'to have just the one brother though, an' I thought his kids were little still. Is Kester from a previous relationship when he were younger then?"

"Kester's nothing t'do with my family."

"I don't get it Rob, yer not making a right lot o' sense."

"It's because I don't know how to explain it so that it does make sense. So that ya'll see it how I need y'to an' not go off half cocked."

The look on Saggers face was one of intrigue, obviously aching to ask questions but leaving Radley to continue. It was killing her to hold back.

"The thing is, last year I found out that I'm not really Robert McAndrew. I'll explain all that in a minute, but my real name, the one I were born with, is Michael Whithorn. I were born here in Scotland an' taken away when I were little, given a new identity an' brought up by my mother's sister. It was all done with damn good reason an' I'm glad it was.

"The thing is, what I've only lately found out, is that the evil fucker that happens t'be my real father, had two other kids before me. My half-brother was called Martin an' he's dead now. Kester Richards is his son."

Radley needed a second to try and keep up with these revelations. "So, you'd a half-brother y'knew nothing about, an' it's his boy that want's t'kill ya?"

Robbie nodded. He knew that what he was saying sounded ludicrous. Even as the words were leaving his lips he knew how unbelievable they sounded.

Radley rubbed his forehead, struggling to absorb things, trying to get them into some semblance of order in his mind. "But why? I don't get why Robbie?"

"Because o' my real father," Robbie laughed nervously. "Because o' the Reverend Eban fucking Whithorn, that's why."

Chapter Twenty-Three

Now clean and smartly dressed, Kester Richards walked out of West Register Street in Edinburgh, turning right along Princes Street. He began to trot down the road at a steady pace just in time to jump aboard the number twenty-two bus heading for Ocean Terminal. It'd been some time since he'd visited his country's capital, but he'd not forgotten his way around, nor all the little nooks and crannies he could secrete himself into.

The stop, start of the journey down Leith Walk was beginning to turn his stomach and he was relieved when he saw the familiar statue of Queen Victoria up ahead of him, proudly sporting a traffic cone for a crown, no doubt the doings of some pissed up students. As the traffic lights changed the bus lurched forward, first turning left, then right onto Henderson Street, just behind the Lidl store. Someone else had rung the bell so he didn't need to. He waited for the bus to come to a stop before he left his seat and got off at the last stop on Henderson Street, right outside Sofie's Bistro. Things hadn't ended well last time he'd been there, so he kept his head down and rushed off towards the waterfront.

The last door on Henderson Street was now painted bright red; it had been black last time he'd been here. He scanned the names on the list next to the buzzers just in case she wasn't here anymore. She was, but he knew she'd probably not want anything to do with him. He pressed number five anyway.

"Who is it?"

She used to always order all kinds of crap from the internet, so he hedged his bets that she'd be expecting some delivery or another. "Package tae sign for."

"Okay, come on up." With that there was a clicking sound where she'd remotely released the lock allowing him in. The stupid cow.

Two flights of stairs taken two at a time and he was at her door. Robbie's rucksack over his right shoulder, he rested both hands on the door frame and waited for her to open it. He was taking a chance; she might not be alone. Shit, there could be some ned living with her by now. He listened for voices but couldn't hear any; he could smell cooking though and it made his stomach rumble. He was hungry.

He couldn't afford to give her any time to panic, so as soon as he heard the latch on the other side of the door he pushed his way in. Quickly closing the door behind himself, he grabbed her by the jaw with his left hand while gesturing for her to remain quiet with his right, then pushed her back against the wall.

"Now tell me Lena; is there anyone else here?" he demanded to know in a stern but whispered tone.

She'd gone pale and was beginning to shake; she could hardly get her words out. "Just me an' Maddie."

He turned his head rapidly, looking down the hallway towards the living room. At least he was between whoever it was and the door. "Who the fuck's Maddie? Where is she?"

Lena began to cry. "Christ almighty Kester, she's yer fucking daughter. Have ya forgotten her already?"

"Where is she?"

Lena pointed towards the door, diagonally opposite where they were standing. "She's asleep in her bed; she always naps after lunch."

He could feel himself getting harder the more she quaked and relaxed his grip on her a little but didn't let go. "Good." He pushed his mouth to hers and kissed her, then dropped his rucksack on the floor before pulling at the front of her jeans and shoving her towards her bedroom. The door was already ajar and so pushing his terrified quarry back onto the bed posed no problem at all.

***

"Victims, you said this is where they interview victims before. Is that what I am, a victim?" Robbie was exhausted. Half laid on the sofa at London Road Police Station, he rubbed at his eyes. He'd told them everything now. Well, that wasn't quite true. He'd told them about the events as he knew them to be, but when DI Saggers had insisted on knowing who, besides Annie Wilkinson, his mum, had been involved with his abduction from the Isle of Stennoch; he'd lied and said that he'd no idea. He told them that, that kind of information had gone to the grave with his mum, with Annie, that she'd never told anyone.

They knew that the Harbour Master had got them away, but Robbie said he'd acted alone. Annie and Jock Maguire were both dead and gone, they couldn't be held accountable now, but he knew that Jamie McGuffie was still around somewhere, and then there was Joe McStay to consider. He couldn't let them be answerable for it either. He knew his mum would understand: let the dead take the blame to save the living, they were safe in their graves so to speak. And even when DI Saggers had pushed him because she didn't believe that no-one else was involved, he'd stuck to his guns. "I don't know! For fuck's sake, I were five an' I didn't even remember any o' this shit myself 'til last year. What d'ya want me t'say? I can't tell y'what I don't fucking know!"

Chris Radley had just stared at him from beneath raised eyebrows. It seemed obvious that he didn't believe him either, but he remained quiet. Saggers had left them alone while she went to see what could be done about verifying Robbie's outlandish tale, leaving the two men in each other's mute company.

The silence seemed to go on for an age, Robbie wondering which of them would be the first to break it. Neither of them looked to have the energy, Robbie exhausted from the effort of retelling that which he never thought he'd need to, and as for Radley, well the poor man looked like his head was mashed; he was all in.

Robbie had made no mention of Izzy and Joe McStay, the couple who'd smuggled him out of the village as a child. Nor of Jamie McGuffie who'd piloted the boat that night. Or Jamie's mother and Gregor (Dredger) Scoular having turned a blind eye to it all. The man had an unblemished career in the police force and even though he was dead and gone now, Robbie had no wish to risk Dredger's posthumous reputation when all the man had done was to help save him.

Robbie had even lied about where he'd got most of his subsequent information from. He didn't want anyone going to Ireland; he'd said that Annie had told him most of it. Even though the truth was that Annie hadn't had a clue about Eban's family, let alone his marriage to her sister Mona, Robbie's mother, being bigamous. The fact remained; there was no way of proving or refuting what he'd said about who was involved.

Radley broke the silence first. "Did y'not think it'd probably be a good idea t'tell the police all about this last year, when y'first found out?"

Robbie snorted and shook his head in disbelief. "I'd just found out that I wasn't even the person I'd grown up believing myself t'be. My head was so fucking mashed that I couldn't even see straight. D'ya really think *doing the right thing* even crossed my radar? Besides, I'd no inkling about Kester Richards back then, I thought I'd just been a random mugging. I didn't even know he existed."

"But y'say you've met with yer half-sister is that right? Elizabeth wasn't it?"

"Yeh, I have. She's been pretty good about it all considering."

"I take it that's where y'were on yer last visit t'Scotland then? Visiting her, collating all this new information ya'd found yerself t'be in possession of."

Robbie was picking up on Radley's less than convinced tone and he wasn't happy about it. "Look, I've had all this shite thrown at me since last year. My whole fucking life's been a lie, an illusion. Turns out I've not even got the right t'be calling myself by the name I thought were mine. How the fuck would *you* feel? What would *you* do about it then?"

"I don't know fella, really I don't."

Eventually Saggers re-entered the room. She had some print-outs in her hands and was flanked by two young, serious looking CID officers. They looked on edge around her too. Bloody hell, she must be a right bitch.

"My DCs are going to follow up on the information you've given us Robbie. DC Simons here will be accompanying DS Radley to visit Elizabeth Parker-Tait in Milngavie." The look on Radley's face told Robbie that this was the first he'd known about it.

Robbie wasn't at all happy about the fact that Peg was going to be troubled by all this. "No! Why? There's nothing more she can tell ya about it. Eban Whithorn's her father as well as mine. End of."

"Her name has come up before Robbie, in relation to Kester Richards."

"Yeh, that's because she's his aunty an' he lived there for a while but that were ages ago, a few years at least."

"We still need tae speak with her. She'll know him better than us, places he might go, that sortae thing."

"Her mother's in hospital, her heart's bad. Her mother can't abide the thought o' me. Please don't make things worse. In fact, let me go too." Robbie turned his plea on Radley instead. "I know she out-ranks ya, but please give the go ahead. Let me come with you an' DC Simons?"

Radley sighed and looked over towards where Saggers was waiting for his answer. "It's no skin off my nose if he's there. An' at least we can keep an eye on him."

Saggers shrugged her shoulders in a nonchalant gesture. "Fine, but go now an' make sure he doesnae warn her yer coming."

She turned to the remaining Detective Constable. "Right, I want you heading out tae Girvan. Any clues ya can gain from paperwork relating to, or past conversations with, this Reverend Whithorn bloke, I want tae know about ASAP. Understand Lewis?"

Lewis. That was Lynsey's maiden name. It made him think about her, how she was, what she was doing, if she was safe. He missed her and even though it hadn't been a tremendous amount of time since he'd last seen her, it felt like a lifetime. Did she miss him too? How long could she remain this angry? Would she ever want to see him again? He knew that she'd be worried about the baby too, even before all this came to light, she'd been worried about being pregnant in her late thirties for the first time. He tried so hard to see things from her viewpoint, but it was difficult. The longer this was going on, the more Robbie was inadvertently convincing himself that he shared some of these personality traits with his father and with Kester. He was talking himself into believing he could be capable of the things they were. Had it started with Martha Richards, or was she just one of many from within the family to be *wrong in the head?* Her father had been hanged for murder; maybe he suffered the same derangement.

The truth was that Robbie needed to know. One way or another he needed to know if he was like them, if he was another apple fallen close to the tree, because the possibility that he *was* frankly, terrified him. Might there come a day when he committed some vile act too? When he was out of control just like the others?

Chapter Twenty-Four

DC Simons drove the pool car they were in. Robbie was in the back immediately behind him and DS Radley was in the passenger seat. They were heading north out of the city and towards Bearsden and Milngavie. Radley leaned round to face him. "Can I have yer phone please Robbie? Just 'til we get there?"

"Why? Because that dragon doesn't trust me?" He noticed DC Simons' face break into a smirk in the rear view mirror. "What on earth does she think I'm going t'do? She must know I want this fucking nutter caught as much as anyone, more even. It's me he hates; it's my family at risk. Why would that hard-faced bitch think I'd do anything t'jeopardise him being caught?"

Radley was losing patience. "Just give me the fucking phone Robbie!"

Just as he handed it over, Radley's own phone began to ring. He pocketed Robbie's and took out his own. "Radley. 'Ey up Bash, what can I do for ya?" His stern expression didn't change at all as he responded to Bash with the odd 'right', 'ugh', 'okay' 'uh-huh'. It wasn't until he asked the question 'how is she now?' that Robbie's ears really pricked up.

"Who? How's who now?"

Radley raised a hand, indicating to Robbie to wait as he finished the brief conversation he was having with Sgt Sajid Bashir. He turned to face him as soon as he'd hung up. "It's okay, it's nothing t'do with Lynsey, but it's very important none-the-less. Do you happen t'know a Katherine Rainey at all?"

Robbie turned both corners of his mouth down and shook his head. "No, who is she?"

"Y'might know her as Kit maybe?"

"No idea, sorry. Why you asking? What's she got t'do with me?"

"She were admitted to hospital after a heroin overdose yesterday morning. Police were called because she looked like she'd taken a beating too. Anyway, once she began t'recover, she started wittering stuff about Chris Hartley being on the run. It seems as though he called her to your flat. She claims she had sex with him there an' that things got a bit rough, more than normal she'd said, so he's obviously used her before. Said he were speaking with a Scottish accent an' she thought he might be putting it on as she's only ever known him t'be a Yorkshireman.

"She'll not know him as Kester Richards y'see. I don't think any of his Leeds connections would. Gareth Dalby or Chris Hartley seem t'be the alias' used down there."

"She's been in my flat?" Robbie was more than a little bit perturbed by that fact.

"Indeed she has, but that's a good thing."

"I don't see how. He shagged his bird in my flat! In my bed most likely."

"Yeh well that's the least o' yer worries fella. Yes, she's been in yer flat…with him. Which makes her a witness; she'll have information she doesn't even realise. Stuff like what he did in yer flat, how he were behaving. If he took anything with him, or anything he might o' said that'll give us a lead on where he could be now. So yeh, her being in your flat from our point o' view, is a good thing."

Simons had asked Radley if he could put the radio on as they drove and Radley had agreed, as long as it wasn't going to be too loud. Robbie had rested his head back and was watching the scenery go by out of the window to his right. He half felt as though he could fall asleep if he allowed himself to. The voice of the radio DJ was talking in the background. It was the only voice talking in the car at that point with none of them paying too much attention to it. That is until Robbie heard him wish a happy sixtieth birthday to Eric's wife, Martha, and dedicated the song Martha's Harbour by All About Eve to her.

It brought a lump to his throat because that was the song that his mum, Annie, had chosen for herself. It was the song that she'd asked to be played at her funeral as her coffin were carried into the chapel, and it was the first time that Robbie had heard it since that day. His initial instinct had been to ask Simons to switch it off or switch channels or something, but instead he just listened, really listening to the words this time. Unlike at her funeral when he'd cried his way through most of it. He could see why she'd wanted that song, it reminded him of the Isle of Stennoch too. Annie must've had so many bad memories of that place, but before that, before Eban, she'd been happy there. Both her and his mother Mona had been happy there. Annie must've held on to those memories of her childhood in the Isle village, playing freely with her sister, of the loving family they'd come from. He was glad that she hadn't allowed Eban Whithorn to mar those precious memories, because she deserved the peace that came with them.

He missed Annie so much, but was glad that she wasn't here to have to confront all of this now. Relieved that whatever wrongs she may have done, she wouldn't have to answer for them. He swallowed down the lump in his throat as the words to Martha's Harbour came to an end.

"Broadmeadow Road; that's right isn't it?" Simons prompted Radley for confirmation that he was heading in the right direction. "We're only a mile an' a half away according tae this." He tapped on the satnav screen with his index finger.

Robbie could feel tension building in his chest at the thought of turning up at Peg's unannounced with two coppers in tow. What the hell was she going to think? Talk about dropping someone right in it. It's not that he was feeling all sentimental about the fact that he'd found himself this long-lost sister or anything, because the truth was, he'd not even known about her until this past year. Not that he wished her any harm or anything, but she knew far more about the Whithorn/Richards connection than he did. She'd known all her life so there could be things she could tell him. He'd no idea what, he just knew that he didn't want her being pissed off enough to shut the door on him, when he'd only just got to know her. He could've been further along with his own search by now if it hadn't have been for Maev's damned heart giving out on her. He sympathised with Peg and how she must feel, but truth be told, he didn't give a flying fuck about Maev and whether she lived or died. He felt like he should, but the fact that he didn't just served to reinforce his own self-doubt about his mental state.

The car came to a stop outside the gate of Peg's cottage. Radley leaned forward in his seat a little and strained to see around DC Simons, into the front yard. "Looks like we're not her only visitors today," he stated upon seeing a bottle green Skoda Octavia parked in front of the cottage to the right of the gate.

Robbie wondered who it could be because most visitors would've just parked at the gate. It'd be too much hassle opening and closing the farm gate just to park inside, which meant that whoever it was must be staying a while.

They left the pool car at the gate and headed in. Radley had instructed Robbie to go in first with DC Simons, so that Peg would see a familiar face first. As they went around the back of the cottage to the door she preferred to use, she was just heading towards it herself from the back yard. Dave barked and ran at them, quickly recognising Robbie and jumping up at his leg, wagging his tail furiously. Robbie bent down to make a fuss of him.

She looked pale and tired as she acknowledged them. "Thought I heard a car pulling up. Who's yer friends Robbie?"

"They're er…"

"Don't tell me; let me guess. Police, right?"

Simons took his warrant card out of his inside pocket and held it up to her. He smiled amiably. "I'm Detective Constable Mick Simons Madam, from Glasgow. An' this is Detective Sergeant Radley, a colleague from West Yorkshire Police. We're here with a common reason."

"My nephew by any chance, Kester?"

"Aye, would ya know of his whereabouts at this present time?"

"Ya'd better come inside." She continued into the house with the three of them and Dave following closely.

As they entered the kitchen Simons jumped suddenly startled by the man sitting at the table. "Shit! Sir it's him, it's Richards!"

The man at the table snorted as he shook his head and turned to address Peg. "Ya can see now why I don't come back Aunty Peg, can't ya? It's always the bloody same when I do, always someone wants him for something an' me having tae convince them I'm not him." He was less than amused.

Robbie spent a few seconds staring at the face of the irritated young man at the table. He'd never seen Kester face-to-face, only from his mug-shots, but this couldn't be him, sitting there as bold as brass. "You're Tavish aren't ya?"

"Aye."

Radley's face began to level out again as he too examined the features of this man. He *had* met Kester on several occasions, but he still needed a really good look at this man before he could assume that it really wasn't Kester Richards. "Tavish Richards I take it, Kester's twin?"

"Aye, like I said. Ya know we're not even identical twins don't ya? We're no more alike than any other brothers."

Peg walked to the sink to fill the kettle. "That's true aye, but ya do both look very similar, always have done. I could never tell ya apart as babies, even as ya were getting bigger the subtle differences weren't easy tae pick out, even tae those of us that knew yae mind."

Peg had told Robbie that she hadn't seen Tavish in years. He wondered if she'd lied about that; it just seemed odd that he'd be here now, when the world and his wife were searching for his brother. "I er...don't know if y'know who I am…"

Tavish stood up from his seat and stretched his hand across the table towards Robbie. "Been hearing all about yae, the elusive Michael Whithorn, aka Robbie, right?" Robbie nodded.

Radley was still wanting some clarification. "Can I ask what the purpose o' yer visit is today Mr Richards? Only, we'd been led t'believe by Robbie here, that y'didn't have much t'do with yer family anymore."

Tavish looked across at Peg, who in turn looked a little lost for a moment before saying anything. "She's dead. My mother, she's dead. Night before last."

"I'm very sorry to hear that Mrs Parker-Tait. Please accept my condolences." Radley was taken aback by the news as it would have obviously impeded his questioning of her as a witness while she was grieving the very recent loss of her mother.

"It's Miss," she corrected him, "Mrs Parker-Tait was my mother. Just call me Peg, everyone else does. Anyway, that's why he's here, because his grandmother's just died."

Robbie knew it was wrong but all he could think to himself was, *damn the old cow for dying now*. He knew it'd be inappropriate to quiz Peg about Kester right now. He wanted to show sympathy but it was a struggle. "I'm sorry Peg. What happened? I thought she were getting better."

"She was, well she seemed tae be at least. Then she had another cardiac arrest in her sleep the other night."

"An' they couldn't save her?"

"They didn't try. She'd got the doctor tae do one o' them Do Not Resuscitate things, said if it ever happened again tae just let her go, let nature take its course, so they did." She was putting a brave face on things but it was palpable that she was fighting with her emotions; it explained why she looked so pale and tired.

"I got here last night, drove up from Luton. Took me the best part o' six hours, but I knew Aunty Peg'd be alone an' I didn't want that."

"I'm sorry tae ask," Simons chanced, "but has yer other nephew been informed Peg?"

She shook her head, sighing heavily. "I wouldn't have a clue how tae find him these days I'm afraid. I keep getting phone calls an' the odd visit from you lot wanting tae know if he's been here, but I haven't seen him for such a long time now an' that's the truth. If that boy's done something wrong then I doubt he'd risk coming here. He wouldn't be that stupid. He used tae live here so he'd know you lot'd be paying us a visit wouldn't he? I don't know what he's done now, but at the moment I don't really care either. I'm sure ya'll understand."

Robbie bit down on his lower lip while he pondered whether or not to continue given the circumstances. He decided he would. "D'ya remember me telling ya about being mugged an' that it were that attack that made me remember things?"

She nodded, though she seemed puzzled by him mentioning that now.

"Thing is Peg, turns out it wasn't a mugging, it were attempted murder an' it were Kester that did it. He tried t'kill me Peg, even before I knew any o' this stuff. He tried t'kill me an' now he's escaped an' he's coming after me. My whole family's in danger; my wife, my brother, all o' them because he's out there somewhere looking for me, an' if he can't find me he could go after them."

Stunned, Peg sat down in the chair adjacent to the one Tavish occupied, the chair that Maev had used the day Robbie had first come here. Peg's mouth was agape in disbelief while Tavish dropped his head into his hands.

"He wouldn't," Peg's voice quivered with emotion as she spoke.

Tavish clenched his jaw tightly together as he shook his head. His nostrils flared and he took deep, sighing breaths. "Aunty Peg he would. Ya can't keep making him out tae be some badly done by wee brat. He's a total bastard! He's my brother I know, but trust me, he's off his head. I grew up with him remember; I *know* he'd be capable o' killing someone. He got just as obsessed with all this stuff about our grandfather as what my dad did. They were as bad as each other. Neither o' them would let it go. My dad would o' never o' taken things this far, but my brother would an' you know it Aunty Peg.

"He's always been dangerous tae know, even when we were kids; you don't know the half o' the stuff he did. That's why I got away as soon as I could. My mother's a piss-head an' my brother a violent nutter. I was always taking the blame for shit he did, because I looked enough like him that folk'd think it were me who'd done it.

"Nobody wanted anything tae do with me; I was *his* brother, guilty by association. He's a ticking bomb."

Peg took her handkerchief out from up her left sleeve and dabbed at her eyes with it, her haggard face contorted in grief now. "Oh stop! I can't hear anymore, I can't take any more o' this now. My mother's just died an' my head is full with her loss an' all that needs doing, needs sorting out. I can't bear it." Dave trotted around the table and jumped up onto his mistress' lap. He knew she was distressed and he wanted to protect her, to make it better. He nuzzled his little face up into her chin and she dropped her head to kiss the top of his head in response.

Tavish reached across and squeezed her hand before looking back towards Robbie, an act that caused the little dog to growl at him. Peg was his to look after. "I feel like it's my responsibility tae apologise for my brother's actions yet again. I'm sorry for what he's put ya through, but I don't know what ya think ya'll gain here. He's no' stupid, he's mental but no' stupid. He won't come back here, it's a known address for him, it's the last place he'd be.

"But I have tae tell ya this, it's only fair. If my brother's got *you* in his sights, if he's locked on tae ya, then he'll no' give up easily. He was a mad bastard when I last saw him an' that must be nearly four years now. Sounds like he's pretty much spiralled out o' control since then. I believe what yer saying here, because I *know* Kester, probably better than anyone else does. I know how he treats people, how he treats his apparent friends, girlfriends, associates etcetera. Other people are just a means to an end for him an' once they've served their purpose he'll discard them like an old sock. He can charm the pants off them one minute, then rip them apart the next. He's a liar, he's cold an' he's cruel an' if he's out there looking for ya then he needs stopping because if he failed at killing ya once, he won't let that happen again if ya understand me."

Everyone in the room understood what Tavish was getting at. Kester didn't like being made a fool of and he considered his failure as having done just that. He was going to be even more fired up than before because of it, and he wouldn't tolerate being made a fool of twice.

Chapter Twenty-Five

Lena couldn't stop trembling and it had cost her a back hander across her face because of it. Kester wanted to sleep, but her incessant bouts of quivering were disturbing him. He wouldn't let her get up, he didn't trust her where he couldn't see her, but she just couldn't relax enough to let him sleep. Then Maddie awoke in the other bedroom and shouted her mum.

"I need tae go tae her Kester…please?"

"For fuck sake Lena, can't ya shut the wee brat up?"

"She's three years old, she'll be scared if she can't find me. Please?"

"Fine!" He released his arm from around her and she leapt from the bed, pulling her clothes on frantically before her little girl came in the room to find her in that state. He got up too, not wanting either of them too far from his sight.

"Mummy yer lip's all red."

"I know sweetie, I just bumped it that's all. Silly mummy."

The little girl giggled as Lena swept her up into her arms. "Ups-a-daisy mummy."

"That's right Maddie, ups-a-daisy." It was taking all of her self-control to stay calm in front of her baby girl, when all she wanted to do was scream, for someone to call the police, anything, just so someone, somewhere would know she needed help.

"Mummy, who's that man?"

Kester was leaning in the doorway, fastening the belt of his jeans, bare-chested. "Hello Maddie, d'ya remember me? I'm yer daddy."

The confused little girl looked to her mother for confirmation and comfort. Of course she didn't remember him, she'd only been a few months old the last time he'd been in the same room as her. He stepped forward and lifted her from Lena's arms, causing Lena to gasp suddenly. Not knowing what was wrong, but knowing something was, Maddie began to cry.

Lena reached to her and took her arm. "It's okay baby, daddy just made me jump, that's all. Everything's alright."

"Aye Maddie, everything's alright. Yer mammy's going tae lend me her phone just now, isn't that right Lena?"

"It's through in the living room."

"Then get it." He followed her along the hallway into the front room with its bow window to one side overlooking Tollbooth Wynd and the front window looking out over the view of The Shore, with its bars and eateries following the banks of the Water of Leith.

Lena unplugged her mobile from its charger and passed it to him. He passed the child back to her mother as he brought up the number keys on the screen. He

stood by the window as he made his call. "Alright pal?
Guess who?"

He laughed out loud in response to whoever was at
the other end of the line. "Aye it is. Listen I need a
favour; I need a car. Aye, aye that's right." He spun
round and looked at Lena as she held onto her daughter.
"That's nae trouble pal, I can get that dropped off for ya
in the next couple o' hours. How well d'ya know Leith?
Aye, well there's a wee road runs between Sandport
Place an' Commercial Street, it's called Dock Street.
Have the motor left there for me, leave the keys under
the wheel arch on top o' the tyre on the driver's side,
okay? Tonight, I need it tonight. Brilliant, I'll sort the
money out now." He hung up his call and deleted the
number he'd just dialled from the call history, then put
Lena's phone in his pocket.

Kester then retrieved the rucksack from the hallway
where he'd left it on his arrival and began rooting
through it. Eventually he came up with a small brown
envelope from which he took out a credit card and

handed it to Lena. She looked down at it. "Mr R McAndrew? Whose is it?"

"None o' yer business! I'm going tae write an address down an' I want ya tae go there with some cash yer going tae get out with that card, right?" He handed her a piece of paper.

She read the street name to herself then looked up at him. "But this is away the other side o' the city."

"Stop yer whining an' get on with it will ya! Two, four, two, nine. That's the pin for that card." He told her how much to get out of the ATM, and to get bits out from different ATMs as she made her way across the city. She'd need to get two buses in order to get to the place he'd told her.

He wouldn't let her have her phone back when she asked, so she got her coat on and began to put Maddie's coat on too.

"What d'ya think yer doing?"

"It's no' so warm today Kester; she'll need her coat."

"She'll no' need her coat. She's going nowhere. Just you."

Panic flooded Lena's face as Maddie began reaching across for her. "I want tae go with mummy, please mummy?" she cried.

Kester picked her up again and swung her round away from Lena's grasp and glared back at her. "Not a fucking chance. Ya think I'd let ya take her with ya an' trust ya tae come back? She stays here with me an' you'll do exactly what I tell ya tae; d'ya get me?" The menace in his tone and expression told Lena that he was going to hold their daughter ransom, to ensure that she'd run his errands without question. It worked.

***

"D'ya think Kester will go back there; to Milngavie I mean?" Robbie asked from the back seat as DC Simons turned the car round and began retracing their journey back towards Glasgow.

Radley shook his head and sighed. "I doubt it. Police Scotland have been keeping an eye out for him around here for a while. He'd be pretty stupid t'risk it."

"Unless he knows I'm here."

"Was there anything on yer laptop that might point towards ya coming here?" Simons enquired.

Robbie thought about it for a moment. There was. "If he's got into my PC, then he's pretty much got into my life: emails, bank stuff, Facebook. If he's been able t'bypass my security, then he's going t'know me almost as well as I know myself."

"How tight's yer security?"

Robbie smirked before answering. "Please…I'm a programmer, trust me, it's tight."

Radley wasn't convinced. "An' trust *me* Robbie; he'll be in. The boy's no fool with that stuff. He's used various identities to cover his tracks in the past, but we know he's more than just computer literate if y'catch my drift?"

"Maybe that's a family trait too then."

It didn't seem to take as long driving back into Glasgow as it had driving out, though that's usually the feeling for most journeys. DC Simons asked Robbie if he wanted dropping off at his hotel, as they would be returning to London Road police station. But Robbie asked if he could be dropped back at the Mitchell Library because there were other records he wanted to look up.

Radley was concerned that things had become a little intense for Robbie. "D'ya think that's such a good idea fella? I mean…well, d'ya not think it'd be better just t'let things go, concentrate on us catching him?"

"Christ; don't you start, I've enough with my lot going on about that. I can't let it go; I need t'know. Why can't anyone seem t'get that? What's going to happen about all the stuff I told ya? About who I really am an' all that?"

Radley rubbed his forehead in thought before answering. "I don't really know what t'tell ya yet Rob.

I can't say it's something I've had experience o' before. There's definitely been crimes committed, but it's not a straight forward case as I'm sure ya'll appreciate. I need t'discuss things further with DI Saggers before any decisions are made, an' I'm guessing further advice will be sought from higher up the chain, but I suspect it could be Police Scotland who deal with it because this is where y'claim to have been abducted from. Y'were a Scottish resident at the time y'see."

There was a mixture of thoughts and feelings running through Robbie's mind. On the whole, he felt relief that he didn't have to lie anymore. It was becoming hard work and so not having to think up excuses and then remember exactly what he'd said and to whom, was quite liberating, though it did nothing to quell the need he had to continue his search into Eban's origins. He looked back towards Mick Simons in the driver's seat, "On second thoughts, is Yoker far?"

"Er...no' so far, why?"

"Can y'drop me there instead?"

Radley was having none of it. "No Robbie, we can't! We'll drop y'back at the Premier Inn. I want ya t'stay there 'til I call ya, okay?"

"Why?"

"Because at this stage yer helping with enquiries, that's why. An' we've got enough on trying t'find this mad bastard who's got it in for ya, without you thinking it's okay t'just bugger off whenever it suits. We can't keep y'safe if we don't know where the fuck you are Robbie. From now on, y'go nowhere without me knowing.

"I don't want y'leaving Glasgow just yet. So you're going back t'yer hotel now, an' yer staying there 'til you hear from me! An' we're off back t'the police station. Once I've had chance t'liaise with the appropriate people, I'll ring ya."

"Well how long's that going t'take?"

"It'll be today, that's all I can tell ya."

"So I'm under fucking house arrest 'til then?"

"If that's how y'want t'see it Robbie. But I'm telling ya now, if I have t'come looking for ya, I assure ya, I'll not be bloody happy about it an' I'll have ya taken into 'protective custody' if that's what it takes. Are you hearing me?"

"Loud an' clear."

The car pulled up on Ballater Street, right outside the hotel and Radley turned to face him. "Go inside Robbie, stay inside, an' don't even think about leaving the premises 'til ya've heard back from me. I'll ring ya in a few hours. I suggest that y'don't use yer email account from yer phone etcetera. You're the IT geek; you know more than I about what he might already have access to. Just be bloody sensible for once. Stay where you are, right?"

Robbie spent a lot of time pacing around his hotel room. He'd had a pizza delivered and eaten most of it. He'd drunk so much coffee that he felt the jitters from the effects of the caffeine, and his patience was wearing thin. He'd spoken to Lynsey again. He wanted her to know that everything was out in the open now, that he'd told the police who he was and how things had transpired.

But it turned out she already knew, they all did. He should've known that they wouldn't waste any time. West Yorkshire police had already been round to his family and Lynsey, Clive, Rich and Jodie had all been interviewed that day. DI Saggers must've informed them at the point when she'd left the room. She was certainly making sure that he didn't get the chance to interfere with their statements before they'd been given. Robbie's dislike for the woman increased somewhat. He'd not had the chance to warn any of them that he'd only given the names of Annie and Jock. He'd been careful to leave everyone else involved. out of it. His family hadn't known that though, and so once it had become apparent to them that the police quite obviously knew about Robbie's origins, they hadn't realised that there could be things he'd held back, and so each of them had inadvertently dropped Joe McStay, Jamie McGuffie and the late Dredger Scoular right in it, not to mention that Clive had explained to them the fact that half the village had been party to events. They'd even been told about Robbie's trip to Ireland and the information he'd got from Jacob Whithorn, so no doubt he'd had a visit too. He'd have some explaining to do. Having told Robbie that the Whithorns had suspected all along that he was in fact alive, how the hell would old Jacob justify that to the police?

He wasn't sure if the police would've been round to see Joe about his involvement all those years ago, but he knew he needed to call him, to explain.

"Aye Robbie, they were here earlier. Asking all kinds o' questions about my Izzy they were."

"I'm so sorry Joe. I never mentioned either of ya, but I didn't realise how quick they'd be t'follow up with my lot. I'd not had chance t'warn them an' they didn't know not t'say anything."

"Och, it's nae bother son. My Izzy's dead an' gone an' they cannae touch her for it now, an' as for me…well, I couldnae give a damn if I'm honest. Let's face it, how much d'ya think they're likely tae want tae chase this up now, all these years later? Money's tight, they'll no' have the wherewithal tae do it an' there's no benefit in them sending an old man tae prison. Don't worry yerself son. I'm not. I told them everything I know; they were fine about it, just asked that I no' go anywhere without informing them for the time being."

Robbie wondered if they'd been to Girvan too, to corroborate what he'd told them about Eban. Silly really, of course they would have. They'd probably gone there as a priority. He wondered what they'd made of Eban, trapped in his body with nothing to offer them but his contemptuous expressions, and Dieter wondering what the hell was going on with no idea at all about the past of the disgusting creature in his care that he respectfully addressed as Reverend Whithorn. Spending his time, carefully catering for his needs, washing him, feeding him, changing his catheter bags and wiping his arse. Would he still do that if he knew? To be honest he probably would, because he was the sort of person who cared about people. He likely wouldn't judge Eban on his past atrocities but would deal with him in the here and now, a helpless soul with no one else to take care of him.

Robbie's phone rang, startling him briefly. It was Chris Radley calling, just as he'd promised to. "There's a pub just round the corner from your hotel, Sharkeys Bar. D'ya know it?"

"Yeh, that's the one I were in when you called to say you were on yer way up here."

"Oh, right. Good. Meet me there in ten."

Chapter Twenty-Six

Radley was already at the bar, pint in hand, when Robbie walked in. He didn't say much about his meeting back at London Road with DI Louise Saggers, but he did ask Robbie a lot of questions about his own search into Eban's past. "Any investigation material you've done yerself fella, could prove t'be of interest to us. It all helps y'know."

"I don't like that woman, DI Saggers. She's a bitch an' I don't trust her."

Radley laughed. "Yeah well you an' me both, an' yer right, she is a bitch, but d'ya know what Robbie? She's a bloody good copper. An' if Kester Richards has got her biting at his tail, then I'm pretty confident he'll be found soon."

Robbie didn't see the point in hiding anything now, they pretty much knew from the thread to the needle everything relevant. So he set about explaining as best he could. He told Radley that he knew about the police visits to his family back in Leeds and Lynsey in Blythe. He asked if Jacob had been interviewed too.

"The Irish Uncle? Yeh Robbie, he has."

"He's Scottish not Irish, he just lives there."

"It seems ya've been busy. Ya got a lot of information from Jacob Whithorn didn't ya? An' Gregor Scoular o' course. I'd be interested t'know where he got *his* information from."

Robbie shrugged. "He never said. Everything he gave me, I didn't get 'til after he'd died, so I never got the chance to ask. I'm guessing he still had some contacts maybe seeing as he were one o' you lot."

Radley suddenly aborted his attempt at a slurp from his beer in surprise. "A copper? Was he? I didn't know that. DI Saggers never mentioned that part."

"He'd been retired a long time, but maybe he had mates still, y'know, old colleagues or whatever, snitches too if that's what y'call them. For all I know it's stuff he'd been sitting on for years. He never said. He only ever told ya what he wanted ya t'know."

"D'ya still have his last letter that he wrote?"

Bloody hell! They even knew about the letter, was there anything these people didn't know. Was there any part of his life that wasn't an open book anymore? Lynsey? It had to have come from her.

"Your lot haven't said anything t'Clive about what were in that letter from Dredger have ya? Only, I never told him y'see. I didn't want him thinking badly o' my mum. He loved the bones of her an' I didn't think it were right t'tell him something like that, if she'd chosen not to all those years."

"Don't worry Robbie. There's nothing gets passed on in these matters that doesn't need t'be. We're looking for anything that might give us a lead in finding Kester Richards an' also, now that we've been made aware of it, anything that might help in the investigation into a child abduction, even if it is a few decades down the line."

Robbie didn't like that term, 'child abduction'. It made it sound as though he'd been plucked off the street and sold to a group of paedophiles or something. "I wasn't abducted; I were rescued. I'll never resent or regret what my mum, Annie, did. I don't think I'd o' survived childhood if it wasn't for her. She saved me because she loved me an' because she loved her sister, my real mum Mona. Y'can't tell me that if you'd been put in that position, that y'wouldn't o' done something similar?"

"Luckily times have changed now haven't they? We'd like t'think that people are more answerable for their abuses now than they were back then. I understand accusations were made, an' ignored. So yeh, I can see the logic in what she did, but it doesn't make it right. She still committed a crime."

"Joe didn't seem t'think the police would bother doing anything about it all these years later."

"It's a crime Robbie; it needs looking into just like any other crime would. But, the fact is that the Procurator Fiscal would have to be satisfied that there was enough evidence t'bring such a crime t'court. An' Annie Wilkinson isn't here to answer for any of it."

"Is that like the Crown Prosecution lot, The Procurator Fiscal?"

"Pretty much. It's a Scottish crime, so it'd be the Scottish Judicial system that took it forward if they chose to. The English lot will look into the fraud aspect though."

Fraud? He'd been taken from Scotland to England. Surely that was it, kidnapping or something. "What's fraud got t'do with anything?"

Radley put his glass down; it was close to being empty anyway. He wiped a beer droplet from the corner of his mouth. "Yer Aunty claimed child benefit for a child that was no longer living; that's fraud."

"But that were for me."

"I know, but it doesn't change the fact that she claimed it in the name of a dead child, not a living one."

"Well it's not like they're going t'get it back now."

"True, but what happened needs acknowledging legally, none-the-less."

"Surely anyone in their right mind would know why she did what she did. It's not like she was getting child benefit in order t'profit from the system."

"I know what yer saying Robbie, but you have to understand that the law's black an' white. There are no grey areas. A person has either broken the law or they haven't. It's not up t'the police t'look into the whys an' wherefores. Just into whether or not a line has been crossed. Any mitigating circumstances are dealt with by whoever presides. They'd normally be put forward by a defendant's legal representation an' then taken into consideration by a magistrate or judge at the time o' sentencing. It's just the way it is. It's the law."

"So we all might have t'go t'court? To testify?"

"I'll be honest with ya fella, I've never had t'deal with anything like this before; I don't think any of us have. So it's hard t'say what the next steps are going t'be, but if I were a gambling man, my money would likely be on it not going much further. I think if you'd have come to any harm as a child things might get looked at differently because ultimately, legally speaking that is, *you are or were,* the victim of a crime. As y'didn't an' if I'm t'guess at it, yer unlikely to uphold or help us with any complaint about yer abduction, which means it'll be expensive an' time consuming with nothing t'be gained by pursuing it. But don't quote me on that. I'm surmising, I don't know anything for sure."

Robbie wasn't sure, but it seemed to him as if Radley had just dropped a massive hint; basically, don't give too much away with regards to his own abduction, and they won't have enough to go on for a prosecution. Police Scotland were likely to be scratching their heads anyway, wondering how the hell to take a case like this forward. They were probably hoping they didn't have to as much as he was.

Radley finished his pint and got up to go order another, he asked Robbie if he wanted one too. When he came back to the table with their drinks, he was carrying a bag of crisps and a packet of dry roasted nuts between his teeth too. Once he'd sat back down he ripped the two bags open and tipped the nuts onto the crisps, telling Robbie to help himself. He took a swig from his fresh pint before asking him about his own mind set.

"Thing is, I can understand that ya'd be curious as t'where y'came from an' all. I mean, that's not going t'be any different to anyone else who's been adopted I suppose. But what I don't get, is why yer so het up about yer father's family. Why are y'so insistent on following all that up? Why's it matter t'ya so much? Especially seeing as it appears to have caused ya such grief with yer wife."

Robbie smiled as he thought about it. "It's funny, but I remember Dredger, Gregor Scoular, warning me off chasing things up. He told me no good would come of it an' that instead o' getting any answers t'my questions, I'd just get more questions. An' d'ya know what? He were right. That old bugger knew what were what.

"I can't explain it to ya. Only in so much as…I just need t'know. The more I've found out about Eban Whithorn, the more I've needed t'know. I only started following the lead Dredger had left, thinking I'd find out about him before he went to the Isle o' Stennoch. I'd learned that he'd been married before, that I had an older half-brother an' sister. But when I looked for them I ended up in Ireland with Jacob Whithorn filling in some o' the blanks. I found out that Eban's marriage t'my mother had been bigamous for a start, so technically, I'm illegitimate. I found out that Eban wasn't a Whithorn by birth, he'd been adopted. But then all these elements of mental illness seemed t'be dripping through the generations o' the family that he truly belonged to. Then from him t'my half-brother, Martin, an' now Martin's son, Kester."

"I think y'getting carried away Robbie, y'letting yerself get blinded by scion fella."

"By what?"

"Scion; s…c…i…o…n. silent 'c'. It's generally a botanical term, it's when traits are passed down to the offshoots o' the original plant."

"Right. I suppose so then. Anyway, it scared the shit out o' me, I can't help thinking I might be like that too. What if that madness, that depravity's inside me too? An' now Lynsey's expecting, I'm terrified my baby's going t'be affected. I know I sound paranoid, but I need t'know, even though she hates me for it, I can't give it up 'til I know. An' t'be honest, even that scares me shitless, the fact that I know I've got so obsessed by it all, but I still can't stop. Why can't I? Am I proving myself t'be a head-case after all? I don't know."

"Where does Yoker come into it then?"

"What?"

"You asked t'be dropped off at Yoker earlier. Why there?"

"Oh right. When I saw Jacob Whithorn, he told me that Eban had been adopted from an orphanage when he were about four or five I think. Anyway, he were in the orphanage because he'd been born to a young lass who were an inmate in a lunatic asylum. I've tried getting into his adoption records, but they're sealed. The guy at the records office told me I'd have to apply to the Sheriff in the district the adoption took place."

Radley laughed. "Pfft, good luck with that then. Ya've no chance Robbie; they'll not let y'see those. It's all data protected stuff."

"Yeh well, I needed t'give it a go. But anyhow, I knew his mother were called Martha Richards. That guy said if I came t'the archives here in Glasgow, that there might be something about her in old newspapers, an' there was. It said she came from Yoker."

"What else did it say?"

"That she weren't right in the head. She ended up in Glasgow Royal Mental Hospital, but a woman in the library told me that doesn't exist anymore; it turned into the Gartnaval General an' the whole place got rebuilt or something."

Radley sat back in his seat, rubbing his chin between his thumb and fingers as if he were giving great thought to something. "Fact is fella, yer never going t'get access to yer old man's adoption stuff. Why did y'want it anyway?"

"T'find out more about her, where she came from, why she were in the loony bin, that sort o' thing."

"Okay, well I reckon adoption records are an avenue that's closed to ya. There's other ways o' finding out about her y'know."

"How?"

"Leave it with me Rob, I'll have a think."

Robbie's heart suddenly lifted again. "Are y'going to help me? How?"

"Like I said, leave it with me. I'm making no promises, but I'll have a think about it."

***

A silver Ford Mondeo pulled up on Coalpots Road in Girvan, on the Ayrshire coast, opposite the driveway of St Ninian's nursing home for retired clergy. It was getting dark now and the occupant of the car decided against going in given the time. There was no rush. Waiting a while longer wouldn't be too much of a hassle. He'd just come through a roundabout with the sculpture of a boat in the middle of it, and written into the side it had read 'Whit's yer hurry?' which seemed an omen if nothing else.

The map on the built in satnav seemed to show that there was a fair bit of open countryside once he went a mile or so further on the road. He decided to find somewhere quiet to pull off the road and spend the night in the car. He soon came across a dirt track that looked to lead into some woods, so he followed it in for a quarter of a mile, then pulled off that and into a wooded area where he knocked off the headlights.

He got out of the car and walked round to the boot and opened it. The smell of vomit hit him straight away. "Fucking hell Maddie, ya dirty wee bitch!"

She looked pale and was crying for her mother again. Kester resented having to bring her, but felt he'd no choice. He needed to ensure her mother's compliance and the only way he could, was by bringing the brat with him.

"Daddy…" she cried.

"Shut the fuck up! Don't call me that!" He lifted her out and told her to take a drink of water from the bottle he gave her. She did so, sniffling the whole time. "Now go an' have a piss!"

"What?"

Christ, how the fuck anyone put up with these wee pains in the arse, was beyond him. "A pee, a wee-wee. Just go tae the fucking toilet!"

"Where toilet?"

"There isn't one. We're in the middle o' nowhere, ya'll have tae crouch down an' pee over there, behind that tree."

Poor Maddie began to cry. "I'm scared, I want my mummy."

"She's no' fucking here. Now go an' pee!" he yelled at her. She flinched as he raised his hand as if to smack her, and ran behind the tree like she'd been told to.

Kester wondered if Lena had managed to raise the alarm yet. He'd left her tied up on her bed with no way of getting free without help. Even if she could get her hands free, she couldn't phone for help because he had her phone. The duct tape over her mouth would take some shifting and the tape and cable ties he'd used to lock her firmly to her bed frame could only be cut off. No, she wouldn't have got out very easily. Though that didn't rule out that she could be found by someone else but he was willing to take his chances. He needed to think of what to do with this kid though, and fast,

because he wanted rid. She was in the way and she was
a pain in the arse. She'd have to go.

Chapter Twenty-Seven

One of the cleaners had left the front door to St Ninian's propped open while he loaded some boxes into the back of the small van that was parked outside. He didn't notice Kester slip through the doorway while his back was turned. Nor did Dieter Richter notice the intruder as he was heading towards the resident lounge, ready to brief the day staff on the previous night's events. The only person who did see Kester was some mad old bat who came out of the room just beside the stairs as Kester had been about to ascend them.

"Oh hello there Bertie, back from manoeuvres I see?" he called out to him.

Kester wondered what the hell he was on about, and was about to tell him where to get off, but then decided that to go with it might be more effective. He ducked down and lowered his tone to a virtual whisper. "Come here," he gestured to the old man. "I'm still on manoeuvres," he glanced around himself as he spoke, as if suspicious of his surroundings. "Top secret mission ya see. Ya mustnae tell a soul ya've seen me, d'ya understand? Lives are in peril."

The old man suddenly looked both scared and exhilarated. "Oh, oh I see," he mimicked Kester's whisper. "Yes, I understand. Mum's the word. Shhh!" He tapped the side of his nose with a finger and winked.

"Maybe *you* could assist me in a matter of national security?"

"Oh, yes, yes I can. What do you need Sir?"

This was like taking candy from a baby. "We have intelligence that a chap known as Reverend Eban Whithorn is an undercover enemy agent. D'ya know him?"

"Damn an' blast it! Right under our very noses…" the indignant response was too loud.

"Shhh, keep it down. D'ya know where he is?"

"I'll take you there myself Sir." The old chap was
incensed to think that an enemy spy was among them.

"No, no need, it's too dangerous. Just tell me where
he is an' let me deal with the blighter, okay?"

"Understood, very well." He gestured up the stairs.
"Top of here, left, third door on the left."

"Right."

"No, no, left."

"Aye, o' course, silly me. I'll be sure tae let the
powers that be know what a service tae yer country
ya've been. Now, yer tae forget ya ever saw me
Remember, tell no-one."

He took the steps two at a time. They were quite
wide as this seemed to be some kind of converted manor
house, so these would have been the main stairs. It was
an impressive building, plenty of original features.
Kester considered that if he managed to keep himself out
of jail, that he might return one day and steal some of

these things. The wood panelling alone must be worth a fortune, not to mention the original fire surrounds; it was a gold mine.

Outside the third door on the left he hesitated, listening to see if he could hear any voices coming from inside his grandfather's room. He'd never been here before; he'd never met his grandfather. But it was his grandfather at the root of all this ill will. It was his grandfather and that bastard Michael he saw whenever he remembered the sight of his dad swinging by his neck, dead. And it was high time his grandfather saw him in the flesh. He pushed the handle down and slowly opened the door.

Eban was sitting in a wheel chair in front of a table by the bay window. He was slumped to one side, just staring out towards the sea in the distance. Kester closed the door behind himself.

"Morning," he called. There was no response, so he walked slowly over towards the old man. He noticed the photographs on the side. Unbeknown to him, they were the same ones that Robbie had first seen the previous year. Mona, various others and an old one of Eban as a boy with his adopted parents and siblings. But there were none with Kester's grandmother in them, none of Maev or Elizabeth, none of his dad, Martin. As if they'd never existed. The rage began to rise in him. He picked up Mona's photograph, put it gently on the floor, then crushed it with the heel of his boot. Though the noise wasn't very loud, it was enough to draw the old man's attention. He'd barely moved at all, Kester wasn't even sure if he was capable of movement, but his eyes had fixed on him and his nostrils flared slightly.

Kester sat at the table within Eban's eye line. "So, yer the old fucker responsible for all this shite are ya? Responsible for fucking up everyone's life, for ditching yer kids, replacing them, for killing my dad, your son…responsible for me you old cunt!" It was taking everything he had to stay calm, to keep the volume to a minimum, when all he wanted to do was to bounce this old bastard off the walls.

That familiar expression of contempt crossed Eban's brow. But for the grey hair and withered features, these two men could be the same person: both nasty, contemptuous, self-absorbed monsters. Kester leant in towards Eban.

"Aye, you know me now don't ya? You know yer own blood when ya see it. Well let me tell ya something old man. Take a really good look at my face, because my face is the last one ya'll ever see. I bet ya've spent yer time wasting away in here wishing death'd come an' grab ya by the balls. Well today's yer lucky day ya fucked up old bastard, because today's the day yer going tae die an' I promise ya this, it'll no' be painless."

Kester normally thrived on the look of fear he'd get from the people he threatened, but the distinct lack of it in Eban's face really got to him. His rage just escalated in a heartbeat. He lunged forward and tipped Eban backward onto the floor, then knelt with one knee on his chest, just enough that he began to struggle for breath. He could breathe, but not quite enough and the appearance of desperation it caused invigorated Kester.

Just when Eban looked like he might pass out, he released him then he'd do it again. This went on five or six times. He noticed the catheter bag strapped to Eban's leg, so he pulled on the tube. Eban made a strange noise, no doubt expressing pain of some sort. Kester then unstrapped the bag and emptied the urine contents all over Eban's head and face. The old man coughed as he tried not to choke.

Kester got up and walked over to the bed where he took a pillow from it before walking back. He put the pillow on top of the table then bent down over Eban again, placing his hands firmly around his wizened throat and squeezed.

Eban's feeble body found a little more strength as his dying brain fought for life, causing him to jerk and thrash under Kester's grip. His grandson released his grip, just before it was too late. He allowed Eban to recover some gasps before doing it all over again, and then boredom hit him, so he reached up for the pillow and placed it hard over Eban's face, holding it there. He looked around the room, admiring the fixtures and fittings and wondering on the value they'd hold, all the while pressing the pillow harder and harder into his grandfather's face. Even once the bodily jerking had stopped and the old man lay still under the hands of the young, he maintained his grip on the pillow. He had to be sure; he needed to know that he wasn't going to have to come back here again to finish the job.

Finally satisfied, he removed the pillow and looked down into the wide-eyed, desperate face. Mouth open and faced cyanosed, blue around the lips and grey in skin tone, the whites of his eyes all blood shot, he reminded Kester of his dad and how he'd looked, hanging there dead, though admittedly his dad's face was more purple than blue and his eyes were bulging slightly. He ran his fingers down the side of Eban's face and onto his neck; he pushed them in, feeling for a pulse but there was none. Job done.

He took his time, washed his hands in the sink, walked around the room drying his hands on the towel as he did so. He dropped the towel on top of the table then began opening cupboards and drawers, looking for anything of interest or value. He even stepped over Eban's lifeless body a couple of times as he searched.

Some men's jewellery and a small amount of cash were the only things he came across as he headed towards the door, pausing for one last look back at the dead man on the floor. The pathetic creature who had been the all-consuming force that had driven his dad's paranoia, had been the cause of all the vitriol spouted by his grandmother. The nasty, venomous man who'd taken pleasure from the pain he'd caused. Well now it was Kester taking pleasure. He got such a buzz from being the one to finally end the days of Eban Whithorn, though he'd been surprised that no-one had got there before him and a little annoyed with himself for leaving it so long. One down, one to go; anyone else would be collateral damage.

Exiting the building had been even easier than entering it. There were a few cars outside, staff probably for the most part anyway. He found himself back out on Coalpots Road in a matter of minutes, still buzzing. Now all he needed to do was to get himself back to the car and deal with the kid, before moving on. She did nothing but snivel and whine for Lena and he was fast losing patience. She'd served her purpose and she'd have to go.

Jumping back into the Mondeo, he drove down the road and turned up the same dirt track he'd spent the night at. He pulled into a small layby that led to a farm gate. He got out and walked round to the boot, but just as he was about to open it, a Springer Spaniel appeared at his side, sniffing round his legs, jumping up at him and wagging its tail furiously.

"Jake!" a woman's voice called. As she got closer the dog ran back to her. "Sorry," she apologised to Kester, "he's only young an' he's no' learned his manners yet."

"Nae bother," Kester nodded as she carried on her way, relieved that she hadn't appeared a moment later when he already had the brat out of the boot.

He gave her plenty of time to be well out of the way and to check there were no other dog walkers around, then opened the boot and lifted Maddie out. She'd cried that much that she was exhausted, probably dehydrated too. She wasn't complaining any more, which was a relief, and just let him lift her over the farm gate and carry her down the bottom edge of the field into the woods.

***

Mick Simons pulled the car to a halt on Dumbarton Road, just outside Yoker Parish Church, an old, red stone church with a huge arched window. He pointed across the road to a row of shops. "That one there, the red one, a news agents now by the look of it. According tae the old newspaper article ya showed me Robbie, that's what used tae be Murray's Grocers, the one Martha Richards was caught stealing from."

It was difficult to imagine it in days gone by, now that there was a traffic light junction close by with lots of traffic moving in all directions. But back then, in the war years, it would've looked different no doubt.

"I'll drive us round tae the road that was given as her address if ya like, but like I told ya this morning, those old terraces have been demolished years ago. I think it's some industrial units there now."

Radley didn't seem as patient as his younger colleague though. "I don't get why coming here's important Rob; there's nothing left here t'give ya any clues." He turned to Simons. "What about that contact y'spoke about before? Have ya heard back?"

"What contact?" Robbie was intrigued.

Simons seemed a little uncomfortable about it. "I know someone that's all. I didnae want tae say anything just yet, in case there was a problem. But I'd been chatting with this mate o' mine on the force, he said he might be able tae do me a favour."

"What favour?"

"He can get access tae records from the archives, as long as there's nothing too sensitive. He said he'd have a look."

Robbie's heart missed a beat or two at the thought that he might be able to learn more. Simons explained that he was just waiting for his mate to call him back and let him know if there was anything worth seeing.

They headed back towards Glasgow centre and had just discussed stopping off at a café or something for a late breakfast, when Simons' phone began ringing. He pressed the button on his headset and began speaking.

"Hello. Hiya Ben, aye, yep. Oh really? Aye that's great. What time? Right. Listen Ben thanks for this, I owe ya. Ha, aye okay…"

If it wasn't for his seatbelt holding him in place, Robbie might have been on the edge of his seat in anticipation. Was this the call Simons had been waiting for or was it just a random friend organising a night out and a game of pool or something? "Was that the mate y'mentioned?"

"Aye it was. Change o' plan; we're heading up tae the Gartnaval General Hospital instead now, the GGH."

It didn't take long to cross Glasgow and arrive at the GGH. Rush hour was over now, so the traffic had calmed down a lot. As Simons indicated to turn into the hospital grounds, Robbie felt a little bemused. It was a huge place, but very modern looking, just like the woman in the library had told him it would be. She'd said the old mental hospital had been taken over by the Gartnaval, that there was nothing left of the old place and judging by what he could see, she was right. He said as much to DC Simons.

"I can't say as I blame her for telling ya that Robbie, I've lived in Glasgow my whole life an' would o' told ya the same 'til now." He continued along the driveway around the front of the vast building, but then carried on around the side where there were various out buildings as the drive seemed to narrow and dip downhill a little. It wound round a couple of shrub-lined bends before opening out again slightly to reveal an, almost as vast, old Victorian building, much of which had scaffolding around it with boarded up windows, but one side appeared to be in use. They drove around into what looked like an old courtyard of some sort. To one side of them was the back of the disused part which looked to have two, bricked up archways, old stables maybe. But the other side, which was the back of the section still in use, had a set of four stone steps leading up to green, double doors with a sign to the right which read: *Estates and central workshops* at the top, then at the bottom, *Medical Records and Archives.*

Radley was taken aback. "Bloody hell, even though this place is huge, ya'd never know it even existed from the road would ya?"

Simons agreed as he explained why they were there. "My mate Ben, the guy I mentioned, well when he looked into this for me, he realised he knew someone who works in the records department here, a John Ward. When he spoke t'the guy, it turns out that his Aunties an' his old mum all worked here when it were still the mental hospital.

"He's going tae see what strings he can pull with regard tae seeing some o' Martha's old notes, but he's apparently brought the old girls intae work today. Apparently they'd be happy tae talk tae ya about the old place, what it was like, that sortae thing."

This was great as far as Robbie was concerned. Although the old birds might not know much that'd be useful, they'd be able to help him understand at least. Radley however seemed a little more dubious. He frowned at Simons. "Does yer DI know about this? Does DI Saggers at know? Yer stretching it a bit lad, getting unauthorised access t'stuff like this."

Simons looked a little sheepish. "Er...no, not exactly. But if we had tae go through all the correct channels then Robbie might never know."

The thought that Radley was trying to put the kybosh on it now, left Robbie with a sense of desperation. "Oh come on…y'can't let me get here, get this close an' then just throw a spanner in."

Radley clearly wasn't happy about it, but he had agreed to help Robbie in his search for the facts, in return for Robbie's compliance in finding Kester. He reluctantly agreed, but made both Robbie and DC Simons swear that they'd never reveal his presence if any complaints were made.

"Okay, but I was never here, d'ya understand?"

They both agreed to not even introduce him as a police officer once inside. He was happy with that and so joined them as they got out of the car.

Chapter Twenty-Eight

John Ward looked to be a lot older than any of them
had probably expected. He explained that he was
already semi-retired and was only planning on staying
for another six months before retiring completely. He
took them around to what looked like some kind of staff
canteen, though it was only small and had vending
machines in place of proper food: one for hot drinks, one
for cold, one that dispensed pre-packed sandwiches and
another with crisps and chocolate inside. There were
only half a dozen small tables there, one of which was
currently occupied by two elderly women, one in a
wheel chair and the other with a walking stick resting
against the table next to her.

John took them over to the two women. "These are
my Aunties," he said. Pointing to the wheel chair bound
lady, he introduced her. "This is My Aunty Wendy,

Wendy Towers. And this is my Aunty Karen Durkin.
My mum Susan's in a home now, she doesn't really get
out at all now ya see. She's no' got many of her
faculties left any more tae be honest, no' like these two.
Still going strong aren't ya Aunty Karen? Sharp as a
tack!"

She chuckled. "Och aye." She nudged her sister.
"There's no flies on us now is there Wendy? I say
there's no flies on us," she raised her voice a little as she
repeated herself. It seemed Wendy was a little hard of
hearing.

Old Wendy just smiled, nodding her head in
agreement. Karen continued. "We all worked here back
in the day though, all three of us ya know. Och it was a
harsh time some of it, but it was lovely too. Me an' my
sister here, we often talk o' those times. We talk of it
when we visit our Susan too, but she's no' in her right
mind now ya see; I don't think she remembers so much
anymore." She rocked back slightly and laughed.
"She'd certainly have qualified to live on the dementia

wards here eh? Good job it's no' an option now. Imagine that."

John looked a little embarrassed by her 'too much information' stance. "My er...my mother's no' quite as sprightly as her sisters here," he smiled.

Robbie decided to take the lead; he smiled and held out his hand to shake. "I'm Robbie an' these are my friends, Chris an' Mick. We've been doing a bit of a family tree, an' I think I might have a relative that used t'be a patient here."

Wendy, who so far hadn't really said anything, suddenly straightened herself in her chair. "Well yer no' a local boy are ya? Ya sound English tae me; och my Frank hated the English ya know."

Poor John flushed the colour of a beetroot. "I'm so sorry, there's no holds barred sometimes with old folk is there? Ya know how it is."

If anything, Robbie found the two ladies amusing. He thought it was so funny that she would just come out with a comment like that without a care in the world; he liked her. He took the seat next to her. "Well, we're not all so bad, honest," he smiled.

She smiled back at him and laughed. "Now don't *you* be flirting with me young man. I can see by the ring on yer hand there that yer already taken. Besides…I'm outae yer league."

They all laughed as poor John walked away embarrassed, "I'll be back in a wee while tae let ya see what I've been able tae dig out."

"Who's yer relative?" Karen asked.

"She were called Martha Richards. She came here in the early forties."

Old Karen pulled down the corners of her mouth in thought. "Martha Richards, Martha Richards…what was wrong with her?"

"She had problems, she'd stolen things an' attacked people, police officers. She'd been t'court for those kind o' things, but I think she stabbed someone the last time, an' she'd been living rough. She were only young when they brought her here, fifteen. She were pregnant too by all accounts."

"Martha Richards, Wendy. D'ya remember her?" Karen said in a raised tone so her sister would hear her. Wendy shook her head, but explained that Susan would've been the sister working there in the early forties; Wendy and Karen hadn't started there until later in that decade.

They went on to chat about how life had been in the institution back then, the laughs they'd had, the sadness they'd witnessed. Some of the patients they *did* remember fondly and some not so. They giggled to each other as they recounted the day the 'dishy doctor' had started work there and how all the nurses swooned in his presence. This chatter went on for about twenty minutes before their nephew, John, returned carrying a box file.

He pulled one of the other tables up to join them, giving himself enough space to place it down in front of himself as he sat with them. "It seems she was admitted tae here in nineteen forty-two an' remained 'til the facility closed in eighty-eight. She was then transferred tae one o' the new, smaller facilities for three years before moving tae a mental health unit outside o' the city."

Robbie couldn't help but feel a little pity. "So she was never released? She never got out?"

"No, indeed looking at her notes, I don't think she was ever well enough tae leave. She only died a few years ago though son. Two-thousand an' nine, she was eighty-two; died of a..." he read the words slowly so as not to mispronounce any of them, "catastrophic cerebral vascular attack it says. That's a stroke I think." He dug around in the box file. There were various things there as well as the expected official documentation. Several, child-like drawings were piled together, the name 'Martha' written at the bottom in crayon, as if scrawled by an uncoordinated five year old and not the adult that she would have been by then.

Radley seemed a little overwhelmed. "Good lord, isn't it sad?"

John found three black and white photographs in amongst everything else in there. He took them out and examined them; two were group photographs and one was of the same pathetic face that Robbie had seen previously.

Wendy reached across and took them from him. "Let me see."

The sisters spread them on the table and looked closely at the two group photos for a minute or so. Karen suddenly called out and started jabbing her finger onto one of them. "That's our Susan there," she was pointing at one of the nurses at the edge of the group, "an' that's me; look, in the middle o' the back row, that's me."

She scanned the other group photo and gave names to some of the nursing staff pictured, before looking back at the first. She ran her finger along the faces in the front row before stopping at one. "Ah, Mad Martha, I remember her now." She took the third picture and held it up. "Aye, it's wee Martha, look Wendy, d'ya remember her? She were only a tiny wee thing, but feisty as a lion, ya remember her don't ya Wendy? She were the one that took Sister McTeel's eye out when she stabbed her in the face with a fork. Took four big orderlies tae hold her down for sedation. D'ya remember Wendy?"

"Aye, I do now ya've said that. She were a real nasty piece o' work though."

"Who? Martha?"

"No, Sister McTeel. I'm no' surprised one o' them went for her. She were terrifying when she'd a mind tae be. She'd wallop the nurses as easily as she would the inmates. Horrible woman."

Robbie looked more closely at the photographs. They were right; it was Martha. He recognised her from the photograph he'd already seen. She had the same sullen expression, though he wondered now if it might actually be a sedated expression on her face, given what the sisters had just mentioned.

Karen continued. "This is one o' the secure unit groups. They were the ones deemed as criminally insane, violent an' unpredictable a lot o'them. I remember escorting Martha for her electric shock therapies just after I started work here, but that all stopped after her leucotomy."

Radley cringed at the thought of the barbarity that was considered normal practice in those days. "Christ, that's awful."

DC Simons hadn't said much at all until then. "What's that, leucotomy?"

John Ward decided he'd be the one to give the young man a history lesson. "It's what ya might've heard termed as a front lobotomy."

"Euw, d'ya mean where they drilled intae their skulls?"

"Aye. The surgeon would cut in here," he pressed his index finger into the upper temple area on the left side of Simons' head, "once the skin was pulled back, they'd drill a section out, so as they could get at the pre-frontal lobe. The idea was tae sever the nerve pathways so the patient would be calmer, easier tae manage. It had some nasty side effects though an' that's why they don't do it any more; it's pretty archaic now. But it was in its heyday at the time Robbie's relative would've been admitted."

Robbie looked back at the two elderly sisters. "An' Martha definitely had this done to her?"

"Oh aye, right enough she did. There were this German doctor used tae perform the surgeries. He were some old colleague o' the Superintendent I think. They'd worked together in Germany before they'd fled Europe an' the Nazis. The inmates'd be taken tae theatre at the infirmary an' he'd operate there. Then they'd be brought back the next day tae recover. He'd sometimes do a couple a day, but he was only ever around for a week or two, once a year. I think he travelled around the country performing the procedure. So when he came tae Glasgow, he'd do a job lot."

Wendy looked saddened by the memory. "Some o' them were never the same afterwards ya know. Yer Martha was one, she'd sealed her own fate when she attacked Sister McTeel. Och she'd given her such a skelping with a leather belt, had her in the corner, well the girl just flipped, had a sparey an' grabbed the fork. But that was enough for her tae get herself on the list for the next time the German came round."

John explained that many of the inmates who had undergone the leucotomy procedure had been left with permanent deficit. None had died, and while one or two had shown some improvement afterwards, the rest had been left almost zombie-like. The surgeon, Mr Werner, had been one of the most revered neurosurgeons of his time and given that he was a German in the United Kingdom during what was at the time the post-war years, the psychiatric societies felt very privileged to have access to him and followed his lead enthusiastically. And so for six years, from nineteen forty-four until nineteen fifty, the Glasgow Royal Mental Hospital had put dozens if not hundreds of its inmates into his hands for the 'cure'. Martha, unfortunately had been among them. In early nineteen fifty, the Doctor Superintendent of the institute changed, and the new man in charge stopped any more from being subjected to leucotomies. He was more in favour of drug therapies and electric shock treatments.

"How was Martha effected?" DS Simons seemed horrified.

Karen piped up. "Well she couldnae hold her pee again, an' she never spoke after that, not a word as I recall. Can *you* remember her talking after that operation she had Wendy?"

The old girl shook her head. "No, I don't think I can, but I'd no' swear tae it mind. None o' them were right after seeing Mr Werner, no' just her. Ya'd tae feed them, cut their food for them, wash them, dress them. Och they'd been quieted alright, but dear god what a price they'd paid."

"Aye, it was like they'd been disconnected from their souls; lights on but no-one home. D'ya know what I mean?"

Unfortunately, they all did. Robbie wanted to know more about his Grandmother's admission. He asked John if there'd be anything in among the box file he had.

"Aye, I do have her admission report in here an' some o' what looks like assessment reports by Dr Hellmich; he was the Superintendent here at the time. I can't hand them over or give ya copies I'm afraid, but I'm happy for ya tae take a look." He handed the first of seven papers to Robbie. He skipped past the usual patient information notes at the top and began reading the doctor's report on her initial assessment upon arrival at the facility. Wincing at some of the more brutal language, which was no doubt acceptable back then.

The patient is very mal-nourished and dirty in appearance. She spits, screams and bites anyone who gets within striking distance and she is clearly imbecilic and retarded in intelligence. I needed the assistance of

*three orderlies and a nurse in order to have the girl
stripped and examined for lesions, lice or any signs of
venereal disease. She was negative for lice, but had
various sores on her body, some of which were infected
and requiring treatment. Among these sores were many
injury sites in various states of healing and she also had
a strong, odorous, vaginal discharge leading me to
suspect that gonorrhoea were present. An internal
examination was nigh on impossible as the patient
fought and screamed threats to kill throughout, but I was
able to establish at this point that she was approximately
at four to five months gestation, the foetus being very
small and barely noticeable to look, but could be felt
clearly. The foetal heartbeat could be heard on
auscultation and normal movements felt.*

*The patient was taken from this point to the wash
rooms where she was scrubbed with antiseptic soap.
According to Sister McTeel, the girl's hair was so badly
matted that there was no other option than to have her
held down and it shaved off completely.*

On her return to my office, though cleaner in appearance, the patient was less than grateful for the help she'd received. The cuts to her scalp were explained by the difficulty the nurses had encountered on shaving her head, some small patches of hair were still present due to the same problem. Sister McTeel had been unable to remove the pubic hair as requested but assured me of the patient's cleanliness.

A more thorough psychological assessment will be scheduled in a week's time.

Robbie didn't know what to say as he handed the report on to Chris Radley so that he could read it. DC Simons got up to stand behind Radley so that he could read it over his shoulder.

Robbie asked to see the next report. John smiled sympathetically as he handed it over.

Given the deeds and behaviours of this patient, it has been difficult to come to any concrete conclusions with regard to a diagnosis of her condition. She has in this past week since our last meeting, had two sessions of electric shock therapy. Though she is still what I would deem as 'a danger', she is definitely calmer in her manner than she was previously.

She remained strapped in the chair throughout my consultation with her, but did respond in part to some of my questions. When asked her name for instance, she responded. She told me of her family, which I believe to have once consisted of her parents, three older brothers and herself. She tells me that she has no recollection of her mother in recent years and no clue as to her whereabouts. Her manner is very child-like and she talks in phrases more usual of a child of six or seven years, rather than fifteen. For instance when describing her father she stated that he was 'a bad man what got hanged for doing a bad thing to some folks'. The police report that came with her had indicated to her father having been a dock worker, but a quite unpleasant character who had been found guilty of a double murder for which he had been executed by hanging some months previously.

She described how she had been living rough on the streets and alleys of Yoker since his death, that her brother had thrown her out. She tells of some kindnesses, but for the most part it seems she has very much had to be self-preserving.

One wonders, given the clear mental vulnerability of the patient, what sort of man would take advantage of her, leaving her with a child inside her that she would have no clue as to what to do with or how to take care of. She seems at this point, completely oblivious to the fact that in a few short months, she will give birth to a baby.

She displays outbursts of a paranoid nature, jumping suddenly and going into what can only be described as a panicked state. She rages when attempts are made to calm her down. It is for these initial observations that I believe the patient to be suffering from a form of paranoid schizophrenia, on top of which, I don't believe her mental age to be above that of a child of seven.

I have no clue as to how her family have managed her until her father's execution, but I have serious doubts as to the effectiveness of any such methods they may have used, given the amount of old injuries on her body that I saw on her arrival, I doubt very much that great care of her needs has taken place at any point in the past.

These reports made for uncomfortable reading as Robbie passed them one by one onto Radley and Simons. It would be bad enough to have to see this about a stranger, without knowing that this was the life of his own paternal grandmother. He was silent as he read through the other reports, occasionally sighing heavily. He noticed that the reports were being passed from Radley to the sisters, who were both weeping quietly as they read them. He caught a glimpse of Karen passing a hankie to Wendy while neither of them shifted their gaze away from the words they were locked on.

The last report left in the first file of seven made for equally tough reading. It had been written a short time after Martha had given birth and had contained something both revealing and disgusting. Martha had obviously built up a bit of a relationship with one of her nurses by this point and Dr Hellmich had obviously used this relationship to learn more about her. It seemed the nurse had a way of putting Martha at ease better than most and was able to subtly question her without inducing violent outbursts. In this report, the doctor was clearly reporting what he had witnessed as well as his opinions on what he'd learned.

The patient gave birth some five days ago now. She was not only delivered of a son, but there was the remains of a second foetus which had clearly not developed as it should and must have been dead inside of her for some months. This twin foetus was in some state of decay and may account for the patient not responding as well as expected to treatments given for infection. The fact that the second foetus went on to develop and survive is something short of a miracle in my opinion. The live infant is of a premature nature, but has maintained and I'm told is thriving. The patient is clearly unconnected to the child and shows no interest in him. The terror she suffered during the birthing process may have some bearing on this, and she won't tolerate the baby to suckle. She has been deemed unable to function as an adequate mother and so the decision has been made to hand the child over to the Sisters of Charity of St Vincent de Paul at Smyllum Park Orphanage in Lanark, next week.

During the labour the patient would only allow Nurse Malloy to attend to her. She has built up a communication with Nurse Malloy and seems to be in wonder of her strong Irish accent. The nurse has been in a position to discuss things with the patient that have so far eluded me. I asked Malloy to make endeavours to find out what she could from the patient with regard to her life prior to her incarceration here. The following is an account of the things told to Malloy over several weeks:

When asked about her mother, the patient had said that her mother had gone. She had little memory of her and couldn't account for where her mother had gone; she had no idea if her mother still lived or not. She told that she lived in a house with her father and big brothers. One went to jail, one went to sea and she had spent the last few years living with the remaining brother and their father.

When asked how it had come to be that she had become pregnant, Martha had no idea of the concept. Nurse Malloy explained that in order to have got a baby inside of her that she must have laid down with a man. The girl's reply caused much distress to Malloy who hails from a good Catholic family and she had to make her excuses and defer to me for advice.

It seems that the patient disclosed that she had done nothing bad and had only laid down with her father or her brothers and that she was a good girl 'because daddy said'. She told that sometimes she lay with some other men whose names she didn't know, but that it was allowed because her father knew of it and would buy her a bun from Mr Murray's if she were a good girl. She also told my nurse that she had 'done the pain' before, referring to giving birth, but that the 'thing' hadn't moved or made any noise last time.

I am horrified to think that this patient, a mere child herself, has been abused in such a despicable manner. It is clear to me that this patient has been used for intercourse by the men of her own family and occasionally rented out to other men by her father for his monetary gain. The living infant now in our care is very likely the result of an incestuous union, though which of the male family members is responsible for this may never be known. The father would still have had access to her at the time of conception, though two of her brothers would also, the older one being on shore leave. It is not clear if the eldest brother had abused her as he has been gone from the family, serving a life sentence in jail for several years. But the patient was unable to recall a time where she didn't 'lay down' for any of them, indeed she seems totally unaware that this is anything less than normal. Which leads me to believe that this has occurred for most of her life as she has clearly never know it to be different.

Robbie couldn't bring himself to read any further. He felt sick. Eban, his father was, for want of a better phrase, inbred in the most appalling way.

John could see his discomfort and asked sympathetically if he would like to see the later reports. He offered to read them out, most of which were much the same as each other: Martha had spat at an orderly, Martha had attacked another patient, Martha had tried to climb onto the roof, until eventually, Martha, having been caught disrobing in the dining area, was punished by Sister McTeel for her lewd behaviour. She then grabbed a fork and attacked McTeel, stabbing her first in the arms and then twice in her face, resulting in irreparable damage to the right eye and permanent scarring. This was the point that it was decided that 'for her own safety' she be put forward for a leucotomy procedure upon Mr Werner's next visit to Glasgow the following month.

John went on to summarise the remaining reports of assessments that had been done following Martha's surgery. "This one's from straight after, when she were first returned here. It pretty much states that the surgery went well an' that she made a good recovery. It states that she was incontinent of urine on her return, but that this was a common side effect which was usually transitory. He says that she didn't speak an' wouldn't make eye contact with him.

"The others are much the same. It looks as if she were only ever reassessed twice a year thereafter. Dr Hellmich retired a few years after that, but the remaining reports on her seem tae indicate that these so called *transitory* side effects remained. Her daily care included her having tae be changed frequently, wearing things for incontinence etcetera. It seems my Aunties are right, she never uttered a word afterwards. Even in these reports from the other facilities she lived in, they're all much of a muchness. She'd get up an' walk with a nurse if held an' instructed tae do so, she'd sit in a chair if physically encouraged an' instructed tae do so, but she couldn't feed herself or dress without assistance any more.

"It's very sad Robbie, I'm sure ya didn't want tae be hearing this sort o' thing about yer relative. But I can assure ya that this last place she lived in, the one she spent her final years at, they're brilliant there. I know the treatment she received here was far from ideal, but it was the norm back then. Unfortunately folks like that Sister McTeel were ten a penny then too. They'd no' be allowed near vulnerable folk in this day an' age, but things were different back then. They'd no' the understanding o' mental health that they do now."

Old Wendy put her hand on top of Robbie's and squeezed gently. "I'm sorry for ya son. They were all tragic cases in one form or another back then, no' that it helps ya tae know that," she smiled lifting the mood. "Yer no' so bad for an Englishman." She winked at him which raised a smile on all their faces.

Chapter Twenty-Nine

DC Simons had left the building just before the others in order to take a phone call as his mobile had been ringing incessantly throughout. Robbie thanked John Ward for the time he'd taken with them. "I know ya've bent a few rules today John, so I appreciate it. Ya've been a big help, thank you."

John smiled, a little embarrassed by the gratitude. "I'm just sorry it wasn't a happier tale for ya son."

He showed them back through to the entrance lobby and they headed back out through the green, double doors and into the daylight. Simons was leaning against the car bonnet still on his phone. He ended the call when he saw them coming and beckoned for DS Radley to go over to him. The two of them turned their backs on

Robbie and walked a little away from him, heads together in some sort of conflab.

He took the time to read a dedication encased in a wall cabinet, which explained that the plaque it contained had been rescued from the site of the hospital's pauper graveyard, which ceased usage almost a century previously.

Here lie the feeble dead, side by side
Their tortured minds and sufferings, line after line
Hushed whispers of lives, no longer lived
No weepings at the graveside, seeking to forgive
Two thousand, eight hundred, lunatic souls
Two thousand, eight hundred, who ne'er went home
May they rest in peace now, in God's warm embrace
May they sleep in his arms, with love and with grace

Anon.

How sad, all those people unclaimed and buried in the cold, lonely earth with no-one to mourn them. Robbie hadn't given much thought to what Simons might have wanted, until they turned and walked back towards him with more purpose in their stride. "Get in the car Robbie," Radley instructed.

"What is it?"

"Just get in, I'll fill you in on the way."

"How far's that orphanage in Lanark?" Robbie asked Simons, relying on his local knowledge.

"We need tae go back Robbie, I'm sorry but we've tae go back tae the station. Something's happened."

Robbie glanced quickly in Radley's direction, wanting to know more, worried in case the 'something' had anything to do with Lynsey.

Radley sighed, not too sure how much would be appropriate to disclose at this stage. "Our colleagues in Ayrshire have been called to a murder this morning Robbie."

Robbie wasn't quite catching on. Did they mean that there was a more serious crime they needed to afford their time to or what? Mick Simons noted the confusion in Robbie's face through the rear view mirror. "Ayrshire's the region where Girvan is Robbie. It's where yer father is…he's been found dead this morning by one o' the staff at St Ninian's. He's been murdered."

"Fuck!" The news took Robbie by surprise. He'd been beginning to think that Eban, old and frail as he now was, was pretty much indestructible. "Kester?"

"We think so but we need tae get back tae London Road a.s.a.p. for more information. It seems it's no' just about Eban Whithorn there's…"

"That'll do Simons!" Radley cut him off.

Robbie was even more concerned now. "What? There's what? Y'can't just stop him like that. What else's happened? Tell me."

"It's t'do with Kester Richards, Robbie. It's nothing t'be concerned about for you. Now, we're going t'drop you back at your hotel. There should be a uniformed officer there waiting. Yer t'stay in yer room, d'ya understand me?"

"No. I'm not staying anywhere!"

"Ya'll do what I tell ya fella!"

Robbie was having none of it. "If I'd wanted someone barking orders at me I'd have joined the fucking army! I've done nothing wrong an' I'm not being confined t'quarters again. Now…*d'you* understand me?"

Radley was clearly annoyed by his defiance but knew that Robbie was correct in what he was saying. If he'd a mind to, he could've invented something appropriate to have him arrested on just for the sake of knowing he'd be safe and he'd know where he was, but he couldn't bring himself to. Given all that he'd learned about the man in the short time he'd known him, he'd have felt very cruel adding to his difficulties. "Right then, have it your way! Come back t'the station with us, but y'stay there Robbie. We need t'meet with DI Saggers, so I need t'know ya'll stay where I put ya, okay?"

"Fine."

As soon as they arrived, Robbie was shown into the same interview room he'd been in previously. A uniformed police woman was sent in to 'babysit' him. Robbie thought it a bit ridiculous; she was only about five foot three and slightly built. Unless she was some kind of secret ninja, she'd have no chance of stopping him from leaving. Those thoughts were dispelled quickly when Radley introduced them.

"This is PC Gabrielli. She's not here t'stand guard but if yer going t'bugger off, at least she can let us know, though I'd rather y'waited Robbie, 'til we know what's what at least."

Gabrielli made him a coffee and for the best part of an hour, they chatted about her Italian heritage, her parents meeting, her dad's work, her nonna's favourite pasta recipe and the band she used to be in when she was a student. She was sweet, but he thought his ears might be bleeding by the time the door opened and he was rescued from her.

"Thank you Constable, ya can go now," DI Saggers instructed abruptly, holding the door ajar for the young officer to leave the room. "Thanks for waiting Robbie."

Radley, Simons and two other plain clothed officers walked in. "This is Detective Sergeant Glenn Frobisher an' Detective Constable Carolyn Hames. They're part o' the investigation intae Kester Richards an' I think it's time they met ya an' everyone's brought up tae speed."

Something seemed to be afoot. It was as though the whole search for Kester had gained a new momentum. He'd killed Eban, or at least it looked that way, but there was something more; had they found him?

"Eban's dead isn't he?"

"Indeed," Saggers informed him. "How do ya feel about that Robbie?"

"I don't know. Cheated maybe."

"Why? Would *you* have liked tae have been the one tae kill him?"

He laughed; he didn't really know how to answer her though. "I once stood in his room, last year. I could've done it easily if I'd wanted to."

"What stopped ya?"

He shook his head, a wave of emotion washed over him for the briefest of moments and he worried it might show on his face, unsure of what his answer should be but Radley knew.

"Because yer not like him Robbie, that's what stopped ya."

He was asked to sit down as the DI wanted to inform him of events and see if there was anything he might be able to shed a light on. "No-one's entirely sure how he managed to gain entry, but the manager…"

"Dieter Richter?"

"Aye, well he says that one o' the other residents was talking of a spy living among them, an' how outrageous he found it that someone would have the audacity tae disguise themselves as a man o' the cloth. From what Mr Richter could ascertain, this old guy saw someone who he described as secret service, looking for the spy. We don't know if there's anything in what he's saying or if it's just the ramblings of a senile old man, but it could be that he saw the intruder."

"I know this might be a daft question, but how d'ya know it's definitely Kester?"

Saggers looked round at the other officers for a moment, as if she were trying to decide how far to go. "Look, there's things that should be kept under wraps for the time being Robbie, but I…we, believe yer life tae be in immediate danger now, so I'm going tae tell ya some things that I need ya tae understand are sensitive information. It's no' for the public domain as yet an' it's vital for the investigation that it remains that way. I need yer word that ya'll no' repeat any of it, not even tae yer nearest an' dearest?"

"Is my wife safe?"

"Aye, she is. Yer family's been looked after, don't worry."

"Okay then, whatever y'tell me I'll keep t'myself."

"Like I said, yer only getting this info because I believe ya tae be in danger an' I'd rather ya worked with us than give us more of a headache than we've already got.

"Kester was seen in the Girvan area; we've sightings of him that match his description. A woman walking her dog says she saw a man early this morning. She says he was acting suspiciously and so she took a mental note o' his number plate."

"You said *sightings*, not sighting," Robbie pushed for more information.

"A wee girl was found on the farm adjacent tae the land where the witness placed him. A three-year old, it turns out she's Kester Richards' daughter."

"What the fuck! He's got kids? Didn't anyone know? What d'ya mean she were found? She's not…"

"Dead? No, thankfully. But what happened tae her's more than a wee bit disturbing if I'm honest.

"Once we identified her, it didn't take long tae trace where she came from: Edinburgh. We traced her home address an' some officers went round there with a warrant an' broke in. The child's mother was then found, alive thankfully, trussed up tae the bed where he'd left her. It seems he'd sprung a visit on her out o' the blue, caught her unawares an' then used their daughter as collateral so as the mother would run some errands for him without raising the alarm. She was terrified he'd hurt them, so she did what he asked. Told us he'd arranged for a car tae be dropped off nearby an' then tied her up an' taken the girl. He told the mother that she'd maybe come in useful if he found himself cornered, a hostage so tae speak.

"Trust me Robbie, we'd no idea he'd a daughter either. Any way both mother an' daughter are okay, a little worse for wear, but they'll survive. The wee girl told officers in Girvan a bit of a chilling tale though. She referred tae the man as 'daddy', an' told officers her mummy called him Kester, that's how we made that connection. She said she'd been in the back o' the car, where the shopping goes, meaning the boot. Said he'd shouted a lot an' she'd been very afraid o' him.

"When the specialist officer, DC Hames here, asked her how she'd come tae be on the farm; ya see the farmer had found her wondering when one o' his dogs started barking frantically. Well she'd said that 'daddy' had taken her out o' the car an' carried her intae some trees. She said he hurt her neck because he squashed it an' it hurt an' made her cough an' cry. He was staring at her with an angry face…Hames, do ya want tae pick it up from here?" Saggers seemed ill-at-ease.

DC Hames stepped forward a little nervously. "Oh right, aye okay." She faced Robbie. "She was pretty much describing the fact that Richards was strangling her. She's only three ya see, so she's no' the appropriate vocabulary tae explain it. She said he was squeezing her neck an' she couldnae catch her breath, even crying had become impossible it seems. Anyway, she said it was making her want tae go tae sleep, like she was losing consciousness I suppose, but then she felt him shaking her an' she opened her eyes. She said he picked her up again an' carried her intae the place where the cows were mooing. He told her tae go find the farmer. Strangely, he kissed her forehead then pointed her in the direction o' the farm house. That's when the dog's barking started an' alerted the farmer."

Robbie was confused and appalled by what he was hearing. "Hang about. So yer saying that he tried t'kill the poor kid, then changed his mind, is that right?"

Radley was the one to answer. "It looks that way but it looks as if it wasn't a case of him changing his mind, but more a case of he couldn't bring himself t'do it. He actually seems to have encountered some emotion from somewhere including affection because he kissed the girl before letting her go, not t'mention making sure he let her go where she'd be found quickly an' be safe. I'm assuming it were an alien concept to him because the cruelty he's shown in the past, including t'the girl's mother among others, is somewhat lacking in any kind of empathy or compassion."

"Oh my god! But they're alright, they're okay now aren't they?"

"Physically yes, but Christ knows what that encounter's done to a bairn like that."

"What's their names, the little girl an' her mum?"

"We can't give y'that information at this stage Robbie. I'm sure you'll understand."

"Yeh, course." He rested back running his fingers through his hair and trying to take it all in. "You thought I were in immediate danger y'said; why?"

DS Frobisher stepped forward and put a sheet of paper down on the table between them. "The licence plate the witness gave us. We've run it through our database an' found the car was stolen in Aberdeen two weeks ago. I then put the details intae our number recognition system. There's number recognition cameras all over the place ya see. Anyway, the car's been logged heading back here tae Glasgow. We even picked it up outside here on London Road around three hours ago it seems. It's since been found abandoned at the King's Park railway station in the south o' the city. So right now, we don't know where he is, but we know he's in the Glasgow region somewhere. We've got officers up in Milngavie in case he's headed for Elizabeth's. He may know his grandmother's dead ya see, or else hoping for help or something, an' be wanting tae go there or, he knows that *you* are here."

"D'ya think he'd be that stupid?"

"Tae go tae Milngavie? No, unlikely. But if he's in Glasgow because he's traced you here Robbie, then I think he's past caring about stupid. Ya've no' been using yer social media have ya? Even if ya don't say where ya are it can tag yer location. He'll have access tae yer accounts if he's got yer laptop."

"No of course I haven't, I'm not daft. I've not even sent any emails, nothing electronic."

Frobisher raised his eyebrows. "Forgive me if I'm teaching ya tae suck eggs here Sir, but how do ya pay yer mobile phone contract?"

"Oh fuck!" Of course, why the hell hadn't he thought about that? And him the bloody programmer too. It would all be on there, his mobile phone account information, and if Kester had worked out his password he'd have access to it all. His number, his frequent contacts, everything. He'd used his mobile to call

Lynsey, his brother, his family, Jacob, St Ninian's, he'd even used it to call the records office in Edinburgh. He'd used it to call Peg too, so if Kester had access to his phone usage, he'd know that Peg had spoken to him. So maybe he would be heading up there after all. Was she safe or would he just want information from her? "What do we do now?"

DI Saggers held out her hand. "I think ya'd best leave yer phone with us. We can use it tae try an' draw him out, lay a false trail if ya like. We'll give you a burner phone, ya know a disposable one. Then I think the best thing'd be for ya tae return home tae West Yorkshire with DS Radley here, go see yer wife."

"There's still things I need t'do here; I haven't finished in Glasgow yet."

"Yes ya have Robbie. Yer no' staying here d'ya understand me? It's no' safe for ya." She turned towards DC Simons. "I'm well aware mi'laddo here's been, shall we say, assisting ya with yer own enquiries."

Simons blushed. He'd obviously had a telling off from her.

"You tell him what it is ya still want tae know, an' I'll see if I can't release him tae do yer digging around for ya. But you Robbie, *will* most definitely be on a train out o' here by tonight, even if I've tae drag ya there kicking an' screaming myself, right!"

Chapter Thirty

Robbie had wanted to take an east coast train so that
he could go to Blythe and see Lynsey, but when he'd
called her to ask if she'd see him, she told him not to
bother. She planned travelling into Leeds the next day
herself because she had an appointment for an ultrasound
scan at the pre-natal clinic. He felt guilty again. All this
effort he'd spent in his search for answers and very little
on the here and now. He almost didn't dare to push
himself forward; he'd neglected her so much lately. But
as it turned out he didn't need to because she was the one
to ask if he'd meet her, if he'd go with her to the scan.

Maybe it was a 'man thing' or maybe it was just
him, but he'd been finding it really difficult to muster
any kind of feeling towards his unborn child thus far. It
just didn't seem real, like when something exists in
theory but you've never known the reality of it as yet.

He decided that going to the scan would be a good opportunity to try and get on board; he needed to make it up to his wife and he didn't ever want to risk things getting this bad between them again. He told her that he and Radley were leaving for Leeds that evening, but that he'd meet her in the Costa at Leeds Railway station the next morning, when her train arrived.

Now that Blythe was no longer an option, Robbie and DS Chris Radley got tickets for the next train from Glasgow to Leeds, which as it turned out, went down the western route instead. They'd had to hang around in Carlyle for almost an hour, waiting for the connection, but all in all the journey wasn't too bad. Radley had been a little twitchy on the platform at Glasgow Central but DI Saggers had assured him that the CCTV was being heavily monitored and that if there were to be the slightest sniff of Kester Richards, then he'd be lifted immediately.

Radley was picked up at Leeds by a marked police car, while Rich had driven over to collect Robbie. He'd have to spend the night at his brother's because his own place was still a mess and evidence was still being collected apparently. He'd been told that anything he wanted from there could be collected by a police officer and delivered to him, but there was nothing he wanted. He'd no idea what or how much had been stolen or damaged, but the very thought that Kester had been in there, in and around his and Lynsey's things, had somehow marred everything else. He had no desire to go there because he didn't even feel it to be home anymore; it was sullied.

Jodie had made a shepherd's pie and had plated some up for him which he polished off quickly. He hadn't even noticed himself to be hungry until she'd put the food down in front of him. He took his empty plate through to the kitchen where she was just about to start washing up the dishes. "I'll do that," he offered.

"It's okay, I've started now. D'ya want a drink Robbie? There's some beers in the fridge, or we've wine, red and white."

"I'll have a glass o' wine I think; I've not had wine for ages."

"It's in the fridge. Help yerself."

Robbie looked round at her, assuming she'd meant the white wine. "I think I'd prefer red if that's okay."

"Yeah, whatever Rob. Like I said, it's in the fridge, help yerself."

He began laughing. "Wait a minute, y'keep yer red in the fridge? That's almost sacrilegious isn't it?"

She wasn't going to be drawn. "Do I look like I give a shit? Really? Don't give a damn if red wine's meant t'be served at room temperature or not; I like my rioja cold…end of."

His sister-in-law really was one of a kind, both in the way she looked and dressed and in character, one of the most genuine people he knew and confident enough to stand her ground against all opposition if she felt it justified. She was certainly the guiding influence in his brother's marriage; Rich would be lost without her.

"Leeds Rhinos are playing Robbie," Rich yelled from the living room.

They'd followed Rugby League from their teens, Clive's influence no doubt. He'd been the *Give Blood Play Rugby* die-hard of the family, though not so much in recent years. But the brothers still liked to watch; it'd been a long time since they'd sat down in front of the tele and watched a match together though, and even longer since they'd actually gone to one. "We'll have t'go t'the Carnegie again Rich, when this is all over an' everything's back t'normal I mean. It must be three or four years since we went up to Headingley. Who were they playing last time? Can y'remember?"

"Wigan Warriors?" Rich seemed a little taken aback.

"Yeh that's right. Me, you, Clive an' that fella from the pub, Barry. D'ya remember? His hotdog fell out o' the bun when the Rhinos got that last try an' he threw his hands in the air cheering, onions an' mustard all over himself. It were hilarious at the time."

Rich sat forward, grinning. "Bloody hell mate, the last time I talked rugby with ya, ya'd no memory o' that day. I remember trying t'make ya remember it but y'just couldn't. Mind you, y'were only a couple o' months out of hospital then," he smiled at the memory. "Anyway, it's St Helens tonight, so sup up, I'll get you another."

A pensive moment hit Robbie. "Have you ever resented me Rich? Y'know, me not being Annie's real son an' you are? Has it ever pissed you off since finding out?"

"Y'what? Why would it? Yer my brother; I've never known any different have I? I wasn't even born when mum took you on. Ya've always been there my whole life so why the bloody hell would I start resenting ya now? Get a grip soft lad," Rich seemed more offended by the suggestion than anything, so Robbie let it drop.

The soporific effect of the rioja meant that Robbie didn't even make it as far as half time. He'd fallen asleep on the sofa, long before the whistle. He woke up as the daylight was pushing through the cracks in the window blinds, a quilt with a Bratz themed, pink cover was resting over him. Very manly…not.

No-one else in the house appeared to be awake and so he took advantage of the empty bathroom while he could. Rich was in the kitchen when he came back downstairs, freshly showered and wide awake. "I'm off out Rich. I'll get something to eat in Leeds, then I'm going t'meet up with Lyns; her trains due in at half ten. It's the scan today."

Rich nodded, unable to speak as he'd just shoved a whole, folded up slice of toast into his mouth in one go and was trying to chew, a habit he'd had from being a kid, despite the number of times he'd almost choked himself doing it. He did a thumbs up to his brother, to let him know he'd heard him, then held his hand up to the side of his head with his thumb and little finger extended, indicating that he wanted Robbie to call him later.

"Yeh I'll give you a ring after the scan. Let y'know how things are."

A couple of hours later Robbie found himself sitting in the Costa at the railway station. He was nervous, really nervous and he was beginning to regret the bacon and egg buttie he'd eaten for breakfast earlier; it was making him feel queasy now. He knew that his wife's train was due in at any minute and he was anxious about seeing her again. He'd missed her so much, but he didn't know how this meeting would end. Well, he hoped, but what if she were wanting to make the split final? What if she just didn't want to be with him anymore? Not that he'd blame her. He knew he'd been an arse but he was finally beginning to realise where his priorities lay. They were going to have a baby and that mattered. He knew he was struggling with the concept of fatherhood; it had never been something he'd planned for or expected. And now, with this ingrained fear he'd allowed himself to adopt, the fear of passing on some genetic, psychological aberration to the baby. The 'what ifs' were astounding, but he needed to be realistic now, even Peg had told him so.

He knew he'd have to mask the fact that he just didn't feel anything towards the baby. He couldn't tell Lynsey that, not now, she'd be mortified. All he could do would be to hope that as time went on, he'd start to love the kid, just like she did. He really needed to stop trying to auto-analyse his own mental being too, always jumping the gun, always assuming the worse. So what if there was a fucked-up gene running through the family tree? It didn't mean he was affected, nor did it mean he'd pass it on to his baby either.

"Hi."

Robbie spun round to find Lynsey standing behind him. "Oh, hi love." He stood up, unsure of whether or not to lean in for a kiss. He took the risk and luckily she responded. He glanced down at her belly. "Are you okay? How's the baby?"

"Fine and fine, thanks. We've got nearly two hours t'kill before the scan. D'ya want another drink?"

It was awkward for the first twenty minutes or so. He felt like he was walking on egg shells, but as they got into conversation he felt himself relax more.

"I just need y'to know how sorry I am Lyns. I know I've been a twat, but I never meant t'be. I never thought…well t'be honest, I'm not sure what exactly I thought, I just seemed t'get swept up an' carried along somehow. I'm sorry."

"Me too."

"What're you sorry about? You've done nothing wrong."

"I'm sorry because I should've told you it were getting too much. I thought I were being all supportive an' that, but it were taking a toll on me Robbie, more than I realised."

He reached across the table and took hold of her hand. "I've put everyone in danger if this nutter comes looking: you, the family. I've put you all in a god-awful position."

Lynsey sighed and took a few moments to respond. "Truth be known, this guy, this Kester Richards, he would've come looking for you anyway. It was always going to happen. Even if you'd never been attacked, even if Annie had never told y'the truth. He were still coming for ya, because he knew, even if we didn't."

She was right. Kester was going to find him one way or the other. It was probably best done this way because at least they weren't alone in the situation like they had been before. At least now the police and the powers that be were able to help.

"Have y'been home? Have y'seen our apartment at all? Y'know, since he…"

"No love. I stayed with Rich an' Jodie last night; I couldn't face it. Besides that DS Radley said we can't go in yet, not 'til they've finished collecting evidence etcetera."

Lynsey nodded, though the sullen expression on her face gave away the feeling she held about going back there. "I want t'move, I don't want t'go back there

Robbie. A fresh start'd be good, besides there's the baby t'think about now too. We need somewhere with a garden really not a balcony. I'd be permanently paranoid."

The relief he felt in his heart was almost overwhelming. She was talking about them moving forward together. *She* wanted to stay with *him* after all. He couldn't ever let things get this close to destruction again. He knew there was unfinished business, but he knew he'd need to pace himself from now on, not hit the ground running. Taking a breath before making any decisions would be better than being as spontaneous as he had over the past few weeks and more.

She looked down at her watch. "Come on, if we set off now we'll be there in plenty o' time. God I need the loo."

"They're over there." Robbie pointed to the ladies toilets across the foyer of the station. He rooted round in his pocket. "Here, I think y'need twenty pence t'get in. Bloody rip off."

"I can't Robbie; I have to hold it, it's the scan y'see. They need my bladder t'be full so it pushes my womb forward an' they can see the baby better."

"Right, so ya've got to hold it all that time?"

"Yep, and while they push down on it with the ultrasound. Come on, let's get there an' get it done."

He could tell she was uncomfortable in the waiting room by the way she kept shifting position in the chair, so it was a relief when they were finally called through.

"Just get yerself comfy on this bed if y'don't mind Mrs McAndrew, an' if you could just pull yer pants down to yer hips, that'd be great, thank you."

The lights in the room dimmed as the sonographer set to task, her conversation light hearted and superficial. She apologised for the temperature of the gel she squirted onto Lynsey's belly, the smallest of bumps now apparent. When she pushed down with the device in her hand, the images appeared on screen immediately.

She wasn't saying too much for the first minute or so, while she scanned around the lower part of Lynsey's abdomen, looking for her quarry. "There," she suddenly announced. "See, that's the head, can y'see it?"

They could. Lynsey gasped in awe. "Oh wow, that's our baby! Look Robbie, that's our little baby. Oh my god!"

He was looking; he could see, but he was still not feeling it. He'd have to pretend, for her sake. "Wow, yeah, that's brilliant."

The sonographer pointed at the screen. "Can y'see the little heartbeat, just there?"

They both squinted as they looked at the pulsating mass in the middle of their baby. Lynsey was overjoyed. "I can see it Robbie! Look can y'see it?"

"Yeh," he feigned pleasure.

"Oh, wait a minute," the sonographer was surprised. She moved the scanner around a little then pushed back in. "That's yer other baby," she grinned. "Best start thinking up two names instead o' one."

Robbie smiled and kissed his wife, but inside all he could think of was the twins who'd gone before. Eban and his twin that never even made it to the end of the pregnancy. Martin and his dead twin, the first Michael Whithorn, and then of course there was Kester and his twin, Tavish. Christ only knows how many there'd been before that, but it was very likely there *had* been some, because it appeared that twins were quite prevalent in the…what was it DS Radley had called it? In the scion, the genetic offshoots: twins and insanity. Though he had to be honest with himself, he hadn't *really* given too much thought as to how many heartbeats he might see at this scan.

Lynsey must've picked up on a brief flash of a despaired expression in his face, because he felt her squeeze his hand. As he looked at her she smiled. "It'll be fine. Our babies will be fine. You'll see." Nothing was going to spoil this moment for her and Robbie wanted to keep it that way.

The sonographer gave them a print out from the images taken, though truth be known, it was barely recognisable now that there was no movement. "You can get more at yer next scan," she explained. "As y'know Mrs McAndrew, the fact that yer over the age o' thirty-five, and now coupled with the fact that there's two in there, we'll be keeping a close eye on yer progress."

"Yeh, I understand. Can I ask though, am I more at risk carrying twins? Only, don't they tend t'be premature?"

She smiled reassuringly. "It's more common that they're premature, but it's not a given. You could still go full term, but I'm sure yer midwife or GP's best placed to answer those questions for ya." She reached across and rubbed the top of Lynsey's arm, trying to put her at ease. "Don't worry. Don't go inventing problems where there are none."

Those words probably hit home more with Robbie than they did with his wife, because that's exactly what he'd been guilty of, 'inventing problems where there are none'. What a bloody idiot he'd been.

As soon as Lynsey was decent again she made a bolt for the ladies. She'd been holding it all this time and looked as if she might explode if she couldn't pee soon. While he waited for her he felt the burner phone in his pocket vibrate. It was a text message from DS Radley.

DC Simons from Police Scotland's come through, got info on that orphanage & Eban before adopted. Faxed it here as your email might be compromised. Where you staying? Can drop it in, or you pick up here. Let me know. Chris.

Bloody hell that was quick. He hadn't expected to hear anything back so soon. It seemed that having a badge to wave around at the right people had opened more doors faster than he ever could've hoped to on his own. He'd have to tell Lynsey. No more lying about all the Eban stuff anymore. He'd learned that lesson the hard way.

Chapter Thirty-One

From the clinic they'd gone straight to the estate agents. The sympathetic agent agreed that once the police had finished and their apartment had been cleaned up, that she would put it on the market for them. "It's a city apartment. They're very desirable now. I'm fairly confident you won't be waiting too long for a sale."

"We'll be staying at my brother's for the time being, but do ya have a list of rentals we could take with us?"

She obliged. The thought of moving seemed to lift Lynsey's spirits no end, so Robbie thought it might be a good moment to tell her about Radley's text.

"If y'want me t'leave it alone Lyns then just say so. I don't want t'get into a bad situation about it again."

She took in a deep breath, then sighed heavily. "No, let's just do it, find out what we can. Ya've come this far already, it seems daft not t'see it through now I suppose."

When they arrived at the police station, DS Radley wasn't available, but Sgt Bashir was. He took them round to a quiet room and passed Robbie the fax. "I have t'say Robbie, I never expected any o'this," Bash admitted.

"Me neither."

"Why didn't y'just tell me? Last year when y'found out, why didn't y'tell me then? I could've helped an' who knows, thing's might not've got t'this point."

"I didn't know who he was back then. That's something that caught us all out Bash. I don't know, I didn't want anything t'come back on mum for it I suppose. I'm sorry, really I am, if I've made yer job that much harder, but who could've known all this shit would hit the fan?"

"We had him in custody Robbie. We had him, but we'd no idea about his relationship t'ya, it mattered."

Surprisingly it was Lynsey that got defensive. "Why? Why did it matter? He would still've been in custody, he would still've had t'go t'court, an' he still would've beat the shit out o' that prison guard an' escaped. It wouldn't o' made a blind bit o' difference at all."

Bash relented somewhat. "Perhaps yer right, but we'd have known the danger y'were in, done more t'keep ya safe."

Robbie felt bad about not telling Bash the truth. After all, he'd been the first copper to deal with his family, to make the connection to him in the hospital bed. He'd looked after them. He deserved to be kept in the loop; he was a good bloke. "I really am sorry Bash. All I can say is that I had my reasons. Maybe they were a bit arse-about-face, but I thought I were doing the right thing at the time."

He nodded his acceptance of Robbie's apology, then left them alone in the room to peruse the information that DC Simons had sent through.

Robbie picked up the fax and read it aloud. "Hi Robbie, it wasn't too difficult to find out what we needed. It seems that the report from Dr Edgar Hellmich was pretty much on the ball. Do you remember the report saying that the baby boy was to be given to that orphanage? Well he was, but I've found another report from Dr Hellmich to do with the actual handover. It's a bit creepy, so am sorry, but it seems that at the time, Martha Richards was asked if she'd like to give her baby a name. She said she wanted him to be called Michael, after her daddy. I know, doesn't sit well does it, not when you consider that the kid's dad could very well have been his grandad too. Anyway, the nuns at Smyllum Park Orphanage decided that it was abhorrent to use that name considering the circumstances of his birth, so it was them that changed it to Eban."

He broke off from what he was reading, a sense of horror burning deep in his gut. "Oh my god Lynsey. Eban's really Michael too. He must've known all this, he must've been told somewhere along the line about this. Why else would the sick bastard keep calling his sons Michael?"

Lyns was just as horrified. "Surely any right minded person would want t'stear clear o' that name. He can't possibly have thought Martha's father was some sort o' bloody hero, could he?" It was a chilling thought and made her shudder.

Robbie continued reading from the fax. "There's plenty of historical evidence that the so called Sisters of Charity were anything but. Over the years there's been dozens of reports from various former residents about the cruelty that went on in their orphanages, many of whom wrote testimonies about how they were treated, starved an' beaten. One even wrote about witnessing another child being forced to eat their own vomit. Sadly there doesn't seem to have been any formal investigation, but to be honest, the fact that so many have said similar things makes me think there should have been. Ultimately, I think what I'm saying is that it's probably likely that your father spent his early years in this sort of environment, which I'm sure didn't help.

There's no documentation on his time there other than when he arrived from the mental hospital and then when he was adopted by the Whithorns. The only report on him talks about him being healthy and free of lice an' a bit small for his age, which was five at the time, but that's it. The only thing about his character that's mentioned is that he's described as 'a quiet child'. Strictly speaking, there should be much more written down about all of the kids there: check ups, doctor visits, school etcetera, you know the sort of thing. But I couldn't find any of that. Their records were very sparse, which makes me wonder if they've not been 'lost' if you understand me, whether by the Sisters themselves, or by someone later who didn't want any recriminations brought on the holy women of god for their treatment of some of the kids. Anyway, that's about it. He was adopted by the Whithorns in nineteen forty-seven, which you already knew." He stopped reading.

"That's sick." Lynsey wasn't impressed. "I mean, I can almost feel a little sympathy for the child he was, but that doesn't excuse his behaviour as an adult. An' t'call two of his sons Michael. How did he know about that? The Whithorns must've told him at some point. Did Jacob mention it?"

"No. Maybe he didn't know, or he might not have known the whole story behind it. Maybe none o' them did."

"How d'ya mean?"

"Well just suppose you were the one running an overcrowded orphanage full o' kids that y'wanted rid of. If someone came along an' offered t'take one, would y'risk them backing out because ya'd told them something like that?"

"But they'd known about Martha being in an asylum."

"Yeah but that's different isn't it? Remember the Whithorns were missionaries, religious people, the kind o' folk that'd feel it their duty t'pity someone like her, but maybe the rest would've just been a bit too much information for them. Or maybe these so-called Sisters o' Charity, were too prudish t'come out an' say that Martha grew up being fucked by her dad an' brothers an' that one of them's very likely the sire of her illegitimate sprog."

Lynsey looked down at her own belly and stroked her small bump. "I'm still glad Eban's dead now. It might be wrong, but I am. However he started in life doesn't excuse how he ended up, the things he did. Plenty o' people have shitty childhoods, but they don't end up like that." She looked up at him. "How d'ya feel about that? Really? Knowing he's dead, how d'ya feel?"

He shrugged and took a few moments to consider the question. "Truthfully? Numb, I don't feel anything really, one way or the other. It's not like he could tell me anything. Even if he were able t'talk, he were still up for mind games. It'd have been nice if he had to answer for some o' the stuff he did, even if it were only the bigamous marriage they could get him on, but the fact is, he'd never have gone to court, not in the state he were in. He's no loss t'me though if that's what y'meant?"

The door opened and Bash popped his head round. "DS Radley's here now. He'd like t'see ya Robbie if that's okay?"

Robbie looked round at Lynsey, reading the expression on her face for any signs of annoyance. "I won't be long, I promise."

"It's okay, I'm sure Bash'll be able t'get me a cuppa, won't ya Bash?"

He smiled and gestured for her to follow him. Radley entered the room shortly afterwards.

"So Robbie, makes for interesting reading don't y'think?"

"Raises a few eyebrows doesn't it? My father, the bastard child of an underage lunatic and a sick murderer who also happens t'be his grandfather, or maybe it was an uncle. Who the fuck knows." It wasn't worth him thinking too deeply about it.

Radley tried t'be sympathetic. "Look fella it's shite, I know that. Like I've said t'ya before; it's the first time

in my career that I've had t'deal with anything like this,
so I've had a lot o' head in books moments myself. This
is a new one on me.

"One thing I didn't pass on that Simons sent, was the
fact that the extended family o' Martha Richards has
been traced. Her brothers are all dead now. One o' them
were hanged not long after she were incarcerated; he'd a
wife an' a couple o' kids. The sailor emigrated. He died
in Quebec years ago, an' the third lived in an' around
Yoker his whole life. He were the one still at home
when Martha were homeless, he died twenty years ago.
They've all left kids behind. We haven't approached
anyone yet, but we know where they are. The point
being that if y'were wanting t'find out exactly who
fathered Eban then, with their cooperation, DNA tests
could be done for a sibling match."

Robbie didn't even need to think about it. "No.
Absolutely not. I'm not blaming them; I don't know
them. But I don't want to either. It doesn't matter which
o' their fathers is my natural grandfather, if any. I don't

care because it won't serve any purpose, so no. Thanks but no."

Radley smiled, relieved. "Good, I were hoping ya'd say that."

He asked about Lynsey's scan and appeared a little stunned by the news it was twins, just as Robbie had been. "Really? Brings it home I suppose doesn't it? Genetics, I mean."

Robbie couldn't look at him, nor could he think of anything to say. His inaction obviously prompted Radley's next suggestion. "Look, I might be able t'sort out a visit for ya, to a chap we use a lot for psychiatric assessments. He's a university professor too, does a lot o' research into this sort o' thing. As it happens, he were the one that did the assessment on Kester Richards."

"You had him assessed?"

"We had to."

"So you had yer suspicions, even then?"

"I can't go into it too much Robbie, code of ethics an' all that. Look, d'ya want me t'try an' sort this out or not?"

"Will it cost loads?"

"Unlikely, he's a research professor. It'll probably benefit him as much as you."

Robbie agreed and so Radley said he'd let him know.

Back at Rich and Jodie's house, Lyns began looking through the properties to let pages in the Yorkshire Evening Post, as well as those in the booklet the estate agent had given them. It was hard to look at the rentals; she wanted her own home, but knew they'd need to sell the apartment first, and so rented accommodation was their only option. She was using Jodie's laptop and found herself searching out holiday lets in the Isle of Stennoch. Despite everything, it was peaceful there, Robbie felt at ease there and it'd be nice to spend some time there, out of the way until this madman were found. Robbie had agreed when she mentioned it to him. She'd looked at the little chalet lets in Laigh Isle, just around the back of what had once been the village school. "Number twenty-three's free at the moment. We could go there for a couple o'weeks while we sort out somewhere to rent back here. If we see anything we like quickly, I'm sure your Rich'd go round an' have a look on our behalf."

She rang the number and enquired. "The day after tomorrow Robbie, Friday. We've got it for two weeks, okay?" She was beaming, the relief at not being in Leeds for a while was shining out of her. And much as she loved Jodie, Rich and the kids, she didn't like having to impose on them. She wanted her own space.

That evening Radley got back to Robbie about the university professor he'd mentioned. "Can y'make Friday morning, ten-ish?"

"Oh, right. We were going up t'Scotland on Friday, but we can set off a bit later I suppose."

"Woah, hang about. Y'can't just keep going for a wander Robbie. We need t'know where you are at all times just now."

"Isle of Stennoch, not Glasgow or Edinburgh or anywhere like that. We won't say anything to anyone. It's out o' the way an' t'be honest, me an' Lyns just need some time together, y'know?"

Radley sighed heavily, but knew he couldn't prevent them. "I'll have t'let Louise Saggers know where you are Robbie; she might need t'get hold of ya. So, Friday then. Try an' get there a bit early. It's Professor Waterman yer looking for. Anyway, he's expecting ya. Ya'll find him in the main campus building for the University o' Leeds off Woohouse Road."

"Yeh, I know where that is. Thanks Radders."

"Bloody hell, not you an' all!" Radley didn't let many people get away with calling him that.

"D'ya know what this assessment entails, how long it'll take, that sort o' thing?"

"Not a bloody clue Robbie, sorry mate. I think there's blood tests an' the like, but I don't really know anything about what he does up there. Just that when I told him who y'were, with relation t'Richards that is, he almost bit my hand off. It's all free because it's all part of his ongoing research into that sort o' thing. All a bit doctor Frankenstein t'me though."

Robbie laughed. "Thanks, that makes me feel a lot better," he quipped sarcastically.

<h2 style="text-align:center">Chapter Thirty-Two</h2>

Lynsey stayed behind with Jodie on the Friday morning. She wanted to finish packing the few belongings they had with them before setting off for the Isle. She'd had a weepy moment the previous night when she'd come across the panic alarm button that had been installed by the police; it'd upset her, crashing her back into reality and the potential danger they were all in.

She'd begged Robbie to find out about the little girl, Kester's daughter. For some reason this mattered to her and she wanted to know that she was alright. Jodie had blamed her hormones, 'baby-brain' she'd called it. Explained it away as the random panic modes all pregnant women experience, even if only momentarily. But the thought that Kester would use his own daughter like that had brought it home to her, just how dangerous he was: ruthless, pitiless and completely barren of any compassion for his own little girl's terror, not to mention what her mother had gone through.

Robbie had tried to reassure her, but couldn't promise the police would tell them anything more specific. He left her in Jodie's care while he went off to meet Professor Waterman.

His phone rang as he was parking at the university. It was DI Louise Saggers. "So yer off on a wee jaunt again?" She didn't sound amused.

"Yeh, don't worry, we'll stay where y'can find us."

"I'm more concerned that yer where Richards might find ya."

"Any news on that front?"

"Nothing concrete. We've got a few more o' his contacts up here thanks tae his ex, the wee bairn's mum."

"I wanted to ask about her. Are they okay? I mean…I know y'can't tell me too much, but my wife's been concerned about them too."

"More shaken than stirred I'd say. He was never named on the wee girl's birth certificate an' he'd no' made it public among his so called friends either, so no-one knew he'd a kid. Some o' them in Edinburgh must o' known I suppose, because that's where they are, but outside o' there we don't think anyone had an inkling."

"What about Peg, Elizabeth I mean? She must've known; she never said, but surely he'd have told her, an' Tavish. He were there when I went with Chris Radley."

"Aye I know. He's gone now though, headed back home tae England, work commitments apparently. Elizabeth was quite upset when we told her what had occurred. Couldnae believe Kester'd do such a thing tae his own flesh an' blood. But she didn't react so much when we told her we'd reason tae believe he'd killed Eban. But then I don't suppose there was any love lost between Elizabeth an' her father."

"She's not seen him since she were a kid herself. She never spoke about him with any kind of affection, put it that way."

"Look Robbie. I've spoken in length with the Procurator Fiscal here in Glasgow. There *has* been an historical crime committed under section two o' the child abduction law. There's nothing for ya tae answer yerself as yer viewed as the victim in this case. But if Annie Wilkinson had still been alive, then it would've been a possibility."

"She didn't do anything wrong!"

"Yes, Robbie…she did. The law's there for a reason an' it's no' the job o' Police Scotland tae look intae why she did it. We only look at the facts, an' the fact is, she broke the law. Any reasons she had for doing so would be taken intae account in court. Our job's just tae bring it tae court, nothing else.

"However, due tae the fact that she's no longer with us, the PF feels it'd be futile tae try such a case. In addition tae which, no one has ever actually made a

complaint about yer abduction. She took ya away an'
helped fake yer death, both o' which are highly illegal.
As for the matter of any fraud committed, in other
words, the years o' claiming child benefit that she wasn't
entitled to…"

"She was, she had me."

"No, because she was claiming it the name of a
deceased person, not you. Whether ya were using that
identity or not is irrelevant. Anyway, that's an English
crime as that's where she settled with ya, but the PF has
made a recommendation that no further action be taken
for both. It's up tae the Crown Prosecution Service in
yer area now as tae whether or not they want tae pursue
it, but it's highly unlikely as no remuneration can be
made now."

Robbie thought he got where she was coming from,
but wanted clarification. "So what yer saying is that
nothing's going t'come of it? No-one's in trouble for
it?"

"Right, but there is one more thing."

"What?"

"Yer still living under a false identity, legally yer Michael Whithorn, no' Robert McAndrew."

"It's who I am. Surely I don't have t'go back t'being called Michael Whithorn?"

"No, but the law requires that ya change yer name tae Robert McAndrew by deed pole, make it official. The 'presumed dead' order has tae be revoked, so technically all yer documentation's illegal now, yer passport, driving licence. The PF said they'll need tae be re-applied for once ya've changed yer name. If ya don't, ya'll need tae re-apply for those things in yer true name, Michael Whithorn."

Robbie's head was mashed with the thought of it all. "How do I go about all that? I don't even know where t'start."

"Start by getting a solicitor. The ball will be started rolling by us, an' soon. So don't waste time. Ya can still go tae the Isle o' Stennoch, but maybe contact a family solicitor before ya go, find one who'll take ya on, then Police Scotland can deal with them about it all."

"How long have I got?"

"Now that yer aware of it, yer supposed tae start dealing with it straight away. Put it this way Robbie, if ya don't then when yer baby's born or should I say babies, it'll have tae be Michael Whithorn on their birth certificates."

It was all he could think about while he lay in the MRI scanner in Professor Waterman's lab. He'd already had blood samples taken and had to answer a million and one questions. He'd been there longer than he thought he'd need to be and so was glad when the scanner finished and the Professor appeared beside him.

"Right then, I think we're done Robbie. Thank you very much for participating, I can't tell you how much our research here depends on the cooperation of people like you."

"But what category do I fall into? Normal or nut-job?"

Waterman grinned, amused by the question. "It's not that simple I'm afraid. I'll need some time to collate the results of all the testing we've done today."

"But what about that first test, all those questions?"

"Ah, the Hare Psychopathy test. Well, you did score in the slightly higher than average region, but on its own, it's not conclusive enough at that mark. I need the results of the blood tests and time to analyse your brain scans."

"So this Hare test, this shows that I'm a psychopath to some degree?" Robbie's heart was pounding so hard that he could hear it pulsating in his ears. He was mortified to think he was like Eban in any way.

"Not exactly, it shows that in a characteristic way, you have some psychopathic tendencies, but don't go jumping the gun. A large percentage of the human race have some marginal tendencies in one category or the other. And it may surprise you to know, but most psychopaths live among us, getting on with their lives as are the rest of us. Don't assume that this particular disorder means that a person automatically becomes deranged because they don't. It's a personality disorder, not a psychotic condition, however when it's combined with a psychotic condition it can make for a very dangerous person."

A very dangerous person, like Kester then. Great. "What exactly is it then? What tells y'the difference?"

Waterman went on to explain to Robbie the relevance of all the tests he'd done. He explained that up until the age of around three, our impulses run riot, then our pre-frontal cortex, that part of our brains that controls impulses, develops and gives us the ability to control those impulses, kind of like applying the brakes where necessary, and we learn to live in a more civilised manner. How that pre-frontal cortex develops, very much depends on our early experiences. And so that's why Robbie's brain had been scanned, to look at the amigdala in the pre-frontal cortex.

He had also been asked the personality questions to gauge his responses and form an initial impression.

He'd been wired up to electrodes, measuring his brain activity and shown a whole host of both still and moving pictures of various kinds, some cute and fluffy and some pretty appalling, for the same reason, to see how his brain reacted to such information. And the blood tests were looking for a heightened level of testosterone and a lower than normal level of serotonin.

"In combination these factors can make for a very dangerous psychopath, a killer in many cases. But I doubt very much that this will be the case for you. Let's face it, you're in your early forties. I think that were this going to be your make up, that it would've been evident by now."

"It's the head injury I had last year. Is there a chance that it could've brought things on?"

"It's true that certain genes that have been dormant previously, can be switched on after a serious event. But those genes would need to be present in the first place."

"When will I know? How long am I going to have t'wait?"

Waterman shrugged. "As long as it takes for me to collate everything Robbie. I understand your anxiety given your family history, but I'm afraid you're just going to have to be patient. I wouldn't be too concerned though. The very fact that this worries you, is a good thing. If you were genuinely as bad as you thought you might be, then I doubt very much that you'd care."

Explaining all of this to his wife on the drive up the M6 motorway wasn't easy. He'd forgotten half of what was said and wasn't sure he was getting it right.

"Just remember Robbie, this is for yer own peace o' mind more than anything isn't it? No-one else thinks there's anything wrong with ya, just you."

He daren't tell her that all this worry and excitement over their impending parenthood was one-sided, that he just didn't feel it. Did that make him abnormal? Maybe. He'd told all of this to Professor Waterman, strangely enough the only person he'd been completely honest with about his feelings, or lack thereof. But he'd seemed quite an open person. He didn't try and flower anything up with explanations of, 'oh don't worry, many new fathers feel that way,' or 'well there's a lot going on in your life at the moment.' He was up front about it; he'd explained that it could well be due to his psychological make up, or…it could be down to extenuating circumstances. He'd pretty much said that if psychopathy were present, then it's present, end of. That there's no reason he couldn't continue as he had been doing.

Robbie's biggest fear now was that he could end up being the father of another Eban or Kester and even if the mental deficit wasn't quite that bad, would he and Lynsey be spending their lives caring for a child who couldn't live independently, like Martha? Would they be visiting an institution on a regular basis, or sat anxiously at home awaiting a phone call telling them that one of their kids had hurt themselves, or someone else? He knew in his heart that if Lynsey turned round and said that she wanted an abortion, that he'd be secretly relieved. He didn't want her to miscarry because he didn't want to see her pain and anguish over an event like that. But if she were never pregnant in the first place he'd have been so much happier. How could he ever tell her that, how could he ever admit to feeling like that to anyone? They'd just think he was a total bastard.

Four hours after setting off, one motorway, several 'A' roads, even more 'B' roads and one stop for coffee later, and they found themselves pulling into the parking space of their rented chalet. It was cold, but the waves lapping up on the rocks only thirty yards or so away made for a welcome sight.

"It'll be unlocked," Lynsey called as Robbie headed round to the door. "The owner said the keys would be left in the fruit bowl on the table inside."

Robbie took their bags inside. It was small; the entrance was directly into the kitchen which was long and narrow, but had everything they'd need. Beyond that was the living/dining room with big sliding patio doors at the far end, which meant they could see the sea from there. There was a small hallway with the bathroom on the right, next to the tiniest bedroom

Robbie had ever seen. Then to the left was a bigger double bedroom, still not huge but it was all more than adequate for their needs, and so close to the sea that he thought he'd easily be able to throw a stone from their patio and have it land in the water. It was nice; he liked it.

"Can we go t'the Solway Harvester for tea? Can't be arsed making anything an' I don't fancy any more driving today."

"Sounds good," she replied. "Did you call Joe yet, let him know we're up here for a couple o' weeks? He's bound to want t'see us." She picked up the visitor notice that the owner had left on the table, with all the information of how everything worked on it: washing machine, cooker, heating, that sort of thing. "Oh good, there's a landline here. That's good because the mobile reception's crap. The only time I picked up any signal here, it was from the Isle o' Man service; the charges were phenomenal." She looked around the living room before spotting the telephone round the corner, just beside the sofa.

They heard a dog bark by the door, so Robbie went to look. As he opened it a little black and tan dachshund trotted in straight past him.

"Ash! Come on out ya wee terror!" a dark haired woman of around fifty called after him. She held out a pile of towels to him. "Sorry, he's so cheeky. I'm Mandy, I look after the place when the owner's away. I forgot tae leave these when I was getting the place ready for ya earlier, sorry."

Lynsey came to the door with Ash in her arms. "Don't worry about it Mandy. Here, I'll do you a swap." She gave the dog back to Mandy who passed the towels to Robbie.

"Do ya have everything ya need? I just live in the castle cottage over there if there's any problems. Just ask anyone if ya need tae find me, tell them yer looking for Mandy the artist an' they'll point ya in the right direction."

Lynsey's eyes lit up. "Oh yer an artist? D'ya have a studio in the village?"

"Aye, I do. Come for a visit while yer here if ya like. I might even manage a cup o' tea an' a Wagon Wheel if yer lucky," Mandy smiled.

"I think I probably will. Me an' my husband are be moving house soon. It'd be nice to have a new painting for the new home, something t'remind us of here."

"Good, I'll look forward tae it."

Once Mandy had gone, they dumped their bags in the bedroom and set off across the grass towards the passageway that took them through what would've been, the school playground when Robbie had lived there, and through the gap in the houses that would've been the school gate. It brought them out in the middle of Main Street facing the harbour. It looked beautiful in the last of the evening sun. The small church, Eban's former kirk, just to the left looked quite quaint too. The angle that Robbie was looking at it from made him stop in his tracks briefly.

"What is it?" Lynsey asked him.

"I'm not sure. Some kind o' sense o' familiarity maybe. Just when I looked at the church from here, with my back t'the school yard, it just felt…I don't know, a memory maybe." He looked round the other way, to his right, half expecting to see his mother, Mona, waiting for him. He felt a warmth wash over him that brought real tears to his eyes.

"Oh Robbie, oh what's wrong? Have y'remembered something?"

He nodded and smiled. "My mother. I've remembered my mother." He took a moment to gather himself before rallying and taking hold of Lynsey's hand. "Come on, let's go an' see what's on the Solway's menu. What's the landlord's name again?"

"Angus Maguire."

"Joe said he's started one o' them micro-breweries now, got his own beers. Five Kingdoms it's called. Let's go give them a try before tea. Don't worry, a woman in your condition an' all," he laughed. "I'll try yours for ya."

Chapter Thirty-Three

As was becoming a habit whenever Robbie came to the Isle of Stennoch, there was a phone message waiting for him when he arrived at the Harvester. Angus remembered him and said a Chris Radley wanted him to call.

"Yer McAndrew right?" he asked.

"Yeh, why?"

"There's a message for ya that's all; ya've only just missed the call. I only put the phone down no' thirty seconds before ya walked in my door there. Here." He passed Robbie the note paper he'd just scribbled on.

"Thanks…again. It must get a bit annoying."

"It's nae bother man. Are ya having a drink?"

Robbie scanned the bar pumps. "These must be the new beers Joe McStay told me ya've been brewing."

"Aye, going down a treat too. Will ya try one?"

Robbie pointed to the pump clip that read 'Five Kingdoms Brewery, Summerisle'. There was a picture of a winking sun below what looked like the white tower out on the Cairn. Robbie ordered a pint of that one and a Britvic for Lynsey. He took a couple of menus from the bar as he paid.

"Yer okay having a look, but I'll no' be taking any food orders 'til half six." Angus informed him. That was an hour away yet so he bought some crisps and left them on the table with Lynsey while he went to call Chris Radley.

"Just missed ya apparently. Sorry."

"No problem Robbie. Listen, Police Scotland are putting out a public plea for information. They're going to show Kester Richards photo, asking for information on his whereabouts in relation to the murder of Eban Whithorn and I just wanted t'make you aware. DI

Saggers called me t'say that it'll be going out tonight all over Scotland and throughout the north of England too. Look it might piss you off a bit because she's going t'portray Eban Whithorn as a defenceless old man. There's a reward for anyone offering him up."

"For fuck's sake!"

"I know, but it'll play on the public's sympathy. It's more likely to reap results that way. I just wanted to make you aware so it didn't catch you off-guard if ya happened t'see it."

Robbie thanked him and passed on the landline number for their chalet before heading back through to the bar area.

It was a few days before he actually saw the appeal though. They'd both made a deliberate effort to avoid the television and only happened to see it while they were visiting Joe.

"Och it's been on a fair few times now laddie. They've no' caught him yet though have they?" Joe seemed less than impressed.

A photograph of Eban was displayed as the 'poor, defenceless victim'. It made Robbie's blood boil. Then the outside of the nursing home was shown and Dieter Richter, the manager was interviewed, a mandatory expression of remorse on his face that this could've happened on his watch. Next they showed a mugshot of Kester with a brief description, including some of the alias' he was known to utilise. Some CCTV footage of him getting out of a Mondeo at Glasgow Central Railway Station and leaving the site was shown. All areas where he'd been known to have contacts were mentioned, mainly Scottish, but Leeds and West Yorkshire were mentioned too. 'A substantial reward' was offered to anyone providing information that led to his capture, though no actual monetary figure was stated.

They'd agreed between themselves that they didn't want to let the outside world and all it entailed into the peaceful quiet of their time away. They'd needed this time, they'd needed to be together, to talk, to plan for the future, but more importantly they needed to start getting over the past. Rich had already been tasked with three visits to rental properties and because they knew it was going to be a short term option, they'd decided to just go with whatever him and Jodie thought was suitable. They trusted them.

Robbie had a message to call Professor Waterman for the results of all the tests he'd undergone. He was nervous and half ready to just not bother, but it was something he'd wanted and he knew he'd regret it if he didn't find out. He made the call, anxiously running his hand back over his hair while he waited for the rings to be answered.

"Hi, it's Robbie McAndrew. You've got the results I understand?"

"Ah Robbie, indeed. Now the first thing I'm going to say, is that you need to listen to the explanation of each one in order to get the whole picture, alright? No random conjecture, okay?"

"Yer not filling me with confidence Professor."

"Trust me. As discussed previously, your initial assessment from the Hare Psychopathy test *did* show that you share some characteristics on that scale, and as I mentioned previously, a large percentage of the population have some of those characteristics also. I would say that you were at the high end of average, if not just above, so borderline in effect. This is corroborated in your neurological responses to the stimuli you were shown. For the most part, there was very little difference in your responses from fluffy bunny rabbits to images of tortured captives and dead children in warzones."

"What does that mean exactly? Dead kids is nothing like fluffy rabbits. Of course I'd find that grim."

"You need to understand Robbie; your psychological conditioning and your psychological make up, though both relevant of course, need to offset each other. Let me explain.

"Having spoken in depth with you, it's apparent that you know right from wrong, good from bad etcetera. This is because of the upbringing you've had. But neurologically, your brain doesn't induce those emotions

in you to the same degree that someone else's might.
This will feel normal to you because it's all you've ever
known and has nothing to do with your head injury.

"The blood test results show that you have higher
than normal testosterone levels but that your serotonin
levels are normal. The scan we did of your brain, to look
at the development and function of the pre-frontal
cortex, in particular the amigdala, showed a normal size
and development in that area. There has been no damage
sustained there from your injury."

Robbie was struggling to keep up. "Look, can y'just
break it down for me please? Simple Saxon."

"Of course. Basically, you *do* measure in the
positive for psychopathy, in that you don't feel or
empathise in the same way that others do. That's not to
say you have no feelings or emotions, of course you do.
It's just that your emotional responses are not quite the
same. You also have a tendency for obsession, but you
know this, you said as much yourself, and to be honest,

this tendency is very likely what makes you very good at your job.

"However, I wouldn't put you in the category that others might find themselves in. You're not dangerous, but you could be ruthless if you'd a mind to be. Dangerous psychopaths tend to come from very disturbed backgrounds for the most part, though there are exceptions. And yes, I'm aware of your background, but the fact remains that physiologically, your pre-frontal cortex is intact and normal. As I said before, this is your control centre, the braking system if you like. This is what makes you stop when impulses of anger hit you. This is what makes you as safe as the next man on the street."

Robbie was confused by this apparent barrage of information. "So I am a psychopath?"

"Borderline, yes."

"But how come my pre-frontal whatsit is okay then if it isn't in others?"

"To be honest Robbie, that's down to your experiences as a child. It's down to the love you must've been shown by your mother."

"So Annie really did save me after all?"

"I'm sure she did Robbie, but it's your very early experiences that I'm talking about. This factor is very much down to your real mother and the care she gave you as a baby and toddler. Despite what you tell me about your father, I think you must've been sheltered from his behaviour when you were that young, or else his behaviour wasn't that bad back then, but developed later on.

"She was obviously a very good mother and role model as your physical brain has developed normally. So in answer to your original question; *yes*, it's more than likely that these factors are genetic given your family history, so *yes*, you too have inherited some of them. *Yes*, there's a possibility that you may pass these genetic codes onto your own children, but *no,* this does not mean that they will become deranged or have mental health issues. They may have the genetic coding for such, but their own early experiences are what determines if those codes are switched on or not, just as your early experiences were.

"Be a wonderful dad Robbie and I'm pretty sure that they won't be."

"Why am I noticing these things about myself now then? Why is it that these things are only coming to light since my head injury?"

"Because you're looking for them. Those personality traits have always been there, but they're perfectly normal to you. Since finding out about your true background though, you've been 'obsessed' shall we say, with making a square peg fit a round hole."

Robbie laughed; he couldn't help it. It all fit into place now. He was right, he had let his own obsession create this paranoia. If he were honest, he *was* always this way, he'd just never really thought about it before. *Don't look for problems where there are none.* Simple words that the world had been screaming at him for a year, but he'd ignored because he knew best, or at least he'd thought he did. Between them Mona and Annie had raised a *good* man. He was a good man, he'd always been a good man, he'd just lost his way for a while. All that time he'd wasted searching for the answers that he could never possibly hope to get. Even Dredger had warned him what a pit he was dropping himself into, but he hadn't listened to any of them. His whole chest seemed to inflate as he felt the huge weight of this false cataclysm lift and disintegrate. It'd taken up too much of his time already and it sure as hell wasn't having any more. Eban Whithorn was scum, as were all that went before him, Martha's father, her brothers, Kester. The only one he didn't attach any blame to was Martha herself; she was a vulnerable child abused appallingly by those who should've loved her the most. And Kester's daughter, a little girl, in the same position he'd once been. Had her mother, Lena, saved her too?

It felt like a new day and all he could think about was how much he loved his wife. He still felt nothing towards the babies inside her, but one thing he didn't feel anymore was fear. He wasn't afraid of them being born or of what they might become, because he knew that they'd never become like Eban.

Chapter Thirty-Four

The shrill of the phone ringing in the middle of the night caused both Robbie and Lynsey to jump, as they were both woken from their sleep by the sudden onslaught coming from the living room. Robbie rubbed at his eyes as he ran through, wondering who the hell would be calling at half past two in the morning. He grabbed at the receiver and almost dropped it in his semi-slumbered state. "What?"

It was Rich and he sounded distraught. "He's got her Robbie. That bastard's got my Jodie!" His sobs were almost uncontrollable. "I swear t'god if he hurts her I'll kill him with my bare hands. I'll fucking kill him!"

Robbie's heart was pounding as he tried to absorb what his brother had just said. He could hear voices in the background and Rich crying. Robbie called back through to the bedroom. "Lyns! Christ Lynsey y'need t'come in here!"

The panic in his voice drove her. She didn't even query his reason at that point; something dire had happened and that was obvious.

The familiar tone of Chris Radley's voice picked up the line at the other end. "Robbie, we got feedback from that television appeal. A couple o' sightings placed him near Lockerbie and three more from the Leeds area here. One in particular sounded more valid, a woman by the name of Angela Overend saw him in North Leeds, at a petrol station she works at, not far from yer brother's place. Yer brother were out, working late an' by the time we got here she'd gone. We think he's got Jodie. There's signs of a scuffle an' a small amount o' blood on the carpet by the door. The kids were asleep upstairs, didn't know anything about it, but she'd gone. I'm sorry fella, we thought he'd be following you."

Robbie couldn't speak. He'd been prepared to face Kester Richards himself; he'd even rehearsed the things that might be said. But he never thought for a minute that his brother would be involved. Not Jodie, oh Christ he's got Jodie! The depravity of the man left Robbie in no doubt whatsoever that he wouldn't think twice about hurting her. "I'm coming home, I'll set off now. Make sure my brother's looked after."

"No, no absolutely not. You are not coming back here at the moment Robbie! Do you understand me?"

"My brother fucking needs me you prick. Of course I'm coming back."

"DI Saggers is fully aware of events and I promise y'this Robbie: you set one foot over that border an' I'll have you arrested."

"What for?"

"For making things fucking worse, for obstruction, I don't care. You just stay where we can find ya an' y'go nowhere else now, Alright!"

He could hear Rich in the background asking for the phone. "Listen t'me bro, do what he says because I can't risk y'making this shit worse. Don't make it fucking worse…please."

"Okay, okay. Christ Rich I'm so sorry, I'm so, so sorry."

Lynsey was in tears; she'd got the gist of events from what she'd heard. She listened, shaking as her husband begged DS Radley to use him as bait, as a bargaining chip in order to get Jodie home safely. Radley told him it was something they'd considered already, but that unless he heard otherwise from the police, that he were to stay where he was.

"How's he doing this? How the fuck is he managing to stay ahead o' the game?" Robbie was perplexed.

"Kester's getting help Robbie, he must be. There's no way he could move around this freely without someone somewhere being complicit. I think we've underestimated his reach. Please don't compromise things though by wading in. Y'need t'trust us now Robbie. This is our remit. Let us deal with things.

"Listen, does Jodie know where you an' Lynsey have gone? I mean precisely. Would she be able t'give him yer address for instance?" Radley was keeping things calm, but Robbie could detect the undertone of anxiety in his voice.

"Er…I don't know, I…"

"Don't worry. We'll assume he knows or soon will. Listen, stay there. DI Saggers is on route t'yer location as we speak, an' the local guys are putting a presence in the area as well. We'll get him Robbie, I promise. An' we'll make sure yer brother's taken care of too. Yer step-father's been collected and is on his way here; he's safe. Lynsey's parents and sisters are covered too, don't worry. We let our guard down, misjudged his next moves. It won't happen again, I assure you."

The rest of the night seemed to drag on forever; no-one slept at all. Then the early morning sun began casting long shadows across the grass as Robbie stood outside on the patio, staring out to sea. The seemingly bejewelled Solway Firth glistened immensely as the horizon was broken by the ascending orb lifting slowly from the east. He'd not slept a wink but didn't even feel tired. The chalet was bustling now. DI Saggers had been and gone but there were two uniformed officers, as well as DC Mick Simons and DS Glenn Frobisher. DC Carolyn Hames had taken Lynsey into Newton Stewart. They needed supplies and it seemed like a good idea to get her out of there for a break. She'd been tearing her hair out, inconsolable at times and the more anyone tried to reassure her the worse she got.

DS Saggers had gone to meet up with someone from Serious Crimes. They were wanting to secrete armed officers in and around the village, partly in the hope that Kester was heading there and partly to ensure he didn't. They needed to treat Jodie as their priority now, awful as the concept was. They didn't know if she was alive anymore or not, and if she was, what had he done to her? Given the things he'd put his daughter's mother through and given the way he'd tortured Eban before killing him, it just didn't bear thinking about.

Robbie had spoken to his brother again, tried to reassure him that Jodie was tough, a survivor. But it'd just pissed him off; everything was pissing him off. Her parents were beside themselves and it had fallen to Lynsey's sister, Natalie, to come and get the kids. They didn't understand what was happening but Rich just couldn't deal with them. All he could think about was his wife, his beautiful, quirky Jodie. Despite all of his lashing out, the person Rich really blamed was himself. He should have been there for her. It was all he repeated to Robbie when they spoke. "I should've been here. It's down to me, if I'd have been here. I'm going t'kill him Robbie. I swear he's a fucking dead man!"

Lynsey and DC Hames arrived back from the twenty-four hour Asda in Newton Stewart, the boot loaded with shopping. Lynsey looked wrecked, pale and drawn, her eyes pink. Robbie went up and took hold of her. They hugged for the longest time, neither of them saying anything, just holding each other.

Frobisher came out of the chalet and rushed past them both hastily towards his car. He was wearing an ear-piece, plugged into the radio he was talking into as he passed them. He jumped into the driver's seat and set off. DC Simons came outside.

"What is it? What's going on?" Robbie began to worry.

"I'm no' too sure at this point," Simons replied. "But don't worry, I'm sure we'll find out soon enough if it's anything relevant."

Lynsey wanted to know how come they had reception on their radios when she and Robbie had no mobile reception in the Isle.

"They work on satellite, they can use mobile services too, but they don't have to." He seemed glad of the distraction; it was very likely that he didn't know what to say about the current state of affairs either. It was bloody horrible trying to reassure someone when you know full well that you're just insulting their intelligence.

Hames called them all inside with the promise of a hot drink, while one of the uniformed officers was still unpacking the shopping bags. Once there, she asked them to sit down.

"Why? What's happened?" Robbie could feel a sense of dread in the air.

"We're no' sure yet, so I don't want tae say too much at this point, but we think we've located him, Richards. DS Frobisher got a call just before he went off. West Yorkshire Police had checked the CCTV footage from that sighting at the petrol station last night. It confirmed that it was indeed Kester Richards. It also gave us the licence plate o' the car he was driving an' that car's now been picked up an' tracked on the number recognition system. He's just outside Dumfries; the car's surrounded."

Lynsey burst into tears. "An' Jodie? Please God let her be okay. Is she? Is Jodie with him?"

"I don't know anything else as yet I'm afraid. I promise I'll tell ya the minute I hear."

Robbie got up and began pacing the room, both hands on his head. "Does my brother know?"

"Aye, he does."

"How long 'til we know? I mean what are they doing now? Why don't y'know if she's there?"

DC Simons stepped in as Robbie's tone was becoming a little aggressive. "Be patient, I'm sorry but that's all we can do now. As soon as we know, you'll know!"

Robbie rushed towards the phone on the wall. "I'm calling Rich. Oh fuck if it's bad news I don't know how he's going t'cope." He dialled his brother's landline number but the call was taken by a police officer. "It's Robbie, let me talk t'my brother please."

"I'm sorry, not just at the moment Robbie; he's in no fit state," the officer said. In the background Robbie could hear the sound of crashing and swearing, Rich must be frantic. He could also hear the sound of Clive's voice shouting at him to calm down, that he wasn't helping anyone.

The sound of his brother's pain was awful. "Is he wrecking the house? What's going on? Have you lot heard something we haven't yet? Is it Jodie?"

Just behind him he became aware of Simons answering his radio. Almost simultaneously the officer at the other end of the phone did the same thing. The first voice he heard next was the officer there at Rich's house, shouting above the din his brother was making. "She's okay. We've got her she's safe now Mr McAndrew. Did ya hear what I just said? Yer wife's okay. She's with our officers. She safe."

Robbie spun round and looked at the others in the room with him. "They've just told my brother, Jodie's safe. Is it true? Have they found her safe?"

Hames was smiling, as were the two police constables. Simons confirmed it. "Aye it is Robbie; they've got her. It's just come through tae us too."

The cry that Lynsey let out could only be described as midway between a sob and a laugh. "Oh thank god, oh Robbie thank god." Turning to Simons. "Is she okay? Has he hurt her? Have they got him? They have got him haven't they?"

He raised his hands in a gesture to gently fend off her barrage of questions. "All I know at the moment is that when they surrounded the car, it was Jodie in the driver's seat. She'd driven the car intae the city on her own."

"So he's still out there?"

"I don't know, I'll tell ya more as I find out myself. No-one's trying tae keep anything from ya, ya know."

It was hours before they heard anything else. They were told that Rich was being driven up to Dumfries to be with his wife. She'd been taken to the hospital just to be checked out, but there were apparently no serious injuries.

It wasn't until about four that afternoon before they found out anything more. It was Rich himself who phoned them. Robbie took the call.

"She's okay mate." He sounded so much calmer than he had been, exhausted but calm. "She said he was in the kitchen when she'd come downstairs after putting the kids t'bed. No idea how he got in, but he did. She said she lunged for the panic button but he shoved her away. He made her stay quiet, said he'd hurt the kids if she didn't. He asked her about y'both staying here. She told him ya'd gone now, but she didn't know where, said the police had told ya not t'tell anyone, not even us. I think he believed her because he went on my laptop. He'd got into Lynsey's email somehow an' pulled off where you are now. No idea how Rob, sorry."

Rich might not have known how, but Robbie did and he was angry at himself for not thinking of it before now. "Lynsey's used my laptop before, her email would've been in the history. He took my laptop remember, if he'd hacked her email with the information he got there, then he could get in from anywhere. It's my fault, I should've thought o' that."

"Yeh, anyway. He took her with him. The bastard shoved her into the boot. She'd no idea where she was or where he were taking her. She said all she could think about were the kids because they were on their own. She were worried that one o' them might wake up an' be scared. Typical Jodie."

"But she is okay isn't she Rich? I mean he hasn't hurt her, he didn't…"

Rich interrupted him before he could finish his sentence, not wanting to hear those words. "Oh he's hurt her alright. She wouldn't get in the boot without a fight. He's battered her; y'should see the state of her Robbie." He had to pause to compose himself. "She'd no idea where she were when he dragged her out o' the boot; she'd lost all sense o' time she said. She said it were dark, but she could hear traffic in the distance. He started grabbing at her, saying stuff…y'know."

He didn't know for sure, but Robbie could only guess at what Rich was alluding to.

"She said she'd stayed calm the whole time, tried to keep him calm, said she'd tried chatting with him, y'know befriending him or something. Anything she thought might keep him on side."

"Did it?"

"No, he grabbed her by the throat when she wasn't having any of his crap. She said he pinned her t'the ground an' tried t'throttle her, but she managed t'wriggle free. She got up an' tried t'run. She said she were shouting for help but no-one came."

"I don't get it. How did she get away from him then? Did he just let her go?"

"No did he fuck," Rich began laughing at that point, not a rolling on the floor kind of laugh, but a nervous tension kind of laugh. "He would o' killed her Robbie, I'm sure of it. But the stupid fucker didn't reckon on my wife. He didn't think my Jodie'd pose any problem for him. But that stupid bastard doesn't know my Jodie. When she'd been in the boot, she'd managed to get her hands under the matting that covers the spare wheel, she'd got the tyre lever up to the surface. He made another grab for her an' she booted him square in the bollocks then grabbed the tyre lever an' wrapped it round his head, jumped in the motor an' just drove t'where she found a load o' people. She said she were going t'get help, but the next thing she knew, a load o' coppers were pointing guns at her."

Robbie couldn't help but laugh at what he'd just heard. What a schoolboy error! Never underestimate your enemy; wasn't that a basic rule? "Is he still out there then? Have they got police with y'both now?"

"The heat's off Robbie. He's in intensive care. She's only gone an' cracked his fucking skull...poetic justice or what? She were able t'show them where she'd left him an' now he's under armed guard. He's going nowhere. It's over Rob, it's over."

Robbie could barely find the words to pass on the news to his own wife, but the relief in his face was almost palpable. He didn't need to say anything.

Lynsey took his face in her hands and cried, tears streaming down her pale cheeks. "They've got him, haven't they?"

Chapter Thirty-Five

Lynsey had been on a high ever since the news that Jodie was okay and Kester Richards was in intensive care. They'd both had a good night's sleep and planned setting off back home that evening, cutting short their break but neither of them wanted to stay any longer given recent events. They'd got the place back to themselves and regretted having to leave, but they both wanted to be with their family now. Lynsey had gone round to Mandy's where she'd previously chosen one of her original paintings, a trawler moored in the Isle harbour called 'Stennoch's Pride'. She'd paid her a deposit already, but wanted to settle up and collect the artwork.

Robbie had gone for a walk, stopping off first at the Solway Harvester for a half of his new favourite brew, Summerisle. Angus gave it to him on the house and asked when he'd be back. For the first time Robbie looked at this man and wondered if his father, Jock Maguire, had ever made mention of the part he'd played all those years ago.

Angus nodded towards the bar stool Robbie occupied. "That was always old Dredger's perch too. I often think I've caught a glimpse o' the old duffer out o' the corner o' my eye some days," he laughed out loud. "If he's looking down from wherever he is now, he'll no' be very happy tae have missed out on my brew. It were him gave me the idea in the first place." He pulled himself a half pint too and raised his glass. "Tae Dredger Scoular, wherever he may be. Here's tae you old friend."

"Dredger," Robbie toasted him, glass held high. He looked out of the window and across the harbour to where he could see Dredger's cottage on the Brae, the 'For Sale' sign now a little lop-sided, and a thought hit him. They could buy it, him and Lynsey. It'd need work doing, updating and possibly an extension building, but what if they bought it? Would she agree?

Would she move to the Isle of Stennoch? There were a whole host of reasons not to, all of the bad things that had happened here for one thing. But he could still continue working for Fletcher Dean's, that wouldn't be an issue. He already did most of his work from his home office anyway; he didn't need to be in Leeds. And with the twins on the way, he felt sure that Lynsey would want to stay at home with them for the first few years anyway. He wondered if what Professor Waterman had said about his psychological make up was clouding his judgement. Did he not feel all the negative connotations around this village because of how he was, or was he just being reasonable after all? He wanted to do his best to delete all the bad and replace it with good memories. His mum had come from here, both of them had, Annie and Mona. They had happy childhoods here, so why shouldn't he, Lynsey and their family be happy there too? Why let the random arrival of a psychotic vicar forty-odd years ago ruin what they could have here? Because despite everything that had happened, he actually felt a sense of belonging here.

He left the pub and stood outside for a few moments, resting on the railings on the harbour side, taking in the view of the moored boats, bobbing gently up and down, listening to the sound of the soft mast bells as they rang with each movement of the tiny waves. The fields on the other side of the harbour, leading up towards Burrow Head and the sight of Dredger's home on the Brae. He'd ask her, probably when they were ready to leave. Drive her up there for a look, let her see the view out over the harbour and out to sea, let her imagine it for herself and hope that she could see it the way he did.

He wanted to walk out onto the Cairn, sit up by the white tower for a while and watch the sea. He'd agreed to be back at the chalet by five, ready for leaving at six, so he wanted to use the last of the afternoon sun to enjoy the peace. Apart from someone heading off the Cairn with their dogs, there was no-one else around. There was a cold chill in the breeze which probably kept most folks at home, but he didn't mind it. It was still warm where the sunny bits were.

Once he'd reached the tower he sat on the bench facing out to sea. He loved this spot. It was a clear enough day that he could make out the Isle of Man on the horizon. When he looked to his left, he could see a couple of line fishermen balanced on the rocks on the far side of Laigh Isle where the chalets were. He almost felt that he was welded to the spot for a while, half an hour maybe. When he looked down at his watch he realised it was getting on, almost half past four, so he decided to have a steady walk back. It'd only be a ten minute walk anyway, if that.

The 'Bright Horizon' was just heading back towards the harbour on his right, home after a day's fishing, disappearing from his sight once it got close to the harbour mouth. And as he began walking again, following it with his eyes; he noticed the form of a man heading onto the Cairn in the distance, as he was rounding the tower. Probably the early evening *walking the dog* routine that most dog owners do when they get in from work. He lost sight of him when he dropped down onto the pathway though. When he got to the memorial bench down the side of the tower, just under an overhang of rock, he stopped again for a few moments to watch as the 'Bright Horizon' entered the harbour and passed just below him. The wind was picking up and the sea looked to be getting a little rougher as the evening drew in because the rocks below him were taking crash after crash of white water. It was nowhere near storm-like, but choppy to say the least. He turned around ready to head back, and that's when it hit him.

An almighty thud on the back of his head, enough to take him off his feet. He got himself onto his hands and knees wondering what the hell had just happened. Had something fallen from the overhang of rocks above him? The answer to that question came in the form of a hard, solid kick into his right side. Robbie looked up. Kester.

He jumped to his feet with nowhere to run, the wall of rock now flanked his right side with the sea both behind him and to his left. The only way he could leave the Cairn was forward, and Kester was blocking that path, grinning at him. How could he be there? How would it be possible that he'd recovered enough from a fractured skull in one night, been able to slip past armed guards and find him here? It wasn't possible and there wasn't a mark on him. Then it dawned on him.

"Tavish, Jesus fucking Christ, you're Tavish!" he said.

"Ya think?"

"Well yer not fucking Kester, ya can't be. Yer brother's in intensive care in Dumfries."

"Aye, I know that, my brother's a fucking joke. It's his own fault, if he'd o' done what I said in the first place he'd o' been home free. But he's a fucking idiot, always has been. One job I gave him, one fucking job!"

Robbie didn't understand what he was getting at, and it was now hurting to breathe too deeply; his ribs must be broken. "What job? What d'ya mean?"

"Well if he'd o' just, shall we say, *taken care o' her*, then he'd no' be where he is now."

Jodie, he was referring to Jodie. Robbie was struggling to get his head round everything. Had Kester been the one responsible for the original attack on him, or had it been Tavish all along? "But he might die."

"So fucking what, like I said, it's his own fault. But I'm no' here tae discuss my brother's possible death. I'm here tae discuss yours, you fucking freak!"

Robbie's initial fear switched quickly to a sense of rage. "Why the hell you ever held me responsible for the fuck-up that your lives have been, I'll never know. Yer sick, just like that piece o' shit y'killed in Girvan, or he killed. Whichever one o' you it was, yer just like him, both o' ya!"

"Och that'd be me right enough, credit where it's due eh? I dispatched grandad. I doubt yer exactly gutted by it though?"

"An' the kid, didn't have the bottle t'kill yer brother's kid though did ya?"

Richards suddenly lunged forward, the grin now replaced by a grimace. "Fuck you!" he spat, his teeth gritted together.

But Robbie couldn't stop himself. He knew his nephew was younger than him, in better physical shape and far more likely to come off the victor in any physical conflict with him, especially since he'd already been nobbled with a blow to the head and a couple of rib fractures. But his own rage was at a level he'd never experienced before. Adrenalin had kicked in and though he knew he'd been injured, he felt no pain anymore. All he saw in front of him was the reason for his nightmares, the reason for his wife's fears, the reason his brother had suffered the trauma of his stolen wife, and worst of all, the reason Eban was still here, right here in front of him now, staring at him through the eyes of this young man, wishing him dead through the words he spoke and trying to kill him…again, through his hands.

For the briefest of moments it crossed his mind that his own psychopathy, however borderline that might be, had now taken over. That he was now capable of killing this man, he knew he was and he knew that the first sign of weakness in his defences and he'd be in. He knew that he was ready to kill him, just like he knew that he was willing to die trying. There was no fear any more, none at all. This was the day that one of them would be going to breathe their last, and if it had to be Robbie, then he was going to make damn sure that his nephew didn't get out of it unscathed.

Richards came at him with a rock in his hand, he'd raised above his head in readiness. From nowhere, Robbie's old karate training suddenly took over. He didn't see the rock; he wasn't looking at it. All he saw was the unguarded right flank on his nephew's right. In a flash he'd landed a roundhouse kick right in the ribs. Richards cried out but seemed more enraged than before. He ran at Robbie, blind fury oozing from every cell of his being.

Robbie stepped back, the undulating ground causing him to lose his balance. As he crashed to the ground, Richards soon followed, his upper torso heading straight down on top of Robbie. But he'd raised his arm and as

Richards' face came crashing down towards him, Robbie grabbed his own right fist with his left hand and swung his elbow up to meet Richards' jaw. The force of the blow sent him off to Robbie's left side. As both men jumped to their feet again, Robbie was now in the prime position and Richards left with his back to the sea instead.

"What now?" Richards taunted him. "Come on then, what now, eh?"

Robbie became aware of the sound of voices approaching but he didn't pay too much attention. He had one thing on his mind and one thing only. It wasn't until he caught a glimpse of movement in his peripheral vision, just above where they were standing on the edge of the Cairn that he glanced up.

An armed police officer was pointing a gun straight down at Richards. He'd seen it too and he laughed, now waving around a knife he'd pulled out from his jacket. "Go on then fucker, shoot me!"

Robbie was partially aware that his own name was being called behind him. It sounded to be off in the distance but when he looked round, he realised it was DI Saggers and she was only a couple of yards away. She was wearing a stab vest over her clothes and she kept on shouting his name. The sound had started off faint, but the more she shouted at him, the louder she got. There was a buzzing in his head, almost like tinnitus. It was masking the outside world, but she was breaking through it.

"Robbie! Robbie McAndrew! Don't you dare! Stay right where ya are now! Do ya here me? Robbie!"

He spun back to face his nephew, who was still laughing, blood splattering from his mouth with every word. "Do ya no' need tae tell the bitch she's got yer name wrong eh…Uncle Michael?"

The buzzing was getting louder again as his rage maintained control over his common sense. All he could hear was Richards and all he could see was Richards. They both lunged for each other at the same time.

There was the crack of a gunshot and Robbie fell face down onto the ground, his shoulder catching on the memorial bench as he landed, the weight of a body on top of him. He looked across to the cliff edge and saw Richards laid out but still moving and he tried to get to him, but DC Simons was laying on top of him. Robbie fought to get out of his grip but when DS Frobisher joined the effort he knew it was futile. They had him pinned down; he was going nowhere. All the pent up rage came out in one long almighty yell of frustration as he felt himself finally relax beneath their combined weight. "Knock it off now Robbie," Simons shouted at him. "We'll put the cuffs on if ya can't get a lid on it, d'ya understand me?"

Robbie's body began to shake uncontrollably. The adrenalin that had driven him so far was now subsiding, but he still couldn't take his eyes off of Richards. "It were him all along; it's Tavish who's been behind all this. All this time an' we were after the wrong brother."

Saggers stepped forward and nudged her officers to get them to allow Robbie to sit up. He looked back at

Richards, who'd now sat himself up too, blood pouring from the wound to his upper arm. He looked up at the officer on the rocks above him, still with his gun trained down at him. "Ya shot me, ya fucking shot me ya bastard!" He stumbled to get himself to his feet, almost losing his balance and toppling over the edge. He was clutching the bullet wound, blood seeping through his fingers.

"We didn't get it wrong Robbie," Saggers broke into his thoughts. "This *is* Kester Richards; Tavish is the one in Dumfries." She looked towards Kester. "They think he'll very likely survive by the way, in case yer interested. Ya can maybe write tae each other from yer jail cells."

"Like I give a fuck!"

Robbie thought he was caught in some weird nightmare. "Wait, this is Tavish, surely?"

Saggers went on to explain that DS Radley had gone through the Leeds CCTV footage himself, just that morning. When he'd seen the footage from the petrol station, not only had he recognised that Richards was indeed there, but he'd recognised the car too. "A dark green Skoda Octavia, DS Radley recognised it as being the same car that was present when the two o' you an' DC Simons here, paid a visit tae Elizabeth Parker-Tait."

Kester was laughing hysterically now. Still clutching his arm, but almost doubled up, he could barely get his words out. "Ya bunch o' fucking numpties! *Och, I'm sick o' been blamed for my brother's deeds, och poor me,*" he mocked them. "I was so sure that fucking stupid Radley'd know it were me, but he didnae…idiot!"

"That was you?" Robbie was stunned. "You were sat there right in front of us all that time an' we thought y'were Tavish?" He tried to get to his feet, but Frobisher held him still. "So Tavish got Jodie then, not you?"

Kester grinned, almost beside himself with joy at his uncle's obvious confusion. "Me again, sorry," he mocked, "I got the lovely wee lady in his car, took her for a nice wee drive, met up with my brother who

swapped cars with me. He was meant tae dump her an'
the fucking motor in the loch, but he decided she was a
bit tasty, ya know; thought he might help himself tae a
bite before bed so tae speak. Seems she's a bit of a live
wire that one eh? Ya know, I've been puzzling; are
we're related, me an' her? You being my uncle an' all."

"Shut it Richards!" Frobisher could feel that Robbie
was tensing up again and didn't know if he could keep
holding him back.

Saggers tried to clarify things again. "We knew he
must be getting help. He couldn't o' got as far as he did
without it Robbie. We just never realised it was a family
affair. We'd no reason tae believe that Tavish was
involved in any way, probably still wouldn't if DS
Radley hadn't o' recognised the Octavia. The public
sightings up by Lockerbie weren't false leads after all it
seems; they were sightings o' Tavish, the ones in Leeds
were him, Kester."

As two uniformed officers began to approach Kester,
one of them began to read him his rights. As he did so,

Kester stared past them and glared at Robbie. "Ya think yer bairn'll be safe do ya…eh?"

That was all it took; Robbie snapped. He was on his feet in a heartbeat; he broke free of Frobisher's grip and shoved his way between the two uniforms. Kester raised his arms when he realised he'd nowhere to go, but it was too late, both men hurtled down the rocks and into the white water below.

Kester had taken the brunt of the fall and hit the rocks below him, Robbie had bounced off of him and landed in the water, still gripping onto Kester's jacket for dear life. He wouldn't let go. Even when he felt the current pulling him under, he refused to release his grip. The screaming and shouting from above them on the Cairn was barely audible above the sound of the crashing waves and the water was freezing.

It took a few moments before Robbie realised that Kester wasn't moving at all, his body lifeless in Robbie's hands. His eyes were open but the back of his head was smashed in and his whole body was being thrown around like a rag doll. He was dead. Both of them were being thrown against the rocks with each incoming wave and Robbie knew that he'd have to release his grip on Kester if he'd to stand any chance of saving himself.

When the next wave hit, Robbie let it wash him into the rocks and he used the opportunity to try and grab on. He was able at least to use his feet to try and reduce the force of the impact. It was far too rocky for any boat to get in close enough to be able to help him, so he knew he'd need to try and climb in as far as he could.

He looked round at Kester's body which kept disappearing out of sight beneath the water before it finally came to rest, wedged in the rocks, right beside him. He looked into his face for one last time. He looked like a boy, a child almost with the rage in his expression now gone and the contortions of his anger washed away by death, leaving the fresh look of youth. For one brief moment Robbie wanted to reach out and touch his face: his nephew, his brother's child, dead beside him. But the next wave took away that desire as fast as it had come.

Ropes began appearing from above along with calls of *'hang on Robbie'* and *grab the rope.* A nearby voice startled him. He could've sworn he could hear Dredger Scoular. "Yer alright laddie, hang on, I'll get ya son."

He swung his head round in confusion. It couldn't be Dredger, could it? But it was Angus Maguire, along with the skipper from the 'Bright Horizon'. The two of them had come under the Cairn and were holding each other up on the lower level rocks as they edged nearer to him. Angus threw a rope towards him.

"Grab it lad! Quick get a hold!"

He did so and as they held him steady at the other end, he was able to drag himself closer and closer until he could reach Angus' outstretched arm. He looked up into the big man's face and Angus winked at him.

"That's two Maguires pulled ya out o' this water now eh?"

He knew. He'd known all along.

Epilogue

Tears streamed down Robbie's face as he held his two tiny babies in his arms, two daughters. All the fear of not loving them disintegrated the moment he saw them. He loved these two perfect little human beings, how could he have ever doubted it. They had arrived a little early as Lynsey had feared, but only four and a half weeks. They were perfect. He couldn't take his eyes off them. Lynsey walked slowly back onto the ward; she'd been for a shower. She'd apologised for looking a mess as she'd called it, but she was far from that, she was beautiful, the most beautiful woman in the world, and these were the most beautiful babies in the world and they were his. He'd never before experienced this intensity of emotion; it almost took his breath from him.

"Have you decided which names you like Robbie?" Lynsey asked him as she climbed back onto her bed.

They'd been discussing names for weeks, but not coming to any decisions.

Robbie looked down into the eyes of his tiny daughters. "Ramona Rose," he said as he looked at the tiny face of the one laying in his left arm.

Lynsey smiled, unsurprised. "Good choice, and what about this one?"

He looked down at her, fast asleep on his right arm. "I don't know, I just don't know."

"How about Lily Ann? That way, both o' yer mothers are honoured." she suggested.

Robbie smiled, touched by her reference to them. "Yeh, I like that, but we'll call them Rose and Lily. We'll honour Mona and Annie, but our girls should never feel they aren't individuals."

In the months that had passed life had become peaceful again, the status quo had returned. They'd not bothered renting a house, instead they'd moved in with Clive and he was glad of the company. It was a temporary arrangement though, because when Robbie had brought up the possibility of them buying Dredger's old place on the Brae, Lynsey had jumped at the suggestion. She loved it as much as he did. In all the time since Dredger's death, there'd not been a single offer made for his cottage. It was as if the old man had been keeping it for them. It needed a fair bit of work doing and they'd got planning permission for a two story extension on the back so that they could make a bigger kitchen diner and add a bedroom upstairs. They'd moved in with Clive while the work was getting done, it wouldn't be long now. The builders had finished and the decorator was in there. They'd bought most of their furniture new, only one or two small items from the old apartment remained, and they'd had their beautiful wedding canvases reprinted too. The days of digital photography made such things a breeze now.

They planned on staying in Leeds with Clive for the first month or two after the babies' births anyway. It made it easier all round especially for Lynsey, as it meant her mum and sisters would be on hand to help while Robbie had to work. Fletcher Dean's were on board with their move too. They were happy to accommodate Robbie working from two hundred miles away. Most meetings could be done by video link now and on the odd occasion he'd need to be there in person, it was manageable. Their hearts had already moved to the Isle of Stennoch, and they wouldn't be far behind. The past was becoming a distant memory, especially since their minds were now full to the brim with their beautiful newborns.

As for the Richards twins, Kester's body had finally been recovered the next morning, after the tide had gone out leaving him broken on the rocks below the Cairn. Robbie was due to attend the inquest into his death but DI Saggers had told him he had nothing to worry about. He still thought she was a bitch, but Chris Radley had been right about her, yes she was a cow, but she was a bloody good copper and he was glad it hadn't been him she'd been hunting down.

Tavish did survive Jodie's wrath, but it'd caused a bleed on his brain that had left him with the effects of a stroke. He had partial paralysis down his right side and his speech was a little slurred by all accounts. They couldn't say if he'd ever recover more, but it was unlikely. He was currently on remand in a secure mental facility unit near Edinburgh. It had become apparent that he'd been complicit all along. Kester had always been the driving force, the stronger of the two brothers, physically and mentally, but Tavish had been no shrinking violet. He'd a cruel streak and despite his disability he'd still attacked a member of the unit's staff and had to be restrained. Imagining Tavish as he was now, put Robbie in mind of Eban, living with the effects of a stroke. Though Tavish was such a young man to be so inflicted and would likely recover to some degree, Robbie felt no compassion.

They'd had a pay-out, compensation for what they'd been through, but Lynsey had refused to spend it. She'd asked DS Radley if he could find some way of getting the money up to the little girl and her mother in Edinburgh. Robbie and Lynsey only learned of Lena and Maddie's names when they received a thank you letter from them. Maddie had drawn a picture of some fireworks that Lena had included. along with an explanation that it was the Edinburgh Tattoo, which had recently taken place. Lena said that she was using the money to get them out of the flat they were in and they were moving to the other side of the city instead, a fresh start. It made Lynsey happy to know that they were going to be alright, all of them.

Lena had invited them to visit whenever they wanted, which was nice of her, but they weren't sure they could face it for the foreseeable future. Robbie was glad they were okay, but didn't really want to look into that little girl's eyes and see her father looking back. They'd refused to allow Kester and his madness to sully what was to become their new home, and bit by bit, they were cleansing him from their lives completely, but one step at a time.

Jodie had taken everything in her stride, like Jodie always did. It was Rich that still struggled from time to time. He'd started suffering from panic attacks after what had happened. He couldn't leave the house for a while, but he was having counselling and doing really well. He'd been back at work for the past few weeks now and things were slowly returning to normal for them. His counsellor had recommended hypnotherapy too, which had really helped. His sense of humour was pretty much back now, especially with regard to his wife's 'prowess as an assassin'. He'd laugh when they were all together and tell Robbie not to piss off his wife. "Just look at what happened t'the last bloke who pissed off my missus."

Peg, or Elizabeth, had been questioned about her knowledge of the Richards brothers' identity switching. But it seemed that Police Scotland were satisfied that she'd played no part; they'd used her too. Relying on the fact that she'd not seen either of them in a very long time, it hadn't been too hard for Kester to mislead her, especially as she was grieving for Maev at the time. She'd sent them a long letter, apologising for what the brothers had done to Robbie and his family. He hadn't replied. He didn't want to, but Lynsey had persuaded him to phone her that morning, to let her know about the babies.

Robbie told her later that Peg had cried as soon as she'd heard the news, relieved that everyone was safe. It was only then that it occurred to Robbie how alone in the world his half-sister was now. A few chickens and a Jack Russell called Dave. He remembered how that little dog had growled at Kester when he'd tried to touch Peg. If only they'd all known what Dave knew then.

He had no particular feelings one way or the other towards Peg, but as ever, Lynsey wanted them to stay in contact with her once they'd made the move to Scotland themselves.

He'd discussed his feelings in length with his wife now, all the content of the tests he'd undergone with the research Professor, the results. He'd even told her how close he felt he'd come to committing murder himself. She was brilliant about it all. "You're no different now than y'were nine years ago when we met Robbie. All those same things would've been there then too, y'just never noticed back then that's all. I'm not surprised y'wanted t'kill Kester either. Even Jodie admitted she'd felt that way about Tavish at the time. Please don't start obsessing about all this shit again will ya? Promise me?"

He *had* promised her because he knew that he meant it. That desire to dig into Eban Whithorn's background seemed ridiculous to him now. History had been repeating itself down the Richards' generations: some victims like Martha, some perpetrators like Eban. But here is where it had come to a stop.

Right here is where Robbie knew for certain that he was neither a victim, nor a perpetrator. He was a husband and a father and *his* twins would grow up loved.

* * * * * * * *

The End

Author's Note

At this point I feel it's important to make mention of my colleagues and to thank them for allowing me to 'borrow' their names for some of the characters I've written into this story and the previous one. The character names are by no means a representation of the real people I know, but as these people would tell you, the reader, I am notoriously bad at remembering names and so using ones I'm already familiar with and swapping and changing them really helps, so apologies and gratitude in equal measures to my wonderful colleagues, much love to you all; you're amazing. In particular I must thank Mr Kester Richards who offered up his own name for use knowing that the character who would be using it, was going to be especially vile. The real Kester is a lovely, happy (and sane) family man and nothing like the one you've just read about.

Just like the first book in this story, Ramona's Angel. This one is also set in part, in the beautiful Scottish village of the Isle of Whithorn. The latter part of the name borrowed for the family name I've given to Eban. Again, the local history has been an inspiration to me in my story telling.

In particular I would like to draw your attention to the pub mentioned in the story, The Solway Harvester. The real village pub is called the Steam Packet Inn, Alastair Scoular is the real landlord, though the mention of the micro-brewery is in fact true. He really does brew his own beers and they are well worth a sample should you find yourself in the vicinity, the food's pretty damn good too.

I chose to call the pub The Solway Harvester for a specific reason. It was a decision made to pay tribute to the crew of a scallop dredger with that name that sank off the coast of the Isle of Man on 11th January 2000, with a loss of all hands during a force nine gale. All seven crewmen were from the Isle of Whithorn and it's surrounding areas. A memorial to these men is by the

White Tower on the Cairn at the far end of the village. May they rest in peace.

Thank you for reading this novel. I hope you have enjoyed this sequel to Ramona's Angel and I hope that you found Like Eban to be just as good. The best reward for an author is to leave an honest review of their work so that other readers can make a balanced decision as to whether or not they would like to read it too. If you bought your copy from Amazon, then reviews can be left there, if you bought from elsewhere, then reviews can be left on GoodReads too. Writing is a very solitary trade, which is why the reviews and feedback from readers are so important to us.

Thank you so much for your purchase and support and keep your eyes peeled for my next work.

Kind regards, PLJ.

<u>Other books by this author;</u>

Ramona's Angel – book one in

the bilogy, where Robbie first

discovers who he really   is, an

emotional rollercoaster of a read

with amazing reviews.

Contact, Like or Follow this Author here;

https://twitter.com/Eyyuplass

www.facebook.com/PLJenkinson

www.goodreads.com/author/show/9212104.P_

L_Jenkinson

If you have enjoyed works by this Author then

please leave a review of the book you have read on

Amazon or Goodreads. Reviews are the most valuable gift you can give to an Author. Thank you.